The Awakening

Cassandra Morphy

Chapter One
Regret

The hot, thick liquid oozed down my hand. His life's blood. The last his heart would pump. It quickly became sticky around my fingers. It pasted them to the keys that still stuck out of his neck. I watched, with pain, with sorrow, with regret and mercy, as the life slowly drained out of his eyes. My heart broke all over again as the man slowly died in my arms. The man that I loved for so long. His weight was on top of me, pressing me downwards into the firm ground beneath my back. The blood turned it into a mud that I couldn't escape. Pinned as I was, I could barely move, could barely draw breath. I tried to look elsewhere, to look anywhere but in his cold, dead eyes. They stared into my soul with a level of accusation so much worse than that which they had in life. It had been so long since we had been together. Yet the scent of his skin, masked as it was under the pungent stench of his blood, was too familiar for me to not remember the good times, the best of times, of our short, but blissfully happy, marriage.

I looked around us, around at the yard that was supposed to be ours. The swing set that he had gotten for our child the first time I was pregnant, before the miscarriage. The bushes that I had painstakingly planted from seedlings. I couldn't help but wish things had been different, had ended differently. But, with a glance up at the house, up where so much pain and suffering had happened, I knew that I couldn't have lived there. Not with him. Not for another day.

She was there, up in the window, looking down at us. His second wife. She had been pregnant with his child while we were still married. As I lay there on the ground beneath him, she was just standing there, holding the child that would never be mine. The reminder that he had been unfaithful. She glared down at me, the phone to her ear. She was no doubt calling the police. Calling to report what I've done. Calling for them to come and take me away.

And I couldn't move. I couldn't flee. I couldn't get away from the man pinning me there. No, the body pinning me there. Greg wasn't there anymore. The part of the body that had been him had fled. It had gone to wherever such souls go to. There was no telling which of his many sins would damn him. Or, perhaps, if he would be forgiven all of them in light of what I had done. I dreaded the thought that I might be soon to join him, wondering if they had the death penalty in New York.

"You'll just have to kill her as well," came the voice, unbidden, into my ears. I knew that I was the only one to hear it, to hear either of them. I knew that no one would ever believe me if I told them about it. They never had before. The unhelpful witness, my ex-husband, wouldn't have helped even if he could speak. The only thing that saved me was my denial.

"No," I insisted. "No. You're not real. I know you're not real."

"Oh, I'm real, alright," he said, as they always did, even from the beginning. "I'm as real as you are."

I pushed on the corpse, pushed against its dead weight. Trying to slip out, to get free of him, once and for all. I could never get free of him. Even now. Even when he was dead. Even when he was gone from my life, never to return. It was his voice in my ear. It came so quickly, far quicker than those that had come before him.

I started to feel the familiar tingling in my right hand as it fell asleep. They were still pinned beneath him. Still held the keys that killed my love. I wished I could pull it out, could shake it out, could flex the fingers so as to stimulate the blood flow. But I couldn't move it. My breathing became difficult, with the weight of the body pressing into my chest. I could still see, could still feel the wind blowing through the open yard. Yet, all my mind knew was the box. The eternal darkness. The constant pressing inward from the unyielding wood. My breath became quick and shallow. My vision became blurry, the darkness closing in around me.

I almost welcomed the sound when it came. The cacophonous claxon call. The siren heralding my impending imprisonment. Even as I could see nothing around me, the flashing blue and red lights still registered, still came through the darkness that threatened to overwhelm me. It blinded me, stunned me into submission. The remainders of my resistance quickly fled, limited as it was beneath the weight of the body. I closed my eyes, letting the darkness consume me. Wishing for the end that quickly approached to absorb me, to bring me to the same place that my lovely, wonderful Greg had flown to. Perhaps they would be merciful to us both and bring us into the warm embrace of the light, along with all of our lost little ones.

My breath came in with a harsh gasp as soon as the body was removed from me. The backyard slammed back into focus almost painfully. The brown, dead grass surrounded my place on the ground, a sign that the yard sorely missed me. It seemed to perfectly frame the four officers standing over me. Two of them were holding my Greg, pulling him off to the side. Another was putting cuffs on my dead wrists. The blood flow returned to them, painfully. It took me a few moments before I realized that I was no longer holding the keys. The murder weapon. I couldn't hear what the fourth cop was telling me, was droning on to me in his long, drawn out, overly practiced tone. My eyes were still scanning the area around me, looking for those lost keys. The last connection I had to what had been before.

There they were, still sticking out of Greg's neck. The imprint of my hand was left behind in the void, the stretch of metal where the blood didn't reach. They betrayed me, just like Greg had. Just like Angela, his second wife, had. Just as these four officers did. Blue gloved hands reached out to the keys, stabilizing them in the wound. The two officers that had peeled Greg's body off of me still stood over him. They stared down at him as if unsure what to do. I knew that it was too late. They wouldn't be able to save him. Just as I knew how horrible it would be if they had. Greg deserved to be dead. He needed to stay dead, for the good of all involved. The only one who would benefit Greg's swift return to the land of the living would be Greg.

I mean, sure, I would love to see him alive again. To see the love in his eyes that had long since fled from the world. And, yes, I knew that, legally speaking, attempted murder is better than actual murder. Still, I couldn't bare it. Couldn't think it. Couldn't bring myself to wish him back for my account.

Not that wishing it would have made it true. My mind whirled around in circles, giving the voices no purchase. No clear way to the surface. No one, not any of them, had any right to be in my head right then. I needed to be alone with my thoughts. Alone with the misery that would be my life without Greg in it.

"Ma'am, do you understand the rights I have just read to you?" the officer said. From his tone, and the general shaking he was giving me, it sounded like he had asked me that question more than once. He and the one that had cuffed me were starting to pull me to my feet. My body resisted. My legs didn't have the strength to hold me up. The mud beneath me didn't want to relinquish its claim over me. Still, I rose. I stood. My feet found their places beneath me. The officers' steadying hands held me up, supporting me where my legs would not.

"What?" I asked. Their words slowly registered in the dull fog that had become my mind. A low, deep laugh found its way out of that fog. I ignored it, shook it off as I tried to focus on the world around me.

"Do you understand the rights I have just read to you?" the officer asked, again.

"What? I, no, I... What?"

The officer gave a deep sigh, a guttural sound that seemed to echo in my head louder than his words had. "Come along," he said, dejectedly. He and his fellow officer started leading me through the yard.

I looked back up at the window, up where the second wife, up where Angela, had been standing. The curtain was swinging back and forth, still not having settled. They showed that I hadn't imagined her being there. She had been standing there, watching me from the safety of the house. Calling in my sin to the police. I wanted to hate her, to curse her very name. For taking my Greg from me. For giving him something that I couldn't. For turning me in for what I had done. But, I couldn't; I couldn't feel much of anything. I could barely feel the ground beneath my feet as the grass turned to asphalt.

The lights were still flashing as I was led around the house, the red and blue whirling in place, coloring the walls, despite the sun still overhead. The clouds were hiding it. Hiding my shame from it. Hiding the joy that I would never feel again from me. One of the cars was parked in the driveway. It blocked the minivan, the present that Greg had given me on our anniversary but took back during the divorce. The other police car, the one the officers were dragging me towards, was on the street. The narrow avenue, not designed to house cars while letting others pass, was overcrowded. With no place to stop on the crowded street, the cruiser was double parked. Cars were on both sides of it, blocking the traffic.

Though no one was going anywhere on the narrow street. Even now, even after so little time since the incident, a crowd was already starting to form. The cops hadn't put up the tape yet. Nothing showing that this place was anything but the happy home it had pretended to be since we had first moved in there. And, yet, still, the neighbors, some I recognized, others I didn't, stayed off the yard. It was as if the tape really were there, visible to everyone's eyes except mine. But I knew that wasn't the case. I knew that the voices couldn't hide that from me. I knew the neighbors were just keeping their distance, not just from the crime scene, but from me.

Those few neighbors I recognized in the growing mob, the ones I had once called friends, once upon a time, averted their eyes, avoiding making contact with mine. Their own shoes suddenly became the most fascinating thing in the area. It should have hurt. It should have caused the voices to come, to point their words at me like knives, stabbing viciously. But it didn't. They didn't. I had put those so-called friends behind me a long time ago. There was no shame, no fear, no loss in them seeing me like that. They had already seen me in far worse situations than that one. Like my screaming match at the vacant house back in February.

One of the officers moved one of his hands from my back to my head. He pushed it downwards, motioning me towards the open door. I hadn't noticed it being opened, didn't notice the loss of the hand responsible. My wrists pressed hard into the leather seat, a new source of restraints replacing the officers' hands. The car door slammed with a finality. The final nail in Greg's coffin, though I knew he was still back there. Still lying in the dirt, his blood soaking into the grass that had been ours.

And, yet, I couldn't seem to bring myself to care.

Chapter Two
The Station

Eyes were staring at me from all over. I had to keep reminding myself that no one was actually looking at me. The officers that filled the station were all preoccupied with their paperwork, staring at screens that didn't stare back. The ringing phones held more interest than little old me. I was just sitting there in that chair, off to the side, out of view of most of them. I could run for the door, make my escape, flee from the station, and no one would notice for several seconds. Perhaps it would be enough time for me to get outside. To get to the freedom that was promised there. The sun had chased away the clouds. It was shining brightly through the windows. Teasing me. Tempting me to join it.

And, yet, eyes were staring at me from all over. I couldn't escape those eyes. The worst ones were those directly across from me, reaching out from beneath the more recent postings pasted over it. I knew those eyes. I had seen them often enough over the past few months, ever since that stupid stunt last summer. Some idiot had dressed up as an alien and climbed down the George Washington Bridge. Nothing came of it. No one was ever caught, ever found, ever arrested for the stunt. All it did was lead to a record number of people going to the pop up geek fests that had happened all that month. No one would have even cared. No one would have even remembered the stunt. Except for what had happened a little over a month afterwards.

Someone strutted their way down the hallway, some punk kid who didn't own a belt. The voice of my father snarled at the kid. Despite agreeing with the sentiment, I didn't voice it. Happily, the distraction broke the lock that the eyes had on me. It released me from the grip that was keeping me in the chair. The chair was one of the most uncomfortable ones in the world. It reminded me of the ones at home… at Greg's house. The chairs in the dining room that Greg had proudly picked out. I stood, taking a few tentative steps down the hall. Down towards the front of the station. Down towards freedom.

"Now where do you think you're going?" the familiar voice asked. I turned in the direction of the voice, knowing who I would see before I did. It was Detective Bently, the man in charge of the case. He smiled his Cheshire cat grin at me. A flailing tail hung from his lips where the mouse was trapped. "It's so good of you to come in, Natalie," he said, as if I had much of a choice in the matter. "I believe you know the way." He pointed in the opposite direction from where I had wanted to go.

My eyes turned to the red carpeting that spread throughout the station. Whenever I came in there, and it was nowhere near my first time, I always thought the color choice had been to hide the blood of those who go against them. As usual, the sound of my footsteps on the carpet sounded like the carpet was drenched in the liquid. The one time I tried to feel it, it was as dry as it should have been. I took the two steps away from the sitting area, passing the entrance to the bullpen, the stretch of the station where everyone on desk duty would sit while they filled out papers or talked to suspects. The noise from there immediately engulfed me. It rooted me to that place as easily as the detective that followed me down the hallway did.

The station had two interrogation rooms at the end of the long hallway that ran the length of the ground floor. Every time I came there, both rooms were open and empty.

Detective Bently would always lead me to the one on the left, though. That day, the one on the left was occupied. The door was closed firmly and solidly, blanking out whatever it was that was happening inside of it. Reluctantly, I turned to the right, heading for the room I had never seen more than a glance of. Much like the one on the left, the carpeting ended at the door. It left a cold, grey tile that filled the floor inside. A table took up the center of the room. A metal ring protruded from its surface on the side farthest from the door. Knowing that Bently would put me in that seat if I didn't go there myself, I sat heavily into it. The metal legs of the otherwise plastic chair scraped against the tile as I settled into it, easing the weight off my still weak legs. My cuffs, still attached to my wrists behind my back, banged noisily into the plastic.

Bently closed the door and all noise of the outside world disappeared, though the room was anything but quiet. The voices had sprung up during my perp walk, though I had been doing my best to ignore them. To focus on the noises of the station rather than their insistence that I run. My father insisted that I hit Bently over the head with the cuffs, that I kill the good detective so that I could find freedom. Bently stalked towards me, his hips swaying, his tail wagging in the air. Without a word, he nudged me forward, pushing me a little to give him access to the cuffs. I felt the coldness of the metal keys in my hand for a moment and I shied away from it. The voice of my father snarled at me to grab them from him, to twist the cuffs around on the detective. The metal clicked and my right hand was suddenly free. To spite my father, I placed my hands, submissively, on the table, my palms upwards to the ceiling, on opposite sides of the metal loop.

"There's no need for that," Bently said. He removed the other cuff before taking the set away from me. He flipped them around in his hands a few times, teasing me with them, before sticking them in a pouch on his belt. "You're going to be a good little girl, aren't you?"

"Yes," I croaked. My voice was hoarse from lack of use. I couldn't remember the last time I had spoken. Was it when I was arrested? Before the attack? Back before Greg was dead? After clearing my throat, I tried again. "Yes, sir."

"Good," he said, nodding at me.

He made his way to the other side of the table, easing down into the chair over there. It was an echo of the one I was sitting in. But as he sat on his, it creaked, groaning under his heavy frame. The detective seemed to have put on some weight since he had first introduced himself to me. He was large to begin with, his belly hanging over the waste of his pants like one large boob that finally had fallen. It had only been a few weeks ago when I first had met him, back when they found her. As the reminder hit me, like a punch to the gut, I tried not to picture her. I tried not to see her there, bruised and bloody on the side of the river. I closed my eyes, pressing my fingers into them. Trying to blot the image from my sight. But it only made it stronger, more vivid as the colors, the reds and browns, settled in, painting the image in my mind. I saw it so often in my dreams, it had become a paint by numbers.

"Now, then, we've come full circle, haven't we?" he asked.

"Now, then." I flinched at the phrase. It was a simple oxymoron. And yet, this moron seemed to start every sentence with it. Did that mean he was on oxy? Still, it was his room, and I was his prisoner. I couldn't afford to anger the beast. "It would seem so," I placated him. However, I had no idea what he meant by it. He had pulled me into the interrogation room almost every day. Every time a new piece of evidence showed up with my name on it, sometimes literally. Did he still think I was guilty? Did he think that my killing my ex-husband was further proof of my guilt, building on my one-way ticket to death row?

I looked all around the room, anywhere but at the man's face. The mirror that took up most of a wall was to my right.

I stared at that for a good minute, trying to make it turn into the window that I knew it was. Trying to see through it to the crowd on the other side. They were the mob with their pitchforks and torches, just waiting for the word. The go ahead to stone me alive. The rest of the walls were blank. A subtle, boring grey that didn't catch my attention in the least. There weren't even marks to indicate the blocks that made it up. They were flat, unremarkable walls, meant to drive people insane from staring at them. What would happen if someone was already insane?

I looked to Bently's watch, a black plastic piece of crap that doubled as a calculator so that he wouldn't need to use his own brain for math. Tom, one of my more boring voices, is great at math. I never needed to stoop to such levels. The screen was angled just so, catching the light from the overhead fluorescent bulbs, throwing it in my eyes whenever I tried to see the time. I wondered, briefly, if he was doing it intentionally. If he knew just the right angle to hold his arm to keep anyone from telling the time. The lack of a clock in the room, meant to disorient those stuck in it for days at a time, led me to believe it was. My father's voice agreed with me.

"Well, now's the time," he said, when he finally got tired of waiting for me to say anything. "Now's your chance to tell us why you did it, why you killed them. We have you dead to rights for both murders, now. So, you might as well confess."

My eyes dropped to the desk. Both murders? How could they have tied me to the first one? Had they found some new, completely irrefutable evidence that tied me to her murder? Her eyes flashed in my mind, locked in an accusatory stare at her attacker. At her killer. Lost to the rigors of death for all time. Condemning any who walks in their path; just as I had done when I found her. I shook my head, jarring the image out of it, not a denial of anything. I had already denied my involvement in her death for days, weeks now. No one had believed me; certainly not Bently.

"There's no sense in denying it now. We have Angela in the other room, singing like a canary. We'll have the whole story soon enough. Wouldn't it be better to have your side of things on the record?"

Angela. Of course, it was Angela. She never liked me, even back when she was cheating with my husband. She must have been in on it as well. I should have killed her when I had the chance, back when I killed Greg. My father snarled his agreement. Of course, she will be spinning any story she could come up with. Anything to make it seem like Greg was an angel. A wonderful man that shouldn't have died. That should have lived a long, happy life with her and the baby. The only one that had my sympathy in that family was that baby boy, little Doug, who would grow up never knowing his father.

"I have nothing to say," I mumbled. I could have told him the truth. Everything that I had uncovered that day. Everything that had pointed me right back to that house. But, I knew, from weeks of experience with this man, that he wouldn't believe a word I said. No, he didn't like me. He never liked me. Anything I said, he would just twist around to make me look more guilty than I already did.

"Fine, why don't I do all the talking then. We know you killed Emily. Her blood was all over your clothes, as yours was on hers. Your skin was under her fingernails from where she defended herself against your attack. We even have you at the crime scene when the murder was taking place, by your own admission, I might add. What else do we need?"

I laughed at the thought of Emily defending herself against me. My skin was under her fingernails. Of course, it was. It was from when she tried to scratch my eyes out less than an hour before the murder. I had gone to her, tried to warn her about Greg. About his anger. About how she wasn't the first, and she certainly wouldn't be the last. Well, I was at least wrong about that last part, anyway. Greg worked fast, but not that fast. Not with the police looking everywhere for clues and Angela breathing down his neck.

"As for Greg, well, that was just sloppy," Bently continued, ignoring my little outburst of mirth. He probably just wrote it off as part of my condition, something he had uncovered on day one. Well, not so much uncovered as was told, flat out, by Greg. Thanks a lot, Greg. I'll see you in hell for that. "Doing it in full view of witnesses. That house is a complete mess right now. We'll be collecting evidence from there for a week. All of which will point directly at you as the killer. Hell, we have you holding the murder weapon, while it was still in the victim. You're not going to get away with it. With any of it. So, you might as well just confess. I've heard it's good for the soul."

Victim, yeah right. Greg had never been a victim in his life. He became a lawyer so that he would never be a victim, not even of the justice system. There was no way he wasn't going to get away with it. Get away with killing Emily. He would have gotten away with killing me, if he had succeeded. But there was no way I'd be able to tell Bently that. No way that he would believe it in a million years. It would just be the same as me admitting that I murdered my ex-husband simply because of the "ex" part of that equation.

Tom perked up at the thought of ex's and equations, coming to the forefront of my mind and beating Dad back to the background. I sighed, feeling the relief that I always felt at his absence. At the removal of that toxic cloud that I always carried around with me. Bently leaned back in his seat when he saw my reaction, no doubt thinking that I was about to confess. That I was ready to relieve myself of the burden of my guilt.

I leaned forward in my chair and Bently smiled. His grin grew beyond what his face should have been able to contain. His crooked front teeth sprung out from the cover of his lips. A gasp of the bad breath he subjected everyone to flowed through the air. A spritzing of dust and saliva flowed through the beams of light from above, unerringly heading my way. I inhaled quickly before it got to me, letting out the air to push the debris away, giving me space to breathe in. "I want a lawyer," I said, in that same breath.

The smile faded instantly from his face. "You just killed your lawyer," he spat at me, before getting up from the chair and leaving the room. The door slammed loudly. The sound resonated more in my head than in the rest of the room. It jarred my voices from their perches on my shoulders.

Of course, he was right. Greg had been my lawyer. No wonder why I was so screwed.

Chapter Three
Departure

The metal table was cold against my cheek. My reflection stared back at me with a look that was somewhere between boredom, fear, and loathing. Of course, since she was me, that would make it self-loathing, wouldn't it? Or perhaps it was for the men and women on the other side of the glass. I still had no doubt that a crowd grew over there. Perhaps they were eating popcorn, waiting for the crazy girl to snap. To turn on them. To start smashing things in the room. Or, maybe, just to confess. I almost wanted to confess just to get the whole mess over with.

When Bently had first left the room, I tried to count off the time until his return. I tried to keep track of the time in a room with no clock. But I had lost count of my irregular time keeping long before I heard from anyone. It didn't help that, while Tom helped count off the numbers in my head, Greg shouted out the numbers of his favorite sport stars. I knew that my newest of voices, the echoing remnant of my now dead ex-husband, was there mostly to spite me. No matter how justified I felt in killing him, he would always hate me for it.

The door opened up suddenly, bashing loudly against the wall behind it. It sounded like the door knob broke through the wall, as the metal of the handle slammed into the stone blocks behind the drywall. Bently stood there, framed by the doorway. His body was silhouetted against the much brighter light of the hallway outside. It seemed like the sun was hitting the building just right, its rays channeled down the hall and into his back. He looked glorious, godlike, and vengeful. He stepped a menacing step forward. His fists were clenched at his side, preparing to swing a blow.

It had been what I was expecting. What I had always expected from him and his ilk. Dad cried out, cheering the giant on as he came towards me. Fearful, I jumped up from the chair, backing away from the man. Backing away into the wall behind me. Until there was nowhere to back away to. When I could see his face, there was a rage there that I hadn't seen in the weeks since I met him. His hands went up, into the air. I flinched away from him, slinking down into the wall.

"You're free to go," he said, through gritted teeth. I looked up at him, from between my guarding arms, to see him gesturing to the door behind him. He had stepped aside, giving me free and clear access to the door. To the hallway beyond. To the freedom that I had thought I would never experience again.

He didn't need to tell me twice. I made my way out, waiting until I was free and clear before I tried to collect myself. The clock on the wall showed that I had only been in the interrogation room for a couple of hours. It was almost three o'clock in the afternoon. As I passed the covered flier of the costumed freak and his brethren, I paused. Not because of those eyes, though I did notice them again, staring into my soul as if it were that easy to see.

I stood there, not two feet away from the seat I had been put in when I first got there that day. Reluctantly, I turned back towards my captor, the detective. "I need a ride," I said. On the main occasions that I had been pulled into that station over the past few weeks, I had always left with Greg. He had always come to act as my lawyer. He would always come to inform the police that I would have nothing to say and they might as well just let me go. Then he would drive me home. Now that he was dead, I had no one to turn to. No support structure in place to give my life form. This is, of course, not including my shrink. But I had already burned that bridge too many times to count.

"I'll have an officer drive you by your apartment," Bently said. His voice had softened, though not by much. He still looked like he wanted to lock me up and throw away the key. I wouldn't put it past him to do so.

Unfortunately, Tom wouldn't shut up until I asked a stupid question that would only make Bently more mad at me than he already was. It was a dangerous question that could prompt the worst outburst I had ever elicited in another human being. "Why are you letting me go?"

"Shut up," Greg shouted at me. His voice drowned out Tom's incessant babbling and put him in his place. "Don't say another word."

"You're not my lawyer anymore," I whispered to Greg. I tried not to move my lips too much. I tried not to look crazy.

"You have a better friend in Angela than I would have thought, considering the state of your relationships," Bently said. It was a strange comment that I hadn't been expecting. I didn't even understand how it applied to my question. Although, apparently, Tom did. However, he wasn't offering an explanation, and neither was the detective. Instead, Bently just left me there, alone in the hallway, as he headed off to his desk. I knew where it was, though I had only been there once in all the times I had been in that station. It was the one in the far corner, buried by a large pile of folders and right next to the water cooler. As if to greet him home, the water cooler let off a new group of bubbles. The top two folders fell off the growing pile into his lap as he slid down into his overworked chair.

I sat back down into a chair as I waited for an officer to offer me that ride. It was the same chair that I had been in earlier, though this time without the handcuffs. Sitting there, I should have been feeling the relief that I wasn't under arrest anymore. That, for some reason, I was free, despite having killed Greg just a few hours earlier. I should have been thinking about the symbolism, or the symmetry in my day. I had woken up innocent of any crime but still under suspicion. By the cops. By Bently. I had assumed by Greg, though that turned out to be a lie. And, now, from the look on Bently's face, it would seem that he still suspected me. But he had nothing to prove definitively that I had done anything wrong.

And I had done nothing wrong. However, that wasn't what I was thinking of. Instead, those stupid eyes claimed me once more. Now that my hands were free, I could pull the newer fliers off of the one that had been haunting me, revealing the stupid man in the alien costume. Or, perhaps, it was supposed to be an orc or something. It had been a big debate on all the talk shows and the news for days. What the stunt had meant. What it was supposed to be about. Then, when the plane suddenly disappeared, that plane that had been flying towards the towers, everyone insisted that it was the aliens. That the aliens had abducted the plane in order to save it, and that the stupid stunt had really been an alien climbing down that bridge.

I pulled the flier off the board, letting the newer ones fall back into their place, hiding the spot that my pilfered plunder had been moments before. The "Information Wanted" flier had been everywhere. They had papered the town even as far north as we were, up here in Tarrytown. It was a sloppy picture, taken hastily on a cell phone. But it was the only one discovered of the strange man. So, it had made all the rounds. The picture was as famous as some of the better ones of bigfoot had been, back in the day. Back when people actually believed in that creature. It was hard to discount this one, though. The crowd that had been there, had been at the base of the support structure of the bridge, had been too large to discount.

"Ready to go?" someone asked. His voice jarred me out of my thoughts. I looked over to the source of the voice, the familiar face of Eric. He had been the officer who had first brought me in. He had been the first on the scene when I had found the body. I smiled at the friendly face, the first one I had seen that day, nodding my approval of their choice of escorts for me.

"Sure," I said, shrugging. Dad imitated the sound of a shotgun. It was not easy to do when you're nothing but a disembodied voice. But he accomplished it admirably. He had nothing to worry about, though. After Greg, I had sort of sworn off men for a while. I was in no hurry to find a replacement husband. Not concerned with finding love again. It had been nothing but a disaster for me most of the time anyway. What with my condition, I couldn't exactly expect the best of men, the best of loves, to come my way. Instead, I settled for the dregs. Greg had seemed a prince next to the frogs I had been stuck with before meeting him.

I did have to admit that Eric was cute. Perhaps now, now that the case was solved, that I wasn't at risk of being arrested, imprisoned, maybe it was time to consider trying again. I gave Eric my patented half smile. He only nodded at me, gesturing towards the front of the station.

"My car is just outside. I hope you won't be disappointed with a regular sedan. I just got off work, so I'll be taking you home in my personal car."

My smile broadened at the thought. Perhaps I wouldn't need to spend any more time in a cop car ever again. If I ever saw the back of another cruiser it would be too soon. Though, I had to admit, I was a little disappointed that I wouldn't be able to experience the front seat of one of them. "No, that's fine," I said, simply.

"Great," he beamed.

As we passed the front desk of the station, Eric waved at the two officers behind there. The front desk was the place that most visitors never get past, those that come to report crimes rather than be interrogated for them. I only glared at the officers, daring them to stop me. To arrest me. To pull me back into the dungeon of the station behind them. They, on the other hand, didn't so much as look up from their paperwork. Not to return the wave. Not to stop me. They barely even acknowledged my existence as I left the station, hopefully for the last time.

The sun beamed down on my face the minute that I stepped out of the glass doors that led to my freedom. It was glorious, feeling that instead of the dreadful dreariness of the cells within. After what I had done, I never would have expected to experience freedom again. I wasn't sure what to do with it.

Not wanting to test my luck, I quietly followed behind Eric as he led me to his car. I held the zillions of questions that were flooding my mind. Most of them were mine, though Dad and Greg added their own to the growing collection. As usual when I was confused, Tom was quiet as a mouse. He was neither curious nor lending his own analysis of the situation. He knew something, but I knew from experience that I wasn't going to get anything out of him. At least not until he was good and ready to tell me what was going on. And, usually, by then, I had figured it out myself.

Tom was an asshole.

Chapter Four
My Apartment

The remnants of the flier were still in my hands when Eric pulled into the parking lot of my apartment complex. I had been picking at it since leaving the station. Bits and pieces had been raining down onto the floor of the car. Onto the legs of my jeans. Even into my sneakers, sprinkling through the cracks and creases to tickle my toes. All that was left behind of the notice were the eyes, those hideous eyes. The special-order contacts that made them look so alien had been the most popular costume for Halloween that year, less than a week before the murder.

"Um, Natalie?" Eric said. His voice pulled me out of the vortex of those eyes. When I looked over at him, he was pointing out the front window of the car, out over towards my building. In front of it was a flock, a gaggle, a... what's the collective word for a group of reporters? From how they were approaching the car, I would have gone with swarm. "Do you want me to get us out of here?"

"No," I said, dejectedly. "They've only been getting worse over the past couple weeks. I guess it makes sense that they seemed to have doubled since this morning. It'll be better for me to get it over with. Or, at the very least, get in there to get a change of clothes. I've been wearing these since yesterday when..." I trailed off when I remembered the events that led up to my revelation, led up to the death of Greg. The flash of his dying eyes made me flinch. I shrugged in on myself when the reporters started banging on the window next to me.

"Well, maybe you shouldn't have killed me," Greg suggested. His voice made me flinch again. He was whispering in my left ear, so I flinched back towards the window, back towards the reporters. Despite the fact that Eric was sitting right next to me, right where Greg's voice had come from, I knew he wouldn't have heard a thing. He was kind enough not to mention my weird reaction, though.

"Just get me as close to the door as you can," I said. Flashes came from all over as the reporters tried to take decent pictures of me in the car with the officer. I just glared at them, daring them to bust open the windows and pull me free. "I'll make a break for it. Hopefully I can make it inside in one piece. Once I get out of the car, drive out of here as quickly as you can. Save yourself; there's no need for us both going down to these vultures."

"You don't have to answer any of their questions," he said. Eric had always seemed so sweet, despite his involvement with the detective.

"I know," I said, as way of a good bye, before opening the door. I ducked down, putting my arms over my head as I forced my way through the crowd. The last few bits of the flier were still clutched in my hand, but it did little to help me. Over the past few weeks, I had never once offered them a statement. I barely even acknowledged their existence there in front of my apartment. Yet their numbers only grew.

I found the curb the hard way, with my foot. My sneakers were little protection from slamming my toes into the cement, and no protection at all for my face. I fell forward, my hands barely coming up in time to break my fall. I faceplanted into the sidewalk. The reporters swarmed around me, their flashes going off, attacking me from all sides. Their cameras were plastered to their faces like third eyes, zooming in on my soul. Not a one of them bent down to help me up. All of them seemed to take a new level of pleasure in my plight. They wouldn't even give me the room that I needed to stand back up, leaving me to crawl forward to the front door.

The door opened, seemingly automatically, at my approach. It gave me enough room to dart inside. I came to a standing position, leaning forward against the far wall. The hallway headed off in both directions on either side of me. I breathed deeply, trying to steady my heart rate, trying to not pass out again. The general panic I had been feeling ever since finding Emily wasn't doing me any favors. Looking over my shoulder, back out at the throng that was barely held at bay by the glass door, I saw my landlord. He was holding the door closed against their banging. He must have been the one to open the door for me. It wasn't an automatic door and I didn't have a spare set of keys on me.

"Thanks," I huffed.

"No more," he said. I could never place his thick accent, though it was probably something middle eastern. I hadn't caught his name when he gave it to me a year ago when I moved in. "No more of this, no more of them. There are other people living here, you know. They need to be able to get in and out of their units without being accosted by them."

"I need to be able to get in and out of my own apartment without being ambushed by them," I pointed out. "I never asked for this, never wanted this. If I could go back, I'd never find that... never find Emily..."

"No, no, no, I don't want to hear of it. Get rid of them or I get rid of you."

"You can't evict me over reporters staying in front of the building," I said, exasperated. "I pay my rent on time and don't bother the other tenants."

"Watch me. Mark my words, number 403, you'll be out on your ass in no time."

The elevator dinging behind me drowned out the low, prolonged growl that Dad was giving off. Greg was quiet as he tried to mull over all the rules and precedents that would help me fight any pending eviction, though it wasn't his specialty. Tom was just sitting there, smug as always, as he hid from me the revelation that he came up with earlier. The landlord angrily stomped off towards his apartment, 114, the one facing the swarming sociopaths outside, just to the left of the entrance. I could see two of the reporters pressing their faces into the glass, trying to see me through the glare of the evening sun at their backs.

Someone pushed past me as they came off the elevator. The man took two steps towards the front doors before stopping dead in his tracks. "Ugh, not these people again. Why won't they just leave us alone? Who are they even here for anyway?"

"Who knows," I muttered, knowing his questions were rhetorical. He glanced back at me for a moment, before doing a double take. He rolled his eyes, as if to say he knew the answers to his questions just by looking at me. With a small huff, he headed off to the right hallway, towards the fire exit at the far end of the hall. After the reporters had started to camp out on our doorstep, the landlord had been nice enough to disable the alarm from using the fire doors. It allowed people easier access to the outside without having to pass by the mob. This had led a mass migration of the parking from the center of the lot towards that side. However, seeing as how I had been the source of the issue, I had kept parking in the middle, I still used the main entrance to do my penance. This only worked for the first week, before my car was lost beneath the throng. I knew it was still there. I had seen signs of it beneath the swarming insects. But I haven't had access to it for days. It had forced me to spend more time walking around and using public transportation. Of course, it had been walking that had gotten me in trouble in the first place.

The elevator doors threatened to close behind me before I could get on. I quickly, brazenly, threw my arm between them. They closed around the limb, but opened up quickly enough not to cause me any pain. Dad blustered his outrage at my supposed stupidity, repeating all the stories he had told me growing up about people getting stuck in elevator doors. They usually involved them being pulled through the shaft, their bodies bloody messes afterwards. I just shook it off, trying to ignore him as I got on the elevator and hit the "4" button.

I had to pry open one of the lamps hanging on the wall to get my hide-a-key. My own set was still in an evidence bag somewhere. Dad's bluster ended the moment I stepped back inside my apartment, the place that I had feared I would never see again. I looked all over the place, already feeling the underlying sense of dread that was emanating off of him. It wasn't the usual kind of quiet, when the voices would finally be silent enough for me to think properly. It was the paranoid kind of quiet, the one that had kept me alive for as long as it had. The kind that had kept me from being committed twice already. The one time I ignored it, I had spent two years in Holy Trinity Psychiatric.

I looked around at my apartment, searching for anything out of place. My purse was still where I usually left it, on the table right by the door. It had gone forgotten last night when I went for that walk. My wallet was still sticking out of it from where I took out the cash that I figured I might use, though I had thought I had pushed it back down afterwards. The answering machine next to the purse was blinking that I had a bunch of messages. Seeing as how most of them were going to be from the reporters outside, begging for my side of things, I didn't bother listening to any of them. The low light from outside struggled to come through the blinds that I had started keeping closed, trying to avoid being seen. It was something that I started after I had found a picture of me eating in my dining room on one of the tabloid rags the other day. I reached for the light switch next to me, hesitating with my finger extended. It was edging closer to it as my eyes continued to wander around, waiting for Dad to find some clue. Some evidence that his suspicions were right. He was still messaging me that turning on the light would be a bad idea, that it would only draw attention to myself. It would draw the attention of someone there that shouldn't have been there, more so than my opening the door had.

But there wasn't anything there. No one was hiding behind the couch that seemed out of place in the apartment, largely due to the fact that I had chosen it for how well it would look in the living room back at the house. No one was hiding in the closet that I always kept open, because the door dragged across the carpet and was too much of a pain to keep closed. The small kitchen, open up to the rest of the apartment, was empty. Although, the trash needed to be taken out and the sink was full of dishes that I was too lazy to wash. I even looked over to the bedroom, the door closed to keep that room cooler than the rest of the apartment. Nothing seemed out of place.

Just as I flicked on the lights, giving off a steadying sigh of relief that there was nothing to Dad's suspicions, someone knocked on the door behind me, making me jump in place.

Chapter Five
Angela's Arrival

"Go away," I yelled through the door. I bristled at the boldness of some of these reporters, invading my building in an effort to get a statement. When this whole thing first started, back when everyone just assumed that I had done it because I was standing over the body with blood all over me, they hadn't bothered to stay outside. Instead, they assaulted me at my door, camping out on my doorstep. It was ever friendly Eric that had repelled them. He made it clear to all of them that they weren't allowed inside. Apparently, the "No Solicitors" sign on the front door to the building hadn't been enough.

"Natalie, it's Angela. We need to talk." I cringed at her voice.

"Go away," I repeated, wanting nothing to do with that woman. I'd sooner jump out the window to talk to the reporters than open the door for her.

"We need to talk," she said. "There are things we need to discuss now that Greg's..." Her voice broke when she said his name. Sobs were clearly audible through the thick wood door.

"She's right, you know," Greg said, in my ear.

"Well, who asked you," I muttered to him.

"What?" Angela asked.

"Nothing, I was just... Nothing."

"Let her in," Greg insisted. "At the very least, you need to know what she told the cops."

I rolled my eyes at his insistence. Still, reluctantly, I pulled open the door that I hadn't fully closed just yet. I had been waiting until I knew my home was safe before latching it and putting on the five locks that I had gotten installed last week. The landlord was not happy about that, and had threatened to take it out of my security deposit.

Angela's blond hair hung loose and wild around her face, making her seem like she had just stumbled out of bed. Greg cooed guiltily at the sight, as if he had just been in bed with her. Of course, that was completely impossible now. Other than him just being a voice in my head and, well, you know, dead, there was no way that Angela would have slept with him after knowing what he did.

Or would she? I wouldn't put much past her, given the fact that she had been sleeping with my husband while we were still married, supposedly happily married. She held the evidence of the affair in her arms, the sleeping baby cradled against her neck. His hand was unconsciously reaching for her breast. He seemed so much like his father in that way.

"Can we come in?" she asked. She looked behind me as if inspecting my apartment. As if trying to see if my home was up to her high standards. This seemed a bit ironic to me, considering her appearance.

This had to be the most unkempt that I had seen her since I had met her. Since I came home to find her and Greg in our bed. Even then, wearing nothing but a sheet, she had looked like a golden goddess. Perfectly framed by the sunlight streaming in through the bay windows, as if God himself wanted nothing more than to bask in her beauty. Now, though, she wasn't wearing any makeup, her t-shirt had spit up and other, less identifiable, stains all over it, and I was pretty sure the jeans she was wearing had belonged to Greg, from the small pile of jeans that he never wore. Seeing her like that whittled away at my hatred of her the slightest bit. It was enough to allow me to keep my pride intact as I stepped aside, granting her access to my sanctuary from her and the cheating asshole that now haunted me.

Angela eased down onto the couch. She repositioned her son from her shoulder to her lap so that she could free her arms. I went over to the little dinette in the corner, turning around my usual chair to face her. As she sat there, comfortably, I tried not to think of the fact that this was probably not the first time that she had sat on that couch, despite having never visited my apartment before. Dad's continual laughing didn't help that effort much.

"You wanted to talk?" I prompted, after a moment of awkward silence.

"Right," she said, though she didn't pick up the cue immediately. Instead, she sat there for a while longer, just staring at me as if she had never seen me before. As if she hadn't been sitting next to that ingrate in every single divorce mediation meeting that we had.

"Be nice," Greg said. I rolled my eyes at him again, the only possible response I could give to him right then without seeming like a complete lunatic.

"Look, it's been a long day," I said. I didn't qualify how it had been a long day, but my eyes went to my hands, still stained red with Greg's blood. I hadn't been able to wash up, hadn't been able to get him off of me all day, and I desperately wanted to crawl into the shower, curl into a ball, and cry for the next three months.

"I'm sorry," she said.

"It's fine, let's just get it over with." I wasn't quite sure what I was saying was fine. It was just my default response to any apology, no matter how heartfelt.

"No, I mean, I'm sorry, about everything," she said.

"Everything is a lot," I said.

"And I'm sorry about a lot. About the affair. About Emily. About... about today. I'm very sorry. If I had known--"

"You never would have slept with him?" I asked. "Yes, you would have." She had known that he was married from the beginning. If she hadn't, I couldn't have been as angry with her as I was. At him, sure, but I could have forgiven her ignorance. He was just a lying piece of--

"Not if I knew that he was going to kill someone. Someone he had been sleeping with. I had known Emily, and-_"

"So had I," I yelled. She scooped up the baby, rocking and shushing him before he even woke up. It was obviously an over-practiced maneuver. He barely even flinched at my outburst. She was just tending to the little one, giving him exactly what he needed to stay calm, to stay asleep. It reminded me of some of Greg's more fiery outbursts, and his gloating guffaws in my ear weren't helping. "So had I," I repeated, at a more sensible volume. "I had known her a lot longer than you even knew him."

"I know," she said. "I wasn't trying to... I never wanted to diminish what you had with him. You two were together for--"

"Fourteen years," I said. Two years ago, I would have called them wonderful. But he had put an end to that long before she had ever shown up. In my most self-demeaning moments, I knew that what we had had been destroyed before she entered the picture. If it hadn't been her, it would have been someone else. That didn't mean I had to like it.

"Exactly," she agreed, she placated. "I didn't even have him for fourteen months." I glared at the three month old baby in her arms, the symbol of those months. The proof that she had no trouble getting pregnant, of carrying a perfectly healthy baby to term. "Either way, he cheated on us both. He lied to us both. We have more in common than we have differences."

"I somehow doubt that," I said with a grunt. Dad grunted his own agreement.

"We also both need to learn to live in this world now that he isn't in it anymore."

"What is that supposed to mean?" I asked. "I haven't needed him for anything for a long time."

"So, you haven't been taking his alimony? You've been working this whole time? Paying for this apartment all on your own?" That took some bluster out of me for the briefest of moments. But, once I got over the shock, I glared right back at her, reflecting her statement back on her. "Yes, I've been just as guilty of relying on his money as all that, though I've been living in the house that is fully paid off."

"Yeah, my house," I said. Greg had been far too busy to help in the house hunt. I picked out everything, from the town, to the neighborhood, to the house, to the furniture, and what we were going to do with it. When we got married, it had suddenly become my full-time job to take care of everything that he was too busy to deal with. What did I get for all of that effort? A husband that suddenly had far too much time on his hands.

"I'm just saying... I don't really know what the state of everything is going to be. But there might come a day when we're forced to... consolidate."

"Pfft, you mean live in the house? With you?"

"Or, maybe we'll move into a duplex somewhere else, somewhere cheaper. It might be better to move at this point. I saw you have your own growing collection of lawn ornaments outside."

"Lawn ornaments?" I asked. I moved towards the window to look down on the courtyard below, hoping, more than believing, that the reporters had departed. The second I pushed aside the blinds, I got blasted again by a barrage of flashes from their cameras. I immediately pushed the blinds back in place, not even having gotten a proper look at the grounds below. Dazed and blinded, I felt my way back to my chair. I held on to the familiar feel, the support that I desperately needed.

"That's what I call the reporters," she explained, too late. "It's not exactly like you can call them human beings. Humans would have left us alone by now."

"They haven't gotten their story yet," I said, finding the explanation obvious. Tom blew out a breath in my ear, as if to say that he was about to say that. "Unless, of course, you've already talked to them. Have you?"

"No, of course not," she said. "Not without discussing it with you first. We need to stay a united front on that subject."

"I don't want to be united with you on anything," I sniped. "I just want to be left alone."

"Fine," she huffed. She flapped up her free hand, the one not cradling her child. It hit the couch at her side loudly, though not loud enough to disturb the baby. "Fine, I'll leave you to your... aloneness. I know that a lot has happened today, and you probably want to... well... Anyway, think about it."

"Think about what?" I asked, confused. What exactly had she said that hadn't been complete nonsense?

"Think about what you're going to do, now that he's gone. Now that you have no one to hate. Now that the money isn't coming in anymore." In one fluid movement, she moved the baby back up to her shoulder as she stood up. It seemed overly rehearsed, though she didn't seem to think much of it. Her eyes never left the face of her child. The love she had for him was plain in her eyes. It hurt me, to see that kind of love. To know that I would never experience it for myself.

She smiled at me, encouragingly, as she made her way back across the room towards the front door. Tom perked up the moment she placed her hand on the knob. He reminded me that I really did have something that I needed from her. Something that I needed to know. "Angela?" I asked, hesitantly.

"Hmm?" she mumbled, turning around to look at me as she pulled open the door.

"What exactly did you tell the cops today? What did you tell them that made them release me so easily?"

"The truth," she said, simply, as she walked back out of the door.

Chapter Six
Shrink

It was nice of Greg to die the day before I was already scheduled to see my shrink. Dr. Mendez was one of the staff psychiatrists at Holy Trinity, but he had his own practice just a few blocks away from my building. It gave me an excuse to go for a walk around the neighborhood once a week, sometimes twice when the voices were overly verbose. His ground floor office looked out into an internal courtyard. It was one of those areas inside the building itself, open only to the sky above, that usually looked unkempt and that no one could actually get into without picking a few locks here and there. Greg would have never been seen dead in a place like that, which was part of its charm for me. Admittedly, I didn't know about the office before building a rapport with the good doc back at HTP. However, it was one of my excuses to continue seeing him. That, and the fact that it was a term of my release. If I missed too many sessions, even if it was for something like, say, spending the day in jail, I'd find myself right back in a padded cell.

The waiting room outside the office was small. Dr. Mendez, unlike some doctors, never got backed up far enough to have more than one person waiting at any given time. It had a single chair stuffed in the corner next to the door, one with a metal frame and thin leather padded seat and back. There was also a button to indicate to the doctor that you were there. He didn't have a receptionist, though I imagine that made it easier for those people with social problems. I had met quite a few of them during my stay at HTP, even having to room with one. That was an interesting experience, to say the least. The waiting room was narrower than the office itself, so it didn't have a window. Instead, the walls were covered with inspirational posters, mostly cats in odd situations. As if seeing cute creatures in precarious positions would make our problems seem not as bad. Dad always hated those. He hated cats in general. He always begged for me to pull them all down and set fire to them. It was easy to ignore him when he went on about that, though. No setting fires for me. That's another guaranteed one way trip back to the nuthouse.

I had been sitting there for twenty minutes before the light switched off and the door to the office opened up. My wait was more because Dad insists that I be early everywhere than that the doctor was running late. I stood up, expectantly, but had to take an awkward step into the corner to let the last patient by. "Hey, Mark," I said, recognizing the patient. Mark usually had the time slot before me, so we ran into each other often enough. We also had spent some time together at HTP, but I had left almost a week after he was committed that time.

A shocked expression played across his face as he saw me there. "Hey, Natalie," he said. "I-I hadn't expected to see you here." His voice quivered noticeably as his eyes seemed to grow disproportionately large. I squinted my eyes shut, shaking my head a little, to dislodge the delusion. But, when I opened my eyes again, he only looked more distraught. "Well, I-I'll see ya... I guess." He darted through the open door, not turning his back towards me as he left. His footsteps thundered down the hallway, echoing around the small room like thunder.

"Come on in, Natalie," Dr. Mendez said, drawing my attention back towards his office. As usual, he was sitting behind his desk. His tall backed office chair was stuck in the far corner, preventing it from turning more than an inch in either direction. He gestured towards the large leather couch that took up much of the wall next to the door, knowing full well that I preferred the small chaise by the window. This wasn't me being paranoid, not wanting my back to the door, or anything crazy like that. I just didn't like sitting on something that was so soft that it would swallow me whole if given half the chance. "I've heard you've been having a few... issues since our last session," he said, as I closed the door behind me.

"You can say that," I said. I automatically, almost robotically, walked over to the chaise, sitting down heavily. I leaned against the wall behind it, as the back only came up to the small of my back. But I put up my legs on the rest of it. The light blue leather smelled like something out of a dream, but it did little to chase away the nightmares that have been plaguing me as of late. I could still see Emily's eyes whenever I closed mine.

"I saw you on the news yesterday, though I can't say that I caught the gist of the story. Care to explain what's been happening?"

"Not really," I said, simply, honestly. "The case is over, or, at least, I hope it is."

"So, no more talk about sending you to prison, then? That's good. Have they apprehended the killer?"

"Uh... no... he... he died."

"Oh, well, that's a shame. At least he's not on the loose anymore. How are things with you?"

That apparently wasn't the right question for him to ask as, suddenly, quite unexpectedly, even for me, I started to break down. To cry harder than I had in a long time. Dad just gawked at me, stunned by my reaction, much like I was. I didn't actually see him do it, but I could feel his gaze on me. To Dr. Mendez's credit, he waited patiently in his chair, knowing that him trying to comfort me would be no comfort at all. He knew that my... history, shall we say, would prohibit me to accept any support from him besides quiet patience. Dad, on the other hand, didn't know this about me, despite being with me constantly for the past several years. I could sense him trying to hug me. I flinched away from his touch, as I always had back when he was alive.

Dr. Mendez must have noticed the movement. When I finally managed to bring myself back together, he had a solid frown on his face as he watched me. "Have you been taking your medication?" he asked.

"Of course," I lied. Well, it wasn't exactly a lie. I had been taking it, just not as directed. The dosage he had put me on back in HTP often left me in a fog, one that I could barely function in. So, after leaving the forced medication environment, I had backed myself down to half dosage. It had mostly kept the voices at bay, though never completely silent. However, with the stress of the investigation, I must have missed a few doses. Dad and Tom had, almost instantly, come out to play, making the whole situation that much worse. "It's just the stress," I said, trying to write it off as nothing.

He eyed me warily, his eyes drilling through me like he could see down to my soul. I focused, instead, on his diplomas and certificates that papered the wall behind him. None of his credentials were all that impressive. He went to Rutgers for crying out loud. But they must have been enough to make him a fully certified shrink. Admittedly, it wouldn't have been enough for Greg, but he never had much of a choice in the matter. Not when we were married, and certainly not now that he was...

The reminder of him drew my attention to his absence. Ever since my keys found his neck, he had been an almost constant companion to me, much as Dad and Tom had become over the years. I tried to think back, tried to remember, just when I shook him. I could have sworn that I had heard him say something stuck-up on the walk over. Perhaps the thought that Greg wouldn't find himself dead in that building had been more appropriate than I had thought.

"And, yet, you seem to be having a conversation with one of them right now," Dr. Mendez said.

I looked at him, confused. "I wasn't talking to anyone," I said, in all honesty. "I was just... thinking... about... about the case."

"Uh, huh," he said, unconvinced.

"No, really. I... well... okay, you'll probably find this out eventually anyway. Hell, it's probably going to be on the news for weeks more. It... it was Greg."

"What was Greg?" he asked.

"Greg killed Emily," I said.

"But you said the killer is dead."

"Yes."

"Greg's dead?"

"Yup."

"The police killed him?"

"Nope."

"Oh... oh... oh... I'm... I'm sorry. Are... are you going to be alright? I mean with the police and all."

"Oddly enough, I think killing Greg is going to be the least of my worries," I said, trying to laugh it off. It wasn't working. "Angela was there. She heard him confess. She saw everything. And, miracle of miracles, she actually told the cops what really happened, rather than trying to get me sent to jail for the rest of my life."

"That was... considerate of her," he said.

"Yeah," I said, hesitantly. "Yeah."

"I imagine that wasn't easy for her. Not only admitting that Greg had been the one to kill Emily, but that she had married someone that was capable of doing that without her knowing it. She hadn't spent the past two weeks out of town, had she?"

"What? No, why? She had been one of the many people trying to get me sent away for the rest of my life."

"And, yet, she had been sleeping beside the real murderer the whole time, without her knowing it."

"I guess... but, they have a newborn. Aren't new parents supposed to be sleep deprived?" I joked.

He nodded towards me, not so much granting me the point as much as trying to change the subject. The new subject that he had come up with took me a little by surprise. "Have you spoken to Angela since then?"

"Yeah, she actually came by last night, when I got home from the police station. She must have come right over herself, 'cause I hadn't been home for long before she was there. I'm not entirely sure when they let her go though."

"They had arrested her?"

"No, they had her in for questioning, or whatever. I was the one holding the... when... when they came by." I tried not to picture it, the blood oozing down my hand. But the feeling wasn't going away. The ever-prominent box of tissues was on his desk, just out of reach. It was usually used by those that come to therapy to cry. I leaned forward, scooping up three of them, before lounging back again. The wad of tissues did little to wipe the blood off my hands. The blood that wasn't really there.

I had taken three long, hot showers the night before, only to give up on feeling clean ever again. The blood had seeped into every crevice of my hands, stretching down my arms and into my pits. Fortunately, it hadn't gone much further. But it had dried onto my skin, seeming like some alien disease, slowly converting me to something I wouldn't be able to recognize. Even after my skin was clear of the red, brown, and black crust that had formed on it, I could still feel it there. Still feel my skin slow to move as I continued to scrub at it. And the tissues, scrubbing at that sensation that would never go away, did little to abate it.

"You're not turning OCD on me as well, are you?" Dr. Mendez joked. He got up from his chair, something I rarely saw him do, and moved around to sit near my feet. Dr. Mendez was a large man, though thin as a stick. His broad shoulders made navigating his small office a feat all its own. Yet he made it look effortless, with his almost graceful movements. The chaise leaned over slightly under his weight.

The far leg popped up a centimeter, jarring me out of my frenzied state. He took the wad of tissues, pulling them from my hand and tossing them into the trash with the same movement. They had already broken apart into so much lint under my fevered scrubbing, and rained down like snow into the can. As I watched them fly, he took up my hands in his. He pulled me closer to him, to force me to look him in the eyes. "There's nothing there," he insisted. "There's nothing wrong with your hands. You need to calm down."

I nodded. Taking a deep breath in, I started performing some of the relaxation exercises that he had taught me during my stay at HTP. He did them with me, his breathing in tuned with mine, as I tried to let go of the stress that had been plaguing my life for the past few weeks. Even before finding Emily's body. It had been like I had some kind of premonition, Tom being smug again for weeks as he hoarded a revelation that he had had the last time we had seen Greg. I tried not to picture it, tried not to think of seeing him and her at that work function that I had stumbled upon during one of my walks. As I gradually got a handle on myself again, my heart slowly finding its usual rhythm, Dad perked up again. He was never one to leave me to my peace.

"Is this guy trying to make a move on you?" he mumbled, directly into my ear. I smiled, a single laugh flitting out, unbidden, from my lips. A single blip of madness in my otherwise, relatively, sane mindset. Dr. Mendez, sitting next to me, didn't seem to notice it.

"Now, are we better?" he asked. He looked into my eyes with a level of concern that he had never seemed to show with any of his other patients. At least not while I was around. It took some of my bluster away, making Dad's words seem not as insane as they should have been.

"Sure," I said, nodding.

He gave me a small smile before dropping my hands and making his laborious trip back around his desk. "So now what are you going to do?" he asked, before plopping down, heavily, into the chair. As he did so, I wondered just how many of his patients had managed to get him to stand up during a session. He always seemed plastered in that thing, as if he was incapable of standing up under his own power.

"What?" I asked, when he sat there, staring at me, expectantly.

"What are you planning on doing, now that the case is over. Certainly, you were going to do something."

"I... was going to go looking for a job?" I asked, more than said.

"Yes, we had discussed that at one point, hadn't we?"

"It does seem like the logical next step, doesn't it?" I echoed Tom's words as he whispered them into my ear.

"Especially since the alimony payments should be ending, now that you... now that Greg is dead."

"Yeah... funny you should say that... Angela had mentioned that yesterday. What is the protocol for that? Shouldn't I still be getting my checks?"

"Well, I don't think Angela is going to be picking up that responsibility," Dr. Mendez said.

"Certainly not," Tom agreed.

"I'm no lawyer," he said. This made me wonder, yet again, just where Greg had disappeared to. It would be just my luck to lose a voice right when I might actually need him. "But I think you should be covered once the will is executed."

"Yeah, like Greg kept me in that," I laughed.

"If that's the case, then you would definitely need to consult with a lawyer. In the meantime, it's a good idea to start looking for other sources of income. Plus, there's the whole 'getting out of the house and socializing with other people' aspect that I can't herald enough."

"Right," I said. "It's also a much better idea than the one Angela had come up with."

"What idea was that?" he asked.

"She was actually suggesting that I move in with her," I laughed.

"That... might actually not be that bad of an idea."

"What? No, it would be a terrible idea. I'd have to live... with... her. And that spawn of hers."

"Did she say why she was suggesting it?"

"Money. It's always money with her." And Greg, but I didn't add that last part. I, grudgingly, had to admit that they made a good fit between the two of them.

"Did it ever occur to you that money might not be the only reason why she suggested it?"

"What?" I asked, completely surprised by that suggestion. Tom, the ever over-analytical one, was similarly thrown by this thought. Dad, on the other hand, was picturing something quite different, which would have earned him a slap across the face if I was able to do so.

"As you said before, she does have an infant to take care of. When she had Greg around, she had at least some help. Maybe she's looking for that from you. Plus, maybe, just maybe, she might actually feel bad about how that whole thing went down. Maybe she wants to make it up to you."

"By inviting me to live with her?"

"By allowing you to move back into the house that you yourself had picked out, as you had said on multiple occasions. Maybe this is her trying to bury the hatchet, as they say. I'm not telling you to move in with her or anything. I just want you to honestly consider it. Not just from your point of view. Not just from the point of view of the scorned ex-wife. But from hers. From someone who might, just might, need something similar in return."

"You really are insane, Doc," I said, shaking my head. No wonder why they say all shrinks are in therapy.

"Well, on that note, it looks like our time is up. I do have some time open on Friday if you think--"

"Nope, I'm good," I insisted. I didn't want to spend another hour discussing Angela's weird suggestion, and all the reasons that might have gone into it. Instead, I stood back up, grabbing a couple of tissues along the way, for the road, and headed back towards the door. "Same time next week is more than enough for right now."

"You might be surprised," Dr. Mendez said, as a parting analysis. "You might find you need my help more than you think, particularly to get over what you were forced to do. I did notice that we didn't spend much time on that."

"When I figure out just how I feel about that, I'll let you know."

"That's not really how therapy works. You know that."

"I also know that I'm smack dab in the middle of denial right now. I like it here. I think I'll stay."

I nodded towards George, the guy with the standing appointment after mine, on my way out into the hall. He was in the middle of reading one of the three magazines that have been in the waiting room since I first started going to Dr. Mendez fifteen years ago. Or, perhaps, he was just in the middle of avoiding eye contact with me. I wondered, briefly, if he had seen the news. If he had known what I did to Greg. If he was just worried that, if he looked at me, I might end up killing him as well. Last I checked, though, George hadn't killed someone, tried to frame me for the murder and, when that didn't work, tried to kill me. So, he was safe from my wrath... for now at least.

As often happens after my sessions, Tom and Dad were arguing over some of the more relevant revelations that had come up during the session. This time it was mostly around the thought that Angela might need me as much as she said that I would need her. Dad was of the opinion that he doubted the woman needed anyone, other than inside her sheets, and if I wasn't prepared to fulfill those needs, I needn't bother moving in with her. Tom, on the other hand, was in full agreement with the good doctor. He was throwing up my memories of the strained look of Angela when she was at my apartment. Usually, I tried to stay out of it, content to let them battle it out, knowing their conclusion would have no impact on my own decision. But I had to put in my own two cents on this one. I did admit that she had looked rather ragged. However, that was probably more related to my just having killed her husband right in front of her, and less with her being overstressed by the baby. After all, until yesterday morning, she had had Greg's help with everything.

The three of us were right in the middle of an argument, with my words as silent to the outside world as theirs were, when we left the building. Suddenly, it was no longer the three of us, but the four. Greg stomped over towards us. How voices can stomp is beyond me, but he somehow managed it. Unfortunately, I don't actually see these people, just hear their voices in my ear. So, I couldn't tell just where he had disappeared to. However, seeing as how I had last sensed him by my side when I entered the building, I had my suspicions that my original thoughts about him were completely true. Greg really wouldn't be caught dead in that building.

"What did I miss?" he asked, interrupting our internal diatribe.

Chapter Seven
Nightmare

The phone rang in the middle of the night. I swore loudly into my pillow, once. Then Dad started up a long list of swear words that would impress the most foul-mouthed sailor. I wanted to just let it go, let the phone ring to the machine. Or, better yet, pick it up and slam it back down loudly. However, Tom is one of those people that just can't let a ringing phone go. Begrudgingly, I got up out of my nice, warm, comfortable bed and stumbled over to the phone. On the way there, I begged Dad to shut up long enough so that I could hear the other line. I promised him that, if given the chance and excuse, I'd give him free reign of my mouth to spout out all the foul words he wanted to the actual person responsible for waking me up at... I glanced at the clock on the TV as I passed it, 1:20 in the morning.

The silence of the night returned to the apartment when I managed to pick up the phone, but that wouldn't be the end of my discomfort. "What?" I yelled into the phone, before it even made it all the way to my ear.

"Oh, sorry," came a small, high pitched voice on the other side of the line. "Wrong number." The line went dead before I could give Dad the go ahead. Instead, I slammed the phone back onto the cradle, grumbling under my breath as I started to head back to bed.

I took two steps away from the phone before it started ringing again. "God, damn it," I yelled, loud enough to wake the neighbors. I've noticed on multiple occasions that the walls of my apartment aren't all that thick, so that was easily accomplished. I reached back, not even bothering to move my feet, and scooped the phone back up. "What?" I yelled, again.

"Oh, sorry," the voice said, again, the line immediately going dead.

Dad's line of profanity started up again, beginning from the top of his long, overly practiced list that, at one point, I almost had memorized myself. Agreeing with his sentiment, I unhooked the phone, from both the wall and the machine, and slammed it back down. The small end table that it had been on for years, even before moving into the apartment, collapsed under my unexpectedly strong slam. On my way back to bed, the neighbor to the right started banging on his wall, our shared wall being in his bedroom. I glared at that wall, wondering what it would take to bash it open. To rip a hole large enough in it to pull him halfway through it. Instead, I simply ignored him as I headed back to my bed. Once I closed the door to my own bedroom behind me, his banging was no louder than the ticking of the clock hanging in the room. It had been a fifth anniversary gift from Greg, an antique wooden cuckoo clock.

After climbing into bed, that ticking was all I could hear. Dad had finally gone silent, having fallen back to sleep much more easily than I ever do. Tom had barely woken up to start with; just enough for him to be irritated by the ringing phone. I lay there, listening to the ticking of the clock, until the little bird popped out, once, to tell me just how crazy it thought I was to be awake that early in the morning, before slamming his door closed behind him.

"No kidding," I said to it, as the general silence of the room resumed. I rolled over, so I could stare at the wall, trying to see through it. Trying to see the impertinent phone that had interrupted my perfectly good sleep, something that didn't often come easily to me. As it slowly became clear to me that I wasn't going to get back to sleep anytime soon, I decided to take a walk. Those late-night walks were something that I had often done back when I still lived with Greg. I hadn't felt the need to do them since leaving. It was almost like leaving Greg had solved most of my insomnia issues. I would never truly be rid of them, though. Not without getting rid of the voices while I was at it.

After grabbing a pair of comfortable sweats to put over my usual sleeping outfit, a tank top and a pair of panties, I threw on a pair of flats. Once ready for the cold outside, I grabbed my keys and headed out into the night. My night walks were always such a mystical experience. I was seeing the world while everyone else around me was asleep. It was almost like the world itself was at sleep as well. The street and traffic lights still worked, still followed their usual patterns. But the rest was darkness. Even the nighttime insects and birds had gone to sleep, leaving only the sounds of my own footsteps on the cement.

I don't know why I decided to head towards the river. Perhaps it was just that it was downhill from my apartment. Or maybe it was something else, some internal messaging system that knew that I needed to go that way. All I knew was that I couldn't blame it on the voices. Dad and Tom still slept soundly despite my waking state. That was another reason why I used to have those midnight walks. It was the only time that they were silent. When I wasn't overly medicated that is. It was the only time that I could be alone with my own thoughts. Not someone else's. And not with the numbing nothingness of the drugs. Every time I stepped out into the darkness, alone with myself, I'm always reminded of how amazing it is to be truly and completely alone.

Three blocks over from my apartment is a long stretch of woodlands, surrounding the river on the east. The land was set aside as a park over a century ago, a protected woodland and nature preserve that had survived generations of rezoning of the area. It often made me smile to think that that little piece of nature was just a few miles north of the city that never seemed to have enough room. But, of course, in recent years, with climate change starting to affect the level of the river, it also doubled as a flood zone. No one wanted to risk building in there anyway. Not with plenty of room further upstate or closer to the city.

There was a much-used path that led into the woods, starting at the end of the street as if it were a continuation of it. My feet found the path without much prodding from me. The sounds of my footsteps immediately changed from the clap of leather against stone to a more subtle, subdued sound of wet leaves underfoot. The ground was littered with beer cans, cigarette buds, and less pleasant signs of the passing of humans through that path. With the area less visible to the outside world, people were less inclined to keep it clean and clear. Still, the signs of human life of the area tapered off the further I went into the woods. As did the light from the streets behind me.

When it got to be too dark to see the ground in front of me, I waited, allowing my eyes to adjust to the darkness of the woods. I knew that I should have turned back. Should have headed home. Should have gone back to bed. But the draw of the woods, of the wilderness in front of me, was too much for my half-asleep mind to listen to my better judgement. Half of me wanted Dad to wake up, to revel in that wilderness with me. When I was growing up, my father and I would go camping every once in a while. It was on those rare occasions, and only on those rare occasions, that he actually acted like he was my dad. It was as if the removal of the temptations of modern life, the return to the wilds of our forefathers, suddenly made him a decent human being.

The sounds of water rushing past got gradually louder as I approached the river. It drew me further into the woods. It was so gradually, in fact, that I never noticed when I first heard it. Still, I continued onward. My eyes searched everywhere for the signs of the river, for that final stretch of woods that would break free into the open space over it.

There were several places in the woods where that break, the bank of the river itself, was sudden and treacherous, with several feet to fall before hitting the water.

A familiar rock came into view before I saw the end to the woods. It was a place I had often gone when walking through there. I knew that I would be able to see the river rushing past when sitting on the rock. Knew that it signified the end of the wooded area, the safe, solid ground for me to walk upon. Not wanting to risk falling into the river, I headed straight for it. That familiarity was the main reason why I had come to that rock so often. As I did, I realized that that rock had always been my target, my destination, even as far back as when I left my apartment, with none in mind.

The wet, slick sounds of my footsteps changed again as I stepped around the rock, coming to sit in my usual seat. It was a small divot in the otherwise random surface of the stone. The divot looked surprisingly seat-like, and worked well as one, almost as if it were carved just for me. Or, perhaps, I was just one of many that have gone to that stone over the years, with so many of us using it that it had worn down into that form.

I thought little of the change of the sound of my footsteps, figuring it had more to do with the proximity of the river than anything else. My hands draped down on the rock, feeling around for armrests that didn't exist, as my eyes turned to the horizon. The break in the tree line, not five feet in front of me, overlooked a big drop into the river. The moon was visible over there, setting on the horizon that was no longer blocked by the woods. The far side of the river could be seen in the distance, though it was too far off to see much of anything specific.

It was the smell that I noticed first, before anything else. It was this wet, coppery smell, the smell of old pennies. That smell always reminded me of a bad day in my childhood, a day that I tried my best not to think of. I squeezed my eyes shut against the onslaught of the memory, the almost physical attack my body goes through whenever my mind goes amuck. I could feel the beast, Dad, stirring at the memory. But I shook my head, trying to dispel it from my thoughts. Instead, I thought of an old lullaby he used to sing to me, back before he became that monster that needed to be destroyed. I tried to lull him back to the slumber he hadn't quite escaped from.

But, then, I remembered what that smell was, what it signified. And, suddenly, it was all I could smell. Freshly spilled blood. Death if not tended to quickly. I started to look around, my eyes darting around the dark ground I could barely see. The moon, flirting with the horizon, was little help, leaving me in the utter darkness that had surrounded me since I took to the woods. I stood up, planning to run back to the road, to get help from the first person I saw. Not that I expected to see anyone, as early as it was. I didn't get that far, though. My foot slipped on something, tripping over a branch. I spilled forward, perilously close to the cliff, close to the water's edge. I fell to the dirty, blood soaked ground.

That's when I saw it. Saw them. The eyes, staring into mine, reaching down into my soul to pull it free, to drag it along to the afterlife with hers. Emily, her lips locked in a scream of denial, her eyes cold and dead to the world. I was covered in her blood. It was everywhere. It was all I could see.

I screamed.

Chapter Eight
Evicted

I continued to scream as I jumped up in bed. My covers clung to me, restraining me in their embrace. Dad tried to comfort me, shushing me, as his incorporeal hands slid through my hair, pressing it into my scalp with the cold sweat that was already there. When I ran out of breath, I gasped for more, my scream winding down in the process. As it faded, the echoing remnant bounced around the room. My cuckoo clock told the time, telling me just how crazy it thought I was being. Still, the lingering memories of the dream would not fade. The cold, dead eyes of Emily as they were the night that I found her continued to stare into my soul.

I closed my eyes, trying to dispel the image. Trying not to think of the rest of her, naked and alone, and more than anything else, dead, in the woods. I hadn't been back there since, and not just because it was a crime scene. Her body, torn asunder by... well, by Greg; now that I knew who had done it, it didn't make the sight any less terrifying. If anything, it had made it that much more real, that much closer to my soul. I had slept beside the man that could do that to a person. One he had, no doubt, professed to love at some point.

Still, the thoughts stayed present, perverting my bed as much as they had that rock in the woods. With how I had contaminated the crime scene in the dark, it was no wonder why I had become the prime suspect. To some, it was easy to see that I had a reason to kill Emily. To me, she was proof that there hadn't been anything wrong with me. That Greg hadn't left me for reasons I had any control over. Had I not had my miscarriage. If we had our own child. If I had been raising our little girl instead of mourning her loss. He still would have cheated on me. He still would have left me. Emily was living, breathing proof of that fact.

It was Angela that had the motive to kill her. But it hadn't been her, had it?

I got up from the bed, slowly, painstakingly peeling the covers off of me, letting them fall into a soiled pile at my feet, before heading out of the bedroom. The sun streamed in through the blinds, doing wonders to chase away the nightmare that wasn't just a nightmare. I glanced at the clock on the TV, not having thought to count the cuckoos. I grumbled at my continuing sleeping issues when I noticed it was only 6 in the morning. I would have liked nothing more than to crawl back into bed, but I knew that I would not find any more sleep in there.

As I made my way to the kitchen to make breakfast, I noticed a patch of white on the hardwood floor near the door. Curious, I took a slight detour over there, picking up the envelope when I found it. There was nothing on the outside, but it wasn't sealed. A single sheet of paper was properly folded within. I pulled it out, unfolding it as I did so, and continued to stare at it for the next twenty minutes as my waking brain slowly tried to make sense of it.

"What the hell?" I asked my empty apartment. As it wasn't likely to give a response, I rushed back into my room, just long enough to grab some clothes that would be more suitable for walking downstairs in. Before my clock would have told the half hour, I was banging on the front door of my landlord's apartment.

"What?" he grumbled from within, after a minute of my continued barrage on the door.

"It's Natalie in 403. What's the meaning of this?"

"I should be asking you that," he called through the door. "Do you have any idea what time it is?"

"I know exactly what time it is," I said. "It's half past what the f--"

"What was that?" he asked, in a deep, menacing tone, as he yanked the door open to glare at me. "You've got a lot of nerve storming down here at this hour. Now what is it you're blathering about?"

"I'm talking about this," I said, tossing the sheet of paper into his hands.

He glanced at it for the slightest second, though he would have already known exactly what it was. His signature was at the bottom of the page, and it wasn't on the floor when I went to bed, meaning he would have slipped it under it sometime late the night before. "Ah, yes, this," he said, as if only just then remembering what I might be angry about. "I think it's rather clear what this is."

"You're evicting me?" I asked.

"Then again, maybe it's not," he joked. "No, I'm not evicting you," he said, slowly. "We've elected not to renew your lease."

"What's the difference?" I asked.

"The... seriously? We can't evict you without cause. And, unfortunately, having reporters camped out on our doorstep isn't cause. Believe me, I've checked. However, your lease is up next month."

"What?" I asked, confused.

"It was a one year lease. You moved in last December. Thus, your lease is up next month. You're not getting another one, at least not here."

"You can't do that," I said.

"Why not?"

"Because..." I trailed off. Honestly, I didn't know anything about renting an apartment. This had been the first time that I had lived on my own since college, and that didn't count. Greg? I thought, asking my resident lawyer.

"Don't look at me," he said. "You got yourself into this mess. But, yes, he's completely within his rights not to renew your lease. Granted, I wasn't here when you signed it. But, usually, it runs for a set amount of time and then gets renewed. Either party can decide not to. It's not as bad as an eviction, but..."

"But I need to find a new place to live," I completed for him.

"Exactly," the landlord agreed. I blinked at him, confused, not realizing that I had said that part aloud. "Any place that isn't here would be just fine with me." With that, he slammed his door in my face, managing to hit me in the nose in the process.

"Ow," I mumbled, as I rubbed my offended nose. Shaking my head, in annoyance, in frustration, I started making my way back up to my apartment. The reporters, still camped out at the door, perked up when they spotted me. They banged against the glass, trying to get my attention. It made me feel like I was in a zoo. I wondered which of us were the animals and which the people coming to poke and stare at them. Looking at those reporters, all of them salivating at the thought of getting an exclusive with me, their faces distorted by the glass, and by the early light of the day. It made them seem more alien than human.

"You know, we could probably make a lot of money on an exclusive," Greg said.

"It's not happening, Greg," I mumbled. The elevator dinged the moment I pressed the button to call it, not having left from when I used it to get down there in the first place.

"Why not?" he asked.

"Do you really want me profiting off killing you?"

"Someone might as well. And, since I'm not around to do it myself..."

I just shook my head before leaning it against the wall, hiding from the reporters as the doors closed, barring me from their sight. All I wanted was to go back to bed and wake up to a world where none of this had happened. Where Emily was still alive. Where Greg wasn't a murderer. Where I didn't have his blood on my hands. The thought of blood got me to rubbing my hands again, knowing full well that they were probably cleaner than the walls of the elevator that I was leaning against.

"Well, there is one solution to this whole thing," Tom said. He didn't often talk to me, at least not in words. It was usually more like he would come up out of the fog that is my mind to gloat about figuring something out before I did. To think that he might actually provide a useful suggestion was a bit much for that early in the morning. But that didn't seem to stop him. "We could take Angela up on her offer."

Then again, maybe Tom was just as capable of coming up with stupid ideas. "No," I said, simply.

"Why not?" he whined. "It's not like we have many other options open to us right now."

"We can just find another apartment," I said.

"Yeah, find an apartment. And a job to pay for it. Come up with first and last month's rent and a security deposit. All without letting them know about the reporters that are going to be camped out on our doorstep until this whole thing blows over. That'll really happen."

"It could just be for a little while," Greg suggested, coming to Tom's defense. "We don't have to commit to anything. It just needs to be until we get back on our feet."

"Or, you know, longer," Dad put in, winking at me.

"Will you just shut up?" I shouted, just as the doors to the elevator opened up. The man in 404 was standing right outside, waiting for it. He gave me the weirdest look, as if he had never seen anyone yelling at themselves before. "What?" I snapped at him. He lifted his hands up in surrender before stepping off to the side to let me off. I glared at him as I passed, daring him to say some snide comment about the whole thing. Instead, he, like most apartment dwellers, just minded his own business as he went into the now vacated elevator, heading down to the ground floor.

"Maybe we could approach it more like a job," Tom suggested. "Like we're the live-in nannies or something."

"Okay, first off, you're nothing," I said. "You're just some stupid voice in my head."

"Funny, I don't feel like a voice in your head."

"Well, how would you know what a voice inside of a head feels like if you're not one?"

"She does have a point," Dad said. "All the shrinks agree about our state of existence, or lack thereof."

"And, second, what the hell do I know about caring for a baby? I never... I never got that far, now did I?" I had come to my door, having dragged my feet along the way so I could focus on proving that Tom's suggestion was a bad one. He always needed a lot of evidence to the contrary once he was convinced of something. "And, third--"

"This is a long list," Tom pointed out.

"Yeah, because you always need a long list to drop something," Dad agreed.

"And, third," I continued. "No one is going to hire me to look after a child knowing that I'm crazy. And Angela knows just how crazy I am."

I had just managed to close the door behind me, barely reaching over to the light switch to turn it on, when my front window smashed open. My arms went up, reflexively, to protect my face. The shards of glass never made it past the couch. Something hard and heavy clunked into the hardwood floor, rolling with its momentum, and bumping into one of the end tables. It was just enough force to knock the vase that was on it over. More glass flew as the vase smashed into bits on the floor. The wind from outside blew in the now permanently open window. It played with the blinds, which now had a huge hole in them.

Stunned, I carefully made my way across the sea of glass on the floor. By the table was a rock the size of Greg's fist, twice the size of mine. There was writing on the side facing up, in big, blood red lettering that said "Murderer".

"And, fourth, there's that," I said, finishing the list.

"Well, I don't think we're getting our security deposit back," Greg said.

Chapter Nine
The Call I Don't Want to Make

I called down to the landlord to report the broken window, waking him up yet again in the process. Once I was done getting yelled at, I did my best to block up the hole in my apartment. Three old cereal boxes and a roll of scotch tape later, the damage was temporarily repaired. However, I had no idea how well it would hold up against the elements. Either way, the window would need to be repaired. Fortunately, that wasn't up to me to do. Or pay for, for that matter. Throughout the entire project, the voices were suspiciously quiet, as if trying to avoid doing the work themselves. As I stood back, taking in the spoils of my labor, they suddenly reared their heads once more.

"On the other hand," Tom said, as if picking up the old conversation. "There's now a hole in the wall that's going to ruin everything in here and make it very cold for the next few weeks until it's repaired."

"The heat's been running this entire time and it's already pretty cold," Greg agreed. "I hate to say it, but..."

"Oh, don't give me that. You three love to say 'I told you so'," I snapped. "I know, I know. I don't have many options available to me right now, I just..."

"You just don't want to make that call," Greg said. "I could do it for you, if you'd let me."

"Oh, yeah, like that really works," I said. I would often suggest that one of the voices take over for me. But on those few occasions where I let them try, it was really just me repeating whatever it was they were saying to me. It never really works out that I wasn't an active participant. No matter how crazy I am, that's not one of my issues. "You know, I could just stay at a hotel."

"With whose money?" Greg asked.

"Yours, of course," I said.

"In case you hadn't noticed, I'm not made of money. And I'm not going to be making any more of it. The thought was that we need to spend less of it, not more, until the whole will and alimony situation is settled."

"Yeah, about that, what is the situation on that?" I asked. "You were mysteriously missing the last time that subject was brought up."

"It's... a surprise," he said. "I wouldn't want to spoil that, now, would I?"

I just rolled my eyes at that thought. Of course, he had no idea what was in the will. He was just a voice inside my head. Although, I had to admit, that was very much the thing Greg would do. He would often hold out on critical information, hoping that I would do what he wanted me to do in order to get it from him. Right then, for some reason, he wanted me to move in with his widow.

"Fine," I huffed. "But, let it be on all of your heads that I do this."

"Yeah, right," Tom said, sarcastically. "'Cause it's our fault that you killed that one and landed us in all of this mess. Blame him."

"Well, if you had told me that he was the killer sooner, I might have been able to tell the police that. Instead, I figured it out with him right there, ready to kill me."

"Like the police would have believed you," Tom said. "Greg was one sick, scary son of a bitch--"

"Hey," Greg said, offended.

"But he knew how to play people like well-tuned instruments."

"Yes, he apparently can even play people that don't really exist," I accused of him. "Now will you three kindly shut up while I go throw out what's left of my pride?"

"Hey, I didn't say anything," Dad put in, defensively.

"Until now," I said.

I looked at the clock on the TV, making sure that it wasn't too early to make that call. Then again, I wasn't sure what hours Angela kept, what with the baby probably keeping her up at all hours. It had taken me a couple of hours to get the old cereal boxes to stay in place against the sharp wind long enough for me to tape them in place. Still, it surprised me to see that it was almost 11AM already. With the boxes blocking the window better than the blinds ever had, the apartment was as dark as it would have been at 11PM, with just the kitchen overhead light on.

The answering machine and phone were unharmed during the rock attack. For a moment, I thought they were supposed to be unplugged. Then I remembered that was just part of the nightmare, same as the rest of it. I had plugged it back in the moment I came home, several hours later and after being interrogated by the police. It hadn't stopped ringing since. The machine was stuck blinking 99 on the display. The old tape wouldn't hold that many messages, but the reporters just kept calling. I had long since stopped answering the phone, knowing that no one that really needed to talk to me would be calling me on it. Even as I was about to pick up the receiver, the phone rang again. I waited as it rang twice. The machine always picked it up after the second ring. I watched as the tape slowly rolled along. The machine had been my mom's. I had "borrowed" it when I went away to college. It still worked, so I never felt the need to get a new one. Once the tape stopped spinning, I quickly picked up the phone, making sure that no one would have the chance to call me again before I could place my own call.

Next to the phone was a list of my usual numbers. Right on the top of the list was Home. I had never bothered to cross that out or add that it was Greg's home, and not mine. Even now, almost a year after moving out, it was still my home to me. It was just full of people I didn't want to live with. My fingers skimmed over the buttons in the familiar pattern, not really needing to refer to the list for the reminder. I relied on it nonetheless to make sure I didn't misdial, or worse, chicken out.

Angela answered on the first ring. "That was quick," she said.

Confused, I pulled the phone away from my ear to stare at it for a second, as if it was capable of explaining anything to me. The plain cream plastic revealed nothing. "Um, what?" I asked into the phone.

"I only just got off the phone with your machine. Did you even listen to the message?"

"Wait, how did you know it was me? I never even said anything."

"Caller ID, obviously. I just dialed your number and then it pops up right after. So, if you're not calling about my message..."

"I don't check my messages, or answer the phone for that matter. They're all just from the reporters anyway."

"Well, obviously, not all of them. How do people get in touch with you if you don't answer the phone?"

"Who would even be trying to contact me right now, if not reporters?" I asked.

"Well, me, obviously," she said. I could practically hear her eyes roll over the line.

"Can I hang up on her now?" I thought to the voices.

"No," Greg insisted. "Not unless you know some other way to keep a roof over our heads for the next couple months."

"Well," I said, hesitantly into the phone.

"Oh, good, you are taking me up on my offer," she said, practically jumping down my throat. "I was hoping to bring you around to this. Seriously, like I said, you'd really be doing me a huge favor."

"Wait, when did you say that exactly?" I asked. I tried to play the original conversation back through my head, but the only arguments I remembered her making were about money.

"On the... oh, right. So, you never listened to any of my messages? What if I had an emergency?"

"I would have hoped you would have called the authorities, not me. I have to admit, this conversation is a lot weirder than I was expecting how it was going to go." And perhaps weirder than some of the conversations I had with the voices.

"Hey," Tom complained.

"Oh, quiet you," I scolded.

"What?" Angela asked.

"What?" I asked, confused for a moment. "Oh, sorry, I was... talking to the TV."

"So, you are moving in with me, right? I do sort of need help around the house. Little Dougie is running me ragged these days. I don't think I've had a good night's sleep in... wait, what day is it?"

"It's Tuesday," I said, automatically, remembering my appointment was yesterday, and I always see Dr. Mendez on Mondays.

"Right, um... Wait, what was I talking about?"

I sighed deeply into the phone, not bothering to cover the receiver. She must really need help if she was this ragged after only two days without Greg. I didn't really see Greg being all that helpful even when he was alive. But, to think that she would be turning to me of all people, she must not have any other options. If I were her, I probably would have despised the woman that had just killed the man I loved. Heck, I still loved Greg, and I do hate myself for having killed him. Part of me, a small part, but a part nonetheless, wished I had let him kill me, had let him "put me out of my misery", as he had put it on Sunday. He could have blamed me for Emily.

Claimed I had gone crazy on him, too. People would have believed it. And, yet, in spite of all that, she still wanted my help. Perhaps she was really that desperate.

"Fine," I huffed, trying to forget my own problems, my own need for this situation to work. "But only for a few days, a month at most."

"Thank you, thank you, thank you. When can you get here?"

"Umm," I thought. I pictured the huge crowd of reporters holding the building, and my car, under siege. I wasn't about to give them what they wanted, what they would demand in order to surrender the hostage. I could just go full on crazy on them. But I promised myself I wouldn't do that again. The news already reported that I was nuttier than peanut butter the last time. Then again, maybe I could just ask them nicely...

"Yeah, you're not going to do that," Greg said. "You've never been the kind of girl to ask for something for yourself. That's why you're so crazy."

"Says the voice inside my head," I accused. After another sigh, I resolved myself to rely on the bus to get me uptown, which would take me some time to maneuver. "Give me a couple hours," I promised her. "Then you can sleep like the dead."

"Yeah, you joke, but that's not that far from the truth."

"Seriously, Angela, this is a temporary situation. We're not going to turn into sister wives or... well, I guess that would be sister widows or whatever. Once everything blows over, once the vultures turn to something shiny and new, I'm going to be moving out again. I need my space."

"Yes, of course, you're right. As soon as all the finances get in place, and Doug is sleeping through the night again, we'll figure something out."

"Good," I said.

"Fine," she confirmed. The word had no power behind it as it lulled into a very audible yawn that stretched on for almost a minute.

"I'll be there when I can."

"I'll be waiting."

Chapter Ten
The House That Greg Bought

An hour and two bus rides later, I was standing in front of the house. It had only been a couple days since I had been there last. Yet, it felt like a lifetime ago since I had seen it. The front had large, twin bay windows jutting out into the yard, in addition to the one out the back. The ones in the front flanked the door, which was sunken in by comparison. When I had first seen it, I thought it looked amazing, with the morning light streaming inside that lit up the entire house. When Greg had first seen it, he thought it looked like a butt, with the door acting as the hole. Dad had called him the hole, a comment that I hadn't voiced.

What it looked like right then was my condemnation. My looming incarceration, wrapped in my home. As I rode the bus over there, my paranoia started acting up again. It was more a symptom of the past few weeks than of my mental condition. I wonder, though, can it be called paranoia when someone really is out to get you? Still, I had no reason to believe that Angela was going to pick up where her husband, my ex-husband and newest voice, had left off. I had no reason to believe that she was anything but sincere in her need for my help. Or, more accurately, anyone's help. That she really was willing to accept mine, if it was available.

And, yet, that was exactly what I was worried about. It wasn't that she was going to try to get me arrested for Emily's murder. She could have accomplished that the other day, tying in Greg's murder along with it. There had to be something else to it, though. I tried to think of the last time I had seen her before Monday. It would have been while I was still being investigated, before the other day when I had come to confront Greg. I tried to remember if she had been on Greg's side. If she had said something, anything, that would have led me to believe that she was working with him to frame me. But I couldn't remember much of those two weeks, not outside of the case. It was a long and trying time, and my condition was at its worst in years.

Still, I stood in front of the house, trying to come up with a reason not to go in there. A good reason that wasn't tied to my guilt or my, as of yet, unfounded suspicions of her. I wanted to, instead, turn back around and head to the bus stop. Back to the apartment and the growing horde of reporters.

And then it hit me. I looked around the vacant yard, the noticeable lack of reporters on the lawn. This had been where it happened. This had been where Greg died. His widow still lived here. And, yet, they were all camped out back at my apartment, back where the only one that was related to the case was little old me. Anger and resentment grew in my mind, making me seethe at the very thought that I would be mobbed by the press and Angela should go unassaulted. She was the one that had been sleeping with the real killer all this time, seemingly ignorant of his crimes.

My rage, barely contained, drove me forward, more so than any sense of purpose or obligation I had for her. Or for the little monster she cared for. Instead, all I wanted from her was to know how to get this level of peace she seemed to have achieved, despite it being only days since it had happened. Before I knew it, before I knew what I was doing, before I could stop myself, I was at the door. At the butt crack, as Greg used to call it. And I was banging on the door.

"Oh, finally." Angela's voice came from the right side of the house.

I glanced towards that bay window, only to see the drapes flutter down into place. I barely had a chance to wonder at that new addition to my beloved bay windows before the door was being opened. Angela practically glowed when she looked at me. A punch-drunk smile was spread wide across her unmade up, blotchy face. She was wearing the same outfit I had seen her in last time, two days earlier, and it was looking more destroyed than it did then. There were overlapping stains all over the front of the shirt, with a worry hole at the shoulder of the sleeve. The only addition had been an old belt of Greg's, which matched nicely with his old jeans. They held the pants up enough so they didn't fall off of her. Her hair was in dishevels and looked like it hadn't been brushed in years.

Her appearance took much of my bluster away and caused me to forget what I had been about to say. Instead, I simply said, "Hi."

"Come in," she said, waving me forward, inviting me into my own house. "Shh," she hissed, though I hadn't said anything and she continued to talk at a normal volume. "Doug is asleep. He should be a perfect little angel for the next five minutes before screaming his head off again. Thank you so much for doing this. For staying. Even if it's just for the night, or... wait, what was it that we agreed upon?"

"Why... why don't we just discuss it when you get some sleep," I suggested. She looked like she was about to collapse right there, and sleep for a week on the floor at my feet.

"Okay," she said, simply. She nodded, as if answering her own set of voices. That would have been the perfect end to this story, for Angela to come out and tell me that she heard voices as well. That Greg had dumped one crazy wife for another. However, I knew that, for her, it was more tiredness and stress than any actual condition of her own. "Everything is set up in the kitchen, in case you need it. You know where... oh, of course you know where the kitchen is. I'm sorry," she giggled. "I'm going to bed now."

She stumbled a few steps towards the stairs, grasping the railing to keep from falling over. I watched as she made her way up to the landing, turning around to head up to the second floor. Part of me wanted to follow her up to make sure she didn't fall over. A bigger part of me wanted to watch her fall down the stairs. Once she disappeared from view, I tried to put her out of my mind. To forget the reason why I hadn't been in my house in over ten months, other than these past couple of weeks. Not since the divorce had gone through.

Taking advantage of being left alone in the house, I started to look around the place. To see what damage that they had done to my perfectly designed home. The curtains, blocking much of both bay windows, was only the first change that I had noticed. All the pictures of Greg and I were, of course, replaced with pictures of a supposedly happy family. Greg, Angela, and Doug smiled out at me from every surface. The new couch, put right in the same slot as the old couch had been in, clashed gregariously with the rest of the furniture. The upholstery was starting to peel in places and it had an interesting smell, which made me think that it was picked up from the side of the road at some point. The coffee table and the other half of the end table collection had rubber strategically taped to it in places. I wouldn't have thought Doug was ready to crawl, let alone walk around unattended.

On the other side of the house, towards the left from the door, the den had been completely transformed. The old armchair, inherited by Greg from his father, was noticeably missing. As was the desk in the corner that I used to use when working at home, back when I was teaching. The entrance was blocked by a low fence, barely tall enough to go over my knees. It was obviously enough to keep the little rugrat contained. There was a large assortment of toys splayed randomly across the floor. Two of those weird objects that were something somewhere between a car seat and a cradle were in opposite corners, both with the same objects dangling from above. It seemed odd to see them both there, as if two people had bought the same item without telling the other. They both looked well worn, and the one closer to the door had a very recognizable smell to it.

"You know, I'm thinking it was a good thing that you never succeeded at having a child," Greg said, snarkily. "If you can't even recognize half of this stuff and the smell of the child repulses you so."

"Wow, I really hate you right now," I whispered to him. I closed my eyes, repressing the desire to cry, as I slowly backed away from the playroom. He did have a point, though. I had no idea what I would be doing there, with the baby.

"Hey, lay off of her," Dad said, coming to my rescue. "She would have learned. She's smart, certainly smart enough to dump your ass back when you were alive."

"I'm sorry, who dumped whom?" Greg argued.

"Will both of you shut up?" I whispered, harshly. I backed away from the playroom, as if an argument with my three voices would somehow corrupt the place that should have known nothing but glee. Instead, I headed back over to the living room, ignoring the fact that the couch cushions seemed to move when I wasn't looking directly at them. I plopped into the love seat. The other half of the matching set. My couch's little sister. Thankfully, it was looking away from the stairs and the playroom beyond. "It doesn't matter what I would or wouldn't have been able to do if I hadn't lost the baby," I muttered. "Maybe Greg would still be alive, maybe Emily would too. But none of them are. We need to move forward, as Dr. Martinez always says."

"That's the spirit," Tom said. He seemed unusually chipper, though that might have just been in comparison to the other two.

"What are we even doing here, though?" Greg asked.

"I'm here to help out Angela," I said, emphasizing that I wasn't referring to the three of them. "She's already helped me out." It was such a weird thought, that Angela had helped me out. She had told the truth when she didn't have to. When she could have just let me go to prison for the rest of my life. Or the nuthouse. She had already stolen so much from me, what was a little lost freedom between enemies?

If I closed my eyes, ignored the new items, the new pictures and the rubber linings, just focused on the smells and sounds of the house, it seemed almost like I was back home. Like that whole last year had never happened. Like Greg was at work, rather than in the morgue, or wherever his body was by then. It was just after noon, and I would have only been up for about an hour, having gone back to sleep after seeing Greg off for the day. It would have been hours before I would need to make dinner, so I would walk around the house, tidying up the already spotless place.

I had never gone back to work after my first pregnancy, and not by choice. Soon before I had gotten pregnant, my condition had come out to the dean. And not in a good way. There was nothing like having a screamfest with an annoying voice in your head in the middle of the campus to get you fired pretty quickly. Greg had offered to sue the school, to come to my defense and battle the injustice. By then, we were already on our way to financial solvency, and it didn't seem like it was a fight I wanted. Even if I had won it, I would have still lost. The parents of the students would have demanded my removal or students would have specifically avoided signing up for my classes. It was all just too much for me. Certainly not good for my continued sanity, or what was left of it. So, I just let it slide, let myself be ostracized from academia. It was never my dream, though I had to say I was a damn good teacher.

Don't get me wrong, Greg and I had never been rich. After he made junior partner at his firm, we were no longer struggling. I used to like to consider ourselves as being solidly upper middle class. It was enough that I didn't have to worry about our expenses building up with the baby coming. Or not, as it turned out. It was enough that I didn't have to work.

It just left me with very little to do during the day. That was when the problems really started. The voices started getting loud enough that they couldn't be ignored, even on the medication I was on at the time. The miscarriages didn't help things. After the third one, it got so bad that Greg had to ship me back to HTP for a tune-up.

I shook my head, trying to dislodge the nostalgia that being there, in that house, stirred up. I wanted to leave, to bolt out the door. To flee my past and never look back. But that just wasn't an option, not with Angela counting on me like she was. Looking back on that time, thinking of how it was for me, it made sense that she had had to turn to me for help. Why she hadn't had someone else to rely on. Greg hadn't exactly been the social type, despite his job. The way he looked at it, he was getting paid to be social. To work his contacts. To make his way up the corporate ladder, as it were. But, when he wasn't getting paid for it, when it wasn't helping him to get ahead at the firm, he might as well have been at home in a comfortable pair of sweatpants. He had expected me, and probably Angela as well, to be right there with him. There was plenty of fun to be had at home, after all. It was when he had to look elsewhere for that fun that he had been getting into trouble.

Escaping the living room was much easier than escaping my past. I headed into the kitchen, hoping it would stir up happier memories. This had been my domain, my refuse when Greg was in one of his moods and all I wanted to do was read a good book. The changes in there were much less noticeable. There weren't any childish drawings on the fridge, though I figured Doug was too young for that just yet. The pictures of the happy family stopped at the swinging door that blocked out the view of the front of the house. The only difference from when I inhabited the place was the long line of baby food across the counter, some even on the counter where it had spilled out. I could easily pretend not to notice that. To, instead, focus on the fruit bowl that I had painstakingly picked out one afternoon. I had even gone to five different stores to find the right pattern to match how the sun played across the table in the late hours. I took it down from where it was hiding in the corner of the counter, hidden behind the mess of baby food, and busied myself trying to center it perfectly in the middle of the dinette table. It was the table that Greg never deigned to dine at, though I had used it for lunches alone often enough to excuse the cost. Besides, it was a great additional surface for when the counter was too busy, as it was then.

Once the bowl had been properly situated, I started tidying up the mess. Cleaning up the spilled food. Throwing out the empty or dried out containers. I made my way around the chaos that had become of my domicile, leaving order in my wake. The bare cabinets, containing only a few, mostly empty, boxes of food revealed just how far behind Angela had gotten in such a short amount of time. It would mean I would have to go shopping, but it would have to wait until after she was properly rested and could look after the baby. In the meantime, I started making a list of all the things we would need for the next week. Lists were always a good thing, especially for me. They helped me organize my otherwise unorganized life, giving it some stability where it desperately needed it. The more organized I was, the less the voices came out to play.

"Is it really that easy to get rid of us?" Tom asked.

"Trust me, if it was easy to get rid of you, you would have been long gone," I said.

"No, I mean, don't we mean anything to you?" he asked.

"Ha, yeah, that's funny," Greg laughed. "No, of course, we mean nothing to her. That's why we need to butt into her life as often as possible. To show her just how important we are to her. How lonely her life would be without us. I mean, just listen to all the hell I already put her through while I was alive. What would she do without that continuing after I'm gone?"

"Well, you did have me committed twice while you were alive. Of course, you'll be trying to make it so I commit myself at least once now that you're dead."

"What's a little commitment between spouses?" he joked.

I took a deep breath in, going through my relaxation exercises as I tried to purge them from my mind. It never truly worked completely, but it at least helped me to ignore them. Granted, whenever I simply ignored the voices that were almost always shouting in my ear at those points, it made me feel like a petulant child, ignoring an annoying sibling. But they weren't siblings. They were so much worse than siblings. They were the ghosts that haunted my every waking moment.

Once the kitchen, and my mind, were in order, relatively speaking, I moved on to the dining room. It was in the back corner of the house, and was the last stop on my tour of the ground floor. As usual, the room was immaculate. As it had always been when I had been living here with Greg, my then husband. He had always demanded that the room he ate in was spotless. It had actually gotten to the point that I had thought he might have a little OCD in him. Whenever I brought it up, though, he always turned it around on me. He always pointed out my own mental issues and said I was just "projecting". He had picked up that word during one of our only two group sessions with Dr. Mendez, and he never really put it down.

"Because it's such a fun word," Greg said. "Whenever you think you're seeing something of yourself in someone else, it's just as likely that you're projecting your own issues onto them. Isn't it?"

"Or, it could just be the whole 'takes one to know one' of it all," I said.

I barely glanced through the door into the dining room before backing away slowly. I didn't want my own problems to pervert the otherwise stately room. Perhaps we could set it aside, at least while I was living there. A monument to the crazy that was my ex-husband.

Living there. I shuddered at the thought, at the idea of returning to that place. That house that had meant to be my home, but was more like a prison for the later years of my marriage. Ever since leaving the community college. It hadn't been the most prestigious of teaching roles. But it had gotten me out of the house long enough not to go crazy... well, more so than I already was, at least. And, yet, now that Greg was gone--

"Uh, still here," Greg muttered, but I ignored him.

Now that Greg was gone, I could possibly make it the home that it should have been, the home that it had always meant to be. To me when I picked it out. To the old lady that had sold it to us. To anyone that had ever seen the place.

I backtracked, heading back through the house, back around to the front. Around to the stairs. As I came back to the front hall my hand started to shake. Back to where the confrontation had occurred. Back to where I had first seen Greg's smile turn to something more seditious, more menacing than I had ever thought him capable of. The blood that I always felt on my hands, eternally staining them with the feeling that would never fade. When I had first come into that room, when I first entered the house, I had been able to ignore it. I had almost forgotten what had happened there. However, it had only been because I had been distracted, my mind set on Angela. On the rooms to either side. But, once I was standing there, with nothing but the memories, it was all I could do not to curl up into a ball and cry.

There had been a small table just to the side of the stairs, in the small cubby there. It was noticeably missing. It had been destroyed, splintered into a million pieces, first by Greg's angered, rage filled fists. Then by me in my desperate search for a weapon to defend myself with. The remnants were gone, but an outline of where it had once stood was visible in the paint behind it. It was somehow a shade of white that was several shades darker than the wall around it. I stared at the spot, wondering if it would ever be the same. If left exposed and uncovered, would it become as light as the wall around it? Or would it forever be the dark shadow of Greg's darker soul?

I looked away from the corner, away from the anger that was still there. Back towards my refuge. Back towards the kitchen where I had first fled from Greg when it became clear that he intended to kill me. It hadn't offered any protection that day. Not from Greg. Not from what he intended to do to me. Though, when first confronted by those eyes, the eyes that were behind the mask that he had worn every day that we had been together, it had been the only place I wanted to go. It was the only place that I had sought out. He had followed, had stalked me as his prey. He hadn't let up as the door had swung closed. The back door, tucked into the far corner, behind the fridge, had been my only escape. It led out into the backyard, back where I killed him. My eyes automatically drifted back there, as if I could see where it had happened through the walls. See the pool of blood that was no doubt still there, rejected by the very ground it sat upon.

I purposefully looked away from the playroom as I passed it. It was an eternal stain on the house, on my house, that I would need to get used to if I were to continue there. It wasn't going to be easy, or fun. I knew exposure therapy was the only way to get over the knife to the gut feeling that it had instilled in me. That it still instilled without even looking at it. Just that it existed there, that it showed what Angela had that I never would, was enough to trigger my feelings of inadequacy that Greg had bashed into me every day after the first miscarriage.

The hardwood floors that stretched throughout the ground floor ended suddenly at the foot of the stairs. The carpeting that stretched up them was new, something that Angela must have insisted on. Greg had always loved hardwood floors. It had been the one item that he had insisted on for any house that he would live in. The soft tapping of my sneakers on the floor ended suddenly as I started heading up the stairs, following the same path that Angela had taken barely half an hour earlier. As I climbed further up, my anxiety lifted, as if my soul, too, were ascending as my body did. Perhaps it was distance from the place it had happened. Perhaps with time that room wouldn't affect me so. Then again, what kind of person would that make me if it didn't?

At the top of the stairs, the hall split into either direction, heading off to both sides of the house, with two rooms flanking each hallway. We... I thought that would be good, letting us have room for two kids while leaving a room for guests. Across from the stairs was one of the two full baths, with another off the master bedroom towards my left. I scanned the hallway, looking at all the pictures hanging along the walls. They were the same happy family as depicted below. I noticed that all the doors were open, spilling in the sunlight from outside. The light gleamed off the glass that covered the picture frames, dazzling me for a second before my eyes adjusted. It seemed almost ironic to me that a house as bright as that one should harbor the darkness inside of Greg.

"Well, it had to go somewhere," Greg said. As if that was an excuse for killing Emily. As if the whole thing were my fault for buying that house to begin with. And, yet, I couldn't argue with him. I couldn't hold up proof that he had been evil all along, that the house wasn't responsible for her murder. The fact that he was capable of that surprised everyone. In fact, at Emily's memorial service, he had played the perfect grieving boss. He hadn't let on in the least that he had been sleeping with her, let alone killed her. He even had managed to deliver a few tears, something that I hadn't seen from him in all the years we had been married.

In fact, it had been those tears that had done it for me. They were the first thread that led me down the path of discovery. That led me to his front door with an accusation that I barely believed myself. Not that he had killed her. No, that came several days later. I just knew that he had been sleeping with her. No one would have figured it out if they hadn't known him as well as I did. Angela probably hadn't figured it out either, having only known him for a couple of years herself. But I knew there had to be something else going on, something that he wasn't telling anyone. If only I had known sooner, had figured out the whole thing instead of just part of it. Maybe Greg would have survived, would have come out of it in handcuffs instead of a body bag.

"Or maybe it would have ended exactly the same way," Tom suggested. "You would have wanted to give him the benefit of the doubt. The chance to deny it all. To prove you wrong. You did that morning as well, didn't you?"

"You have some nerve," I accused. "You knew he had killed her for days before I did. You just weren't telling me."

"There's a difference between thinking something was true and proving it," he said. "I could have been wrong. Besides, would you have even believed me if I had explained it to you?"

"Seeing as how you're really just some broken off piece of my mind, I obviously already did know it," I said. "I just wasn't ready to accept it."

"Which is exactly why I didn't tell you," he said.

I shook my head, annoyed, as I always was, with his smug tone. His imagined face perked up the way it always did when he thinks he's better than someone. Trying to leave him behind at the top of the stairs, I quickly took the three steps towards the bedrooms on the left. One of them was the master. The other I had started to make up as the nursery, back when I had first gotten pregnant. First, I glanced towards the back of the house, back towards the master bedroom. I wasn't quite ready to see the nursery in use.

The third and final bay window of the house was there, overlooking the backyard from the master bedroom. It had been there that I had seen Angela, holding Doug close to her chest as she watched me kill her husband. Large curtains were spread out across the breath of the window, hiding it from view, yet not quite blocking out the sunlight streaming in. I was thankful for that obstruction. For not needing to see the place that she had been sitting when it happened. Instead, I glanced towards the bed, towards the same bed that I had slept in for countless nights. The one I had shared with Greg. That she had shared with Greg. She was sprawled out across it sideways, taking up both sides of the bed.

Just as I was about to step away, to leave her to her rest, she cried out. At first, I had thought she had spotted me. That she had thought me an intruder in this room that had once been mine. A denial came readily to my throat. An accusation that she had been the intruder. That it was her that shouldn't be sleeping in my bed. But, then, I realized that she wasn't crying out at me. She was still asleep. She rolled over, pressing her face into the bedspread. Her fists clenched it in places, tearing holes in the cover, stretching and enlarging others that seemed to have been there for a while. I wanted to go to her, to wake her from whatever terrors lingered in her dreams. But I knew that wakefulness would be no true escape from the worst things that had happened to her. I figured she would need her sleep, what little rest she could get when her sleep wasn't restful.

Leaving Angela to battle her inner demons, I turned back towards the hall. I took a long, deep breath in, steeling myself for what was to come next. The door to the nursery was already open. The smaller window that overlooked the street was unguarded by any blinds, leaving the sun free reign in the room. Without needing to take a step inside, I could already tell that the room hadn't been changed much. The little teddy bears that danced across the wallpaper looked out at me, inviting me in to play with them. Tears filled my eyes as I robotically approached them. I had spent weeks narrowing the selection of wallpapers down. Between the dancing teddies, the animal parade, the candy trains that spread all over, and half a dozen other choices that seemed perfect for my little girl. My little darling.

A sound from the crib pulled my eyes from the walls towards it. At first, for one gut wrenching, heart breaking second, I thought it was my daughter. My first baby that died before she could be born, but would forever live on in my heart. Then, I remembered that she could never be. That the rooms occupant wasn't mine. He was a pretender to the throne of the room. The one who had stolen it from the girl that it belonged to. Rage filled me, blinding me to the truth, to the world around me. I took three menacing steps forward, violence on my mind. The only thought I had at that moment was to remove that thing that had stolen my daughter's rightful place, in the house and in her father's heart. No one would know. No one would be able to stop me.

But, then, I saw him, lying there, his eyes wide as they took in the world around him. His little socks were starting to fall off. They were so tiny, yet big enough to cover his feet. His left hand played with his right sock, seemingly unconsciously. His right leg kicked out randomly, as if the whole thing was some weird game to him. When I stood over his crib, his eyes widened as they took me in. Not in fear, but out of curiosity. The little one was so young, so cared for, that no thoughts of his own vulnerability had ever entered his mind. Even in light of what his father had done. What he was. What ultimately happened to him. The child was oblivious to it all.

"So, this is the little monster that's been stealing Angela's sleep?" I cooed, as I looked down at the innocent little baby. "Aren't you supposed to be sleeping, or, I don't know, interrupting your mother's sleep right now?"

As if in answer, Angela's muttering suddenly became a high-pitched scream.

Chapter Eleven
Negotiations

"Greg, no," she shouted, loud enough to wake the dead.

"What did I do?" Greg asked.

I rolled my eyes. Little Doug beside me had a very different reaction, though. He cried out, screaming his little head off. I heard a sigh from the other room. "It's alright, Dougie," Angela said. The bed groaned as she got up. "It's alright. Mommy is here." After a few seconds, she swept around the corner. A robe that she hadn't been wearing before swept out behind her. For a moment, she looked like super mom, coming to rescue the baby from the evil crazy person looming over his crib. She stopped in mid stride when she spotted me. Shock and confusion played out across her face. "Oh," she said, as if she was surprised to see me there. "I, uh, forgot you were here, actually."

"Sorry," I said, not sure what else there was to say.

"No, it's fine. Is something wrong? Does Doug need a change?"

"What? No, I... I don't think so. How do you know when he needs to be changed?"

"Well, it's not one of his diaper cries, I guess," she said. She came over to the crib, scooping him up into her arms. Instantly, Doug quieted down, cooing and giving a few other, less identifiable baby sounds as his hand patted her chest. She gave a small, exploratory pat to the diaper, just to make sure that everything was good down there. "But why was he crying? You didn't scare him or anything, did you? You see, though? This is why I need your help. Half the time I don't even know why he cries out. But he keeps waking me up. He should have been sleeping through the night without trouble by now. He was before this whole mess started. But, since then..."

"Well, for one thing, it's still the morning, so he's probably not sleeping because it's not nighttime. Second, he... he didn't wake you up."

"What are you talking about? Didn't you hear him crying before?"

"Yeah, I did," I said. I looked over at the little fellow, who had gone back to looking around at the blank ceiling above him. It captivated his attention so much that it was as if he could see the imperfections in the paint or that the smooth surface was the most fascinating thing he had ever seen. "I also heard you crying out in your sleep. Then you yelled 'Greg, no' and woke up. That was when he started crying. I don't think this is what you are thinking this is."

"Oh, please, you don't know what you're talking about. You're not a mother."

Ouch, I thought. I flinched at the words as a hot knife of pain plunged deep into my stomach.

"Kill her," Dad insisted.

"Shh," I hissed at him.

"What?" Angela asked.

"Nothing," I said. "Anyway, I don't have to be a mother," flinch, "to know what was happening right in front of my own eyes. The order of the events was that you yelled, then he started crying, not the other way around. I don't think the problem is Doug not sleeping through the night. Although, granted, it's not nighttime, so that might be something else. The problem seems to be that you can't sleep through the night. You're having nightmares. And, given what happened here, I wouldn't blame you. It feels like this place is haunted." I didn't want to say that it was haunted with my own bad memories. I also didn't want to say that I didn't think I could stand to live there, in the house that was supposed to be my home.

"Whatever," she said, though she didn't seem to take my word for it. "Maybe this isn't going to work out after all."

"Maybe it won't," I agreed. All I wanted to do right then was to get out of that haunted house and never return. To leave Angela and Doug to their own devices. It wasn't like I owed them anything. In fact, it could be argued that they owed me. After all, it had been them that stole Greg from me in the first place. Them that had been with him for the past year. Had been living with him while he went off and killed Emily. Had done nothing to stop him, to turn him in after he had. Besides, there was the matter of my own living situation to consider. Even if I had moved back into the house, temporarily, there would have been a time that I would have wanted to move out again. To be on my own, away from the loving mother and her child. I would need to find a new apartment anyway. "Look, there's a problem with my apartment."

"What? Why? What's wrong now?"

"He's... My lease is up next month and they're not going to let me renew it."

"Ah, ha, so the truth comes out. This was never about you doing me a favor. You need something from me, not the other way around."

"Look, Angela, I don't like coming to you any more than you liked coming to me. If I was just going to be coming here for a time, I could get a job and save up enough money to move out again. The alimony from Greg had never been all that substantial. And something tells me that, now that he's dead, I'm not going to be seeing much more money coming from him."

"Damn right," she said. She clutched Doug's head to her chest, as if she could blot out the half swear after she had already said it.

"I just need enough to cover the down payment on a new apartment, once I find one."

"And what about the security deposit at your current place? I'm assuming I'll be getting that back at some point?"

"What are you even talking about?" I demanded. "It's not like you paid it to begin with. Greg did, and that was part of the divorce settlement. Besides, that money is gone, to be spent on a new window, in fact."

"New window? What, you got angry at them for kicking you out? Or did one of your 'voices' tell you to do that?" She said the word voices as if she never actually believed that I heard anything. Like I had pretended to have a condition all this time. Perhaps she was actually the only person who knew me who didn't think I was crazy. And, yet, that somehow became a bad thing.

"No, someone threw a rock through it, calling me a murderer, for killing your husband," I spat at her, trying to insinuate that she should have known what he was and had done something about it without actually saying the words.

"Well, guess what, you're not getting a dime out of me," she said.

"Well, guess what," I spat back at her. "You're getting a roommate after all, then. 'Cause I'm not leaving without a way to afford my own apartment. I'll be damned if I'm going to be living on the streets because you couldn't keep your man entertained."

"Hear, hear," Dad cheered. "About time you started sticking up for yourself."

"Hey," Greg complained.

"Oh, can it you," Dad and Tom said together. It was followed quickly by my own thoughts. I was, thankfully, paying enough attention to not say it out loud. Not with Angela right there.

Angela stared at me for a long time, her nostrils flaring in her rage. I stared right back at her, making it clear that I wasn't going to back down on this. I wasn't going to be living on the streets when my house was half empty. I wasn't even sure if my name had been taken off the deed yet. If I didn't still own the place myself. Either way, I wasn't about to test the point by trying to kick out the pair of them. As much as I wanted to hate the kid, it wasn't his fault that his parents were adultering assholes.

"Fine," she huffed, finally. This surprised me to no end, as she seemed determined to get rid of me. "But if you're not going to be helping out with Doug, the least you could do is get a job."

"Well, obviously," I said, taken aback. "I had been planning on doing that anyway. It was... Well, I'll need to make enough money to get out on my own again, if I'm not going to be getting any more alimony."

"Yeah, I think that's probably a safe bet," she said, glaring at me. "What with you having killed the person who owed it to you."

"Oh, please. If I hadn't, he would have ended up in jail. Or worse, we both could have been his next targets. We could have ended up the ones dead, instead of him."

"Don't you think I know that?" she yelled. Doug started crying again, as if that were the proverbial straw. Or, better yet, that he had understood what we meant by that. She sighed as she started rocking Doug, trying to get him to calm down. Trying to calm herself down in the process, no doubt. When she picked up the conversation again, once Doug had settled down, it was at a much quieter level. "Why do you think I told the cops what really happened here?"

"Why did you tell them that?" I asked.

"Because you probably saved my life. You were obviously saving your own, and I didn't think you should go to prison for it. That doesn't mean I have to like it. Or you, for that matter."

"Well, good," I said. "I don't like you either."

"And I don't blame you," she agreed. "I stole your husband, and you killed mine. I think that makes us about even, don't you?"

"Not in the least," I said. "But I guess it's a start. So, what? I'll be filling in for Greg, then?"

"Well, you won't be joining me in my bed," she said. She laughed, but the humor didn't quite seem to reach her eyes. The laugh quickly turned into a yawn, and I was reminded that her little nap had quickly been interrupted by her nightmare.

"Why don't you go back to bed," I offered. "I can hold down the fort, contrary to what you might think." And, as long as I didn't have to do much with the little one, that would be true. As I looked into his little eyes, still exploring the room, I seemed completely lost when it came to what he would need. Maybe she was right. Maybe I never really was the mother type. "Why don't I take him before you fall asleep on your feet and drop him," I offered. I reached out my hands to take him, but a part of me hoped that she would say no.

"I don't blame you," Dad said. "I never held you that much either. Dang girl seems to be drinking the poor thing up alive. Maybe you should offer to get her a straw."

"No, I got him," she said, pulling Doug in tighter to her chest. The baby gave a little grunt and something sounding like the start of another shout fest. She quickly settled him back down into the crib, letting him lie there. The room would have been the most boring place in the house to me. Yet it seemed to be utterly fascinating to him. "But, yeah, you're right. I'm going to crash. If he cries, though, let me handle it. You seem to be quite lost when it comes to him."

I simply nodded my agreement. Although, I didn't want to admit just how right she seemed to be. At least not to her. Maybe it would get easier, once Doug got older. But I hoped that I wouldn't be there for that long. As long as the job hunt worked out, I wouldn't need to be there past a couple of months. I'd stay just long enough to get enough savings to get my own apartment again.

Angela dragged her feet as she headed out through the door. She headed back across the hall to the master bedroom. If anything, she seemed more tired from her little nap, rather than less. I took one last glance down at the baby, who was busy playing with his now exposed toes. The sock was stuck just outside the crib, lost in the exchange. I followed Angela out of the nursery. I felt a bit like a stalker as I stood by her door, watching as she collapsed onto the bed. She had managed to slide in under the covers this time, taking my old spot on the bed. The side closest to the door. The side that Greg had always refused to sleep on.

Greg's side of the bed was noticeably vacant next to the mound that was Angela. Other than the depression in the covers from the last time she had fallen into bed, that side was remarkably well kept. As if preserved for its former occupant's return. Greg's watch, forgotten the other day, was still situated in its usual spot, on the edge of the side table, centered perfectly beside the alarm clock. The light indicated that the alarm was still active, probably adding to the sleep problems that Angela had been having. It seemed like everything in her life was conspiring against her having a good night sleep.

I made my way silently around the bed, trying not to bump it in the narrow stretch on Greg's side of the room. I ended up needing to sit on the bed so I could find the right switch to disable the alarm. It wouldn't go off for another sixteen hours or so, but I didn't want to risk it. When my weight pushed down Greg's side of the bed, Angela rolled over. She rolled towards me, her arm unconsciously going to my back. I turned around, looking over to her, watching as the loathing and fear that I had seen from her for as long as I had known her eased off of her face. A level of peace that I would have never thought her capable of spread out in its place. Her reaching hand found my wrist, pulling me down next to her. At a loss for what to do, not wanting to disturb her, not wanting to wake her up from whatever dreams claimed her mind, I settled into Greg's spot. The spot she had joked about not five minutes earlier. I froze in place, though, staying as still as possible as she pulled me in. A stiff doll for her to sleep upon.

Chapter Twelve
Those Who Can't Teach, Do

The next morning, after an uncomfortable breakfast with Angela that was held mostly in silence, I found myself in the weirdest place imaginable. It was the waiting room to Greg's law offices. After being chased off the campus of the community college I used to teach at, almost literally, there wasn't much of a chance of me getting a similar position. At least, that is, not without proof that I was completely sane, something that I wasn't about to get anytime soon. However, with my justice degree, teaching wasn't the only thing I could do. In fact, when I first graduated from college, I had started out as a paralegal. It had been how I had met Greg.

The office hadn't changed much since then, though the pictures hanging on the walls had been replaced a couple of times over the years. I think the wife of one of the senior partners was some art collector. She was never happy with the collection on display in the office. A lot of the spouses were like that. Just as sophisticated and high minded as the lawyers. I had always felt like the odd duck left out of those encounters. Truth be told, I had often thought that was one of the reasons why Greg had left me for Angela. He was just trying to trade up to someone who could at least be a mother.

"Trade down is more like it," Dad said, but that was something a dad would say.

"Natalie, I hope you haven't been waiting long," came a familiar voice from around the corner. I stood up, smoothing out the dress that I had borrowed from Angela, before turning towards the hallway and the familiar face approaching me. The dress didn't quite fit me right. It was a little too tight in the backside. But Angela had insisted. She said that it barely fit her anymore and that it would look better on me. Plus, I had forgotten about the interview when I left my apartment. My favorite interview suit was still hanging in the closet, wondering where I was.

I smiled as Sam did. His seemed faker than mine. Sam had been one of Greg's closest work buddies, one of the few he had spent time with outside of work. "How are you doing?" he asked, taking both of my hands in his. He looked deep in my eyes, as if he could read my feelings there. "I had been meaning to reach out to An... well, to you."

I hadn't missed the misstep, a fact that Tom wasn't pleased with. He was starting to get in a gloating mood before he realized it hadn't gone unnoticed. In fact, I thought it was blatantly obvious that he was trying to avoid bringing up Angela. Come to think of it, I didn't think I had seen Sam since before Greg and I separated. Obviously, he was assuming the whole thing would be a sore subject, even after a year.

"I'm... well, I'm getting there," I said, when I realized he was waiting for an actual answer. "How have you been? I know you two were close."

"Not close enough, I'm guessing. I mean, wow, what's up with that? I'm sure you're happy you got out while you still could."

"You mean unlike Angela or Emily?" I asked.

"Um... right, sorry. I'm... Anyway, why don't we head back to my office."

"Uh, okay, I guess," I said.

This took me a little by surprise. I didn't remember the name of the person I was scheduled to meet with. I had it written down on a pad of paper beneath my resume, subtly hidden from view. Both were in my briefcase, which was actually an old one of Greg's that he wouldn't miss. As I remembered from my first time through this process, it always helped to be prepared for anything at these interviews, including a written test. So, I had fully stocked the thing on my way over from the house, filling it with a box each of pre-sharpened pencils and pens of both blue and black ink, a calculator, and three pads of paper. It had been too long since I was in the workforce, and I needed to impress whoever it was that I was meeting with.

However, Sam was a lawyer. On the same track as Greg had been. I didn't remember him having anything to do with the paralegals, at least not from anything I heard Greg talk about. So, it surprised me that he had been the one to come greet me. When I probed the voice Greg about it, he just gave me a shrug. Or at least the closest thing to a shrug as he was capable of. It wasn't like any of the voices could ever provide me with new information that I didn't already have. But they did tend to have access to different memories that were sometimes shut off from me. It helped when trying to remember things. Or, in the case of Tom, when trying to figure things out. I had already gotten a promise from him that he would help me out as much as possible. Anything to get out of that house for at least a few hours a day.

Sam led the way to his office. It was in the back corner of the floor, well away from the bustle of the bullpen. His name wasn't on the door. The window next to it had a faint outline of letterings that looked like Greg's name, above the words Senior Partner, which were still intact. The last time I had been there, this hadn't been Greg's office either. I tried to remember who had been there, but it wasn't like I was taking a tour of the place at the time. Greg had been in a middle office somewhere else in the maze of offices that made up the place. At some point, perhaps when he got his last promotion, he must have scored the corner office. I guess it made sense that someone would get it now that he... wouldn't be around anymore. It surprised me a little that it would be so soon.

Sam motioned for me to sit in one of the two seats on the door's side of the desk, as he made his way around it. The mahogany desk was shiny and unmarred by the marks of use. I wondered briefly if it had been Greg's, something he had gotten with the office. Or if it had actually come with the office. Or if Sam had brought it in when he moved in. It seemed heavy, and awkward, certainly too awkward to get through the door easily. I delicately placed my briefcase on the desk, almost afraid to scratch the fine surface in the process, and looked up at Sam expectantly.

I was nervous, that was probably quite obvious to anyone. And for obvious reasons, too. But Sam seemed just as nervous as I was. He placed his hands down on the desk, his palms pressing into the wood. He took a solid, purposeful breath before letting it out slowly. "So," he said, simply.

"Right," I said. I started flipping open my case, thinking he wanted to see my resume. He didn't seem to notice.

"Look, there's only so much I can tell you right now," he said. "We're executing his will, of course. I mean, I'm his lawyer. But we're still waiting to hear back on some things from the state. The case isn't even officially closed yet."

"Woah, wait, what?" I asked, completely stunned. "What are you talking about?"

"Greg's will, of course. Isn't that... Wait, you weren't here about his will? I would have expected Angela to come down at some point. But I guess you had as much at stake from his death as she did."

"I'm here for a job interview," I said. When his look of confusion only deepened, I explained. "Paralegal? There's an opening here. I applied. And, if this wasn't about that, I should probably get back to the front. Someone might be looking for me."

"Wait, wait, wait a minute. You're looking to come back here? To work?"

"Isn't that what I just said?"

"And, how exactly were you picturing that going, exactly?"

"Probably about the same way it went the last time I worked here, only without falling for the first associate that smiles at me," I said.

"Natalie, you killed a senior partner."

"He was trying to kill me."

"It doesn't matter. The case is still ongoing, both cases are. There's no way in hell that they'll let you work on cases while that's still pending. That would be a lawsuit just waiting to happen."

"Well, then, what exactly am I supposed to do? Get a job as a waitress?"

"You certainly have the legs for it," he joked. I glared at him, daring him to say something else about my legs. "Look, why don't you go back to teaching?"

"Yeah, like I'll be able to get a teaching job after how the last one went."

"But, I mean, you're doing better now, aren't you? You're... properly medicated or... whatever, right?"

"That's none of your business, Sam," I insisted.

He sighed deeply before leaning forward, pressing his elbows into the wood of the desk. His morose face reflected off the surface, showing me a double that was easily dispelled. "Look, Natalie, go home. You shouldn't waste your time on an interview here. Everyone knows about your... issues, both legal and otherwise. There's no way you're going to get a job here. Or at any law firm in the tristate area. Just go home. Lay low for a few weeks. Let this whole thing blow over. Let them close the cases. Bury your ex-husband. When it's all over, when you being here wouldn't cause a huge stir, come back in. I'll make sure you get a slot here. I'll even vouch for you with your mental issues, as long as you promise that it won't impact your work."

"Never has before," I muttered. And it hadn't... Except for that one time. "What am I supposed to do in the meantime, though? Stick my head in the sand? My shrink wanted me to get a job. To get out of the house. And, considering my financial state right now, the fact that my alimony is probably gone--"

"Oh, yeah, that's definitely gone," Sam agreed.

"And I don't know if I'm even still in the will or not," I continued.

"That I can't divulge, not until the reading."

"Which probably won't be until after half the items on your list of things for me to wait for are already over."

"Sounds about right," he agreed.

"So, what am I supposed to do in the meantime?"

"Well," he said, pensively. "Why don't you reach out to Angela? She's probably in a similar state as you, though maybe not financially. Maybe you could work something out between the two of you. Now, I know, she's not exactly your favorite person right now. But you two do have a lot in common. And I'm not just talking about Greg."

Greg seemed to perk up at the mention of his name. He had spent much of the past few minutes slumbering in the back of my head, while we were discussing his death, will, and funeral. He didn't say anything, though he and Dad seemed to be conspiring about something back there. "I'm... actually staying at the house right now. Temporarily, that is. You know, to help out around the place. With Doug and all of that. No big deal."

"Wait, seriously? I mean, I thought she might help you out a little with money, but, seriously? Wow. How did that happen?"

"It was her idea actually," I said. Now that he wasn't telling me to go home or talking about Greg, we slipped back into some of our old habits. It was always easy to talk to Sam, even easier than it had been with Greg. "She's been having trouble sleeping. She is convinced that Doug is keeping her awake. Like he's the spawn of Satan or something." I laughed briefly, but then I remembered who his dad was. And what he had done. And almost done. "So, how are things with you?" I asked, wanting to change the subject. "How's.... I want to say Diane?"

"Diane? Wow, you've been out of the loop for a while. Diane and I broke up a year ago."

"Gee, so did Greg and I," I said, trying to make a joke out of it.

"Ah, right. I guess that's why we haven't caught up since. No, I'm with Jennifer now." He pointed towards the office next door. I looked towards the wall he was pointing at, as if I could see through it to that office. To see the blond sitting behind a desk. Hers was probably a much nicer desk than his was, and no doubt ladened down with piles of papers. Jennifer was one of the other lawyers at the office, one that always ducked out of the social events to "do work", as she called it. I always got the impression that she thought she was better than the rest of them. Or too antisocial for the group or something.

"Jennifer? Really?" I asked, in my gossip voice. "I thought she was gay."

"Believe me," he whispered back. "So not gay."

"Well, I wish I could stay and continue to catch up," I said, pointedly, when I noticed the time. "But I really should get back out to the waiting room. My interview was supposed to be five minutes ago."

"You sure I can't talk you out of going?" he asked. "It really is pointless at this point."

"Even so, I don't want to make a bad impression. Even if there's not a job for me here right now, I don't want to close the door on one down the road."

"Okay, yeah, I guess that makes sense. Why don't I call over there and see what's up? That way I can walk you over there and you won't have to worry about waiting out in the waiting room when you'd already been called in."

"Sure," I said. "That would be nice."

I stood there in his office as Sam went to check on things. Mostly I just looked around, checking out the pictures that were around the office. The large bookshelf against the wall was overflowing with legal books, as well as some other books. Including one that I was almost certain had belonged to Greg. It had been the last gift I had given him, for his last birthday while we were still together. It was an old, first edition copy of his favorite novel growing up, A Wrinkle in Time. Little did I know that, when he left early from dinner to go back to work, he had really been meeting up with Angela in some hotel room somewhere. Part of me wanted to pull the book down, to tear it apart page by page. But I didn't think that would have made the best impression right then.

"Plus, you might be wrong," Greg added. "I don't remember where I stuck that book. Sam might have his own copy of that. Besides, who puts that kind of thing in their office?"

"Pfft, nerd," Dad said.

"Are you ready?" Sam asked, seemingly out of nowhere.

"What?" I asked, turning around to look at him. He was standing by the now open door, holding out his arm towards me to motion me out into the hall.

"I said 'are you ready'. Sarah is waiting for you."

"Oh, sure," I said. I gave him a half smile as I followed his lead. I didn't remember anyone in the office named Sarah. But I had stopped socializing with the paralegals soon after I stopped working there. The only reason why I had kept in touch with all the lawyers was because of Greg, of his dealings with them.

"By the way, you never told me. Why didn't you come to me about getting you a job?"

"Because I wanted to earn it," I said, simply. I didn't want any handouts from people that felt bad for me about what I had to do. Who regretted not seeing what Greg had become. It was bad enough with Angela. But at least she needed me there with her. If I couldn't earn this job on my own merits, then I had no right being there at all.

Besides, it was part of what Dr. Mendez was requiring of me. The last thing I needed right then was to go back to HTP.

Chapter Thirteen
The Party

That night was nothing special. I was simply bored and there was nothing on TV. When you're unemployed and antisocial, you read a lot of books and watch a lot of TV. But that can only take up so much of your time before you go crazy. And, with me, that wasn't a far trip. So, I just left my place and headed off in a random direction. It was still early, barely past five. The street lights weren't on yet. There were so many places you can get to by walking if you just know where you're going.

I found myself in the middle of town before deciding on where to go. There were plenty of stores around that I could window shop in. When you're on a budget, there's not much fun to be had there. Every time I'd try on a fancy dress, I was just reminded that, not only could I not afford it, I had nowhere to wear it to. So, as I was walking along Main Street, I was mostly just watching my feet as they moved down the sidewalk. Making way when other people's shadows disrupted my view.

As the sun set, its rays found the perfect line down the street, glinting off the windows on either side. When I noticed this and looked up, the light blinded me for a moment. I stopped where I was, closing my eyes as I hugged the wall next to me, until the spots faded from my vision.

That was when I heard it. The door next to me must have just opened up, while my eyes were closed. The sounds from within one of the stores reached me as I stood there.

His laugh reached me. It was unforgettable. Easily distinguishable among the masses. Ever since he had broken up with me, his laugh had always sounded so fake, despite it sounding no different than it always had. Yet, that night, it didn't sound fake. Just mean. I ducked aside, thinking for sure that he had spotted me. That his laugh was targeted at me.

When I opened my eyes again, I noticed that I was in a small alleyway that was tucked between the two buildings. The light had faded as the sun edged past the street. At first, I had forgotten which of the buildings had been the one I had been standing beside. Which would have owned the door that the laughter had come out of. The door had already closed again, blocking the voices. Blocking the sounds that were hiding that laugh. Slowly, carefully, I peeked out, first one way, then the other. To my left, as I was facing the street, was a familiar name spelled out over the door. McGrady's was a name I had heard often while we were still together. A place that he had claimed to have gone often. Since the breakup, I had wondered just how many times he had actually gone there. How many times had he gone to see her?

But, as I peeked through the large windows that took up much of the front of the building, I spotted him. Greg was sitting in the center of the group. He was always the center of attention when surrounded by his buddies. It always annoyed me when I saw him like that, because I knew how he was at home. He had always been removed. Withdrawn. Quiet with internal contemplation. It was like Greg only had two settings, off and on in full. Whenever he was with his friends or at work, he was on in full. When he was with me, he was completely turned off. At least in those later years. It was like this person he was with other people was a mask. Or was it the other way around. Was he always hiding the real him, even from me? Was it just so exhausting to be on all the time with me? What was it about me that turned him off so much? I couldn't even remember when it started. When he stopped trying with me. If it had been before or after that first miscarriage. Or if he had started being aloof after the wedding.

Sam was there, too. Greg's constant wing man even when we were together. He was sitting over Greg's left shoulder, taking the place of Greg's angel. The conscience that he didn't listen to often enough. I had never asked Sam if he had ever defended me. If he ever tried to stop Greg from cheating on me. It wasn't like it was his job or anything. But it would have been nice to know that at least one person was on my side. Even Dr. Mendez tried to make excuses for Greg. As if being a man meant you automatically stood up for each other. Why wasn't it like that for women?

Most of the crowd that was sitting around Greg was familiar to me, if not by name, then at least by face. They were all from Greg's office, though I didn't see Jennifer. She, no doubt, had been back at the office, holding down the fort. She would be getting the real work done while the rest of them were out having drinks. Or whatever it was they were doing there. Even Donovan and Lewis, the two name partners, were there. They stood at a table in the back, looking on at the main group as if they wished they were still a part of it, but knew that their presence would only taint the mirth.

I felt like a stalker, standing out there in the fading light, watching my ex-husband from afar. If anyone spotted me there, that actually knew who I was, they would never believe that I had just stumbled upon the group. I no longer had any business being there. No claim to anyone inside. Yet I couldn't bring myself to leave. Tom and Dad were both riveted on the conversation inside. It was as if they, too, missed being part of such a group. Of being social. Of being one of the guys. That was something they could never be when they were just voices inside my head.

Greg's laughter faded, but another voice kept going. It flowed out from the cacophony of the crowd inside. The high pitched, lilting laugh flowed out. A heat seeking missile aimed at my ear. A siren song drawing my eyes forward, unerringly towards her. At first, I thought it was her. It was Angela, the mistress turned wife. My eyes went wide when I spotted her, when I recognized her. Her hand was almost casually, yet, still, possessively on Greg's shoulder. I remembered when Greg had made partner, had first gotten his secretary. He had even looked to me for my advice on whether or not to hire her. So, yes, I knew exactly who Emily was.

Tom saw it, too. He saw the two of them sitting together, practically in each other's laps. The bar was crowded, packed with three other parties. It made sense to me that they would be squished together, trying to hear each other over the general noise that droned on around them, while keeping their own conversations confidential. Tom, on the other hand, saw something else. He saw something much deeper. But he wasn't about to tell me what it was.

"What?" I demanded of him. His smug face was firmly in place. It was something that a person without a face shouldn't be able to manage. And I knew, without him saying anything, that he wasn't about to offer any revelations.

"Oh, let him stew in it," Dad suggested. "It's not like he actually knows anything that you don't already."

"That's just it," I said. "He does. He always does, a fact which delights him to no end. He's the smart one in this group."

"Well, at least you admit it," Tom said. "I'm still not telling, though."

I just rolled my eyes, staring deeper into the inside of the bar. As if staring at the group would reveal the truth that Tom had already figured out for himself. Whatever it was, I couldn't see it from where I was standing. I had to get closer. The sounds within were too much of a draw for me. The level of socialization that I hadn't had in months, in years to be honest. Even if I was just going to be an observer, being inside was better than the perpetual loneliness outside.

The smells of the bar assaulted me as I stepped over the threshold. The barley and hops of the beers that were being slung around freely. The general din of alcohol that exuded from the walls and floors themselves. The door swung shut behind me, hitting me on the butt when I didn't step away fast enough. The extra push forced me in further, rather than letting me sit by the door, unobserved for a few minutes as I acclimated to the social menagerie within. Not wanting Greg and Sam to see me, I skirted the edge of the overcrowded room. I made my way along the wall with the windows, the very same windows I had been spying through all that time, before tucking into a back corner with no table.

"No, don't sit on the sidelines," Dad demanded. "I want to dance."

"God, you sound like you're drunk already," I said to him, relying on the noise of the crowd to drown out my voice.

"We can't get drunk," Dad said, morosely. He had always been one of those men to down about a keg of beer a week. It was one of the many reasons why I didn't drink. Not wanting to be like him. His voice in my head never liked that fact. "That one time you drank yourself silly just to shut me up, I didn't feel a thing."

"Yeah, and you didn't shut up about it, either," I said. "Why do you think I never bothered to try it again?"

"Want anything?" someone called out over the noise around me.

"What?" I asked. I looked towards the source of the voice, a short girl carrying a tray that was about as wide as she was tall. The tray was ladened down with tall glasses, half of them empty while the rest were full.

"Do you want anything," she asked again. "From the bar. That group over there is paying for a round."

I followed her finger to spot Greg and his posse at the bar. They were toasting another round, raising their glasses to each other as if they were the kings of the universe, out to conquer another world. Greg seemed to have noticed the attention, as if he had some preternatural ability to zone in on someone pointing at him. He looked directly at me, recognizing me instantly, even over the intervening distance. His eyes went wide when he noticed me there, his glass, still half full, stuck midway between the bar and his mouth.

Sam looked at me next. His disappointing sneer spread across his lips. As if he wondered how I dared intrude on their territory. As if they owned this half of town and I had no right being there. The look faded quickly, but it still lingered in my mind. A phantom that would haunt me for days. He turned back to the group, trying to ignore me over in the corner by myself.

Though, I never really was by myself. My voices always kept me company, even when the crowd around me was so congested as to intrude on the personal space I try to keep around me. The waitress was still looking my way, her questions still unanswered as she stared me down. She was probably trying to figure out if I was going to answer or not. I just shook my head, no, wanting nothing more than to flee that room. It was no longer comfortable there. Was never comfortable. Never would be comfortable. It felt like the room itself was trying to get rid of me. Like the crowd around me had a force field that was specifically designed to thrust me from their space.

I pulled my purse closer to my chest, more using it as a shield than trying to protect it from the reaching hands of the bar patrons. While making myself as small as I could possibly be, smaller than I already felt myself being, I retraced the path I had only just taken. I fled from the bar as quickly as I could manage. The crowd got louder as it loomed over me. Every laugh seemed like it was pointed at me. Every glance a stare of daggers at my back. I even berated myself for going in there, for trying to be any amount of social, let alone jumping in the deep end like that.

Right before getting to the door, I heard my name spoken behind me. I glanced over my shoulder. Not wanting to turn around. Not wanting to slow my escape even a little bit. Greg and Sam were looking towards me, a look of disdain mixed with pity in an imperfect balance across their faces. Each leaned towards one way over the other. But it wasn't them that had said my name. It wasn't them that had referred to me.

Behind them, the third point to their equilateral triangle, stood Emily. She, too, stared at me, but not with disdain or pity. Her eyes were dead, the irises already whiting over. Though her face was pointed directly at me, her eyes were unfocused. They were staring at something beyond me. Staring at the last thing she would ever see. Greg turned, wrapping his hands around her neck. He strangled her right there in the middle of the bar, though Emily was already dead. I could see the bruises forming around her neck, even as far across the room as she was from me. The sign that she had been strangled to death.

I screamed as she fell to the floor. No one else in the bar seemed to notice either of us.

Chapter Fourteen
The Funeral

It seemed like my nightmares had started up just to compete with Angela's. I sat up in bed, gasping for breath as I tried to focus on the reality that was still forming around me. Angela's hand found my back. It surprised me and made me jump in place. I looked down at her, still mostly asleep next to me, in the bed I had once shared with Greg. That she had once shared with Greg. And, now, it was shared between the two of us.

A few days earlier, while I was at the law offices trying to get a job, Angela had made up the bed in the guest room. I had actually spent part of that night in there. But when Angela's screams woke me, and Doug, in the middle of the night, I moved into the master bedroom. My presence at her side seemed to calm her. To chase away the nightmares and let her sleep through the night again. I didn't know what did the trick. If it was the warmth of my body. The presence of Greg's voice in my head. Or just the added weight beside her. She seemed to think it was my calming influence on her son that was the key to her catching up on her sleep.

Sam had been right, of course. I managed to catch up with Sarah, who, as it turned out, had started at the firm at the same time as I had the first time around. Unlike me, however, she hadn't met and fallen in love with one of the lawyers. Instead, she stayed, worked through the intervening time, and had become the head of the department. Still, despite our connections, as limited as they were, she couldn't hire me while the case was still pending. She, like Sam, had said that I should come back in a couple of weeks once everything had settled down. I'd be starting over from where I had left off, as a first-year paralegal with no real work experience, despite my years of teaching at the community college.

Still, it would be weeks before everything would blow over. The reporters were still camped out at my apartment. I had checked on the way home from the interview. Their numbers did seem to be dwindling. I wasn't sure if that was a loss of interest, the uncertainty of whether or not I still lived there, or if they were eating each other for food. Dad liked the idea of that last one, though Greg thought the first was more accurate. I just hoped it was a sign that things were going to go back to normal soon. Or at least some semblance of normal. I actually thanked God that they didn't find out that I had moved in with Angela.

To her credit, Angela was actually pretty great. Despite her nightmare problems, and the little one, she was surprisingly easy to live with. We mostly stayed out of each other's way. I was holed up in the study that had become of the fourth bedroom, continuing my job search and handling other things that came up. She spent most of her time in the playroom downstairs. The only time we really saw each other was at meals and when we went to bed.

Angela was an excellent cook. It was something that I had never managed to become, no matter how much Greg had pushed me in that direction. She was so used to cooking for Greg that she barely seemed to notice the switch over between having him there and having me. The main difference was that we ate in the dinette, instead of the dining room. Both of us had agreed to save that room as a memorial to Greg. Still, relying on someone else again was a lot for me to get used to. I wasn't sure how healthy it would be. And it was still a couple days before I could see Dr. Mendez again. I would have a lot to talk to him about when I did see him.

Between hiding out in the office and searching for a job, it ended up falling onto me to organize the funeral. Though the case is still officially pending, there wasn't much to look for on the body. I had confessed to killing him... or, technically, Angela had confessed for me. So, not even a week after I had killed him, we were all set to bury Greg. It was something I had been stressing over for days.

With the nightmare fading from my thoughts, I glanced over at the clock on the nightstand. Despite being woken up before the alarm by my own demons, it was about to go off anyway. There was still a lot that needed to get done, especially with Doug to take care of. It helped that Greg had taken the time to spell out exactly what he had wanted from that day. It was almost like he had been expecting it to come. Maybe he had, given how things ended with Emily. The voice Greg had been no help in making the plans. Although, he had been able to read Greg's writing better than I could. His plans had been scratched out long hand on some old pieces of paper, along with some left-over notes from some case he had been working on at the time. There wasn't enough in the notes for me to guess which case. I couldn't properly guage how old the plans were. Even if there had been, it wasn't like I had been following his career all that much since we had broken up. I just had to hope that there weren't any newer plans somewhere, lost in the mess that was his desk. Or when they had kicked him out of his office at work, after he was dead.

With a deep, steadying sigh, I reached back towards Angela. Her hand was still on my back. It was a better fortification against the day to come than I would have liked to have admitted. My arm brushed against hers lightly as I pushed against her shoulder a few times, gently rocking her awake.

"Hmm?" she asked, sleepily.

"It's time to get up," I said. "We have the funeral in a few hours."

"Right," she said, before rolling over and promptly going back to sleep.

I laughed a little, but figured I'd let her sleep while I grabbed a shower and got dressed. Angela was in charge of the food and Doug, and little else. She could sleep in a little longer than I could. Once I was ready for the day, or at least showered and dressed, I woke her up more definitively. I made sure she would stay that way before heading back to the office to double check on a few things. This mostly involved calling the funeral home and the church where the main events would take place. With the funeral home, I just had to make sure that Greg was ready for the day. He wouldn't need to be woken up.

I had found it a little strange that the church didn't have a problem with having the services there. They knew who Greg was. Knew that he had killed Emily. Hers was probably the last funeral service that had been at that church. It was almost odd, the symmetry between the two of them. Both killed by those that had, at least at one point, professed their love for their victim. And, yet, they were both dead just the same.

"What makes you think I ever loved her," Greg said, as I hung up the phone after talking with the church.

"I never said you did," I said. "Or the real you, for that matter. I just figured that, at some point, he told her that he did. Girls tend to want to hear that sort of thing when they're sleeping with their married bosses. Whether or not Emily was looking for that, I'm sure Greg, the real Greg, had said it at least once. I have no doubt that he had never had any real feelings for her, given the fact that he killed her so soon after they had gotten together."

"You make it sound like I was a heartless bastard."

"Well, you did cheat on me. Divorce me. Marry the person you cheated on me with. Then, less than a year later, cheat on her as well," I said, as if that were proof of the accusation.

"You make it sound like that was a bad thing," he said, innocently.

"It was a bad thing, Greg. Very bad."

"Were you talking to someone?" Angela asked. She was peeking her head in around the door to the office. Her black dress streamed out behind her, catching the light from the window. It looked like it was the same dress she had worn to Emily's funeral, which I had crashed. I stayed in the back of the church, my head ducked, hoping no one would see me. At the time, I had been hoping that I could figure out who had killed her by going. Plus, I had actually liked Emily, back before I knew she had been sleeping with Greg. I'm not sure why I had thought the second funeral in less than a month warranted a different dress. It just stuck with me that it looked the same.

"No, it's nothing. I'm just," I started. I waved my hand around my head, as if swatting at a fly. Or several flies that had been stalking me for years. She seemed to understand what I meant, as she let it drop.

"We should get going," she said. "Is everything good?"

"Yeah, I just got off the phone with the church, and the funeral home is already setting up over there. You're right, we should probably get going. I imagine people would expect the widow over there on time."

"Widows," she corrected, as if I qualified for the title. I was just the ex-wife. The one who killed the bastard. I barely qualified for a seat in attendance. Unlike at Emily's funeral, where everyone in attendance, save Greg, had thought I had killed her. This time I really had done it. And, yet, for some reason, instead of hiding in the back, I was getting one of the seats of honor near the front.

I scooped up the much-abused pile of papers that contained the instructions Greg had left behind before following Angela into the hall. The papers had been folded and refolded several times over the past couple of days. Even crumpled in anger a few times. I tried my best to put them back into some semblance of order, and to fold them one final time along the original crease. I failed completely on both counts.

Doug was already strapped into a stroller next to Angela in the upstairs hallway. He was still asleep. Or perhaps asleep again after being woken up to be dressed and strapped in. I wondered, briefly, at why she didn't wait until they were downstairs to do it. I didn't say anything, bowing to her experience. Still, I watched as she awkwardly pulled the thing along, bogged down first by the plush carpeting, then the stairs themselves. I would have helped, but I was afraid to break the whole thing trying. Or worse, Angela or Doug.

Out at the car, I stood back, my mind properly boggled. I watched Angela pull the seat section of the stroller off the rest of the construct, depositing it into the back seat and strapping it in with the seat belts, before packing up the rest of the stroller. The movements looked well practiced, as if she had been in the habit of driving off with the thing. I hadn't seen her leave the house since I had been there. Still, I just stood back, not wanting to get in the way of the maneuver, at a loss for how to help. Or even if she needed any.

Without a word, she climbed into the driver's seat. It was her car, after all, so I figured she would want to do the driving. "We really should pick up your car this week," she suggested, as I climbed in next to her.

"Sure, if the reporters haven't destroyed it yet."

"Didn't you see it when you went by there the other day?"

"A lot can change in a couple of days," I said. "Besides, I only went over there for a change of clothes. I wasn't really taking the time to look around." She nodded, as if my logic made perfect sense to her. It barely did to me.

The church was only a few blocks over from the house. We could have walked it, though I was wearing heels and I never liked walking far in them. Angela was wearing flats, but she had Doug to worry about, and the car might help with that. In either case, it only took us a couple minutes to get over there.

The parking lot was almost vacant when we arrived. The hearse was parked near the front of the church, in one of the handicap parking spots. I spotted a single other car, off to the side in the back parking lot that was mostly used for spillover. I imagined that one belonged to the priest that would be performing the ceremony.

"Well, at least we're the first ones here," Angela said. As if anyone else that was coming to this would bother to show up an hour before it started. Still, I just nodded to her, not wanting to point out how stupid I thought the comment was. She pulled up near the front, in the first non-handicap spot next to the hearse.

With a nod to Angela, I left her to look after Doug while I poked around in the church, trying to find the priest. I wasn't overly familiar with the insides of the church. Back when I lived in the house, I only went to the main room those times that I had gone there. It took me a little while to find the office. Once I did, we spent the rest of the hour hashing out the details of the ceremony. The ceremony was going to be simple enough, not much different from all the others that the priest had performed in his tenure there. But there was one section that Greg had wanted different from any other funeral that I had ever heard of. It was weird, that one section, having someone specifically retelling a person's life, with all the good and the bad. It had been the biggest point Greg had put in his instructions. So, it seemed important to him. I hadn't even heard of anything like that before I started preparing for that day. I didn't want anything messing it up.

So, as I came out into the main room, just a few minutes before the funeral was scheduled to start, my mind was still on getting that part of it in line. The voice of Greg was yelling at me that I didn't do it right, distracting me as I entered the room. I was taken completely by surprise by what I saw out there. I had been expecting a decent turnout. Probably not packing the seats of the large church. But at least the good half of the front seats, and maybe a few stragglers in the back. Instead, other than Angela, Doug, and myself, there were only five others there.

Sam and Jessica were seated next to Angela in the front row. I moved towards them hurriedly. The man in the far back, fumbling around with a stack of note cards, was probably the biographer that I had contacted to do the reading of Greg's life. Off to the side, standing next to a statue of Mary, was Detective Bently, of all people. I hoped, prayed, that he wasn't there to make a scene or cause any trouble for us. As I walked along the aisle towards Angela, he glared at me, as if wondering at the audacity of me attending the funeral at all. The fifth person was sitting almost exactly in the center of the room, as if trying to not seem like a member of the family or one of the awkward people that arrived late. She was a woman in a gray dress and a brown trench coat. She looked a bit familiar, but I couldn't place her. The voices were at as much of a loss as I was.

"Hey," I murmured, when I arrived at Angela's side. Doug was still asleep, still tucked into his transformer car seat. Sam and Jessica were sitting on the other side of Angela from him. I took the seat next to Doug, not wanting to walk around to the other side of the aisle or scrunching past the four of them. "Not that great of a turn out. Do you think people are just going to be fashionably late?"

"I doubt it," Sam said. "People at the office knew about the funeral, but not many of them seemed interested in coming. Greg didn't have any family, did he?"

"We were his family," Angela said, defensively.

"No," I said. "His parents had died a few years ago. Or at least that's what he told me. I never met them, but considering everything..."

"No, that's what I heard as well," Sam agreed. I looked towards Jessica, sitting there. Her arm was tucked possessively around Sam's arm, using it as a shield against the rest of us. As if being associated with Greg was contagious.

"I'm just glad the reporters hadn't crashed it," I said. There was one upside to having the place empty. At least we knew who his real friends were.

"I think that's who that woman over there is," Angela said, pointing purposefully towards the woman in the center of the room. "But there's not much of a story left. I think they're just waiting around for a statement from you."

"I don't know why," I said. "It's not like I stopped a serial killer or anything."

"Hey, you never know," Sam joked. "If he had had his way, he would have killed you, wouldn't he?"

"No, if he had had his way, he would have been able to get away with dating Emily on the side, while still being married to Angela," I said. "I don't think he ever planned for any of this."

"Yeah," Greg's voice agreed. "'Cause what kind of sick person would plan on killing someone they had slept with?"

"You're one to ask," I mumbled beneath my breath, too quiet for those around me to hear.

"Honestly, I'm not even sure why you bothered with all of this," Sam said, gesturing around at the church. "Planning his funeral and all. Dig a hole and drop him in, for all I care. I'm just here for you two... well, three, with the little one over there."

The truth of the matter was, with him dead instead of me, I found myself in desperate need to pick up the slack that he had left behind. It was as if I needed to prove, to myself if not to others, that my life had been worth saving. It was the least I could do, given how our relationship had ended. How Greg's life had ended. I didn't think Angela should have to deal with all of that. She had enough on her plate with Doug. With dealing with the fact that she had been sleeping next to a murderer for weeks without even knowing it. That was something that had obviously been slowly driving her insane.

At one point, I had considered offering her my appointment with Dr. Mendez. But I knew he wouldn't have gone for it anyway. Besides, there were people that specialized in that kind of grief. It would have been better for her to have more than just the one appointment, if she was going to need help to get over it. I just hoped that the funeral would give her the closure she needed.

Someone cleared their throat loudly. The sound of it echoed around the room. It pulled my attention back over to Detective Bently. He seemed at a loss, standing there among the mourners. Even the reporter seemed less out of place than him. She knew how to blend in to the crowd, or lack thereof. I wondered why he was there. What reason did he have to continue bugging us? Perhaps it had to do with the fact that the case still wasn't closed. I made a mental note to confront him about it, even though I knew I would chicken out of doing so even as I made the decision.

The priest tapped the mic up on the dais a couple of times to get everyone's attention, but then quickly stepped away from it. He spoke loudly, his voice easily filling the otherwise empty space. "We're about to get started," he said. "I see that there aren't very many of you here today, and I find that to be a shame. I know that many were disappointed by what Greg had done. But Jesus teaches that we should hate the sin, but still love the sinner. While Greg may not have repented in life, I am sure that he had done so in death, and tried to find some relationship with God in his final moments. For, if he had repented in his heart and to God, even if it weren't through one of his messengers, he could still find a place in heaven by His side."

"Pfft, yeah right," Dad said. "That asshole tried to kill my little girl in his last moments. I have no doubt he's burning in hell right now, and deserving every moment of it."

"Hey, that's not nice," Greg said.

"Why do you care? You're not even him, just some lost piece of my daughter's psyche."

"Yeah, just like you're not really her father," Greg said.

I rolled my eyes, but suppressed my instinct to engage with them. Their continued banter drowned out much of what the priest was saying. It was something that often sprung up those days. That was alright, though. I wasn't there for me. All the grieving I had done for Greg was already over. I had to mourn his loss back when he had divorced me. I reached my hand out, taking Angela's in mine, trying to lend her what comfort I could provide. She looked over to me, her eyes wide in surprise. I simply gave her a smile before turning back to the priest, trying to hear him over the continued banter that only I could hear.

Chapter Fifteen
Dinner Afterwards

It was a long day, and I was exhausted. Angela seemed to have gained a little skip in her step. She had returned to a level of joy in her life that she must have had before Greg had destroyed it... Before I had destroyed it, by revealing to her who he really was... And by killing him. I suddenly could see the person that Greg must have fallen for. Must have left me for.

I sat in my seat at the dinette table in the kitchen, the same one I had back when it was mine. Angela bustled around the kitchen, putting together some semblance of a dinner. Unlike how they usually show it on television and in movies, no one had bothered to dump a bunch of food on us. Greg had specifically said not to bother with a wake. We weren't left with piles of leftovers from no one coming to that, either.

"It was a nice service, wasn't it?" I asked, unsure of what else to say.

"I can't believe that biographer was able to pull up so much information about Greg in so short of a time," Angela said, in answer.

"Well, a lot of it the reporters have been digging up all week," I pointed out. "Well, really the past few weeks. Part of it came out with the Emily investigation. The rest was mostly just dug up out of old records and his own interpretations of the facts of the case. Really, it wasn't anything like I had been expecting from how Greg had described it in his notes."

"I wonder where he had come up with the idea," she said. "It wasn't like anything I had ever heard of."

"I don't know, probably from an old book somewhere. Now, though, I'm wondering if he had come up with the idea simply in case he died without getting the chance to explain why he had killed Emily. That whole thing about him not wanting to ruin his life, his family... I don't know, I kind of get that. If I had been part of this family, I don't think I would have wanted to lose that either. Of course, personally, I wouldn't have cheated in the first place. That seems like the quickest way to lose the family to begin with. Certainly, after what happened with... But, that's not important, I guess. Not now."

"It'll always be important," she said. She placed the large bowl of salad down in the center of the table, replacing the fruit bowl with it. She carefully placed the fruit bowl back on the counter, where it usually spent the time while we're eating, before retrieving a couple of plates from the cabinet. "As long as it affects you, it'll be important. I really am sorry, though, for my part in that whole business. If I had known you before, I don't think I could have done it."

"It didn't exactly stop Emily," I pointed out. "I did know her, at least a little, before that whole mess started. But, then again, she did kind of seem like the type to steal another person's husband."

"Wow, speaking ill of the dead? Maybe I should reevaluate my opinion of you," she said.

"Hey, I speak ill of Greg all the time," I pointed out. "As do you. He was an asshole."

"He was an asshole," she agreed. She laughed a little when she said that, but the laughter turned sour quickly. "But I still miss him. How messed up is that."

"Not at all," I said. "I sometimes miss him myself. It's one of the things I'm working through in therapy. The thing is, though, I'm not really missing him."

"But you just said--"

"I'm missing the person that I thought he was," I clarified. "I fell in love, we both fell in love, with this great guy. But that wasn't who he was. He was... flawed, on some really in-depth level that neither of us saw. I think... I think that was the point of today. Of that whole speech the guy had made. There was a lot more under the surface of Greg than either of us got to see."

"Well, you have to admit, that was one amazing surface," Angela said.

"That it was," I said. I raised my glass in a mock toast. "To the amazing surface and the mask that hid the darkness."

"Hear, hear," she said, tapping her own glass to mine. "So, what's the plan, now that the funeral is over? I know that moving in here was never your long-term plan, but..."

"Well, I still have some stuff at the apartment. Not to mention my car. I have some movers coming by tomorrow to move it all into storage. There's also the matter of me getting a job. If the lack of press at the funeral was any indication, I'm thinking things will blow over a lot more quickly than people had been figuring. So, maybe, in a week or two, I'll try again. In the meantime, I need to work to get some contacts. Some opportunities lined up and all that good stuff."

"Yeah, but... I mean, well," she stuttered. When I looked over at her, she seemed a little flustered, at a loss for words. "I'm just trying to say that you don't need to feel the need to get out of the house right away. Job, yes, that would be good. Especially since we still don't know what's going on with the will and all that."

"Yeah, Sam is taking care of that stuff, right? I'll call him up on Monday to see if there's been any developments on that front."

"Right, but you shouldn't feel the need to get an apartment right away. We still have plenty of room here, in the house, and... well... I'm just saying, it's been... nice having you here."

I smiled at that awkwardly worded complement. "It's been nice being here," I agreed.

"Well, good," she said. She patted her hand a couple times on the table before picking up her fork and digging in. We spent much of the next few minutes eating. Although, I had the feeling there was something else she was trying to say.

"Tom?" Dad asked.

"Hey, don't look at me. I have no idea what she's talking about."

"Can you really look at each other?" I thought to them. My eyes flickered over to Angela, making sure she wasn't noticing the internal conversation I was having. I wasn't sure if this truce could stand a reminder of just how crazy I was. Or blossoming friendship. Or whatever was going on there.

"It's a figure of speech," Tom muttered. "Wait, you don't think..."

"What?" I thought.

"Oh, I'm always thinking that," Dad joked.

"What?" I thought, again.

Angela cleared her throat loudly. I looked back over to her, half expecting her to be waiting for an answer to a question that I hadn't heard her ask. I was too engrossed in the conversation happening inside my own head. But she was just staring at her plate. Her utensils played around a little with the food down there, as if they were lost or something. As I watched, she seemed to shuffle her chair a little closer to me, though I wasn't sure why she would have bothered. Wouldn't it have been easier to move her plate if she was out of alignment with it?

"Um," she started up, placing her utensils down carefully on her plate. I was thinking she was about to say something stupid about the plate settings, which were left over from my days with Greg. Or ask to switch places with me because of a glare from the window. Instead, she said something I wasn't expecting. "About... what the priest said at the funeral."

"Which part?" I asked. I didn't remember anything specific that would have needed further discussion. Then again, it wasn't exactly like I was paying attention to every word the man had said.

"About finding solace in those around you and finding a way to fill the void Greg had left," she said. Yeah, that was definitely a part that I had missed. "I don't know, it's probably stupid."

"I've heard once that there are no stupid questions," I said. I figured that she needed the support.

"God, that's stupid," Greg said.

"Yeah, there are totally such things as stupid questions," Tom agreed with him, for once.

"I just... well, it wasn't exactly a question. It was more... You know what, never mind. It doesn't matter."

"No, seriously," I said. "We shouldn't do this anymore. This hiding what we're thinking. It was something that Greg got us doing, and it's not healthy." Not thinking much of it at the time, I placed my knife down and placed my newly freed hand on top of hers. I had meant it to reassure her.

Angela looked down at our hands for a moment. She bit her lower lip before looking up at me. Her eyes glistened in the light from the window, surprising me with their gentleness. "It's just," she started. "These past few days, with you living here, have been great."

"Yeah," I agreed, unsure where she was going.

"Well, I... Oh, screw it," she said. She grabbed my wrist, pulling me towards her.

I just reacted. My right hand, still entwined in hers, grappled to get free while my left gripped tightly around the fork that was there. I felt the urge to thrust it forward, to protect myself from whatever attack was imminent. I wouldn't have expected that. Wouldn't have expected anything from the otherwise docile woman that was sitting beside me. Neither hand was free to stop what was about to happen. Her hands stayed down, stayed on my wrist, as the momentum brought me closer to her.

My nose bumped into hers and I bounced backwards. Her hands went to her offended nose, freeing me. Without her pulling on me, I tumbled, overbalanced, off my chair and onto the floor heavily. "Ow," I said, as I sat there, confused and hurt. "What the hell was that?" I asked. I pulled the fork in as a shield to cover my exposed chest. I wasn't exactly in the best position to launch a counter offensive, but I was damn sure I'd be prepared to defend myself if need be.

"Oh, my god, I'm so sorry. I'm not sure... I was trying to be smooth and... I'm sorry."

"What exactly was that about?" I asked.

"Oh, my god," Dad said. There was a smile audible in his voice.

"Oh, quiet you," I said to him, forgetting to try to be silent.

"I didn't say anything," Angela said. "I'm sorry."

Her face showed up above me, blocking the light from the overhead lamp. A halo spread out around her head as her hair fell down towards me. The light reflected perfectly off her golden tresses. Her eyes darted straight towards the fork, held protectively in my hands.

"I'm sorry," she said again. "I thought... But, I mean, during the funeral..."

"What?" I asked. I slowly realized she hadn't meant to attack me. She hadn't meant her actions to be anything like an attack.

Dad's gloating words, and continued laughter, took on a much different connotation as I slowly realized what she had tried to do.

"Oh, my god," I said.

"I-I-I was... No, I'm sorry. That was meant to be a joke. But I didn't mean for you to get hurt like that. Are you alright?"

"Yeah," I said. My voice took on a very high-pitched whine. My eyes went wide in shock. "Sure."

Chapter Sixteen
What?

"Seriously, what the hell was that about?" I asked.

"I'm sorry, is that a rhetorical question?" Dr. Mendez asked. "I do believe I've told you before that I'm not a mind reader."

"But... she tried to kiss me."

"So?"

"So? She's a girl."

"Yes."

"And I'm a girl."

"Yes."

"We're both girls."

"We've already agreed on that fact."

"And we're both straight," I said.

"Ah, but how do you know that?" Dr. Mendez asked.

"Because we both married the same guy, the same man."

"That doesn't necessarily mean anything," he said.

I stared at him, sitting smugly in his usual chair. It had been a long day and a half, but he didn't have Sunday hours. Plus, it wasn't exactly an emergency that I saw him. It just felt like one. So, I had to wait for my usual appointment on Monday. I had spent the nights in the guest room, avoiding Angela as much as possible. Fortunately, she hadn't cried out in the middle of the night without me next to her. I hoped that sleeping beside her wouldn't be necessary anymore. It was bad enough living with her if she was having feelings for me. I was just glad that I had already scheduled moving my stuff out of the apartment into storage. It kept me out of the house all day Sunday. I had a feeling that I would be better off moving into storage with it.

"Many homosexual individuals have had heterosexual relationships," he explained. "For some, it's a matter of blending into society. For others, it's denial. However, that might not have anything to do with what's going on here, for either of you."

"Woah, Doc, I have nothing going on here at all."

"For her, then," he allowed. "You both just lost a man that you loved. The same man, in fact. For you, that love had already turned to hate. An anger that you couldn't reconcile. That almost drove you to needing to be committed again."

"Yeah, don't remind me," I said. I closed my eyes against the memories that fought to push through the wall I had wrapped around them. That first week after finding out about Angela, when I was in that office every day. I could barely get up off of that chaise to leave after the hour without reassurance that I could come back the next day. The voices had been stirred up to a level that I hadn't heard them at since before my first time at HTP, after my father died. It was enough to drive even the sanest individual crazy. Although, of course, the sanest individual wouldn't have been hearing voices to begin with.

"It was different for her. More recent. Fresher in her mind. She had him, fully, one day. Then lost him completely the next. Again and again in every way possible. First, that he was cheating on her. Then, that he was a killer. Finally, by his own death."

"By my hand," I said. The reminder brought the feeling of the blood on my hands back to the forefront of my mind.

"I didn't say that, but yes."

"But, shouldn't that mean she should hate me? Why doesn't she hate me?"

"Hate is a strange, and strong, emotion. It can take several forms."

"So, what? You're saying that she tried to kiss me because she hates me?" I asked.

"Or maybe it's transference. You've all but taken Greg's place in the past week. Even sleeping in the same bed as her."

"A fact that I wish I hadn't mentioned," I said. I shuddered at the reminder that I had been so close to someone that might have real, emotional feelings for me that I couldn't return. Whatever they were. It made me feel like Greg, lying beside Emily. Or Angela. Or me even, when his heart was with another. But who did have my heart? Did I?

"But that could be enough that her feelings for Greg have been moved towards you."

"And I thought you weren't a mind reader," I joked.

"I'm not," he said. "These are merely suggestions of what might be happening here. An explanation that would make you at least a little less freaked out about what happened on Saturday. It's something to calm your mind a little. I could no sooner diagnose someone I've never met than I could guess a number you were thinking of. Or an emotion that you were having but couldn't express yourself."

"Yeah, no feelings," I insisted.

He smiled back at me, nodding. "Would it be so bad if there was?"

"Well... no, I guess not," I allowed. "I mean, I don't really see anything wrong with it, but--"

"But a lot of society does," he said. "Are you worried what other people are going to think about you?"

"What? No, no, it's nothing like that."

"Are you worried what I'm going to think?" Dad said. "Cause, seriously, that's kind of hot."

I rolled my eyes at him, an action that Dr. Mendez no doubt had noticed. "Seriously? You do know you're thinking about your daughter having sex with someone, anyone. Isn't that kind of sick?" I thought, loudly.

"Hey, you're not really my kid," Dad said. "I'm not really your dad. Remember? I'm just some part of your psyche that you've assigned the voice of your father to."

"Which, of course, means that it's you that wants to see yourself having sex with Angela," Tom pointed out. I would have expected a comment from Greg, an agreement with Tom's analysis. Or with Dad wanting me to have sex with his widow. However, like the last time I had gone to see Dr. Mendez, Greg hadn't entered the building with us. He had stayed outside. Or, should I say, his voice disappeared when I entered the building. If I could just figure out what affect the building was having on him, perhaps I could use it on the other two and be rid of them forever.

"Now, now, you wouldn't really want to get rid of us, would you?" Dad said. "What would you even do with yourself?"

"Well, for one thing, I'd patent it and use it to rid all people of their voices. I could make a fortune curing people," I said.

"What's that?" Dr. Mendez asked.

"Oh," I said, embarrassed. I had forgotten where I was for a moment. Forgotten not to talk to the voices out loud when around other people. Especially Dr. Mendez.

"You are still taking your medication, aren't you?" he insisted.

"Yes, doctor," I said.

"Maybe I should up your dosage a little," he said. He looked to his notes to see what my dosage actually was.

"No," I said, quicker and louder than I strictly needed to. "No, that's not necessary. It's fine, I'm managing."

"Alright," he said, placing his notes back onto the desk. "But if it gets to the point where I think you need to be committed again..."

"Yes, I know," I said. He didn't have to keep reminding me that the man held my freedom in his hands. But he seemed to be able to get it in every session.

"Alright, then," he said. "So, how are we going to handle this whole Angela issue?"

"We?" Dad asked. I flinched at the word, but tried to let it go. Let it roll off of me, like Dr. Mendez had taught me.

"I'll need to talk to her," I said, knowing that was what he wanted to hear.

"Good," he said, nodding. "This whole avoidance thing isn't healthy, especially with you living with her. You'll need to address it head on, if you want to grow as a person. If you want to ever feel comfortable in that house. And, please, don't just think there's only one answer to this."

"What's that supposed to mean?" I asked, confused.

"Well, I know your initial reaction was to reject her. But, bear in mind, these feelings may be just as strange to her as they were to you. Maybe they might lead you down a path you wouldn't have normally gone down. But that doesn't mean that's a good thing. Or a bad thing. Or whatever."

"Now he's just talking in circles," Tom said.

"No, what h-your saying is that I shouldn't dismiss the idea of Angela and me being good together, as more than just roommates or friends or whatever the hell we are right now. That maybe I'd be okay with a relationship, if I let myself be."

"Exactly."

"Which is, of course, completely stupid," I thought towards the voices, making it clear that I had no interest in anything more with Angela, without letting on to the good doctor. I wasn't worried that he was going to lock me up for not being open to a lesbian relationship. It was just none of his damn business.

"Oh," Dad said, disappointed that I shut the door so emphatically.

"And, with that, our hour is up," Dr. Mendez said.

"What? Already?" I asked. I looked over at the clock on his desk, which, indeed, said that it was almost noon. Almost the end of the session. "Wow, time goes fast sometimes."

"And other times, it doesn't," Tom finished.

"I really think we should pick this up on Friday," Dr. Mendez said. "I have a free session available at your usual time."

"Fine," I said, rolling my eyes. I knew there was no talking him out of it this time. Truth be told, he had given me a lot to think about. Not about actually being with Angela... that way, or anything. Just that her feelings might not be completely directed at me. That my sleeping next to her all that time might have caused things to get worse. That would need to stop. Of course, it already had. But I would need to stick to my room from then on. There was no way I was risking my living situation just yet. Not until after my whole financial situation got resolved, one way or another. "Friday it is, then," I said, before getting up from the chaise.

Out in the waiting room, sitting in his usual chair, was George, as was normal. However, standing right next to him was Detective Bently. He was leaning against the wall with an annoyed look on his face. This was perhaps due to the lack of another chair in the waiting room. His arms were crossed, but I noticed his hand slinking down, inches from the gun on his belt, as he glared over at George. It was as if he was ready to shoot the guy at a moment's notice if the need arose. As soon as I stepped into the waiting room, George jumped up from his chair, rushing past me into the office. As he passed, I noticed a lot of sweat running down the man's face, as if he, too, was just as aware of the detective's gun.

"Hello, Natalie," Bently said, not moving from his place against the wall, despite the now vacant seat next to him.

"Detective, what are you doing here?" I asked. Part of me was confused. What was going on? Did something go wrong? Was Angela alright? But, mostly, I was annoyed. Offended that he would come there. That he would come to my shrink's office, looking for me. Because, no matter what was going on, the one thing I knew for sure was that he had come there looking for me.

"I have a few questions for you," he said. His Cheshire cat smile spread back across his face as he stared me down. It was like he knew something. Something that I didn't know. Something that was going to blow the case wide open. This was, of course, despite the case, both cases, being all but closed by this point.

"I'm listening," I said. I motioned towards the chair, offering it to him. I knew that George would be in with Dr. Mendez for the entire hour, perhaps with a lot more to say given Bently's arrival. The next patient, whoever that was, wouldn't be there for at least half that time.

"I'm afraid we'll have to do this down at the station. Care for a ride?"

"Uh, that's not a good idea," Dad said, beating Tom to it.

"Duh," I thought back to them, not wanting Bently to hear me talking to my voices.

"I actually have my car here," I said. I had picked it up the day before, from the newly vacant parking lot. There had been no signs of the reporters while I had been moving my stuff out of my apartment.

"I'll have someone give you a lift back to it," he said, with a level of finality that scared me. He motioned to the door, inviting me to go first. When I didn't respond immediately, he gave out a heavy sigh before grabbing me by the arm and leading me out.

The hallway outside of the shrink's office was empty, void of anyone to help me. I wasn't exactly sure what help I needed, or who I could even turn to. I mean, Bently was a cop. It wasn't like he was abducting me. Besides, I had gotten used to such treatment over the past couple of weeks, with my many trips into the station. It wasn't until we got to the lobby that we had seen anyone. Bently simply flashed his smile and badge as he passed her. The old woman barely glanced at me to give me a knowing sneer before going about her business. She, no doubt, had seen the news. She must not be surprised in the least that I was being brought in for "questioning".

"What the hell?" Greg said, in total shock, as we came out of the building. "Don't say anything until you have a lawyer present."

"No shit, Sherlock," I muttered under my breath. "This ain't my first rodeo."

"What was that?" Bently asked.

I just shook my head as he led me over to the parking lot. There was a police cruiser, parked quite illegally there. It was blocking my car into its spot, as well as the cars on either side of mine. I smiled at Eric behind the wheel, but he refused to make eye contact with me as Bently pushed me into the back seat. Once I was in, he slammed the door as loudly as he could, ending any thoughts of getting out of my latest escapade with the cops.

As they drove me along the familiar streets, heading for the station, I wondered if I had a case for police harassment. Unfortunately, Greg seemed to go silent once more, so I couldn't ask that part of my mind that might have an answer for me.

Chapter Seventeen
Conspiracy

I could hardly believe that I was back there again. After the funeral, heck, even after the last time they let me out of that place, I was actually starting to think that my problems with the police were over. I knew that the cases were still pending. I just figured that was more a formality than anything else. Obviously, Bently wasn't going to give up so easily. He seemed to have a vendetta against me from day one, from the moment that I was found standing over Emily's dead body.

It was the same interrogation room as always, rather than the one that I had been in before. I was hoping that was a good sign. That, despite being brought in once again for questioning, they didn't have anything more on me than the last time. That other room, across the hall from that one, the one that I had spent a few terrifying hours in last week, just eight days earlier. That was the one for guilty people, right?

"Don't look at me," Greg said. "I've never been in this station before this whole thing started to go down. Remember, I wasn't a criminal defense lawyer." He had made himself known again after I was in that room for about half an hour, with no explanation for his absence. Not that I had any problem with them disappearing on me. Just that they kept coming back.

"You weren't a lawyer at all," I said to him. I glanced over to the one-way mirror on the wall, wondering if anyone was inside. Wondering what they would think of seeing me in here talking to myself. "You're just some inner part of my brain that doesn't work right," I said. It had become something of a mantra for me, reminding myself that the voices didn't really exist. That they were just there to help me handle something that my mind thought I couldn't handle on my own. I tried not to think of the fact that I only seemed to be getting more voices following me around over the years, rather than fewer of them.

Bently had led me to that room when we had gotten to the station, but immediately left me alone in there. He probably just wanted to let me stew for a little, waiting for when I'd break down and confess. The problem was that I had no idea what I was supposed to be confessing to. Not this time anyway. He already knew everything about what had happened, in both cases, after what Angela must have told them the last time we were there. And, yet, I was there once more, waiting for when he came back in and started asking me questions that I didn't know the answer to.

"But, that's good," Greg said. "I think. You don't know anything that would incriminate you this time. Whatever it is that he's trying to pin on you, there's nothing there. Right?"

"I hope so," I said. "But, then, maybe they decided that my killing you wasn't in self-defense after all. Maybe they're actually going to try to press charges. I can't exactly say I didn't kill you. 'Cause I did."

"Yes, but they already know that," Greg said, thoughtfully. "They already have your confession on that. That's not this. If they were going to press charges, it would have been that day. Or at least sooner than this. Maybe..."

"Maybe they're just going to ask a few more questions before closing the cases," Tom suggested. "Maybe there's nothing really to worry about. They just wanted to make sure that we stuck to our story."

"I'm sorry, our story?" Dad asked. "We, the three of us, don't have a story. Not anymore. This is all up to Natalie. You've got this girl."

It felt nice to have Dad on my side, even if it was just his voice in my ear. He had always been a mean old drunk when he was alive. But when it came down to it, it was better to have him on your side than against you. The only problem was he wasn't around to get me out of that station. Perhaps that was a good thing as well. I wouldn't like to see what he would have done to those cops. Not while he was in his prime anger mode. The Hulk had nothing on my old man.

As lost in my thoughts as I was, I literally jumped out of my seat when Bently came in. The metal chair fell backwards, tumbling across the floor to hit the wall behind me. I stood there for a moment, embarrassed. My face turned beet red.

Bently slapped a large pile of folders on the table before walking, slowly, purposefully, around me. He scooped up the chair from its place on the floor, slamming it down onto the tile floor behind me. I looked down at the chair, half expecting cracks in the tiles where the feet hit it. They seemed to have withheld against the onslaught. Bently pushed me backwards as he came back around me, knocking me perfectly into the chair. It was a movement that I suspected was well practiced.

He settled into the chair like a cat, stalking a prey that was about to be dinner. His Cheshire cat smile fit in nicely. His hands grappled with the folders, clawlike, as he dealt them out in front of him. He spent the time, placing them perfectly spaced between, lining them up with the edge of the table. His eyes never left mine as he did this, never blinking as they stared down into my soul, trying to read the lie he expected to find there. I crossed my arms across my chest, folding inward as the voice of my dad stalked forward, ready to defend me. Or join in on the fun that Bently seemed to be having. It was too hard to tell.

When I showed no sign of jumping to an admission of guilt, Bently leaned forward. He templed his fingers in front of his mouth. I thought for a second that he kissed his hands. But, instead, they stifled a yawn that was almost too big to be believable. "So," he said, slowly, carefully. "Care to guess what these are?"

"Folders?" I said, snarkily.

"Watch it," Greg warned. "Better to say nothing at all at this point. Wait for a lawyer."

"I thought you said I had nothing to hide," I thought to him. And I did.

"Care to guess what's in the folders?" Bently asked.

I looked down at them, the three folders on the desk. The one in the middle was familiar. It was the one that he didn't have one of his meaty hands on. It was thick, almost half an inch thick, thicker than I remembered it being the last time I had seen it. Emily's name was faded on the tab, but still legible. I couldn't read the labels on the other two. This was something he had no doubt meant to happen.

"They're case files?" I asked more than said.

"Exactly," he agreed, exaggerating the word so it sounded like several. "Care to guess which case files?"

"Well, that one is Emily's murder," I said, pointing towards it. "I'm not sure about the other two."

"Uh oh," Tom said, but he didn't elaborate.

"Do you think one of them is my murder?" Greg asked.

As if Bently had heard him, as if queued by his supposition, he slowly moved the folder on his right forward towards the center of the table. In the same fluid movement, he placed his elbow onto the tab of the other one. The one on his left. The one that I had absolutely no guess about. "And this one is Greg's murder."

"Murder?" I asked. "I thought that was ruled self-defense."

"It hasn't been ruled anything, yet," he said.

The words were a punch to my gut. This was it. This was why they haven't been closed. This was why he brought me there. That entire week, while I was thinking I was out of the woods, he had been trying to find a way to pin Greg's death on me. To call it a murder no less. And use that to get Emily's murder put on me as well.

"But... Angela told you that Greg had confessed to Emily's murder to me, before he tried to kill me," I said.

Bently blinked a few times as a look of confusion spread across his face. "We weren't talking about Emily," he said. Tom sent a silent word of congratulations to me on my leap in logic, keeping me a step ahead of the detective. It wasn't going to save me though, not while I was still in his crosshairs. "Now that you mention it, though, there is one thing that these three cases have in common. Care to make a guess on that?"

"Me," I thought silently. I didn't have to be a lawyer to know how dangerous saying that one word out loud would be. Instead, I just stared at him, resolving to follow the advice of my onboard lawyer.

"Good girl," Greg said, in approval.

"No?" Bently asked, when it became clear to him that I wasn't going to answer. "You see, I've been looking into you, into your background, for the past several weeks. Ever since we found you standing over a dead body. You can understand how we thought you were responsible."

I simply shrugged as my answer, not trusting my voice in light of the very real chance of getting myself sent away for three murders. I still had no idea what file that other one was, but I had a bad feeling about it. All I knew was that I hadn't been found at another crime scene in the past weeks. It was anyone's guess what was to come from this questioning.

"But, as you said, Angela told us that Greg confessed to Emily's murder," he said, placing his right hand on that folder. "And that he tried to kill you. So, his death could be ruled self-defense." He placed his left hand on that folder, picking it up and placing it lightly on top of Emily's. "The word of one girl clears you of both of these cases. Isn't that... oh, what's the word? Oh, right, convenient."

"Uh oh," I thought, echoing Tom's earlier words.

"And wouldn't you guess what happened after that?"

"I moved in with her," I muttered. My vow of silence was easily broken as my mind reeled at the implications.

"You moved in with her. In fact, the two of you looked rather chummy at the funeral. And that comment about 'finding solace in those around you'. You actually took her hand when he said that. Wasn't that nice of you? And the look on Angela's face when you did that... I gotta say, I never expected you two... I mean, how long have you two been sleeping together?"

"What?" I asked, in complete shock. How could he have known about what happened at dinner the other day? How could he know anything about what was, or wasn't, going on between the two of us? More importantly, what business was it of his?

"Was it before or after the two of you conspired to kill Emily?"

"What the hell are you talking about?" I asked. My eyes darted towards the door behind him, trying to see through it. Through the solid metal to the other interrogation room, across the hall. I tried to remember that other door, when Bently had taken me into the room. Had it been closed? Had there been someone in that other room? Do they already have Angela over there, pressing her to turn on me? No, that was absurd. Wasn't it?

"You found out about Emily and Greg, or perhaps she did. Perhaps she found out and plotted to take revenge. The two of you got together, buried the hatchet between the two of you as they say, and decided to take it out on sweet little Emily. So, you killed her, trying to pin it on Greg so he would go down for murder."

"Except he was never a suspect," I said. "No one ever thought him capable of it. No one except me. If it hadn't been for me, you never would have known Greg..." I trailed off as I realized that the fact that I had been the one to figure it out had already been taken into account. "I called the cops to the crime scene," I said, slowly.

"Maybe you didn't intend for her to die," Bently allowed. "Perhaps you just wanted to scare her. But then Angela went too far. When Emily turned up dead, you panicked and called the police. Angela ran, of course, because you didn't both need to be there when we showed up. She ran home, to give Greg the other half of his alibi. And hers, of course."

"That's... quite a leap," I said, hesitantly. It sounded a little like one of Tom's theories. Like he had just seen something and jumped to the conclusion that the duck did it.

"Hey, I've never accused any duck of doing anything," Tom said.

"Just a goose," Dad agreed.

"That goose had it coming," Tom said.

"And... and you got all that simply from me moving in with Angela?" I asked the detective.

"Yes, of course," he said, as if his conclusion had been the only possible explanation for what he had been seeing. "Why else would two women, who had been fighting over the same man, decide to back up each other's stories and move in together?"

"Fighting? When did we ever fight over Greg? He cheated on me with Angela then married her. I don't remember any actual fighting about it. At least not with Angela. Besides, after what Greg did to Emily, she's as much a victim in all of this as I am. It's not her fault that Greg was a murdering asshole."

"Hey," Greg said, defensively. "And here I am trying to offer some legal advice."

"And here's a perfectly good explanation for us moving in together, because it's the truth. It's because I'm still not working after the divorce, largely due to these two cases and the press coverage related to them. And, now that Greg is dead, we won't have his paycheck to rely on anymore. And

I'm not going to get any more alimony. Plus, there's the issue of my lease not being renewed. We just couldn't afford two places right now, and Angela offered."

"Yes," he agreed. "No more alimony. But, Angela, as his widow. She stands to inherit all of his money, now that he's out of the way. This is, of course, why I'm talking to you, and not her. Once the cases are closed and the will is executed, she'll be rich. And you'll be left behind. Sure, she probably made some promises to you about sharing the money. But once it's in her accounts, what's to stop her from turning on you? You can't exactly turn her in. Not without incriminating yourself in the process."

"And, so, what? You're offering me a deal? Turn on Angela, admit that we conspired to kill both Emily and Greg, in exchange for a lighter sentence? Even if that were true, why would I do that? It's not like you have any actual proof. Because there isn't any. All you have are speculations. Speculations that are way off base, by the way."

"Ah, but you're forgetting something," he said. He patted the third folder, caressing it like a lover. "I have this other case that is very much related to you. I'm sure that it will tie up everything with a nice little bow. Care to guess what this case is?"

"I honestly have no idea what that case is," I said. "I didn't find any other bodies, that I can remember." At least, not lately.

"Oh, but you were indeed found near this body," he said, teasingly. "In fact, as far as I can tell, this is the first body you were found beside. At least, I hope it was the first. I mean, it's not like you're some psychopath that gets off on killing people, is it? Or is it? What exactly are you in therapy for again?"

"That's none of your damn business," I said, through gritted teeth. He knew very well what I was in therapy for. He just liked to tease me about it. It was one of the most infuriating things about the detective, right behind his insistence on accusing me of crimes I didn't commit. I wondered just what crime he was going to accuse me of that day.

"Well, now, I do believe it is my business, when it involves the deaths of three people. At least, three that we know about. Who's to say how many bodies we'll find with your fingerprints on them by the time we finally manage to arrest you."

"You're the one that's insane," I said.

"Are you so sure of that?" he said. With a big flourish, he lifted the third folder up in both hands, as if the folder was so heavy that it took both hands to lift it. It was thick, to be sure, easily an inch or more. But certainly not thick enough to be that heavy. He placed it down in front of me, just out of my reach, rotating it around a few times. It looked like the spinning newspaper they sometimes showed in old movies. When it came to a stop, the tab showing the name of the victim was at the top, facing the detective. The words were barely legible, written and rewritten several times over the years. I leaned forward, trying to see the writing better, my curiosity properly peeked.

My heart stopped dead for a second, a knife plowed through my stomach, as I managed to read the name. Simcoe, Patrick was just barely legible on the tab. I had to read it several times to make sure that I had read it properly. As the realization slowly fell across me, my jaw felt slack, my hands clammy, and my mind refused to quit screaming at me. And, yet, the voices, all three of them, remained silent.

"It's... me," Dad said, his voice breaking the silence after what felt like hours.

"How," was all I managed to say.

"You never told me what happened to your father," Greg accused. I batted away his voice, wanting my mind to myself for once while I tried to figure out just how much trouble I was in.

"I do admit, it was tricky finding this other case," Bently said. "We should have linked it to you a lot sooner."

"That case was supposed to be sealed," I said.

"Yes, that's what made it so tricky. I had to get a court order to have it unsealed. You wouldn't believe what I found out in here. Or, then again, would you? I mean, you were there, weren't you?"

"Yes," I admitted. It wasn't like he didn't know already. It was in the file, plain as day. Clear as print.

"Why, in fact, I do believe that the three victims do have something in common, don't they? Or, of course, according to you, two of them do. What would that be again?" Bently asked. His Cheshire smile had never left his face the entire time, knowing full well that he had the golden goose in front of him. If only he knew that one of the eggs was rotten.

"Greg and Dad were both killed by me," I said. Again, these were facts, already in the case files in front of him. Also in the case files, or at least it should be, was that they were both done in defense. I had killed Greg to stop him from killing me. I had killed my father to stop him... "He was going to beat my mother," I said. "He was going to kill her."

"Or so you say," he said. "So you said back then. And, what? You're sticking to that story now?"

"It's the truth," I said.

"Uh, huh. And, yet, less than a year later you were committed. Why is that?"

I had a feeling he knew exactly why I had been committed. The memories of that day came back to me in a flash, despite my being over them, being past them, for years. Dad had been yelling at Mom, accentuating each accusation with a slap to her face. She backed away from him until she was against the fridge, sliding down its side to the floor, huddling into a little ball. He kept yelling about her supposed affair, which was really just a friendship with one of my teachers who was clearly gay. When her words of denial angered him beyond reasoning, he pulled out a knife from the block on the counter.

"No," I shouted, from my place on the stairs, where I usually hid when Dad got like that. "Don't hurt her," I screamed. I was sixteen at the time, but I had seen him in action for years. This was beyond the angriest he ever had gotten before, and I had no doubt in my mind that he would do it. That he would hurt her. That he would kill her.

He stopped, hesitated, with the knife inches away from Mom's face. He looked back over his shoulder at me. "Stay out of this," he yelled. "This is grownup work."

"Get away from her," I yelled. Then I did the bravest, and dumbest, thing I could have ever done. I ran at him, slamming into him from the side. We both toppled down, hitting the floor in a pile.

The next thing I knew, Mom was pulling us apart. She had never stood up for herself, not against him. But when it came to me, she was always fiercely on the defensive. It was like she suddenly woke up when I jumped into the mix. But it was too late. Dad kept yelling in my ear, his voice only getting stronger, as his blood covered the floor, turning the white tiles red. My pink dress did nothing to hide the blood as it covered me, from my chest down, in several rivulets. I remembered that the dress was ruined. That I could never wear it again, even after Mom had died it red to match the stains.

Mom had, of course, admitted to the cops to killing Dad, trying to take the blame away from me. But, with her almost spotless and me, covered in blood and babbling to myself in the corner, it was obvious who the real culprit was. It was also clear, from the bruises on Mom's face and the hospital records of the broken bones, that I had been defending her. The case was closed quickly. Not like with Greg and Emily. It was sealed soon after. But that didn't stop his voice. Always fresh in my ear. Always yelling at me, telling me that I was just like my mother. That I didn't deserve to be his daughter. I'd say that it drove me insane, except I must have already been there to have heard his voice to begin with. It was only after that first year in HTP that Dad and I got to a place in our relationship that we could actually be civil to each other.

"Well, you did kill me," he accused. "I was really mad about that."

"That was supposed to be sealed," I said to Bently, again, pointing at the offending folder. I pushed my chair away, as if the papers themselves were contagious. As if just being near them set me back years in my recovery. Given the state of where I was, that might have already been true.

"They were," he said. "But when it shows a pattern, when you make a habit of killing people 'in defense', self or otherwise, it makes it remarkably easy to have cases unsealed."

"A habit?" I asked, stunned by the thought. It was two times. Only the two.

"Dropping two bodies in as many months, yeah, I'd call that a habit."

"I didn't kill Emily," I insisted.

"Sure, okay, I believe you," he said, sarcastically. "Letting your girlfriend do the actual killing, though, that's just as bad. What was it? She kills Emily and you kill Greg. Then you both run off and live happily ever after? You don't really believe that's going to happen, do you?"

"No," I said. "I don't think the two of us are going to run off and live happily ever after. It's not even like that."

"Then how is it like? What was the big thing that she agreed to in order to get you to kill Greg? Huh? Did she find out about your dad? Did you tell Greg and he shared it with her during pillow talk?"

"Greg didn't know about it," I said. "No one knew about it. No one but Mom and..." And Dr. Mendez. I didn't want to say it, didn't want to think it. But it was there. If what he was saying was even close to the truth, it would have been Dr. Mendez that would have been in on it. Was that it? Was he sleeping with Angela? Wasn't it his idea for me to move in with her? Wasn't he pushing me closer to Angela? Closer to a relationship with her? Just what was his part in all of this?

But, no, that couldn't be it. It couldn't be some big conspiracy. Not between Angela and Dr. Mendez. Not between her and me. Greg admitted to doing it. He admitted to killing Emily because she was extorting him. Why would he have said that if he hadn't done it? Why would he have admitted to anything? It wasn't like I had evidence to prove it, just a suspicion. Certainly, not enough to get Bently to bend that way. But Greg knew me. He knew that I wasn't going to let it go. He knew that I had figured out enough of it to get me to where I needed to go. To get the proof that I needed to put him away for good. He knew me too well to let me live.

"No," I insisted. "Greg didn't know. Angela doesn't know." I sniffled, rubbing my nose, and was surprised to find tears there. "Can I get a tissue?"

"When we're finished," Bently said.

"What more do you want from me? I already told you that you're wrong. There's no conspiracy. Greg killed Emily. He did it alone. He almost killed me when I found out. I killed him in self-defense."

"Yeah, and you killed your father because he was about to kill your mother," he said, sarcastically.

"Exactly," I said, ignoring his sarcasm. "How is that so hard to believe? I was sixteen. I didn't torture animals when I was a kid. I haven't killed anyone else. You already know everything. Why won't you believe me? What did I ever do to make you think that I'm capable of that?"

"You're the ex-wife," he said, as if that was an accusation. As if there were no need for any other reason than that to think me capable of it.

"There are a lot of ex-wives in the world," I said. "If we all went about killing our ex-husbands, the divorce rate would be a lot lower than it is now."

"That's enough," came a voice at the door. The door opened quickly as Sam came barging in. I could see Eric's surprised face behind him, looking between Bently and me, at a loss for what was happening in there. "My client has nothing else to say to you, detective," Sam said. He was holding his briefcase against the door, using it to extend his reach, to hold the door wide open, as he stood in the doorway. "Unless she's under arrest, we're leaving."

"Fine," Detective Bently said, in a huff. "Just know that I'm on to you. You're not going to get away with killing another person, involved with this case or not. I'll make it my life's work to make sure you see the inside of a prison cell."

"Need I remind you of the rules regarding police harassment, Detective?" Sam asked. "Or should I take this to IA?"

"That won't be necessary," Bently said. He glared back at Sam, his smile long lost to the man ruining his fun. "Just know that you're defending a murderer. She may very well turn on you next. Or maybe on Angela. Mark my words, this one isn't done killing people."

"Well, then, I'd better not give her a reason to kill me, should I?" Sam joked. Now that he knew his weight was enough to spring me, he allowed himself his usual, more jovial mood. "Come on, Natalie. Time to go home."

"Home," I thought to myself. "That would be nice."

Chapter Eighteen
Sam to the Rescue

The inside of Sam's car smelled familiar. A type of musk or aftershave that I couldn't quite place. It reminded me of Greg though. A reminder that I wasn't ready for. The first few minutes of the ride were in silence as I fought against the memories that flooded through me. Even the voices seemed to know not to bother me, knew that I wouldn't stand for them intruding on my inner musings.

"Are you okay?" Sam asked, his question breaking the silence.

"Fine," I said, simply.

"What did they want?"

"What? Who?"

"The cops, back at the station. What were they after? Why did they bring you in again?"

"It wasn't exactly the cops in general," I explained. "Just Bently. He's had it out for me since this whole thing started."

"Okay, what did Bently want then?"

"He still thinks that I killed Emily. Now, he's thinking that Angela was involved, that she was there that night and that she only backed my story about Greg to cover up her involvement with the... with what happened with Emily."

"God, I can't believe that asshole," Sam said. "What is wrong with him? I heard that he's the one preventing the cases from being closed. Preventing us, you two, from moving on. And, now, this? It's insane."

"Not to him," I said. I flinched a little at the term "insane", used so easily, so flippantly. I was the crazy one. Bently was just an old dog with a bone, not quite ready to give up on the idea that I was a killer. And I was a killer, a fact that I never denied. One that he now had indisputable proof of. I've directly killed two people, now, no matter what the circumstances were.

"That doesn't matter. If he has no proof to back up his claims, he needs to drop it. When I get back to the office, I'll get the criminal defense team on this. I'll have Jessica start the paperwork on the police harassment suit. And I'll start putting together the stuff for the will. We'll do the reading on Wednesday and get everything settled so you can start to move on with your life. How does having your own place again sound?"

"Amazing," I said. The comment reminded me of what had happened with Angela after the funeral. It was something that had escaped my mind while I had been being questioned by Bently. It was a bit funny just how close some of his wild accusations had actually turned out to be. If anyone else had noticed the fact that Angela and I moved in together, they would have just seen two grieving widows trying to support each other. However, Bently saw something else. Something more. He had used the term "girlfriend". How could he have known?

Or did he know? Had he guessed right or was he using that word for something else? Like Angela and I were friends and had only meant it like that? And, we were friends. Angela and I, surprisingly. I wasn't sure when that happened. If it was before or after I had moved in with her. It certainly was after I killed Greg. Despite her wanting it to be more, I didn't exactly want to lose her as a friend either. Not now. Not after what we've been through. It wasn't exactly like I had a lot of friends to begin with, either.

"So, where am I taking you?" he asked. "The apartment? The house?"

I looked around, realizing we were back in the main part of town, only a few blocks over from Dr. Mendez's office. And, more importantly, my car. "Turn over there," I said, pointing towards the side street that the parking lot was on. "I have my car over here."

He nodded as he took the turn. I noticed his face as we approached the doctor's office. I watched as it slowly dawned on him where we were. And, more importantly, why my car was here. "That son of a bitch," he said. "He cornered you coming out of your appointment with your shrink?"

I wasn't exactly sure how he knew where my shrink was. Or even that I had still been seeing a shrink. It reminded me of my attempt to get a job at the office. Of the fact that Greg had worked there for years, especially during the divorce. It was going to be hard to determine just how many people there knew of my mental issues and just how much of a problem they might be. I wondered if their previous comments about why they couldn't hire me was just an excuse. A smokescreen over their desire to avoid hiring someone that heard voices. As long as I was medicated, as long as I was continuing to see Dr. Mendez, it shouldn't matter, even when it came to cases. It wasn't like I would be practicing law. Just doing research and processing documents. That stuff could just as easily be double checked if the need arose. If my sanity ever came into question. Or lack thereof. Or its impact on my work.

But would that be enough? Would that satisfy their liability issues when it came to their clients? I had no doubt that, if it came to being between keeping me on as an employee or their clients... Well, it's not exactly like there would be a job for me to have, to do, if they had no clients to work for. Maybe Sam knew this. Maybe his trying to throw everything they had into my case, into Bently's treatment of me and the two deaths, was his way of apologizing. His way of trying to make it up to me. Of trying to get what I really needed out of all of this. I needed a proper social outlet, sure.

But what I really needed was something that Greg could no longer provide. Financial security. Money may not buy happiness, but it's an important part in the process of finding it.

"Well, he knew I would be here," I said, as if that were a proper excuse for the detective coming there. "And it's not like he barged in on it. He was waiting for me in the waiting room when I left my appointment."

"That's definitely harassment if you ask me," Greg murmured.

"No one asked you," I thought to him. But from the look on Sam's face, he had a similar mind to it.

"This won't stand, Natalie. I'll make sure that he backs down. To do all of this on a wild suspicion of wrongdoing, one that isn't even supported by the facts. It's not like you had a choice in killing Greg. It's not like you had any motive to kill Emily. Heck, it's not like you've ever even killed someone before."

"What-what does that have to do with anything?" I asked, surprised he would mention that. That was the whole reason why Bently had dug up my father's old case file, trying to prove a pattern of behavior. I was thinking it was circumstantial at best. Not even admissible if it ever came to a trial. But if Sam knew something that I didn't, maybe I had more to worry about.

"Which part?" he asked, a little surprised. "Motive is rather important to proving a case, right up there with physical evidence."

"No, I mean about having killed someone before."

"It doesn't, not really. Any decent lawyer would get that thrown out, suppressed from evidence. Unless, that is, it had something to do with... well, your mental... issues. That... might cause some problems. But only if the DA is willing to practically give you an insanity plea on a silver platter. He'd need to prove that any previous deaths were part of, or, more importantly, caused by your mental problems. And that you weren't being properly treated at the time of Greg's death, or Emily's. However, now that I think of it, as long as Angela is backing up your story, there's nothing they can do about it anyway. So, you shouldn't have anything to worry about in either case. And your shrink can speak to your state of mind over the past few weeks, right?"

"Of course," I said. "I haven't missed a session yet."

"Good. Then you shouldn't have a problem. Just go home. Relax. Try to put all of this behind you while we handle your case from here on out."

"Thanks, Sam. I don't know where I'd be right now without you."

"Hey, it's no problem," he said. "I kind of owe you, you know. For missing this. Missing what was happening with Greg. He had been all weird for weeks, and I never noticed a thing."

"That's because he doesn't have someone like me whispering in his ear," Tom said. "Now, aren't you glad you have me?"

"I would be if you explained your jumps in logic and told me what to do about them more," I thought. "Rather than just saying 'I know something you don't know' and leaving me in the dark."

"Fine," Tom said, getting all huffy. "I do know something you don't know. Although, really, you should have noticed it yourself already."

"What?" I thought to him, but he didn't say anything.

Sam had pulled up right next to my car. He parked in the spot that had been freed up next to it since the detective's departure. I wondered briefly if, whoever had been parked there, had to wait long before freeing their car from the spot. What with the police cruiser blocking them in. I didn't remember anyone waiting there. But I had been rather focused on being shoved into the cruiser at the time.

"I'll call you to set up a time for the reading," Sam said, as way of a farewell.

I nodded to him. As I reached over to open the passenger door, I realized something. Something that I should have noticed back before leaving the station. Maybe I was getting better at figuring out what Tom was guessing at. Or maybe, as he had said, this one was rather obvious. I turned back towards Sam, a question on my tongue. "How did you know I was at the station?" I asked.

"What?" he asked, confused.

"I never got my phone call. I think I mentioned wanting a lawyer at one point, though I'm not entirely sure when that was. Or if I did. But then, suddenly, you were there. And you're not a criminal lawyer, anyway. So, what were you doing at the station? Why did you come to my rescue?"

"I came to your rescue because we're friends," he said.

Are we, though, I wondered? He had always been Greg's friend. One of the many that he had gotten in the divorce. We had never been all that close. I had met him that same day as I had met Greg, though the two of them had already known each other. He had even given me the stink eye at that one party, back before Emily had died. Back before I knew that Greg had been sleeping with her. Yet, suddenly, he seemed to be trying to make up for something. Perhaps he was.

"As for what I was doing there... well, I don't really have much of an answer for that. It was like... I don't know. It was like I just needed to be there for some reason. I can't really explain it. Maybe it was like some message from God or something. I had this sense that I was needed there, so I came."

I looked at him, one eyebrow raised, lost somewhere between confusion and incredulity. I somehow doubted that God would have had the time to send someone a message on my account. Let alone send it to Sam in order to rescue me from an overzealous detective. If anything, I would have wanted the assistance the day I had to kill Greg. Or perhaps back when I was sixteen and had to save my mom from my dad. No one came to save me for those two occasions. I had to save myself. Yet, I was supposed to believe that Sam had gotten a message from Him?

Then again, why would he lie? What did he gain from lying about it? He could have said something more convincing, like he had been there on an unrelated case. Picking up something for the criminal defense team. Or that he was second chair on a criminal case for one of his clients. Anything but "God made me do it". Just because it didn't make any sense, doesn't mean there was a more malicious purpose in it. That sort of reasoning is what got me in trouble with Bently to begin with.

"Um... Okay," I said, slowly, placating him, at a loss for anything else to say about it. "Whatever. See you on Wednesday, I guess, then."

"Yeah," Sam said. He seemed relieved that I hadn't pressed the issue. "I'll call you."

I nodded as I jumped down out of the car, heading back over to my own.

Chapter Nineteen
Confronting Angela

I wasn't sure what I was going to say to her. I had been working through it the entire drive over from the doctor's office. Perhaps it would be better, easier at least, to just move out. To avoid the problem all together. Certainly, once the will was executed, I'd have enough money to move out on my own again. Even if I did have to work to make ends meet. The only problem was that I knew Dr. Mendez wouldn't approve of that approach to handling the encounter. He would insist that, even after I moved out, I go back to hash it out. Though, the impression that I got from him during my session was quite in line with Dad's thought on the whole thing.

"Bow, chica bow wow," Dad said.

I shuddered at the thought. It wasn't like I never thought about it. About ever being with another woman, it was just that it never really appealed to me. And it was Angela, the woman that had broken my family apart a year ago. I know that my marriage was already doomed. I know that if it hadn't been Angela it would have been someone else. Perhaps even Emily. But it was still something on my mind. Still an impediment to anything really happening between us.

Plus, you know, she's a girl. I never wanted to go down on a guy, why in the world would I want to go down on a girl? The ick factor on that was just too substantial for me to ever go there. I didn't even like looking at my own vagina, let alone someone else's. It just made more sense for me to be with a guy.

So, by the time I pulled up in front of the house, I was pretty sure that I would call it off. That nothing would ever happen between her and I. I wasn't going there, much to the chagrin of Dad.

"Don't leave me out of it, either," Greg said. "I like the idea of you two together."

"Bow, chica bow wow," Dad said, again.

"But not for that reason," Greg said.

He shuddered at the thought of my father wanting to see me with another woman. I reminded him that he had been there every time I've had sex since I was sixteen. Which, of course, was every time. I had gotten over the thought a long time ago, even to the point of teasing him about it. One often loses their inhibitions when they bring their own audience around with them wherever they go.

"Anyway," Greg continued. "I like the idea of neither of you being alone anymore. You'd have each other. That's like second best to having me back. And you two wouldn't need to share me."

"God, your ego is bigger than I remember it being," I said.

"Yeah, there's not really much of a reason to hide it when it's just you to worry about."

"What about us?" Tom asked. "Don't we count?"

"No," Greg and I said, at the same time.

I got out of the car slowly, procrastinating heading inside as much as possible. Now that I was there, all I wanted to do was run away. The familiar wall of anxiety hit me head on. It held me back from the confrontation that awaited me within. It was like walking through water, pushing my way against the pressure that held me. The sludge that kept my feet in place. Trying to keep my mind off of it, I looked towards the one car garage that the minivan was parked in front of. There was always plenty of room in there to park inside. But none of us, Angela, Greg, or I ever bothered with it. It was too much of a hassle to back out of it, not being able to see much around the car as you did. It meant the driveway would always be crowded with the two cars. This seemed a bit of a metaphor for the house within. The house just wasn't big enough for the two of us. One of us, namely me, would have to leave soon enough.

"Hello?" I called out, once I got inside the house. Out of an old habit, I placed my keys on the small end table by the door. They clattered against not only the bowl that was there, but another set of keys. Angela's or Greg's, it wasn't clear which. I still had my old key for the house, still on the keychain that it had never left. It had surprised me that Greg had never bothered to change the locks. But it certainly made things easier after moving back in. "Angela, are you here?" I asked, as if I hadn't just seen her minivan out front. And, yet, there was no response from her in the house.

After glancing over at the vacant playroom, and getting another emotional punch to the gut in the process, I headed around to the kitchen. It was the only other place that Angela would often spend time during the day. It was still early for dinner, and very late for lunch. But it was the next obvious place to find her. She had taken to that little refuse from Greg inside the house just as quickly as I had, once she had actually lived there with him.

I felt a general foreboding as I made my way through the living room over to the kitchen. It was something quite removed from my anxiety over confronting Angela. Maybe it was just my Tom senses acting up again, though he, himself, stayed quiet. Tom seemed as intent on the area as I was. His eyes, if he even had eyes, were as eager to see whatever it was that we could see as we passed through the house. It wasn't until I saw her, outside in the backyard, that I started to breathe easy again. I shook my head, reminding myself that she wasn't having as miserable an afternoon as I had been having. That the cops still haven't circled around to harass her about this new, wild theory of theirs. Instead, she had been having a lovely day home with the little one. I saw Doug out there as well, in the baby swing. He was sailing through the air under her pushes, clapping his little hands.

The scene seemed so sweet and innocent. Far beyond anything that my corrupted mind should be allowed to witness. It felt like I was somehow perverting it just by looking at it. I would never have that. Never have a child of my own to play with like that. Never see that echo of myself in another person. And, yet, I couldn't bring myself to hate Angela for having it. For having something that I never would. She had stolen my life, the life I was supposed to have with Greg. Yet I didn't hate her. That took me more by surprise than seeing them out there like that, playing on the swing set that my daughter was supposed to use.

I didn't want to disturb them. I didn't want to break the tranquility they had found there, in the backyard, overlooking the woods that ran out behind it. They were, of course, the same woods that I had walked through that night, where I had found Emily's body. Although, that specific place was a good several miles further up river. Despite the proximity to that woods that would never be the same for me again, the two of them, mother and son, seemed lost in their little world. Still, I felt drawn to them, in a way that I couldn't explain. Couldn't describe. Slowly, quietly, I drifted towards the back door. To the door that Greg had chased me through just eight days prior. Out to where I had been forced to kill him. That place, that spot where he had died, was just a few feet away from the playing family. Yet they were as oblivious to that place as they were to the woods beyond.

Instead of traipsing through the backyard, I just leaned against the doorway, one foot tilted backwards into the house. It took several minutes of me just standing there for one of them to notice me. Little Doug waved to me from his swing seat. Angela looked over her shoulder at where Doug had waved. Her smile only deepened when she saw me there. I wasn't ready for that. Wasn't prepared to see my presence increasing her happiness. The sun glinted off her hair, once again throwing a halo around her head, making her into the angel that I knew her to be. I nodded to her. When she motioned for me to join her, I just shook my head, turning around to go back inside.

That was when I heard it, the little scream that sent chills down my spine. That shriek that echoed my own feelings of loss when I had found out my daughter was not to be. Instantly, my head snapped around, my eyes ever searching for the danger there. Doug was in Angela's arms and she was backing away from the swing set. Before I knew what I was doing, I was next to them. I was jumping in front of them, pushing them closer to the house.

"There," Tom said. I could sense him, standing next to me, pointing off into the woods, despite his lack of hands to point with. There was a hissing, spitting sound coming out of there, with two beady eyes peeking out from a bush at the edge of the wood. It was nothing, I assured myself. Just some rodent that had gotten too close to the property.

Then it moved forward, stalking towards us across the open field. It was no rodent. I had no idea what the thing was. It was huge, easily a yard from nose to rump, and half as much wide. A long tail, just as long as the thing's torso, stretched out behind it. It twisted and spun in the air, propelling it forward. All I could think about as I pushed Angela and Doug towards the door was that animals were supposed to be scared of humans. They were only supposed to attack when they felt cornered. This thing, this huge, ugly thing that looked like a cross between a beaver and a racoon, was looking at us as if we were lunch.

"Run," I shouted. I needn't have bothered. We were already back to the door, back to the safety of the house, before the thing made it into the sunlight. I slammed the door closed, putting my back against it in a desperate attempt to keep the thing out. As if the creature's bulk were substantial enough to knock it down without my being there.

Despite my shout, Angela and Doug hadn't gone far. They were both in front of the sink. Angela was trying to see through the curtains without parting them. She wanted to see the thing that had made us flee into the safety of the house. Whatever it was, whatever creature had claimed our backyard, it couldn't reach us from in there.

"What was that thing?" I asked.

"I don't know," Angela said.

"Nor I," Tom added, though I hadn't been asking him.

"I've never seen anything like that in my life," Greg said.

"Oh, like you've ever seen anything that I haven't," I said, out loud, too shocked to think it at them.

"What?" Angela asked, looking at me in confusion.

That's when it happened. When the window broke open. The glass flew inward, showering Angela with a spray of shards. I stood there, next to the door, several feet away from them. Completely frozen. Paralyzed in place. Too far away to do them any good. Angela fell forward, pressing Doug to her chest. Her back took most of the glass, but she was defenseless against the creature as it pushed its way into the house. Its beady eyes stared at me as it clawed its way through the crumbling window, trying to find purchase where there was none to be had. The light from outside, the light that should have banished this monster that was attacking us, reflected off its eyes in a strange way. They sparkled all over and dazzling me where I stood.

It felt like I was in a horror movie. Like I was some weak girl being attacked by a psycho killer or monster but didn't know what to do, despite the audience yelling at them. Tom, my resident geek, the one that was supposed to be the most helpful in these situations, was just as paralyzed. He was as much at a loss for how to act as I was. It was Greg, Greg of all people, that pushed me forward. That prodded me towards my family.

"Get that thing away from her," he yelled. His words, his order, snapped me out of my shock. I jumped forward, just as the creature did. Its small arms, barely long enough to reach its elongated mouth, flailed in the air as if it were trying to fly through those last few feet.

I caught the thing out of the air. Its weight and momentum hit me in the shoulder and knocked me aside. As I hit the floor, I lost my grip on it and it rolled under the table. Under my table. Glass was everywhere, and the thing got cut up as it skittered across the floor. A strange, black liquid seeped out of it, splaying across the floor. It was a type of blood that I had never seen before, never heard of before. It caught the light just as easily as the thing's eyes had, reflecting up an orange tint off of it like phosphorescents. Instead of smelling like copper pennies, like Greg's blood had, like Dad's had, this blood smelled more like rotten eggs. The smell was everywhere, making me gag as I tried to get back up.

"Stay down," I yelled over to Angela when she made to get up. "That thing is still in here."

And it was. Still under the table, hiding in the corner, backing away from me like any animal. However, when it looked at me, it gave off a sense of intelligence. A thinking mind that something that small shouldn't possess. Its eyes flicked between me, Angela, and the door behind us. It was as if it had only just realized how stupid it was to attack us like it had. I wanted to jump aside, to give it a free exit to the door. But I couldn't risk it going after Angela and Doug instead. I could hear her cries over the beating of my heart in my ear and the loud, shrill shrieking of the creature.

Not taking my eyes off the thing, I stood up, leaning backwards towards the counter. My hand reached out behind me, searching for the block of knives next to the sink. A feeling of deja vu swept over me as my hand found the gaping hole that once held the last knife that I used from it, back when the block belonged to my mother. Only that time I was protecting her against my father, rather than my ex-husband's widow from a monster. That little hesitation, that precious few seconds as the reminder slammed home, almost cost me everything.

As clever as the creature was, it noticed my movements. It somehow knew that its life was in danger. It ran forward, its teeth bared, hissing at Angela. As I pulled the blade free of the wood, it pounced, sailing towards Angela and the baby still cradled in her hands. Angela must have seen its approach out of the corner of her eye. She flinched inward, giving the thing her back and protecting her son with all that she had. The blade swung downwards at the creature's own back. The entire confrontation felt like it was in slow motion. And, yet, at the same time, it was going way too fast for me to think about anything but stopping it. But protecting my friend from whatever it was.

The creature screamed. I had thought its cries before had been loud. Had been vicious. Had been unidentifiable. Yet its screams were so much more so. The rancid smell of its blood increased three-fold as it sprayed through the air, covering me, Angela, the entire kitchen, and even Doug, protected as he was behind Angela. It was a long time before I realized that Angela was screaming too. That the more familiar smells of her blood mixed with that of the creature. The thing had its mouth splayed wide, wrapped around her shoulder like a large hand, squeezing through the flesh there.

I pulled the knife back across the thing's body, cutting across in a backhand that should have thrown it free. Instead, its now muffled screams quieted as Angela's replaced them, echoing around the house. With a third slash through the creature, this time straight across its gaping maw, it let go of its prey. It toppled off of Angela's back and onto the floor. I raised my foot over its prone form, meaning to stomp on the thing as hard as I could manage. It had rolled with its fall, coming back up to its spindly legs behind me, close to the door. Before I could turn around to face it, the creature ran at the still closed door. It slammed its hard head against the bottom of it. The wood of the door gave way, a huge chunk of it breaking off and giving the thing an exit that it hadn't had before. However, the maneuver had left it momentarily dazed, just shy of the freedom it had just achieved.

My knife swung once more, downward in a final stab towards its torso. It rolled out of the way just in the nick of time, leaving the knife to plunge into the tile floor that had been beneath it just moments before. With one final glare towards me, and a hiss for good measure, it ran from the house, heading off into the waning afternoon light.

Angela's continued screams drew me back to her. Back to the home that had been invaded by the thing. I ran to her side, my hand going to her shoulder before I could think of how bad that idea was. Her screams at my touch had me flinching backwards. Her blood on my hands mingled with the psychological blood that had already been there. With the adrenaline still surging through my body, my eyes darted everywhere, looking for signs of the creature's return. Something in me told me that we weren't finished with that thing.

"It's gone," Tom assured me, though I didn't feel the least bit comforted by that thought.

"Call 911," Dad barked. I nodded, reaching for the phone.

"Are you alright?" I asked, stupidly. "How's Doug?"

"Doug's fine," she assured me through clenched teeth. She pulled him up off the floor, away from the shattered glass. Away from the blood, both hers and the creatures. I could see the strain it took on her, lifting the child with her injured shoulder. But she wasn't going to let that stop her from protecting her son.

"No," Dad said, just as I started to dial. "Drive her to the hospital yourself. It'll be quicker."

"No," Tom insisted, before I could think. "She won't fit in the car like that, not with Doug. We'd need the minivan, which is blocked in right now. Call the ambulance so we can get her there before she bleeds out."

"Will you both shut up," I snapped. I hated when they were like this, when they argued with each other. Talking over each other as if I wasn't there. As if I didn't matter. It made it hard to think. Hard to figure out what is really going on and what is just in my head. Of course, they were just in my head, which only made it harder for me to focus on the real reality that was around me.

"Hey," Angela said. She gripped my hand, holding it with her free hand as she clung to Doug with her other. She stared up into my eyes, demanding my attention, away from the voices that swarmed all around me. Somehow, that connection to her, either through our touching hands or the locked eyes, chased the voices away. It gave me a clear mind that I hadn't had since those early days with Greg, back when there was only one voice up there.

The blood from her wound was running down her arm and covering mine. It mixed with the blood that was already there. She had lost a sleeve in the attack, torn free by the creature at some point. She looked lopsided, with the injured sleeveless side for me and the pristine, late fall side for her son. It seemed appropriate somehow. Like my presence in her life had already destroyed it. Yet, she was still there, still clinging to me. I wondered briefly if that had been why the creature had attacked. If I somehow drew it to the house like a magnet.

With her eyes still locked on mine, she nodded towards the phone that was still in my other hand. "Call the ambulance," she said, agreeing with Tom. "I'm not sure--" She broke off, not managing to finish whatever it was she was about to say. If she hadn't been looking into my eyes, I wouldn't have noticed it. I would have missed when she fainted, from the pain or the blood loss, I wasn't sure. The phone fell from my hands as she did.

The instant that her hand left mine, Tom snapped back on. "Grab the kid," he ordered. It made the most sense at the time, though Angela was already deeply injured and I wasn't sure if she could survive much more of that. She crumpled into a ball at my feet just as the phone shattered into a bunch of pieces. The phone had bounced on its first impact, spinning in the air before hitting onto the tile again. The plastic broke apart like it was glass. Like it had taken on the properties of the debris it had hit. The main circuit board seemed to spin in the air as the plastic around it flew all over the place. As if the board had been what had been restraining the plastic, rather than the other way around.

I had managed to rescue Doug from her failing grip before she fell far. His weight, awkwardly received, pulled me down with him. I overbalanced as I stuck my knees out, trying to use my only free appendages to slow Angela's fall, despite the fact that she was already on the ground. The blood that coated the floor made it slick, and I slipped down to greet it. Doug started to scream as the blood splashed up, spraying him across the face.

"God, you three are a bloody mess," Greg said, his only contribution to this whole thing.

Chapter Twenty
A Quick Stop in the ER

I had managed to get to the phone in the front hallway without dropping Doug into the blood. Then I spent the entire time it took for the paramedics to show up to get Doug into his car seat. I had seen Angela put him in it often enough. I had thought I would be able to do it myself. However, that wasn't exactly the case. It didn't help that he fought with me the whole time, crying his lungs out. He was louder than the siren as we made our way over to the hospital.

The familiar looking building gave me a panic attack as we drove up to the ER entrance of the hospital. I had to remind myself repeatedly that this wasn't HTP. That this was a hospital and that Angela needed to be there. One of the paramedics noticed my panicked state and gave me a face mask full of oxygen as he and his partner unloaded Angela from the back, rolling her into the hospital. I barely managed to hear anything that was said between them and the doctor that had come out to greet the ambulance. Soon afterwards, they came out to get me as well, though they wouldn't let me keep the oxygen. They left Doug and I to fend for ourselves in the waiting room.

At some point, Doug had fallen asleep in his car seat, having grown tired of screaming his head off. This dropped the waiting room into a less chaotic, though not quite silent, level of noise. My panic attack had faded. My breathing regained its steadier rhythm. And the voices came back in full force. They kept me company as I waited to hear back from the doctors. I only hoped they would read into it when I tell them that I'm her "roommate" so they would give me some actual information. It wasn't exactly like she had a next of kin left. At least not one that I knew of. I doubted she would have thought to update her records, seeing as how it had only been a week since Greg died. Then again, perhaps Doug had a godparent that would need to be contacted. They would need to step in to get any information from the doctors. I had no idea who that would have been.

I had just thought to call Sam, who would probably know those things, when a familiar face bobbed into view down the hallway. At first, I didn't recognize Eric. He wasn't wearing his uniform. Instead, he was wearing a white t-shirt and jeans, with a jacket slung over his shoulder. But, when he smiled, I recognized him right away. Dad and Greg recognized him as well. They instantly put up their guards. It was obvious they didn't like him, probably because he was a cop. But I had no problems with him. It was Bently that I had a problem with. I didn't see him there, and I tried not to let one bad egg spoil the bunch.

"Eric," I said, as he came up next to me. "What are you doing here?"

"Subtle," Tom teased, noticing the sound of pleasant surprise in my voice. "Really subtle. Maybe you can give him a lap dance."

I rolled my eyes at Tom. He often thought I was coming on strong whenever I showed any interest in another person. "I mean, I wasn't expecting you. Did someone call you?" I wondered why they would. It wasn't like we were all that close or anything. I've barely spoken to him outside the police station, except those times that he had to drive me to or from it.

"No, why would someone call me?" he asked, echoing my own thoughts. "I heard about it on the police band when I was going off shift, and I figured I'd stop by to see if you're alright."

"The police band?" I asked. "Why would it be on the police band?"

"Someone broke into your house and attacked you," he said. "Why wouldn't it be on the police band?"

"No one broke in. It was some wild animal or something. Like a rabid possum or something. I'm not even sure what it was. The whole thing happened so fast. It broke the window, got stuck inside, attacked Angela, then got back outside. Really, it sounds more exciting than it was. The whole thing is just a blur."

"That's not really what happened," Tom said, but I ignored him.

Eric smiled comfortingly as he took the seat next to me, opposite from Doug. He glanced over at the sleeping baby, perhaps to make sure he was still sleeping. Or maybe just to see him. To see if he survived the attack unscathed and stayed the cute, innocent baby that he was. That wouldn't last, of course. Not with Greg for a father. But we'd do our best to keep him that way as long as possible. Besides, as Eric looked at the baby, I managed to spend some time checking him out.

I never understood the attraction to seeing men in uniform. A well-worn, properly managed uniform would usually hide most of the good parts. Eric was wearing a tight white t-shirt, probably similar to the ones he wears under the uniform. It clung to his chest muscles and abs and left his arms exposed. I had always found him cute before. But seeing that he had a body to match was too much to ask for. I found myself smiling as I ogled him like a well-hung piece of meat. But I steeled my expression when his attention left the baby and returned to me.

"So, you're alright?" he asked. Concern was plain in his voice and etched deeply on his face.

"I'm fine," I said, waving off his concern. It was nice to know that he cared, but I wasn't the one we were there for. "Just a few small cuts."

"And the blood?" he asked, reminding me that I was covered in the stuff.

"It's... not mine," I said, as I examined the mess that covered me. I must have looked atrocious, but no one had seemed to say anything while I was there. I guessed the hospital personnel were used to the sight of blood. The waiting room I was in wasn't that crowded, unlike the main ER waiting room near the front of the building. With that thought in mind, I started looking around, trying to figure out just where I was. The paramedics had led me there when they refused to let me keep the oxygen. "Most of this is..." I trailed off when I remembered the source of the blood. Then my eyes started looking around for a very different reason. Looking for some sign of Angela, of her doctor or someone that knew what was going on. "Angela was really hurt in the attack," I said.

"With how much blood you're covered in, it had to come from somewhere. I'm glad that you and the little one had managed to make it out alright. It doesn't all look like blood though. Is it... did the animal track in mud or tar or something?"

"No, it was bleeding too. It probably crawled under a bush somewhere to die. We'll probably find it in a couple of weeks when the whole backyard starts smelling like a dump or something. That thing was nasty even when it was alive. And it bit her, it bit Angela. Nearly took her arm off." I kept looking around us, trying to find someone to flag down. Trying to figure out just what was happening in there. I should have been focusing on Eric. On the cute cop that had come all the way there to check on me, even when he was off duty. All I could think about was Angela.

"Do you want me to sit with you?" he offered. "You know, just until you find out what's going on with your friend?" I noticed how he stressed the word "friend", like he had heard the accusations that Bently had made earlier but didn't believe it. Couldn't believe it. Not when it was obvious that I was attracted to him.

"Sure," I said, giving him a huge smile and patting his leg. "If you don't mind." He smiled at me as he leaned backwards into the seat, crossing his arms as he settled in for a long wait. "Actually, I was just thinking it might be a good idea to call Sam. I'm not all that familiar with Angela, despite us living together. She was just my husband's mistress until she came to my defense. I'm hoping he would know more than me. The whole family history and all that. Would you mind watching the little guy while I go call him?"

"Sure, no problem," he said, giving me a double thumbs up. "He'll sleep through it, though, right?" His face fell when he stared over at Doug, as if he were a bomb that was about to blow up. I snickered at his face, finding it cute that he had a similar reaction to Doug as I did.

There was a payphone in the corner of the waiting room, so I didn't have to go far and could still keep my eye on the two boys. Fortunately, I had thought to bring my purse with me, so I had plenty of change. I also had Sam's card, so I didn't have to worry about remembering his number or calling the main line.

"Sam Whitlock," Sam answered on the second ring, in a cheery voice.

"Hey, Sam, it's Natalie," I said, hesitantly. I wasn't entirely sure how he was going to react to the news, or how close he actually was to Angela. "Angela is in the hospital. There was some kind of... weird animal attack at the house."

"Oh, my god, is she alright?" he asked.

"I'm not sure, I'm still waiting to hear something from the doctors, but I wasn't sure who to contact. Does she have any family or something?"

"I think she has a sister somewhere out west, but no one she's really close to. She didn't really have anyone but Greg." That sounded rather familiar, like he could just as easily be talking about me. Only instead of a sister, I just have my mom upstate. I don't see her, either, so we had that part in common. "You know what, I'll be right over," he said. "I'm technically her lawyer as well, so I should be able to get information from the doctors more easily than you can. Plus, I'm Doug's godfather. I think that makes me next of kin right now. How is Doug, by the way? Is he there with you? Did he get hurt?"

"He's fine, he's here, he's sleeping," I said, answering his questions in order. "He was there when the animal attacked, but Angela was protecting him the entire time. He has some blood on him, but it's not his." I looked down at the mess that I had become, wondering if I should say the same about me. Sam seemed more concerned with his godson, which was appropriate. "I'm not entirely sure where I am in the hospital itself, but we're at Phelps."

"Right," he said. "I'll be there as soon as I can. Um... I might be bringing Jessica with me. Is that alright?"

"Yeah, sure," I said, a little surprised that he was asking me. Wasn't I the interloper in all of this? If he's the godfather, he's her family. I'm just the roommate, no matter how Angela and I felt about each other. It wasn't like we were dating or anything.

"Does this mean you're open to the idea?" Dad asked. I shushed him, holding my hand over the receiver so that Sam couldn't hear.

"Like I said, I'm not sure where I am right now, so you'll need to ask someone. Eric is here, too, by the way."

"Eric?" Sam asked.

"The cop," I explained.

"The cop? He's there? Is he hassling you again?"

"No, not the detective. The detective is an ass, he'd never come to the hospital except to harass me or something. I'm talking about Eric, the nice one."

"Yeah, I don't really remember a nice cop. But you're nicer than I am."

"Professional hazard," I said.

"Hey," Sam and Greg said together. "Alright, I'm leaving now. I'll be there in ten minutes. Don't let the cop bother you too much."

"Don't worry," I said into the dead line. "He's harmless."

"Armless?" Greg asked. "I'd like to make him armless." I rolled my eyes at Greg's attempt at a joke. "I'm not joking," Greg said. "I don't like the guy. I think he's spying for that other one."

"Hey, leave the leaps in logic to me," Tom said, defending his territory. "I don't see anything wrong with him."

"That's 'cause there isn't anything wrong with him," I said, eyeing Eric over my shoulder. I still held the phone to my ear, trying to make it seem like I was still talking with Sam while I had an open discussion with the other three men in my life. "That man is fine."

"Ugh, don't make me puke," Dad said. "You're my daughter."

"Hey, you didn't seem to mind thinking about Angela and me being together," I pointed out.

"Exactly," he said. "That's you and her. It's him that I don't trust. And it's not like I can go and grab my shotgun or anything."

"Did you even have a shotgun?" Greg asked.

"Don't test me, little man," Dad said. "You're the reason why I'm so protective of my little girl right now."

"Says the man that used to beat his wife," Tom pointed out.

"Guys, will you stop it? Not here. I'm sure the doctors here would love nothing more than to ship me right back to HTP."

"I think they have something here," Greg said. "I had been researching it the last time you went cuckoo."

"Nice," I muttered. "Thanks for the warning."

As I put the phone down, I eyed the few hospital personnel that were visible from the waiting room. There was a nurses' desk across the hall, though the nurses all seemed more interested in the paperwork in front of them than the crazy person in the corner. Eric was still sitting next to Doug, eyeing the child as if he were the dangerous one. After a few seconds of me looking at him, Eric returned the gaze, and the smile. I turned my eyes away, blushing a little at being caught looking at him. It felt nice, normal almost. Something that I don't really remember having. Not even those first few weeks with Greg when Dad fled at the happiness that I felt. Perhaps that was the real solution, just having new loves that consumed my every waking minute. Though, I guess the question was, could I find that with Eric? That level of love that they write songs about, even though it never seemed to last? Or was there someone else that I should be considering right then?

I had to admit, at least to myself... and the voices in my head, this attack on Angela had me rattled a lot more than it should have. She was my ex-husband's mistress. And yet, she was starting to mean more to me than that. More than I wanted to admit. Despite the fact that she was a girl, there was more there than just friendship. The problem was I didn't know if I wanted to explore it. If I was ready to explore it.

"Ah, come on, go ahead," Dad said, encouraging me. "You only live once, right?"

"You just want me dating Angela so I don't start dating Eric," I accused.

"Sure, there's that," he admitted. "Then there's the other thing. Bow chica--"

"Don't you dare finish that thought," I warned. It wasn't like I could do anything to him. If there had been, I would have gotten rid of the voices ages ago, and not just him. They had always made dating awkward. Sometimes, I had wondered just how I managed to get Greg in the first place. It was one of the reasons why I had stayed with him for as long as I had. Even when it became clear to me that he was cheating on me with Angela. I wondered if Angela had a similar reason. If she had known about Emily before this whole thing started. If there was at least a little truth to what Bently was saying.

"Now who's getting paranoid," Tom accused.

"Fine, fine," I said, throwing my hands up. "But don't tell me you weren't thinking it."

"Sure, but saner thoughts took its place."

"Saner? What do we know about sane?" I asked.

"You okay over there?" Eric asked, drawing my attention back to him. Back to the hospital around me. I suddenly remembered that I was surrounded by people who had access to straitjackets, and weren't afraid to use them.

I scowled at my voices, making it clear that I didn't want any more trouble from them, lest I turn myself in to the psych department, before heading back to the boys. "Yeah, I'm fine," I assured him. I sat back down in the seat I had vacated before, right between Doug and Eric, as if I had never left. "Sam will be here soon. We'll probably be able to find out what's going on with Angela at that point." And I had to admit, I really did want to know what was happening with her. It had to have been an hour or so since I had gotten there. I wasn't in any real state of mind to note the time when I did. I wasn't even sure if I was in the right waiting room, though I guessed once Sam showed up, I'd know.

"Well, you know, I am a cop," he whispered, mischievously, as if that fact were a secret. "I might be able to get some information if that will help you relax a little."

I looked at him curiously, one eyebrow raised. Just how relaxed did he want me to be. "I thought you were off duty," I said.

"Well, you know, my badge doesn't know that." He reached into the pocket of the jacket he had been carrying, pulling his badge out of it. "It works just as well when I'm off duty," he promised.

Chapter Twenty-One
Visiting Hours

Eric's badge got me more than just information. He got me in to see Angela. She had to have surgery to cut out some foreign mass that the animal had left behind when it bit her, realign the shoulder so it would heal properly, and close the whole wound. The surgery itself had only taken about an hour. But she had been admitted to the hospital and would need to stay the night for observation. The doctors thought she had an excellent chance at a full recovery in the next few days, and should be able to leave the hospital in a day or so. In the meantime, she had her own room on the recovery floor.

The lights were off as I came into the room. There was a low light glowing near her head so I could see the room enough to spot the obstacles between the door and her bed. Her eyes were closed, so I didn't turn on the light, not wanting to wake her if she was sleeping. I eased into the room, trying not to knock into anything or bump Doug's car seat around any. He was still asleep, but I knew from experience that he was a light sleeper. He'd wake up if I so much as bumped the seat against the door. After making my way across the room, I eased him down to the floor next to the only seat in there, before sitting in the seat myself.

"She does look beautiful when she's sleeping, doesn't she," Greg said, in an only slightly creepy sort of way.

"Well, you did leave me for her," I thought to him. Not wanting to wake Angela, and knowing he could hear me just as easily, I tried to remember not to speak out loud to him and the others.

"There was a lot more to it than her looks," he said. "We were already fighting long before I started dating her."

"Yeah, like that's an excuse," Dad accused. "The least you could have done was make it clear to my girl that it was over, before you started sleeping around."

"I didn't exactly sleep around," Greg said. "It was Natalie, then Angela, then Emily."

"And, yet, you managed to get your mistress pregnant while still being with my daughter," Dad said.

"Well, the fertility clinic did say he had superior sperm," I thought, remembering when we tried to get professional help for the third pregnancy. It hadn't gone over that well. Greg had come away from the meeting blaming me for everything. It was probably the last straw for him, the point when he started seeing Angela in the first place.

"Actually, it was another few months after that," Greg said. "I hadn't even met Angela until the Halloween party last year."

"Well, then you didn't exactly take your time, did you?" I accused. Still, I realized that I never really knew how the two of them had gotten together. Just that they had, and that she had known about me the whole time. Still, for some reason, seeing her unconscious in that bed, her shoulder bandaged, I couldn't blame her for any of it.

"Of course, not," Greg said. "You're too nice for your own good."

"Pfft, nice, right," I said.

Angela stirred at my voice. Her eyelids fluttered a few times before they opened. Her eyes scanned the room before locking on mine. "Hey," she said, sleepily.

"Hey," I said back, smiling. "Someone here wanted to see you." I lifted Doug's car seat, with him still asleep within, carefully placing it on the bed so she could see him. After how she had done everything in her power to protect him from that rabid animal, I knew she would want to see him immediately.

"I hope he wasn't too much trouble," she said. She smiled at her little son, tears of joy finding their way to her eyes.

"Naw, he's been a perfect gentleman. How are you feeling?" I asked, stupidly.

"Groggy," she admitted. "But I'm glad to see you here, glad for both of you being here. Look, about the other day, I--"

"Let's not worry about that," I said. I placed a hand on her uninjured shoulder, meaning the gesture to be reassuring. It seemed to have a very different result. She placed her hand on mine, taking it into hers like she had done after the funeral. She pulled me closer to her. Despite her weakened state, I felt an intense pull that had very little to do with her hand. Carefully, I moved Doug over a little, placing him in her lap, as I took the spot on the bed that he had been in.

"You're my hero," she said, with only the slightest tint of humor. "I don't know what I would have done if you hadn't been there. That thing, whatever it was, it was going after Doug."

"It didn't know what it was doing," I said. "It was rabid or something, just lashing out at anything that moved. It wasn't going after Doug any more than it was going after you or me."

"Even so, you saved me. You saved both of us. How can I ever thank you?"

I snickered a little at that remark. I couldn't help myself. It was just such the damsel in distress line to say. Yet, from her eyes, still locked on mine, I knew she meant it. I knew that I could ask anything of her and she would give it. And, yet, there seemed to be only one thing I wanted from her, and I had no idea why that was.

She seemed to read my hesitation, the thoughts behind it. She pulled me closer to her, pulling me right up to her. My lips found hers before I really knew what I was doing. Before I could think of anything beyond how much I wanted to taste them. They felt chapped, raw, dry, perhaps from the medication she was on. And yet they were still soft, with a flavor all their own, and yielded to mine easily, readily. I breathed deep of her, smelling her own personal scent, mixed as it was with the blood that still covered me and the hospital smells that surrounded us. For some reason, quite unexpected by me, I never wanted that kiss to end. I wanted it to deepen, to engulf the both of us, swallowing us whole. As one being. One entity. Forever connected through that kiss.

A tiny laugh off to the side brought me out of it, breaking the kiss all too soon. We both looked over to the now awake Doug. One tiny hand was playing with his sock while the other reached out for his mother. He was laughing at the both of us, as if he knew something that we didn't. His laugh was infectious, and I blushed a little as I backed away from Angela. Unsure of just what had happened. What had caused it. And what it really meant.

"God, I haven't heard his laugh in so long," Angela said, cooing at her little guy. "Not since..."

"Not since I killed Greg," I finished the thought for her.

"Yeah," she said, drawing out the word.

"I am sorry I had to kill him," I said, looking down at my hands. They were quite literally covered in blood now, though it was the black blood of the animal that had attacked us, rather than the phantom blood of my ex-husband.

"I know you are," she assured me. "You're not the kind of... of person that would kill someone. Not if you had another choice."

Her words reminded me of that first kill. Of that other time that I had to take a life. For some reason, I wondered if she knew, wondered if she had somehow found out about my dad. I didn't know how, though. No one knew. At least, no one had known until Bently went digging. The problem with someone digging into a person's past is that there's always something to find. Some people just won't stop digging until they find something. The only questions are who he was going to tell about it, and if he was done digging.

"She doesn't know," Greg assured me. "I didn't know, and I wouldn't have told her if I had. Do you really think she would have come to your defense if she had known?"

"Yes," I mumbled to him, looking into her eyes, which were locked on her son. I knew that she would have always done the right thing.

"The right thing would have been not to sleep with a married man," Tom said.

"Oh, quiet you," Greg and Dad insisted.

"What was that?" Angela asked.

"Huh?" I asked, wondering if she had somehow heard the voices in my head.

"You said 'yes'," she said, reminding me that I had spoken the word aloud.

"Oh, nothing, I was just talking to myself."

"Well, then, I hope I'll like the question you were answering."

"Let's not worry about that right now," I said. "You should focus on getting better."

"Have you seen it?" she asked, looking over to her bandaged shoulder. "I bet it looks pretty gruesome right now."

"You've seen about as much as I have," I said. "It didn't look pretty back at the house, though."

"Well, so much for my modeling career," she joked.

"They said you'll probably be able to go home in a couple of days or so. It can't be that bad."

"Ah, just in time for the reading of the will, then?" she asked. "You heard about that, right?"

"Yeah, I heard. How did you?" I tried to think back to earlier today, back before the attack. Back when I had left Sam. I had come home right after that to find the two of them in the backyard. So, how would she have heard about it so soon? And what else had she heard at the same time?

"Sam called me right before the attack. Well, before I brought Doug out to the backyard, anyway. He said the cops were just playing with you and that's why they're not closing the cases."

Playing with me. That's one way of putting it. "Well, Bently is a bit of a cat," Tom pointed out. "Cats like playing with their food before they kill it, right?"

"What do you think that thing was that attacked you?" I asked, trying to change the subject.

"Please, Natalie, not in front of the b-a-b-y," Angela said. She reached over to Doug, trying to put her hands around his ears to protect them. But she winced when she moved her left arm. The bandages twisted a bit, restraining the arm to her side.

"Oh, come on, Angela. Doug doesn't even know what a baby is, let alone the fact that he is one. Besides, he was there. If he's capable of understanding us talking about it, he's capable of having his own theories on the thing."

"Fine," she said. She rolled her eyes, though she winced when she did that, too. "Well, I have my theory, but you'll probably laugh at it. What do you think?"

"I've been going with rabid possum," I admitted. "It didn't look like any possum I've ever seen, but..."

"I guess that makes sense," she said. After a minute, though, she looked at me questioningly. "Wait, I thought possums couldn't get rabies."

"Maybe it had something else, then," I suggested. Then, I was suddenly worried about just what it was that she might have contracted from this. "Did the doctors treat you for rabies?" I didn't remember them saying anything about it when they were explaining the procedure they did.

"I only just woke up a couple of minutes ago. You'd know better than I would."

"Well, we'd better have them give you the treatment for it anyway," I said. "Better safe than sorry, especially when it comes to rabies. I wouldn't want to have to put you down, too." It was meant to be a joke. Although, it was a little too soon, given the fact that I had to just kill her husband. She seemed to think so as well, as she turned away from me at the thought.

"Yeah," she said, pensively. "I still don't think it was a possum, though."

"Alright, I'll bite. What did you think it was?" I asked.

"Okay, but don't laugh."

"I wouldn't think of it," I said. I was used to getting some wild theories over the years, mostly from Tom. Many of those had turned out to be right. I was a bit worried that, whatever she was thinking, rang more true than my guesses.

"I think it was some kind of alien," she said, in all honesty.

"Yeah, right," I said. To my credit, I didn't laugh, though I did think the theory a bit of a stretch. Right up there with some of Tom's biggest leaps.

"Hey, I wouldn't put it out of the realm of possibility," Tom said.

"And aliens abducted the second plane," I said, ignoring Tom. "Maybe it's the same aliens."

"Joking is as bad as laughing at me," she said. "And, no, I don't think they're the same aliens, but maybe they're related. I mean, if that lunatic on the George Washington Bridge had really been an alien, then they would have had to have landed at some point. Maybe some vermin hitched a ride down and is on the run, just looking for food to eat."

"And, what? It thought you were its dinner? Would aliens even be able to eat the same foods as us?"

"There were sightings all over the city for months last summer," she said. "It had to have been eating something."

"Those sightings were all people in masks. There were tons of idiots dressed up like the thing going around. It was the number one costume at Halloween last month. It was a hoax. It had to be."

"Then how do you explain that thing today? It wasn't a possum."

"I'd sooner believe that it's Bigfoot's pet on the run than that it was an alien. Besides, wouldn't people have seen it by now, if it wasn't the least bit scared of humans? It would have been on the news or something."

"Not if people keep thinking it's a possum," she said. "We should let people know about it."

"Oh, please, not again," I said, shuddering at the thought of more reporters. "Let's not go crying alien just yet, alright? The last thing we need right now is more press. Besides, there are... other things that I'd rather talk about."

"Oh? Like what?" she teased.

"Like this," I said.

I leaned forward, trying to kiss her again. She backed away, turning her head to the side. All I got was cheek, though I tried to make it seem more smooth than it really was. I gave her a light peck before leaning back. Dejected, I slipped off the bed and back into the chair, but I pulled it closer to her side.

"It's certainly something we'll need to discuss," I said, though I wasn't sure how I felt about it myself.

"Later," she promised. "Like you said, I should focus on getting better. And I'll probably heal best if I get a little more sleep," she said, around a yawn. "Are you alright with him?" she asked, pointing towards Doug.

"Yeah," I said. I had managed to go a few hours with him without breaking anything. Granted, he had been asleep for most of them. "I should probably go home, though." I looked down at myself, at the blood that still covered me. "I think I need to take a very long shower."

"Hey, I wasn't going to say anything, but," she teased.

"We'll both be back tomorrow," I said. "Get some sleep." I got up from the chair, leaning over to give her another kiss, this time purposefully going for her forehead. Whatever reason for the missed approach earlier, I was going to try not thinking too much about it.

"Maybe she's just not that into you," Tom suggested.

"No," Dad and Greg both said, sounding thoroughly heartbroken.

"Maybe you're not that great of a kisser," Tom suggested.

"Nope, that's not it," Greg said.

"Maybe it hurt her shoulder to kiss you," Tom suggested.

"Whatever it was," I said to them, when I got to the door, Doug's car seat in hand. "We'll figure it out later, preferably without you three looking on."

Chapter Twenty-Two
Oh, Right, Eric

"Everything alright in there?" Eric asked, as I stepped out of Angela's room. I jumped at his voice, almost dropping Doug in the process. Doug gave off a little sound of glee as his car seat jumped up and down a little, as if the maneuver had been intentional.

I looked behind me at the door. The foot of Angela's bed was visible through it. Eric's place against the wall wasn't that far away from it. It made me wonder just how long he had been standing there. Had he been there the whole time? Just how much had he heard of what happened in there? How much had he seen?

"Um," I said, as I tried to get over the shock, the uncertainty, of his being there. "Yeah, she'll be fine. I'm just stuck with this guy for a little longer." I lifted up the car seat again, letting it drop down like before, this time intentionally. I laughed out when Doug made the same noise, indifferent to the cause of his ride.

"Sam's out in the waiting room," he said. "Maybe he'll be taking the little one off your hands."

"Maybe," I said, shrugging. I wasn't sure how I felt about that. Angela just wanted to make sure he was cared for. I found myself agreeing with her on that point. If that was done by Sam or me, I didn't much care.

"I don't understand how you can do it," he said.

"What? Taking care of a kid?" I asked. Did I seem that non-maternal to him? Maybe that was... but, no, I didn't want to think of it that way, I couldn't think of it that way.

"You always seemed maternal to me," Tom said. His normally young voice seemed overly childlike when he said that. It felt as if he was some kid that I had adopted at some point without knowing it, rather than one of the voices that constantly drove me insane.

"No," Eric corrected, shaking his head. "Well, I guess that's part of it. I mean being friends with... her."

"What's wrong with her?" I asked. There didn't seem anything wrong with her to me. At least other than her injured shoulder. I was the crazy one, something that the voices in my head refuse to let me forget.

"Hey, we never called you crazy," Dad said. "That's a word other people started using to explain us."

"Yeah, shrinks," I muttered.

"Well, nothing, I guess," Eric said, missing my mutterings. "It's just... well, if someone had slept with my wife, they'd both be dead to me."

"You're married?" I asked.

"No, I meant hypothetically. I'm actually single right now... very single." He winked at me, seeming to indicate that he wanted me to change that. I wasn't sure just how ethical that would be, considering I was still being investigated. Granted, if Bently had his way, I probably would always be under investigation. At least until one of us goes to prison or dies. Preferably him for either.

"Well, I don't know. If it hadn't been Angela, it would have been someone else," I said. "Besides, she's kind of made up for it by coming to my defense for... the Greg thing." I wasn't sure what else to call it. "When I killed my ex-husband," just didn't seem to have the right ring to it.

"Well, yeah, there is that. Still, I wouldn't be moving in with them, offering to take care of the product of the affair." He gestured towards Doug when he said that, giving a little shudder at the thought. For some reason, it just made me laugh. He smiled back, obviously trying to show that he didn't really mean anything bad about it.

"Well, maybe I'm just a nicer person than you are," I teased.

"Sure, let's go with that," he teased back. "Anyway, you came here in the ambulance, right? Care for a ride home?"

"Yes," I said, quicker than I probably should have. "I'd love that. I just want to talk with Sam first before we head out. I'd love to take a long, hot shower and get all this blood off of me." Though I knew that no amount of showering will ever let me feel quite as clean as I once had.

"Yeah," he said, his eyes gazing at mine, mischievously. "That's probably a good idea." He pinched his nose. When he did, the grin stuck out on either side of his hand.

"Oh, ha ha," I said, bumping him a little with my shoulder. He made a show of dusting the blood off of his shirt where I had hit him. The blood had dried on ages ago and wasn't likely to come off without soap and water... and a blow torch. I knew my outfit was a complete loss. I was hoping my skin would recover at least. Though, given the unknown creature that had bled most of the blood, it might never come off.

"Oh, come on," Tom said. "I didn't think you believed that thing was an alien. That means it's just the same kind of blood as the rest of it, no matter what the color is."

"Are you saying you don't agree with Angela's guess on the origin of that thing?" I thought to him, making sure not to speak my words out loud with Eric so close at hand.

"You know me. I don't see any point to any intelligent life form coming to this planet."

"What about the search of intelligent life," Greg suggested. "Maybe they'd come to see us."

"What does one of those have to do with the other?" Tom asked. "If an alien species is capable of interstellar travel, we wouldn't qualify as intelligent to them. We'd be little more than bugs building out of the sand that we infest."

"Well, I think Sam is probably still at the nurses' desk," Eric said, jarring me out of the inner discussion. He pointed the way back down the hall towards the waiting room, which I could just see in the distance.

The entire front of the nurses' desk was in view from where we were standing, though Sam was nowhere in sight. I eyed Eric suspiciously as we headed down the hall. It wasn't like him to mislead me. My hands clung to Doug's car seat protectively, expecting something to jump out at me at any moment. My mind immediately turned to that strange animal. Was it following me? Had it somehow gotten to Eric? Turned him to its side?

Sam's voice reached me before I made it to the desk. It was followed soon afterwards by a woman's laugh. At first, I figured he had just brought Jessica along with him. They must be over in the waiting room, flirting with each other. Then I realized that the voices were, indeed, coming from the nurses' desk after all.

"Ugh," I grunted, as the two of them came into view. Sam was flirting alright, in full form, too. He looked like he was bringing his A-game, something that I had to suffer watching many times over the years. The nurse he was flirting with was trapped in the corner by him, though she didn't seem to mind it at all. "Doesn't being faithful mean anything anymore these days?" I asked.

"What?" Sam asked, looking over at me. "What are you talking about?"

"What would Jessica think of you flirting with her?"

"Who's Jessica?" the nurse asked Sam.

"Jessica and I aren't exclusive. We're barely dating."

"Does she know that?" I asked.

"Yeah, you get him," Greg said.

"You're one to talk," I thought back at him.

"Oh, please, she's out with some other guy right now. Why do you think I didn't bring her? I got the dates mixed up, so to speak."

"Well, then, I guess you wouldn't mind me taking your godson home with me," I said, lifting him up above the desk so he was in clear view of the two of them. "Seeing as how you're so busy right now."

"Oh, like you've never slept around before," Sam snapped at me.

"Excuse me?" the nurse asked. She did not seem pleased by the whole situation. Her face echoed my own expression, somewhere between disgust and annoyance, with a little of her own disappointment mixed in. She bumped into his restraining arm, heading back to the desk and her work.

"I'll have you know that I've never slept around, ever," I said, emphasizing that last word. And that was true. I could barely keep track of one lover at a time, what with the three boys in my head.

"Sure, blame us," Greg said.

"She's not," Tom clarified. "She's blaming us. Dad and I. You haven't been here long. Trust me, you get used to it. She blames us for pretty much everything that goes wrong in her life."

"Not everything," I thought to them. "Just the stuff you're responsible for."

"Fine," Sam said, dejectedly. "Take the kid. I don't really care. I've barely spent an hour with him. I was only his godfather as a favor to Greg, which he still owes me for. Just don't forget about the stupid will reading on Wednesday, when I can finally be rid of the three of you."

I stared after him as he stormed out of the area, heading off to the elevator around the corner. That seemed rather out of character for him. Not that I had spent much time with him besides with Greg. He had seemed so sweet lately, ever since I had gone to the office looking for a job. Perhaps someone had gotten to him, whether or not it was the weird animal.

"Did... Did Bently start announcing what had happened with my father?" I asked.

"Woah, now that's what I call a jump in logic," Tom said. He sounded almost proud of it.

"I don't think so," Eric said. "If he had, he shouldn't have. Why do you ask?"

"I just think that would have explained the sudden change in Sam. Maybe he's starting to think that I had killed Greg because I wanted to, rather than because I had to. They were best friends, after all. And he's my lawyer, sort of. Or, at least, he used to be. I'm thinking I might need new representation after tonight."

"Well, as long as Bently doesn't find anything new, I think you're pretty safe from his wrath. All he has right now is--"

"Circumstantial evidence, most of which is non-admissible anyway," I finished for him. Though I was mostly repeating what Sam had said earlier, Eric seemed pleasantly surprised that I knew this. "I am a paralegal, after all. Or was, anyway."

"Really? I hadn't known that," Eric said. He motioned for us to head down the hall, following the fleeing form of Sam. "You know, I just realized that I don't know much about you, other than what's come out during the investigation."

"Yeah, that's kind of going around," I said. "No one really seems to know anyone in my circle these days."

"You mean you and Angela?" he asked. The elevator doors dinged when we got to them, without either of us having to press the button. At first, I thought that Sam had sent it back up to us as a way of apology. But someone else came off the elevator. The man looked how I had felt back before I knew Angela was going to be okay. He took one look at me and almost fainted, but managed to run past us anyway.

"Yes, Natalie," Greg said. "There are other people in this hospital than you and Angela." I just shook my head, ignoring him, as Eric and I got onto the elevator.

"You do that a lot, you know," he said, pointing at my head.

"Do what?" I asked.

"Talk to yourself. Shake your head. It's as if you're having full conversations with yourself or something."

"Well... I am," I admitted. "Haven't you heard? I'm a little insane."

"A little?" Dad joked.

"Well, given what you've had to go through, killing your own father when you were sixteen, then your ex-husband, you have every right to be more than just a little insane. I think I would have been curled into a ball babbling for years if I had to kill my dad. I love my dad."

"And, what, I didn't love mine?" I asked.

"Aw," Dad cooed.

"Oh, shut it," I thought at him.

"Exactly," Eric said. He smiled, easily taking the bite out of the insinuation. It somehow ended any possible fight before it could start.

The main lobby was packed with people. It was mostly patients waiting to be seen by one of the doctors, and their friends and relatives that had driven them there. Yet, for some reason, I seemed to easily be the most gruesome looking of the bunch. I drew eyes from all around, everyone staring at the blood covered girl, standing next to the out of uniform cop. Eric looked like he couldn't be anything but a cop. Standing tall. His hand reassuringly on my shoulder. His eyes staring down anyone looking at me wrong. His muscles... well, let's just say, I was glad it was him standing next to me rather than Bently. Then again, I was exceptionally glad that I didn't remember coming through there before, when the paramedics had brought Angela inside and I followed behind.

I was a little taken aback when Eric led me to his bright blue sedan parked in the middle of the lot, instead of the police cruiser. Not that I had forgotten that he was off duty. I was just used to him driving me around in the cruiser. Although, I imagined the cruiser would have made getting the car seat into the back harder. It was surprisingly easy to strap Doug in back there, despite never having done it myself before.

It felt weird climbing into the front seat with Eric behind the wheel, but in the best of ways. His car smelled like a combination of old french fries and a pine scented air freshener, though there was no sign of either of them in the spacious interior. Hanging from the rear-view mirror was one of those old saint's medals, though I wasn't sure which it was. I imagined it was the patron saint of cops or something, but I didn't follow that part of religion.

"You're at the house, right?" Eric asked, as he pulled out of the parking lot. I simply nodded in response, though I wasn't sure if he had seen it in the darkness of the night. The street lights flashed by us, flickering light within the car. A slow strobe light that highlighted Eric's tight body. I just wished I was wearing something other than a pair of blood stained jeans and an old t-shirt that used to belong to my dad. I wished I had changed into something else, something sexier, while waiting for the paramedics. Or, at the very least, showered. The stench was starting to bother me, despite having been living with it for hours. All I wanted was to jump in the shower and stay there for a week. Perhaps with a little company.

"God, you're horny," Dad accused of me.

"You're just complaining because she was thinking of the cop rather than Angela," Tom accused.

"So, what if I am?" Dad asked.

"Did anyone do anything with the house?" I asked.

"What do you mean?" Eric asked.

"Yeah, what are you thinking?" Tom asked.

"I mean, am I going to be heading in to see a bunch of cops all over?"

"Why would you?" Eric asked. "It's not a crime scene. At least, not anymore. I thought it was some animal that broke in. Unless you were thinking of pressing charges against the thing." He laughed a little at the thought.

"But you heard about it on the scanner as just a break in," I said.

"All I heard on the scanner was break in and your address. I didn't… Well, I just came over when I heard that. I can check with dispatch."

"No, it's just... well, I mean Bently wasn't thinking I was lying about it being an animal?"

"Oh," Eric said, simply. All humor faded from his face at the reminder of the detective's paranoid nature. "I don't think so. As far as I know, he hasn't heard about it yet. He isn't one to listen to the scanner. I wouldn't put it past him to use this as another excuse to come after you, though."

"Great," I muttered.

"But, no, there shouldn't be anyone at the house when we get there. Unless you were expecting anyone. That probably means the window is still broken open."

"Yeah, second window in as many weeks," I said. "But it's the first damaged door I've had for a while."

"It damaged the door?" he asked. "Just how big was this thing?"

"Bigger than a cat, smaller than a dog, I'd say. It was about your average sized possum."

"A possum isn't going to smash through your window and attack you," Eric said. He sounded more knowledgeable about those sorts of things than I was. "Are you sure that's what it was?"

"Oh, not you, too," I accused. "Angela has it in her head that the thing was some kind of alien. It was a weird, probably rabid animal. That's it. I'm not some kind of animal expert. I'm not sure what it was. Maybe it escaped from the zoo or from some guy's private collection, running up here from the city. I'd believe that a lot sooner than that it was left behind by the bridge climber."

"Well, I can't speak to what the creature was," he said, placating me. "But, I'm with you. I doubt it was an alien. There are plenty of normal explanations to go through before going that route."

"Thank you," I said.

"How about I drop you off at your house so you can shower and change and I'll hit some home repair stores for whatever we need to fix the window and door. You're not going to want to leave those open tonight. Not after the month you've been having."

"That sounds amazing," I admitted.

"Good," he said, smiling a little. "Then perhaps we could spend some time together."

"That sounds even better," I admitted, grinning stupidly at him.

Chapter Twenty-Three
The Reading

I was too exhausted after the long, stress filled day to properly take advantage of the time alone with Eric. He spent some time fixing the door and putting some proper wood over the smashed window. The wood worked a lot better than the old cereal boxes I used on the one at the apartment. After that, we mostly just sat and talked for an hour before I was yawning too much to talk. He did leave his card behind, along with his personal cell number and address, as he excused himself for the night. There was definitely something there. But, then again, there was also something with Angela. I would have liked to have spent more time with him, but he had a night shift on Tuesday.

Angela didn't get released from the hospital until Wednesday morning. I swung by to pick her up on the way to Sam's offices. She seemed quiet while we drove, like there was an inner storm just beneath the surface and it was all she could do to keep it away from me. Her eyes were like daggers out the windshield, zoning out as they followed the road.

We hadn't talked much when I visited her in the hospital the day before. She spent most of the time playing with Doug, getting in that mother son time that she was being deprived of by being stuck in there. Most importantly, at least to me, we didn't mention the kiss or the looming tension between us. I still didn't know what it meant. What was there. If it was anything more than a deep friendship being confused for something else. All I knew was, no matter what happened between us, I didn't want to hurt her. And I didn't want her to hurt me.

She didn't stir from her death stare until we pulled into the parking lot. "Are you alright over there?" I asked. She painstakingly took off her seat belt, trying not to bump her arm in the process. It was in a sling so as to reduce the weight on her injured shoulder, which was still bandaged all to hell.

"Just tired," she said. She popped open the door, keeping it open as she swung around to pull open the sliding door on the minivan. "I didn't get much sleep at the hospital."

"We can put this off, if you'd prefer," I told her. "I can call Sam and say we'd want to do this some other day."

"No," she said, shaking her head. "I want to get this over with. The last hurdle, right?"

"Right," I said. I nodded my agreement, though I wasn't sure that was the truth. Neither of us seemed to be mourning Greg properly, if there was such a thing. Admittedly, he had cheated on both of us, and the loss of the relationship had cut harsher than the loss of the man. Without the man around to hate, how were we expected to move on? Would the division of his worldly possessions give us any respite to that hate?

Angela awkwardly tried to get the seat belt off of the car seat with only one working hand as I made my way around the van. She managed to get it unbuckled, but the belt itself was stuck within the holes that secured the seat to it. Doug started to wail as she tugged feverously at the belt.

"Hey," I said, coming up behind her. I grabbed the belt from her hand before she accidentally hurt the kid. "I'll do that. Relax. We have time. Our meeting isn't for another twenty minutes."

"Can you not do that?" she snapped, though she surrendered the seat belt to my less hindered hands. "Can you just call it what it is? We're about to go up and hear the last words my husband, our husband, had ever meant to be heard. We're about to hear just how much he thought about us, planned for our future in case he died. It's not a meeting or anything else you want to call it. We can't reschedule it. I just want it over with. I want it done. I want him gone. From my mind. From my life. I just want it to be over."

"Hey," I said. I had gotten the seat belt off the car seat, but Doug was still in the car. I left him there for a moment as I went over to her, hugging her close. She felt warm in my arms. Her skin smooth against mine. Her flesh supple around my hands as I pressed her into my chest, trying to lend comfort. Tears tickled my cheek, though I was certain that I wasn't the one crying. "It'll be alright," I said, knowing the words wouldn't be enough. "We'll get it over with and we'll go out later. Get our minds off this horrible mess."

"I just keep thinking it's done, it's over," she cried. "Isn't it enough that we solved the case for the cops? Isn't it enough that we... that you had to kill him? Isn't it enough that we put together that stupid funeral? When will it be enough?"

"This is it," I said, though I knew it wouldn't be. This was just the last hurdle in the process of putting him to rest. Greg would still haunt us for many years to come. Dad still haunted me at times, even after all of those years. I just didn't want to have to tell her that.

"Hey, don't blame me," Dad said. "If it were up to me, I wouldn't be here."

"Do you really want me to go?" Greg asked. His voice was taking on that malicious, mischievous way it had sometimes, when he was intentionally being mean. I don't know why I didn't realize just how much of a sadistic bastard he was when he was still alive. "Hey, I still have feelings, you know."

"No, you don't," I thought to him, as I held his widow in my arms. "The only feelings you ever had in life were hungry and horny. Neither apply to you as you are now."

"That's just mean," he muttered, but let the subject drop.

"Come on," I said, into Angela's ear. "Let's get up there so we can get this over with." She nodded into my shoulder, breaking the hug first. Before I could think to, she scooped up the now free car seat in her good hand. She held it close to her chest as she eyed the area around us. "What?" I asked, when I noticed her looming paranoia.

"I just have this feeling like we're being watched," she said.

"Angela, no one is after us. Not anymore. That creature, whatever it was, isn't stalking us. It probably curled up in a bush somewhere to die, from whatever it was that it had or from the cuts it received when it was attacking us. By the way, did you ever get those rabies shots?"

"Yes, and they hurt like hell," she said. "Please don't remind me about them. They're another thing I'd like to put behind me as soon as possible." I nodded as I followed her into the building.

This time, when Sam came to get me from the waiting room, he really did know why I was there. He didn't say much when he grabbed us up. I could tell from his expression that, whatever was wrong with him on Monday night was probably over. On the way through the corridors, I reminded myself to follow up on the possibility of coming back there to work, knowing full well that I'd forget again by the time I left.

"I'll remind you," Tom promised, sounding extra eager to be helpful.

"Tom, your memory is worse than mine," I thought.

"I'd offer to remind you, but I don't really want you to work here," Greg said. "I spent enough time in this office while I was alive. I don't want to come back here now that I'm dead."

"Well, you're welcome to stay home, or, you know, go off to wherever you're supposed to go," I thought. "You don't seem to have a problem staying away when I'm at my therapy sessions."

"Have you seen that building? It's disgusting. Besides, the thought of going in there with you just seems like I'd be intruding on your privacy."

"That doesn't stop the other two," I thought.

"Hey, we're helping," Tom said.

I just rolled my eyes at that thought, but was saved from having to respond as we had already arrived at Sam's office. Once I was there, I remembered that I had wanted to look in on Jessica. I wanted to see how she's taking whatever was happening between the two of them. When I peeked through the windows into her office, though, it was empty. Sam and Angela went into the office ahead of me, leaving me to catch up to them. Neither seemed to notice me pausing there.

"The will is pretty straight forward," Sam said, while I was still standing in the hall. "Natalie, care to join us?"

"Right, sorry," I said. Angela had already claimed the chair on the left, hugging Doug's car seat to her chest as a shield against the inevitable. Robotically, I slunk into the only remaining chair in the room as I settled in to hear what Greg had to say.

"Well, I--" Greg started to say.

"Not you," I interrupted. "The real Greg, the dead Greg."

"Other than the usual legal stuff, which Greg had a weird fondness for, but I'll save you from, and instructions on his burial and all that, which you had already done rather well, so thank you, Natalie, the document boils down to distribution of assets. We can just skip down to that part, if that's alright?"

"Sure," Angela said. She seemed relieved that we were going with the faster approach. Yet my dread was soon to come to fruition. The thing that I had been putting out of my mind for as long as I could. The very real fear that Greg had left me with nothing.

"Alright," Sam said. He nodded and cleared his throat as he lifted the sheet of paper that had been on his desk. "'After any and all outstanding debts, the remains of my assets are to be split equally between my son, Douglas Fergus Jennings, to be held in trust until his eighteenth birthday, and my wife,

Angela Samantha Brenamin Jennings, to handle as she pleases.'"

I sat there, frozen, staring at the paper, which didn't amount to much in the grand scheme of things. Sam let it fall back down to the desk. It seemed to flutter a little on the way down, showing me the empty back of the paper, with the front filled with a level of legalese that seemed unique to Greg. The words that Sam had just read were highlighted near the end of the paper. Though they were the same font as the rest of the document, they seemed like they were in bold lettering. It was like the words were shouting at me off of the page.

"That's it?" Angela asked, her words barely registering in my screaming mind.

"Wow, man," Dad said. "That's low. You left her with nothing?"

"You'd probably be surprised by how few people have their ex-wives in their wills," Greg said. "Especially when they were getting alimony from them."

"Yeah, but that's just low, man," Dad said.

"Are we going to be living on the street?" Tom asked, in a low whisper. "I don't want to be one of those crazy people that talk to themselves out on the street."

"Well, guess what," Greg said. "That honor is all Natalie's. You get to be one of the voices that those crazy people talk to."

"Don't get too excited," Sam said. I perked up at those words, a slim hope that there was something more. That there might be more to it. That there was another page. That Greg just hadn't used both sides. However, that slim hope died a slow agonizing death. Instead of pulling out another sheet of legalese, Sam, instead, pulled out what looked like a balance sheet. The numbers were upside down to me, so I couldn't make out the final result. But Sam didn't leave us in suspense for long. "I went over Greg's account balances, his student loans, outstanding credit card balances, the mortgage--"

"We didn't have a mortgage," I said. It sounded stupid, even as I said it. Obviously, Greg had gotten one after I left him, perhaps to pay for the new baby or for my alimony.

"Greg took out a mortgage earlier this year, during the brief window between divorcing you and marrying Angela," Sam explained. "I think he was setting the money aside for the buy-in when he made equity partner, which, of course, he hadn't done before his death."

"But that means the money is in an account somewhere, right?" Angela asked.

"After paying off the debts, well, there just wasn't much left," Sam said.

"Just how much is there?" I asked. I knew that none of it was going to go to me. But the hope was that Angela would find it in her heart not to kick me out right away, no matter what happened between us, if anything.

"It's a little over a hundred thousand dollars," Sam said. "Half of that to be placed in a trust for Doug, which I can handle for you."

"So, fifty thousand dollars," Angela said, in a low, detached voice. "H-how exactly was it so little? I mean, even with Natalie's alimony, we weren't doing that poorly. Was it the baby?"

"More likely the mistress," I said. "It's not like I got much in the divorce, either. At the time, I just figured he was very good at hiding his assets. After all, wasn't that part of what he did for a living?"

"Assets, loopholes, clauses that people wouldn't want to agree with," Sam said. "He was pretty much good at hiding everything."

"Including his feelings," I thought to myself.

"Oh, like he even had feelings," Dad said. "The guy was a psychopath."

"I'm right here, guys," Greg said.

"But, anyway, I don't think he was hiding anything in that divorce. You both know how expensive his tastes tended to be. Emily sort of played off of that. She had access to his accounts already, being his assistant and all. She milked him for all he was worth."

"And paid for it with her life," I said.

"Wow, that's a bit morbid," Angela said. "I thought he killed her because she was blackmailing him."

"Maybe that was just the last straw," I said.

"It was a little bit of both, actually," Greg admitted. "Sure, she was blackmailing me, and that was going to be expensive enough. But she wanted more. She wanted all of it. She wasn't going to rest until I was broke and destitute. Who wouldn't have killed her in my position?"

"A lot of people wouldn't have," I thought. "I wouldn't have. Then again, I wouldn't have ever been in your position to begin with. And, seriously, are you still trying to excuse what you did? You killed an innocent woman. Being a slut and gold digger isn't enough of a reason to kill someone."

"Plus, hadn't she already succeeded at draining you dry?" Tom asked. "I thought that was the whole point of this discussion. You're broke, dead, and you left your family with almost nothing."

"But, seriously, what are we going to do?" Angela asked.

"The same thing everyone in America does," I said. "We're going to get jobs. Fifty thousand dollars is enough to get us through the next few months, maybe a year if we stretch it. People have done just fine with less. Speaking of which, would this be a good time to discuss the possibility of me coming back here?" I asked Sam.

Sam stared at me for a moment, seeming at a loss for my segue into the topic. "Um..." he said. "Sure, I guess. Considering how things turned out with Greg's finances, I might have to push for you to be added to the staff. I know we're still looking for a new paralegal, though I haven't spoken with Sarah about it since last week. The notoriety about the case is already starting to fade, though Detective Hard-ass still refuses to close it. There shouldn't be much of a push against you coming back. Besides, it's not like you actually did anything wrong. It's about time people stop punishing you for it."

"Glad to hear it," I said, giving him a smile. His words reminded me about his weird attitude the other night. I didn't want to bring it up, not wanting to reopen any wounds when he was already helping me out with the position.

"Actually, Angela, if you wouldn't mind waiting here, why don't I bring Natalie over to talk with Sarah?"

"Now?" I asked, surprised.

"No time like the present," Sam said.

"Sure, why not," Angela agreed. "I have to feed the little one anyway."

"Just... don't make a mess," Sam said, shuddering at the thought. "I just got this office."

"Yeah, from me," Greg said.

"Wait, she's feeding him which way?" Tom asked.

"I don't have my resume on me," I said. I was trying to focus on Sam and the job, rather than being distracted by the thoughts whirling through the voices' heads; or was that my head, just their territory of it.

"Oh, look," Sam said, gesturing towards his computer in the corner. "I have a computer and a printer. Why don't I just print off a copy, eh?"

Chapter Twenty-Four
The Date

For the first time in a long time, I was nervous. I couldn't explain why, couldn't figure out the exact reason. I mean, it was Angela. The same girl I had been living with for over a week. The one that I already knew liked me enough to kiss me out of nowhere. Still, it would be the first time that we were out together, in public, in... that way. I couldn't even think it. yet I was about to go on a date. With a girl.

I was impatiently waiting by the door, pacing the small front hallway, walking the three paces from the playroom to the living room, and back again. The dress I was wearing hugged me across my front, showing off my assets while tucking in my stomach. Under most circumstances, I didn't usually like to wear dresses. I preferred jeans and a t-shirt or, when in a more business-like setting, slacks and a blouse. But, without knowing where we were going, the dress was the best option.

Angela had insisted on making the arrangements for the date. She hadn't thought to tell me what kind of dress code to expect. I had expected that sort of thing to be one of the perks to dating a woman. They knew better than to keep how dressed up you were going to need to be to themselves. But, it wasn't like I could fault her for it. It wasn't like she had dated a woman before either; at least, not that I knew of.

It felt weird going out, given our financial situation, as it was. We were supposed to be watching our spending, weren't we? Where in that thought process was going out to dinner?

Or whatever it was that we were going to be doing. I was starting to feel like I was going to need to be the sensible penny pincher in this relationship. If we were, indeed, going to have a relationship.

"You seriously need to learn to relax," Greg scolded me. "Seriously, were you this stressed out when we were dating?"

"Yes," Dad said. "But in a completely different way. She was more worried about how it was going to affect her job."

"Thanks for sharing," I said. "And it's not like I was actually dating you. I was... oh, never mind."

"You keep insisting that we're not really who we used to be," Greg said. "Yet, I don't feel any different than I used to. I just feel... well, dead."

"That's 'cause you are dead," Tom supplied. "We're all dead."

"And only one of us wanted to be," Dad put in.

"Well, all three of you were asking for it," I said. I realized after I said it that it sounded a lot darker than I had meant it to. Yet, it went a long way to shut the three of them up.

"Are we ready?" Angela asked, claiming my attention instantly. She was standing at the landing in the middle of the stairs, where it turned around to head back to the front of the house. The dress she was wearing was a lot more revealing than mine was, showing ample breasts that were almost falling out of the top of it. The skirt barely went past her crouch. However, unlike my dress, it was more open, not constricting across her stomach, and was billowing a little as it settled down after walking down the stairs. Her bra straps were visible next to the spaghetti straps of the dress, though they were both the same shade of blue, the same shade as her eyes. She had removed the sling and bandages. There was a little discoloration on her left shoulder from the attack, but, otherwise, she looked completely healed up, and completely amazing. She looked down at me from above, her legs swiveling in place to show them off, as her knowing smile played over her face. My chin was on the floor, and she was loving the effect she was having on me.

"Uh, yeah," I said. I tried to remember her question as I put my face back together, my chin back in place and my eyes back in their sockets. As always, whenever I saw a beautiful woman, I knew that I could never look that beautiful. Only this was the first time that I was actually going out with one of them. I wondered just how she could look that hot so soon after having a baby, though I figured that had been taken into account when she chose the dress to wear. "Where are we heading?" I asked.

"Let's keep it as a surprise, shall we?" she asked. She pulled her keys out of the clutch she was holding. "I'm driving."

"Oh, okay," I said. "Fine with me." I never liked to drive, given the option. Since the divorce, I hadn't been given the option much. I either had to drive myself or had to ride in the back of the squad car.

"Sorry about that," Greg muttered. I knew he wasn't really. It wasn't like he would have gone back and not cheated on me, not divorced me, just for the sake of letting me not have to drive myself around. "No, but I might not have ostracized you from your old college friends back when we started dating."

"Oh, please," I thought to him, as I watched Angela descend the stairs. She was wearing high, strappy heels that looked anything but comfortable, but highlighted her supple legs better than any shoes I had ever seen. "It wasn't like I was that close with them to begin with. And I could have stood up to you on the subject if it mattered."

"Are you sure about leaving Doug with that one?" I whispered into Angela's ears. I tried to mix my concern with a little flirting. I didn't think I managed it all that well.

"I heard that," said the babysitter, from her place on the sofa. She was curled up against the armrest, facing away from us, with a book spayed open in her hands. Though I had never seen the girl before, she, supposedly, lived a few doors down from us. She seemed a bit young to be babysitting, though I knew I didn't really have much of a say on the matter. Doug wasn't my son, and never would be.

"Don't worry," Angela said, patting me on the shoulder. She was an inch taller than me in her heels, yet not quite domineering. "I've used her before."

"Just not that way," the girl commented. I rolled my eyes, knowing full well we'd probably be getting much worse comments if we really did start to date one another.

"We shouldn't be out late," Angela promised the girl. She barely glanced her way, as she moved towards the door. I moved to grab the handle, thinking that maybe I should hold it open for her or something. She had got there first, pulling the door free and towards me. I breezed out the door behind her, following in her wake, and closing it behind us. It banged loudly, sealing my fate for the night. Sealing us to this date that I still didn't know if I wanted. That I still didn't know if I was quite ready for.

It took me a few moments to realize that we weren't heading for the minivan. Instead, she was walking straight for my sedan. I didn't remember giving her a key to it, but she may have found it left over somewhere in Greg's things. He had always been losing his keys, and tended to keep several sets of extras lying around. It was a good thing that he had had this practice. My main set of keys were still locked away in evidence, after having been extracted from Greg's neck.

"We're not taking the minivan?" I asked, stupidly, as she was already opening the driver's side door to the sedan.

"I've been driving that stupid thing for far too long," she said. "I miss Greg's Jetta. Now that was fun to drive. I just figured it would be nice to go a few hours without being reminded of the fact that I had a son at home, from someone else. We're just two girls, out on the town, celebrating the end of an era, and the beginning of another."

"I like that thought," I agreed, as I popped open the passenger side door. It was the first time that I was sitting on that side of my own car, which made it that much weirder of an experience. Although, any reason not to be driving was alright with me.

It wasn't until we got to the restaurant that I realized where we were going. Greg had this one place that he would always take me to that was just outside of town, Rita's Bistro. It was a small, intimate place with plenty of dark, quiet areas where people could be alone together, even when out in public. He always thought the place so much better than those chain restaurants, with the junk on the walls and screaming kids everywhere. I was with him on the screaming kids part. But I had gotten into the habit of going to those places after the divorce, just to spite the guy.

I looked over to Angela as she pulled into the parking lot, wondering if she knew that Greg had taken me there. Wondering if he had taken her there. It seemed a weird place to go on our first date, but I didn't want to say anything. I wasn't sure if she had done it intentionally, if she even knew the history of the place. It would have been interesting to hear what Greg would have said about us coming here. About us rewriting our history in the same restaurant he made his. I would have asked her, but I didn't want to bring up his name. Not if I didn't have to.

"But I am here," Greg said. "And I think it's amazing. Sort of like you're carrying on the tradition without me. Or, well, with me, just not in body." I shuddered at his words as Angela turned off the car.

"Are you alright?" she asked, looking over at me.

I looked back, at a loss for words for a few moments. "Yeah, fine," I said, unsure what else to say.

"We can go somewhere else, if you think... I mean, yeah, it's a bit weird coming here, I guess," she admitted.

"Just a little," I said, laughing it off.

"It's just... well, we still don't know... I mean, I was more interested in what the place offered, rather than any meaning to either of us. Greg used to take me here, back when... well, when we started dating. After... we got married, I started insisting he take me to other places."

"Gee, I wish I had thought of that," I joked.

"It wouldn't have changed anything," Greg said. "I still would have taken you here. She was just more needy than you."

"Thanks for the warning," I thought to him.

"I just thought that this would be a great place to be discrete. I mean, I know the whole 'going out with a girl' thing is freaking you out a little."

"Just a little?" I thought, but didn't want to say it to her.

"Hey, it'd freak me out, too," Tom said. "The thought of going out with a boy like that."

"And, yet, you live with two of them," Dad supplied.

"It's dumb," Angela said, shaking her head. "We can go somewhere else."

"No, it's fine," I insisted. "You're right. I don't want to have to answer questions that I don't know the answers to myself. This... this will be fine."

"Are you sure?" she asked. She looked worried, like her whole night was planned around us coming there. Like she would break apart at the wrong word.

"Yeah," I said.

Her face lit up as soon as I said the word. "Good," she said. She leaned over, giving me a light peck on the cheek. Her hand lingered on my arm for a moment, her nose tickling my ear. The very smell of her, her very real presence so close at hand, danced in my mind. My body reacted faster than I could tell it to do anything.

My lips were on hers before I realized what I was doing. Her hands were on my dress, pulling me closer to her. The gear shift pressed into my stomach, but I didn't mind it. I barely noticed it, as I explored her every facet. I wanted her, right then and there in that parking lot. More than I had wanted anyone before. More than I realized I could want someone.

"Woo," Dad cheered in my ear, instantly souring the moment. But Angela was already in a like mind, and she didn't have pervy guys talking to her at every moment of the day.

"Hey, we're not all pervy," Tom complained.

"Speak for yourself," Dad said. "Greg and I are totally pervy."

"Don't go dragging me into this," Greg said.

"If we don't leave now, they might give away our table," Angela whispered in my ear.

I was about to say "let them," but then my stomach grumbled. The smell of the food within somehow made it through to us. It overwhelmed the smell of Angela's perfume, demanding my attention beyond my hunger of a different variety. "Yeah, that might be a good idea," I said, reluctantly.

"Besides, we have that big house to go home to together later, if we still want to go there," she said.

"I do like the sound of that, a little more than I should," I said.

She gave me one more quick kiss before breaking away from me and stepping out of the car. I sat there for a moment, trying to figure out just what had happened there. Just why this woman had such a strong pull on me. Was it just her? Was there something about her that made me not be able to control myself around her? Or was there something wrong with me?

"There's nothing wrong with you," Greg said. "Even if you were gay, that wouldn't mean that there's something wrong with you."

"I think it's much more likely that she's bisexual," Tom said. "After all, she fell for you just as hard, didn't she?"

"There's just no accounting for tastes," Dad sneered. "At least now she has someone halfway decent to date."

"Hey," Greg said, insulted.

"Will the three of you just shut up," I yelled at them. "Please, let me figure this whole thing out on my own, will you? I'd like to be on this date alone, not with the audience I take around with me everywhere."

"Are you alright?" Angela said. I looked back towards the driver's side door, only to realize that she wasn't over there. She was standing by mine, holding it open for me like she was trying to be a gentleman or something.

"Sure," I insisted. "Just..." I waved my hand around my head, my usual "I'm just talking to the voices in my head" signal.

"Right," she said, drawing out the word. "Are we heading in, or did you have something else in mind?" She smiled impishly, making me want to pull her back into the car for another hour or two. But I settled on doing this night right.

"We're heading in," I said. "That other stuff can wait. We have all night, right?"

"And the rest of our lives, if we so choose," she promised. "But let's try to figure out if we actually like each other first, shall we?"

"Sure," I said.

She backed away from the door, giving me room to hop out. She even closed the door behind me, once I was standing next to her. We proceeded towards the main entrance to the restaurant, arm in arm. I felt like I was heading off on my first date ever, rather than having gone on more dates than I could count, and even been married and divorced already.

The inside of the restaurant looked the same as I remembered it. The low lighting had always made it hard for me to see. But after a few moments of standing just inside the door, my eyes adjusted, throwing the whole room into view. There were several booths around the edge of the room, each blocked off so that no one could look into them without coming to the opening. The bar was in the middle of the main room, taking up most of the bare space between the walls.

There were also three stand-alone tables that were out away from the walls, out in plain view of everyone. I had never figured out why those tables were there, or what determined who was assigned to those seats unless they asked for them. It was one of those mysteries that Tom would always hoard the answer over my head to. Two of those tables were taken. One by a single woman, reading a book that was propped up in front of her. The other by two men, who were busy looking over some printouts that they had spread across the table.

We weren't standing there long before the hostess came back to the stand. She, like everyone there, was wearing a white blouse and black pants, which I had always figured made up the uniform of the place. "Can I help you ladies?" she asked, eyeing us as if we weren't their normal type of clientele.

"Reservation for Jennings," Angela said.

"Oh," the hostess said. She eyed both of us again, as if suddenly seeing us in a new light, then grabbed up two menus. "When I had seen Jennings on the reservations list, I had been expecting Mr. Jennings and his new lady," she admitted. "I was so sorry to hear about what happened to Mr. Jennings."

"Don't be," Angela said, with a laugh. "We're not."

"Well..." I started. "Maybe a little."

"Right this way," the hostess said, whisking us away from the stand. She didn't bring us far, stopping short right by the remaining empty one of the three tables in the middle. She placed the menus on opposite sides of the table before turning to us. "Your waitress, Maurine, will be right with you."

"Uh," Angela started to say, but the hostess fled from us before she could get much else out.

"What was that about?" I asked, reluctantly sitting in the closer of the two chairs. "Not that I have a problem with this table, but I just thought..."

"I had hoped we'd be in one of the more private booths," Angela agreed. She sat down across from me, but she moved the chair over a little so she was closer. "This isn't as quiet and secluded as I would have liked."

"Well, like you said earlier, we have that entire house to ourselves," I said. I tried to make my words sound a little dirty. But, with the business men so close at hand, the last thing I wanted was some extra attention. "Besides, we're not here to make out in some back corner, are we?"

"No, but it makes it a bit awkward to talk when everyone can see and hear us."

"Maybe now you'll explain these tables?" I thought to Tom.

"Isn't it obvious?" he asked, teasing me once more with the information I wanted. He even let out a little maniacal laugh, which always gave me goosebumps up my back for some reason.

"Well, we'll just need to keep the conversation to safer topics," I suggested.

"Like what?"

"Well, I don't think I ever heard how you and Greg met," I said. I didn't particularly like that line of conversation, but it was definitely safer than some of the ones I wanted to discuss. "I know you met at the Halloween party last year, but--"

"Wait, how did you hear about that?" she asked.

"What do you mean?" I asked. "Was that some great secret or something?" I tried to remember just where I had heard that little tidbit before.

"Well, I had been invited there by my then boyfriend, only to find out that he was cheating on me with another woman," she admitted. My eyebrow suddenly rose on its own when I heard this. I found it rather ironic that she dumped a guy for cheating on her, only to turn around and become that other woman with Greg. "I swear, I didn't know he was married at the time," she said, seeing my reaction. "Anyway, I was hiding out in the bathroom and Greg came in. I had forgotten to lock the door. We got to talking and... I thought he was nice. An hour later, he was sneaking me out the back of the house. That should have been my first clue, to be honest. But it felt so... Well, not really romantic, but, well, you know what I mean."

"Yeah, Greg really did have a way to him, didn't he," I said.

"Gee, thanks, Nat," Greg said.

"I didn't mean that in a good way," I thought back to him. "Now hush."

"Anyway, he kept wanting to be discrete and all. It was the second time he brought me here that I heard he was married. By then... well, it's no excuse. But, then, when I confronted him about it, he said he was already planning on leaving her, on leaving you. It just didn't seem that bad by then. I'm... I'm sorry."

"Well, it could have been worse," I admitted. "I mean, I knew Emily. She knew he was married. She went there anyway."

"Yeah, I hate her," Angela admitted. "Honestly, after I found out, if she hadn't been killed already, I might have just killed her myself."

"Don't let Detective Bently hear you saying that. He already thinks we conspired together to kill her."

"Wait, he does?" she asked, surprised. "Why didn't you tell me this?"

"Well, because..." I thought for a moment, trying to remember why I hadn't told her. I knew there was a perfectly good reason for it.

"Can I talk now?" Tom asked.

"Only if you're helping," I thought to him.

"She was attacked by that thing before you got a chance to."

"Oh, right," I said, hitting my forehead. "That was right before we got attacked by the possum from hell."

"You mean the rat from space," Angela corrected. "I guess that's a reasonable excuse."

"Shh," I hissed, eyeing the business men behind me. They both seemed too engrossed in their own conversation to have noticed us referring to aliens.

"Yeah, we really should have gotten a booth," Angela said, her eyes locked on that other table as well.

"Good evening, ladies," someone said. Suddenly, there was a waitress standing next to our table. I hadn't noticed her coming up, so it took me a little by surprise to see her there. "Can I get you two something to drink to start?"

"Well, we're celebrating," Angela said, barely losing a step by the sudden arrival. "Bring us a bottle of champagne, though maybe something in the middle of the rack. We're on a bit of a budget."

"Uh, maybe make it your cheapest," I amended. I wasn't supposed to drink on my medication, and I was already cheating enough by taking the half dosage as it was.

"No, nonsense," Angela insisted. "We have a lot to celebrate, and you're going to get that job at the law offices."

"It was a maybe," I said. "I'm not banking on a maybe. We need to make the money we have stretch as long as possible."

"Yeah, you tell her," Greg said. "She was always spending money she didn't have."

"Oh, you're no fun," Angela said, giving in to me so quick that it shocked Greg. I needed to find more things that did that, because it shut him up for the entire time it took us to order the rest of the meal. "Seriously, though," Angela said, once the waitress was gone. "We need to loosen you up a little. Maybe that's why..."

"That's why Greg left me?" I asked.

"Sorry," she said. "Maybe we should make it a rule to not talk about him anymore."

"That's fine with me," I said. I got enough of him already, with his voice constantly in my ear.

"It's not constantly there," Greg whined, proving my point. "Okay, it's there a lot, but not always."

"We're supposed to be getting to know each other," Angela said, her voice almost drowned out by Greg's.

"A-and we are," I said. "You learned that, when I don't have a steady flow of income, I'm extremely cheap. This date is almost painful. But your smile makes it that much better."

"Well, don't worry about this date," she said. "I'm paying."

"Now, see, I know you want that to make me feel better, but..."

"We'll make the money last as long as possible. Besides, if you don't get the job, I'll go back to work. Better?"

"Well, I don't know," I said. "What did you do before you married G... the man who we're not talking about."

"Subtle," Greg said.

"I was a teacher. I taught at a private school just outside of the city. It shouldn't be too hard to get a new position. I kept up with my contacts after I left. We might need to get a new place, something cheaper. But we'll make it work if we need to."

"A teacher, huh?" I said. "I used to teach, before..."

"Before you started talking to your dead father in the middle of class," Angela finished. "I know. Greg... I mean, I heard about it."

"Of course, he told you," I mumbled.

"Sorry," Greg said. What surprised me most was that he actually sounded sincere about it. Still, it was weird, being on a date with Angela, with both of our ex, who was the same guy, looking over our shoulders. It wasn't helping the whole "she's a girl" of it.

"Is it just me or is it more weird that we both dated, and married, the same guy than that we're both girls?" Angela asked, getting to the root of the issue.

"A little," I agreed. "It's just that, well, he's been such a big part of my life for the past fifteen years. Even after we divorced. I don't really have much of myself left over. I never learned how to be me again. I'm not even sure I'd know how if I tried."

"Yeah, I kind of wish I had kept up with my old friends, the way I had with my old colleagues. I just, it was easier with the colleagues."

"And Greg wouldn't have been so quick to squash that."

"Too true," Angela agreed. "I don't know what we ever saw in that man."

"I think it was his abs," I said.

"Yeah," she cooed. "Those really were amazing."

"And my eyes," Greg added.

"And his eyes," I agreed.

"And, oh yeah, my bank account," Greg said.

"Well, not so much that," I said. As soon as it was out of my mouth, I slapped my hand against it. My eyes went wide as I waited for a reaction from Angela. She just continued to smile at me, seeming to not be bothered in the least by my having talked to a voice in my head. "Sorry," I muttered through my hands.

"Hey, I have quirks, too," she said.

"This is more than just a quirk," I said. "I can be institutionalized for this."

"Hey," she said. She took one of my hands off my face so she could hold it. "As long as you don't start lighting the house on fire... or threatening to hurt Doug, or me, or yourself, your secret is safe with me. Besides, you're still more stable than the last person I was with."

"Your bottle of champagne, ladies," the waitress said. She deposited an ice bucket with the bottle sticking out of it next to our table. Next, she seemed to pull two champagne glasses out of her back pocket, though I knew that wasn't where she kept them. She flipped them over onto the table with a little bit of a flourish. "Your dinners will be out shortly. Enjoy."

"Perfect timing," Angela said, once the waitress was out of earshot again. The bottle was already open, so she just scooped it up, pouring both of our glasses almost full with the bubbling contents. "A toast," she said, raising her glass. "To the end of our marriages, and the beginning of something new. Something better."

"Which will hopefully include one of us gainfully employed," I added.

"Or both," she said.

"Or both," I agreed.

I chinked my glass against hers lightly. The ringing seemed to reverberate around the room, drawing the attention of everyone around us. I took the smallest sip of the alcoholic beverage, not wanting it to go to my head. Not wanting it to have the wrong side effect with my meds. Besides, I'd let Angela get as drunk as she wanted to. I'd be the designated driver if need be. The sweet liquid touched my tongue, slipping down faster than I would have expected.

My eyes were locked on Angela's as I placed the glass down on the table. That's why I noticed it when it happened. Suddenly, out of nowhere, her blue eyes suddenly turned black. And, I'm not just talking about the blue part, or her irises dilating or anything. The entire eye, whites and all, went completely black. It was like ink was spreading out from the center, or watching the bottom of a glass of milk as chocolate syrup is being poured into it.

Before I could properly freak out, the blackness faded. It didn't go all the way, though. There was just a thick ring of blackness surrounding her iris, making it look larger and darker than usual. Her dress, which had once matched the color perfectly, seemed suddenly a lot brighter in comparison. What made it even weirder was the fact that Angela didn't seem the least bit concerned about it.

"Are you alright?" I asked, in a hushed tone. My hand went out to touch her arm, which seemed completely normal under my skin.

"I'm fine," she said. But her voice came out in a low, guttural, husky blast.

I'm sorry to admit that I completely freaked out, screaming as I fled from the restaurant.

Chapter Twenty-Five
The Comforting Arms of a Man

I was halfway down the road before I slowed. My heart was still running a mile a minute, goading me to keep going. To run until I could no longer see the restaurant. I couldn't stand it, though. The thought of the fact that I had just left her there. Left Angela alone at the table, no matter what happened to her.

"No, I'm right there with you," Tom said. "That freaked me out completely. It was like she was some kind of alien or something."

"She can't be an alien," I said. "There's no such things as aliens."

"What about that thing that attacked her?" Greg asked. "That looked pretty alien to me."

"It was a rat. A giant rat," I insisted. "Besides, it was Angela. How could Angela suddenly be an alien? Unless you're saying that Greg was an alien, too."

"Hey, leave me out of this," Greg said. "I'm already dead. Now you want to make me into an alien as well?"

"I mean how else would you and Angela have conceived Doug if she's an alien? Maybe that would explain why we could never..."

"No, no, no, no, no," Tom said. "She wasn't an alien back then. She was still human. It was only after the attack that she became an alien."

"What, like she's just some alien that looks like Angela?"

"No, like an alien possessed her or something," Tom said.

"That sounds more like something we would do," Dad said. "It doesn't work. Trust me, I've tried."

"Yeah," I said. "Wait, what? When did you try to possess me?"

"Oh, don't worry about it. It was a long time ago. And, like I said, it didn't work. You didn't even notice I was doing it."

"Yeah, that's what scares me. When was this?"

"It was during your first stay at HTP," Dad said. "I wanted to make you get us out of there. It didn't work, so I know she can't be possessed."

"She can't be possessed by one of us," Tom clarified. "That doesn't mean she can't be possessed by some alien parasite or something. We have no idea where that alien 'rat' has been. It could have any number of contagions."

"But, wouldn't those be alien contagions?" I asked. "How would they affect humans?"

"As long as they're carbon based life forms, it would still work."

"This is stupid," I said. "There are no such things as aliens. I should go back to her. Find out what's wrong with her. Or what's wrong with me."

"Not on your life," Tom insisted. "There's no way I'm going back there."

"Who said you had to come?" I asked. "I never invited any of you into my head. You're all free to leave whenever you want. In fact, I would prefer it." Half of me wanted to go back just on the possibility that it would chase off Tom once and for all. But the simple thought of those eyes, that voice that seemed to come from hell, turned my legs into jelly. If Angela had been the type, I might have been able to convince myself that the whole thing was some kind of elaborate practical joke. I had no idea how she would have been able to do that thing with her eyes.

"Exactly," Tom said. "The only explanation is that she's an alien now."

"No, there's another explanation," Greg said.

"What's that?" Tom asked.

"What? Seriously? I figured something out that you hadn't?" he gloated. "Then I'm not saying a word. Let's see how you feel about people keeping information from you."

"Fine by me," Tom said. "I don't really believe you know anything."

"You guys, what are we going to do?" I asked. "We need to help Angela, somehow."

"There's nothing to do," Tom said. "She's an alien now. Unless we can come up with a cure, she has to be killed before she kills us."

"Oh, great, now the voices I've been hearing for years are starting to tell me to kill people," I said. "That's definitely a good sign."

"Not people," he said. "Just Angela, or, more importantly, the alien formerly known as Angela."

"We're not killing anyone," I yelled, a lot louder than I probably should have. I looked around me, at the otherwise empty street. There were houses all around me and I didn't recognize the street I was on. "Perhaps I should have taken the car," I said. I fumbled through the purse that I had somehow managed to grab on my panic-stricken escape from the restaurant. I pulled my car keys out, as if to demonstrate that I could have driven off if I had thought of it at the time. Then again, I would have ended up abandoning Angela alone at the restaurant without a way of getting home.

"That's a good thing," Tom insisted. "Then she couldn't go infect Doug and that hot babysitter."

"You thought she was hot?" I asked, not remembering much of what she looked like. "Wasn't she kind of young?"

"Not much younger than I was when I died," Tom reminded me. His voice always sounded so deep in my head. I often forgot that he had been so young. "Either way, it's probably too late for them. They'll all be infected by the time we get back. I'm just glad you never slept with her. You could have been infected as well."

"Ah," Dad said. He sounded overly disappointed by the fact that I hadn't slept with her. Or maybe that I hadn't been infected.

Or had I been infected? "Wait, I was covered in that thing's blood," I said. "How do I know I haven't been infected? Maybe I'm the alien."

"I think we'd know if you were an alien," Tom said. "It probably would have taken on the form of another voice long before it took you over."

"Yeah, but then it wouldn't have taken you over," Dad insisted. "Because we can't possess you."

"God, will you stop saying that?" I asked. I noticed a curtain fluttering in one of the windows of the house on my left and suddenly I had the feeling like I was being watched. "Maybe I should stop talking to myself in the middle of the street," I said, eyeing the window. "But where am I going if I'm not going home?"

"I think you dropped something," Dad said. "It fell out when you were taking your keys out." His phantom limb pointed at the ground by my feet. I bent down, looking at what it was he was pointing at. I was sure that it was just some bit of trash that had been on the ground before we got there.

I was surprised that it wasn't. "What is this?" I asked, as I picked up the small card. The handwriting on the back was familiar, though I couldn't read it all that well. When I flipped it over, I noticed that it was Eric's card that he had given me the other night, when he had stayed with me after the alien attacked.

"So, now you agree with me that it was an alien?" Tom asked.

"Oh, shut up," I said.

"No, this is good," Greg said. "What is the one thing that everyone yells at the screen in those horror movies about body snatchers?"

"Don't split up?" Dad asked.

"Don't go in that room?" Tom supplied.

"Call the cops," I said. I mean, sure, it made perfect sense. Although, I wasn't sure how I felt about turning in Angela on the suspicion that she's an alien.

"But that's the beauty of it," Tom said. "We're not actually turning her in. At least, not really. We just had a bad date and wanted to discuss it with the friendly cop that's been flirting with us."

"Wait a minute, us?" I asked.

"Oh, like he'd ever notice you if it weren't for us talking in your ear this whole time."

"More like I wouldn't have been in trouble with the police so I never would have met him," I said.

"Either way, you owe this whole mess to us," Tom said.

"And a whole lot more," I said, though I let the subject drop. Instead, I focused on the card in my hand. I flipped it back over to the hand-written side, trying to figure out what it said. I hadn't paid much attention to it when he first gave it to me. The writing was barely legible, and it looked like it had faded while in my purse. Fortunately, it was a small town and I knew most of it. He had said he lived a few blocks from my old apartment. That narrowed it down quite a bit. It only took a couple of minutes of squinting at the lettering to see that he lived on Grant Street, rather than Goat Street, which is what the words looked like. There wasn't a Goat Street in town, though, so that was easy enough to figure out. Unfortunately, the numbers were something else entirely. It took me almost the entire walk across town to narrow it down to 582 or 585, both of which seemed completely likely.

Fortunately, as soon as I turned down the street, it was immediately clear that Eric didn't live at 585 Grant Street. Someone was heading out of that house, earbuds in her ears as she started to jog down the street. Eric could easily be living with a teenaged girl, perhaps a younger sister or something. However, the fact that this one was asian, while Eric was most definitely not, had me heading to the house on the left. Just after ringing the doorbell, it occurred to me that Eric might actually be on duty. "Stupid cop hours," I mumbled to myself.

Seconds later, the door opened. Eric was standing there on the other side of the screen door. His shirt was off, his chest and abs open to the air. Open to my prying eyes as I stared him down. "Natalie?" he asked, obviously surprised by my being there.

"Um, hey, Eric," I said, trying to pull my eyes back up to his. "I hope you don't mind me dropping by."

I was pleased to see a smile spreading across his face when my eyes finally got to it. "Not at all, but you... did you walk here?"

"Um... yeah...." I looked down at myself, at the dress I was still wearing. Sweat had started to collect along the edges, despite the chilly night air. I was, once again, very thankful I had worn the flats. If I had gone with heels, I would have ended up taking them off after the first half mile and walked the rest of the way barefoot. It wasn't that unusual for me to walk around long distances. But across the town was still a bit far for me. The walk had been so long that the sun had set a while ago. I didn't remember when that was, though I was pretty sure it had been after I had run from the restaurant.

"Is something wrong?" he asked.

"Well, he is a cop," Tom said, as if that explained his observation.

"Yeah, a cop, not a detective," I thought back at him. I shuddered at the mention of the word, at the reminder of Bently, who was still trying to bury me with evidence for both murders.

"I... well... Okay, now it just sounds stupid to me. Sorry for bothering you."

"No," Eric said, holding his hand out to me. "Come in. Come in. Let's talk. You walked all this way. Whatever it is, you thought it was important at one point."

"What if he's an alien too?" Dad whispered, harshly.

I looked between Eric's welcoming hand and the road behind me, wondering which to take. Wondering if I would be able to walk home from there. The walk from the restaurant had been long enough as it was. My feet had lost sensation halfway through it. "Maybe for just a few minutes, to rest my feet," I said.

"How about a glass of water as well," Eric suggested.

His living room was small, despite it taking up much of the front of the house. He had one of those plush leather couches like Dr. Mendez. Once you sit in it, it would swallow you whole and not let you back up. Despite that, I went straight for it, sitting down carefully but heavily. His walls seemed like they needed a fresh coat of paint, and were peeling in certain places. There was an obvious crack running through it down from the middle of the front window to the floor.

It took less than a minute for Eric to pop down the hall to the kitchen in the back of the house, fill a glass with water, and come back. It was enough time to change my mind about telling him what happened with Angela four times. Why was I there? I was going to sound completely crazy to him. He would just have me call my shrink, who was going to have me committed again.

"It's stupid," I said, again, after taking a long drink of water. "I don't even know why I came here."

"I'm glad you came here," he said. His movements seemed overly practiced as he slid down into the couch. He positioned himself close to me, yet not close enough to have the couch slide him into my lap. "I gave you my address for a reason." His arm automatically went to the back of the couch, around behind me. It seemed like he had a very different idea for why I had come there. I guess the dress would have done that.

"I was out on a date," I blurted out, before he could get too close to me.

"And it went so poorly that you decided to swing by here and see me? I'm touched."

"He's not that far off from the truth," Tom pointed out. "See? I told you that it was a good idea to come here."

"Well, I couldn't exactly go home," I said.

"Oh? And why is that?" Eric asked.

"Because... I was on a date with Angela," I admitted. If I was going to tell him everything, I might as well start with the most awkward parts and go towards the scariest parts. With time and distance, I was losing conviction that those parts ever happened at all.

"Ah," he said. He slipped a few more inches away from me, taking his arm back. "I see. Interesting."

"It... I mean, I've never... Oh, this is going all wrong."

"So, your first date with a girl went wrong and you want to go back to guys?" Eric asked, his smile quick to return.

"Eric, please, let me get this whole thing out before... I mean, it's weird enough as it is without that whole thing on top of it."

"This doesn't have anything to do with the detective, does it?" he asked. "He outranks me, so I really can't help you there."

"No, no, no, this is all about Angela, though... I don't know, maybe, if I'm right... Well, I guess it'll all have to come out eventually. I just don't want to hear what he's going to say about this whole thing." I shuddered at the thought of all the weird conspiracies the detective would no doubt come up with about the two of us, given this latest development.

"It could be worse," Tom said. "You could have found out that she really did have something to do with Emily's death."

"Yeah," I thought to him, sarcastically. "That would be so much worse than her possibly being an alien."

"No, I mean in addition to it."

"So, you know how she had been attacked by that... thing the other day."

"The possum?" Eric asked.

"I'm no longer thinking that it was a possum. I... well... I think it was some kind of alien. Or, at least, it was infected by something alien. Or at least by something not normal, not heard of before now."

"Alien? Seriously?" Eric said. It was clear that I had lost him. He was obviously not going to believe a single word I said after that.

"Eric, please," I insisted. My voice cracked with my frustration. He had always been the one cop I could trust. The one I could believe in, despite all that Bently had been dragging me through. "It's the only thing that I could think of, the only thing that could explain what I saw tonight."

"So, you were on a date, and something happened?" he prompted, though he still sounded like he was just placating me.

"Her eyes went black, I mean seriously black, and her whole eyes."

"Both of them?"

"Yes, both of them, but I mean like the whites of them as well. It was like they turned into two black orbs in her head, without them coming out or anything."

"Is she alright?" he asked. Suddenly he was starting to sound concerned again, though I had a feeling it was more for the alien formerly known as Angela than for anything else.

"She didn't seem to notice the change. Although, I don't know, maybe it hadn't taken her yet, not completely."

"Well, let's head over to your house," he suggested. "If her eyes are black like you say..."

"No, that won't work," I said. He had moved to get up at his words, and my hand went automatically to his chest.

His smooth pecs under my hand felt amazing. All I wanted to do was take my dress off and...

"Focus," Tom blurted, knocking my thoughts back to the matter at hand.

I took my hand back, but Eric had sat back down as well. "Her eyes went back to normal soon after. Well, at least mostly normal. They still have this black ring around them. But, if you don't know what to look for, you could easily miss it. Besides, if we tried to look at it now, it would only tip her off that we're on to her."

"But didn't you do that already when you left? What happened when they went back to normal?"

"I... well, I kind of ran," I admitted.

"Not right away," Tom said. "You asked her if she was alright."

"Oh, right," I said. "I asked her if she was alright first. She had this really deep voice, but it was deeper than I had heard anyone's voice ever be. Like ever. Even Barry White had nothing on her."

"Which is another thing that we should be able to confirm by going over there," Eric insisted. "If we just see her as she is now, maybe we can figure out what happened. Maybe how to help her."

"Don't you get it?" I asked. "She's beyond help. She's an alien, infected by whatever it was that made that possum look like an alien. She'll probably start growing horns and attack us on sight, like the possum did."

"But, Natalie, don't you see?" he asked. "There's a very reasonable, rational explanation here that could be confirmed by going back to your house and just looking at her."

"What?" I asked. "What possible explanation could there be besides the fact that my roommate, my ex-husband's widow, is an alien?"

"Natalie, your diagnosis is in your file," he said, calmly and quietly. My face went cold as his words punched a hole through my chest. From the very beginning, from when I first met Eric, he had always been nice to me, even a little flirtatious. If it hadn't been for Angela, if I hadn't considered going there, I would have been throwing myself at Eric this whole time. And, yet, he knew me. He knew my diagnosis. That couldn't be good. It never is. "What you're describing here, it sounds more like a delusion. Like you're just seeing things that aren't there. Like you're having a..."

"Don't," I said. I put my hand up to his lips, silencing him before he could say the word.

"OH," Tom said.

"Told you," Greg gloated.

"Oh, come on," Tom said. "You did not think of that back at the restaurant."

"Of course, I did," Greg said. "Pfft, aliens. You and your paranoid delusions. Wait, can a delusion have a delusion?"

"But..." I started.

"Why don't we just call your shrink?" Eric asked.

"No," I insisted, demanded. That was exactly what I didn't want. What I had been afraid of the whole walk over. "No, please. Just... Alright," I said. "Maybe I imagined it."

"Hey," Tom said. "We saw it too."

"Again, we're just delusions to her," Greg said. "We only see what she sees."

"Shut up, you two," I thought at them. "Let me walk this back a little, at least for tonight. I just... I don't want to go back to HTP, and I can't go back to that house."

"Maybe it's just my... condition," I said. "I don't usually have visual hallucinations, but that doesn't mean I can't. I just... Let me stay here for the night, let me calm down a little. Then we can both head back to... back to the house together. We'll see what we can see and just take it from there, alright?"

"I'm not sure..." he said, hesitantly.

"I should have never moved back in that house," I admitted. "It's been bad memories the whole way. Even from the start, from the first time I stepped foot in there. It's just...

I need a place to be that's not there. I'll get my head on straight, I promise."

"Okay," he said, reluctantly. "But only for tonight. Tomorrow, we're calling your shrink no matter what. Besides, it's probably too late for us to call him now anyway. Even shrinks have a right to a social life."

"Is that a hint?" I asked. "I imagine cops have just as much of a right to one of those."

He smiled wryly. "This is my social life," he said. "If you needed a cop, the police station was closer to the house than my place."

"I wasn't at the house," I said. "I was at Rita's. And, yes, the police station was closer."

"Exactly. You came to me because I'm a friend who's a cop. And I am, still, a friend. Nothing is going to change that."

"Even if I end up killing Angela?" I asked. His face fell, his eyes going wide with shock. "I'm kidding," I said. I hoped it wouldn't come to that. And it wouldn't if it really was just in my head. But I couldn't ignore the very real possibility that it would happen. That it might need to happen. And soon.

"If you need to kill her, not murder her, then, yes, even then," Eric said. "But it's not going to come to that, right?"

I nodded, more placating him than actually agreeing. With my track record, I couldn't promise that it wouldn't happen. That it wouldn't need to happen. Just that I wouldn't force it.

Chapter Twenty-Six
A Short End to a Wonderful Night

Once the matter with Angela was settled, or at least as much as it was going to be for the night, we moved on to safer topics. It made it much easier to talk with him and, once again, we ended up talking well into the night. We would have talked longer, but a call came in just before two.

"Who could be calling you now?" I asked. "It's like half an hour away from 'why bother going to sleep'." As if to demonstrate, I yawned heavily.

"I don't know," Eric said. "It must be something big, though. They don't usually call in cops when they're off duty. At least not uniformed officers like me. It's not like there aren't enough of us to go around." He picked up the receiver off the cradle, but headed into the other room before actually picking it up. The phone rang two more times as I sat there alone. Or, at least, as alone as I ever am.

"What would you even do with yourself if you were ever truly alone?" Greg asked. "Even when we were married, you were always so needy."

"That's because you insisted that I ditch my friends to hang out with you. Then you'd end up ditching me," I whispered. With Eric out of earshot, I figured it was safe to talk with him openly.

"Yeah, 'cause that usually stops you," Greg joked. "How often do you remember that you're talking with people who, at least according to you, don't really exist anywhere except your head?"

"Ignore him," Tom said. "It took me some time to come to terms with being a figment of your imagination, just as it had you when it was just you and Dad here."

"Don't call me Dad," Dad insisted. He never liked Tom. He never liked sharing room with the other voices in my life. Then again, who would? I certainly didn't, but I was stuck with them.

"What should I call you?" Tom asked, which was a common question he had. Dad had never given an answer. "You would think that, after all these years, you'd have an answer to that."

"It's only been three," Dad said. "I miss those years when I had this place to myself."

"Um, what about me?" I asked.

"Oh, you know what I mean," he said, flapping his phantom hand at me.

"Natalie?" Eric asked. He popped his head back around the corner of the hallway. "I was right. This is big. They found something at the community college. They're expecting to need a lot of crowd control, so they're calling us in."

"The community college?" I asked. "That's not even in your jurisdiction, is it? Doesn't Valhalla have their own police department?"

"Yeah, they do," he said. "And they're the first to jump to our aid when we need it. This is kind of an all hands on deck situation. They need all the help they can get. I'm really sorry about all this."

"No, I get it," I said. "It's not like I've ever had a job where I could be called in at the drop of a hat, but I get it." Even Greg kept steady hours. He wasn't the kind of lawyer that would have these kinds of emergencies.

"Why do you think I went into corporate law to begin with?" he asked. "I like having a social life, as long as the work gets done on time."

"Yeah, it was when it didn't that I was left alone at the house," I thought to him.

"Are you going to be alright here alone?" Eric asked. "I was going to set up the couch for you, if we ever stopped talking. We never really got around to it, did we?"

"I'll be fine," I said. "You don't mind me staying over?"

"Stay the night. We'll handle everything when I get back tomorrow."

"We'll handle everything after you get back and have at least a few hours of sleep," I amended. "I hope they don't have you on shift tomorrow after keeping you up all night."

"Yeah, about that. I'm probably going to be going in for at least a few hours. Which is why we're going to handle all of this before I get some sleep. We're not putting it off for another day. I'll get home tomorrow and we'll call your shrink."

"Well, if we're going to be putting it off until tomorrow afternoon, I already have an appointment with him on Friday," I said. "I'll have to talk with him then, anyway."

"We'll discuss it later," he insisted. His head disappeared back around the corner without him discussing it further. Barely two minutes later, he was coming back out, fully dressed in his uniform. He had a pile of linens in his hands, even a pillow topping it off. "I trust you know how to make up the couch. I'm sorry that I don't have a guest room to offer you."

"It'll do," I said. "If it wouldn't, I could always go home."

"You laugh, but we'll be heading over there tomorrow, whether you like it or not." With that, he headed out the door. I watched him from the window as he headed down the sidewalk for the familiar looking sedan parked at the curb. Once the car was gone, I left the window, letting the drapes fall back into place.

Thinking that I wouldn't get much sleep, what with the stress of the day and the late hour, I barely spread out the sheets onto the couch. However, as soon as my head hit the pillow, I must have zonked out. The next thing I remember was waking up to the phone ringing.

At first, I was thinking that it was just a memory of the phone ringing before. Or maybe I just dreamed that Eric had left and that my head was really in his lap right then. There wasn't anywhere that I would have rather been, anyway. But, as the ringing persisted, my dreams faded from my mind and the glaring sun coming in through the front window chased away the sleep. By the time I was fully conscious, the call had gone to the machine. It gave off a loud beep as the message sounded throughout the room.

"Natalie, pick up," Detective Bently croaked through the machine. "I know you're there. Eric told me everything. We're sending a cruiser over there shortly. You're really in it this time. Don't bother trying to run, we'll just have to chase you down like last time."

I tried to remember what he was talking about when the call cut out. When had I tried to run? Each time I had been pulled into the station had been a complete surprise to me, despite the frequency of the occurrences. Even last time, as he had called it, when I had been at Dr. Mendez's office. I hadn't been running. I just didn't know that they were coming from me. In fact, this was the first time that I had had any warning on the impending arrival of the police. Unless you count when I had been forced to kill Greg. I hadn't run then either.

"That's 'cause you were stuck under me," Greg said. "It made it a bit hard for you to get away."

"Yes, there's that," I admitted. "Plus, I was rather stunned by the whole thing. I mean, it wasn't like I had gone over there to kill you."

"But what could they have on us this time?" Tom asked. I let the plural slide, only because my mind was whirling around on the possibilities myself. "Unless it's another stupid conspiracy theory of his."

"Well, last time it had been Dad's death," I said. "Maybe he figured out something else about that. Wasn't there something last night about..." I trailed off as I tried to remember last night, right before falling asleep. The call that Eric had taken. Why he had left. What he had said about the community college. "You don't think..."

"No," Tom said. "There's no way it's that."

"What are you two talking about?" Greg asked. "Is this something about you flipping out in class that time?"

"Sort of," Tom said.

"It's... related," I said.

"You don't really think it's that, though, do you?" Tom asked.

"You're guess is as good as mine," I said. "Probably better. But, he's right, it's not exactly like I can run. I don't have my car. Besides, where would I go?"

Further compounding the hopelessness of my situation, the red and blue flashing lights of a police cruiser lit up the front window as it pulled out in front of the house. Resigned to my fate, the fate of being blamed, yet again, for something I probably didn't do, I scooped up my purse from where I had left it by the couch and headed out to greet my escort. I delayed only long enough to make sure the door was locked as I left.

I paused near the door when I noticed that the uniformed cop wasn't Eric. He was just starting to make his way up the sidewalk. This surprised me to no end. I figured he would be the first person to volunteer to bring me in, especially since I was staying at his house. Bently had said Eric had told him "everything" though. That must have included our blossoming friendship. Maybe he had thought that Eric was too close to me. That he wouldn't be able to keep his neutrality when it came to me. Or, maybe, Eric was still out at the college with Bently and would meet me at the station.

The cop, whom I hadn't met before, had taken out his cuffs as he approached me. His hand was conspicuously near his firearm as he eyed me dangerously. I guessed he wasn't used to the suspects coming out to greet him. This was just more of the same crap that I had had to put up with for weeks. More fodder for the harassment lawsuit Sam was putting together for me.

"Dang it, you should have called him before leaving the house," Tom said.

"Gee, now you tell me," I thought to him. Still, not wanting to make waves with this new officer, I raised my hands to show that I wasn't going to make trouble. My purse slid down into the crook of my arm, awkwardly hanging there heavily. "Maybe he'll just know I'm in trouble and need his help again, like last time."

"Oh, please, Eric obviously called him last time," Tom said. "That's why he came in with him. He's bound to have called him again this time. Sam will probably beat you to the station. Or, better yet, one of his criminal law colleagues."

"In the meantime, at least we have our resident lawyer," I thought to them.

Unfortunately, the uniformed officer insisted on the handcuffs. He didn't bother to read me my rights or even say what, if anything, I was under arrest for. I knew that Bently would go over all the formalities anyway, once I was in the room with him. So, I just settled in. I went with the regular, all too familiar process of being brought into the station. When we got there, once the cop opened the back door for me, I practically marched my way through the station. I didn't bother to wait for the guy, already knowing my way to my favorite interrogation room. Fortunately, it was vacant this time as well.

"You know, the least you people could do is get a more comfortable chair," I said to the cop. He had followed behind me into the room, seeming at a loss for my reaction to the arrest. I settled down in the usual chair, the one I knew I would be expected to sit in from all the other times I had been there. The cop undid the cuffs, taking them with him as he departed the room.

"You need to get a watch," Tom said, as soon as the door was closed.

"Why is that?" I asked.

"So that we'd know what time it is while we're in here," he said. "You're always complaining about losing track of time. If this really is going to start becoming a regular occurrence, we might as well be prepared for next time."

"They might start taking it off me when I get here," I said. "I think they like disorienting me. Isn't that the whole point of this room? To disorient me and make me uncomfortable so I tell them all my secrets to get out of here?"

"Besides," Dad said. "This should be the last time. We'll insist that the suit be filed after this. They shouldn't be able to pull us in here every time they find something. It seems like every time there's a crime in this area, they try to pin it on you."

"And even in other places," I said, thinking of Dad's death.

"Yeah," Tom said, pensively. "I really think they did it."

I was almost certain I knew all too well what 'it' was. Before I could ask to what he was referring, Bently came in. His Cheshire cat smile was back, bigger than ever. There even seemed to be a little bit of a jump in his step, the three he took between the door and the other chair. He seemed unaffected by whatever it was they found at the community college the night before. Or by the lost sleep. The folder in his hand was thin, as if it were empty. I knew, from my weeks of experience with him, that it wouldn't be. It would no doubt have some freshly printed photos of another grisly crime scene, perhaps the one they found last night.

"Natalie," he said. "So lovely to see you here."

"Not like I had much of a choice," I said. I raised my hands, as if to demonstrate the cuffs that were no longer on them.

"Did you enjoy your time at Eric's house last night?" he asked.

"Yes, I did," I said. "I probably got a better night's sleep than you as well. Now that we have the pleasantries out of the way, care to tell me what new crime you're trying to pin on me this time?"

"Oh, this isn't a new crime, it's an old one. I really do like it when we can close some cold cases. Bring some peace of mind to people that have been waiting a long time for answers. I just wish that this one had a happier ending. Well, before we get started, we should get the formalities out of the way." He lost his gloating and superior tone as he regurgitated my rights in a monotone voice. This time, I let him continue, going through the whole speech. I glared at him with my arms crossed over my chest. He revealed nothing. His hand was solidly placed on top of the folder where it sat on the table. Once he was finished, he put his gloating smile back into place. "Now, any guess as to what's in this folder?"

"Yeah, we were right," Tom said, dully, at a loss for anything else to say.

"It's a picture of the body of Tom Morison," I said.

"E-exactly," Bently said. His smile lost a little of its power, as a bit of shock got mixed in it. He recovered quickly. "I'm so glad we're past pretending--"

"I reported his suicide the night it happened," I said, interrupting his attempt at returning to the usual cat and mouse game he loved so much. "I didn't kill him, as the coroner's report will no doubt show. As I said at the time, he jumped from that roof all on his own. I have no idea how it took this long to find his body. It's not like the forest in the area is that thick."

"That's the thing, though," he said, regaining his composure and his gloating. "His body wasn't found in the woods. It was nowhere near the building you said he jumped off of."

"What?" I asked, surprised.

"What?" Tom said, completely shocked. "I was there when you told the campus security officer what happened. It's not like my body was still walking around on its own after I died. I even saw where I fell. I should have been found years ago. What game is this guy playing at?"

"I don't know," I thought to him, while keeping my face as calm as possible. "It's not like he would have moved the body three years ago, back before he even knew me. Before he would need to find something to pin on me, just for this occasion. Besides, if that were the case, he probably would have come up with the body sooner."

"Now, I'm sure you're going to tell me you have no idea why the body was found... where it was found."

"Of course, I have no idea why it was found there. Or where, for that matter. It should have been at the base of the building. Unless some wild animal ran off with it or something. I remember that it was a big mystery at the time, some of the best fodder for urban legends."

"Yeah, which isn't much fun to hear about when you're the subject of those legends," Tom said.

"I don't really know what happened too long after that," I said. "Well... you know what happened a few days later."

"Yes, the guilt over killing yet another person started getting to you and you freaked out in a class," Bently said.

The truth of the matter was Tom didn't like being stuck with me. At least not at first. "Actually, I'm still not thrilled about it," he said. "I just started realizing that you didn't have much of a choice in the matter either, and that I shouldn't make things harder for you. It's not like you chose to be haunted by three spirits. Then again, who would? I think Scrooge is the only one that ever benefited from it."

"And that instance is debatable," I thought to him. "Some might say he was better off being a miser."

The point is, when the Tom voice started showing up, he really ran with it. He joined in with the Dad voice in their constant attempt to drive me insane. Or, as some would say, the constant reminder that I was already insane. After a couple of days of a constant stream of questions that I couldn't answer, he started singing the song that never ends. The one that was in that stupid sheep puppet show back in the 80s or whatever. A couple days of that non-stop would be enough to drive the sanest person crazy. I was already halfway there to begin with.

"I'm sorry, only halfway?" Dad asked. He was, of course, responsible for a similar break back when I was still a teenager. By comparison, Greg was by far the calmest of the bunch. He seemed to be the quickest to assimilate into the twisted psyche that was my mind.

"Ooh, maybe it was Greg," Tom said. "You were married to him at the time, right?"

"You know I was," I thought to him. "You were there. Or, at least, you were afterwards."

"Right. And you two were already having problems. Maybe he moved my body so as to make you look more crazy than you already did. After all, it wasn't a far push. And it wasn't like he could have known that I would have done the work for him. Sorry about that, by the way."

"Where is Greg?" Dad asked. "I'd like to know what he has to say about it."

"Oh, like the voice that took on the Greg persona would know anything," I thought. "I don't know what happened to the body, so it's not like he would know either."

"Besides, it's not like he would admit to it if he had moved it," Tom said.

"Still, I'd like to know where he went off to," Dad said. "And how. I've been trying to get out of here for decades now. I'd hate to think that I should be taking lessons from the new guy."

I just shook my head, trying to put them out of my mind, despite my inability to get them out of my ear. I tried to focus on the room around me. Bently was still there, still in that other chair, staring at me as if waiting for a response to something. "What?" I asked.

"You freaked out in class because you couldn't handle it anymore," he repeated. "It must have been eating away at you all these years. Don't you think you'd feel better if you just told me the truth?"

"But... I have told you the truth. When, in the weeks and weeks that you have been accusing me of crimes, have I ever, once, lied to you?" I asked.

"You've done nothing but lie to me," Bently said. "Oh, sure, some of the things you've been saying turned out to be true. At least from your perspective of things. That doesn't mean anything in the long run, now does it?"

"Doesn't it?" I asked. "Shouldn't it? You have nothing. Nothing but your own accusations. Nothing but a bunch of circumstantial evidence that tells me a very different story than the one you are convinced of."

"And what story is that?" he asked.

I stared at him for a moment, a bit confused by his question. "Which story? Mine or yours?"

"Let's start with yours for a moment, shall we?"

"Oh, you mean about the abusive father? The troubled kid who killed himself in front of me? My terrible taste in men, that probably stems from the abusive father part? Or, at least, that's what my shrink keeps telling me. I'd say it was all just some big coincidence, except--"

"Except it's not," he agreed. "It can't be. There's no such thing as a coincidence. Not on this scale. This, here, is a conspiracy. A conspiracy to commit murder, again, and again, by a troubled young woman. And, now, I hear you have your sights on your next target already. This is a sign of escalation, when the murderer always makes their biggest mistakes."

"What?" I asked, completely taken aback. What did he mean that I had my next target? Who does he think I'm planning on killing?

"Didn't you just tell Officer French that you needed to kill Angela? Your roommate? Because, why? She's an alien?"

"I... I never said we..." Did I say that we needed to kill her? Could he actually be right about something, for once? I said that we needed to get her help, didn't I?

"No," Tom said. "You said we needed to kill her. And we do. There's no help for the infected."

"That, alone, is enough for me to hold you," Bently said. "I just wish I could arrest you. Send you to prison for the rest of your life for the murders you've already gotten away with. Unfortunately, there is quite a different policy in place for people like you."

"What do you mean people like me?" I asked. "People that you can't prove anything against?"

"No," Bently said. His smile was firmly in place, getting broader by the second as he sat staring at his dinner. "People with prior diagnoses of mental instability."

My face went cold as I realized he was right. He really did have me this time. He had me dead to rights. Maybe not the way that he wanted me. I wasn't going to be going to prison anytime soon. But I was stuck nonetheless. I knew it, and he knew it. And it only got worse as I slowly realized what this really meant.

"No," I whispered, barely having enough strength to get the word out. "No, you're not sending me back there."

"I've already spoken with your doctor, this Dr. Mendez fellow. He believes that sending you back to Holy Trinity Psychiatric is the only way to go right now. They already have your old bed prepped and waiting for you. We'll be starting with a seventy-two hour hold, which is quite standard. I wouldn't be surprised if your stay wasn't a little more... open ended, shall we say?"

"But, no," I said. "You can't do that." Though I knew he could. That he would. That he had wanted to do just that ever since Emily's murder fell onto his desk. Still, my mind couldn't wrap itself around it. Around the idea that I would be going back there. Back to that hell hole that I had only just escaped last year, for the umpteenth time. And I would need to do it again. I would need to get out of there. To prove that I was "sane" enough to make it on the outside. Then again, maybe they wouldn't bother. Maybe they'll just lock me up and throw away the key. Wouldn't that be exactly what I deserved?

"Why?" Tom asked. "Why would you deserve that? Why would any of us deserve that? Remember, it's not just you that suffers in there. Dad and I will be muted again, forced to be silent to a world that already doesn't hear us. Doesn't believe that we really exist."

"That's because you don't exist," I thought to them. "You don't exist. You're just voices in my head. My condition forcing its way past the medication."

"And whose fault is that?" Dad asked. "You were the one that stopped taking the medication."

"It was only half dose," I said. "It should have been enough. Why isn't it ever enough." I continued to shake my head. To deny what they were saying. What I already knew was true. I was doomed, and there was nothing anyone could do to stop it.

As if to amplify my hopelessness, Sam, once again, barged into the room. He was out of breath, as if he had run the entire length of the building from the parking lot. His face was beat red and sweat was already finding its way down his face. The officer that had brought me in was standing behind him. The officer's arm restrained Sam, preventing him from entering the room. "She's my client," Sam insisted. "I demand to speak with her immediately."

"Oh, it's quite too late for that, I'm afraid," Bently said. "She'll be heading off to the psych ward shortly. It's just a matter of a little paperwork and having the doctors show up to take her away. There's nothing you can do on this one." His laugh sounded maniacal to me, though I knew that it had to sound completely normal to everyone else. Or, at least, as normal as a laugh could sound when it was about sending someone to the nut house.

Chapter Twenty-Seven
The Missing Cop

"I'm sorry," Greg said. They were the first words I had heard from him since we had arrived at the precinct. I would have yelled at him, for once again disappearing when I really needed my lawyer. But he just sounded so sincere that I couldn't take it out on him. "I got here as soon as I could."

"What do you mean?" I said. I was alone in the waiting room, waiting for my ride back to HTP. With my return trip ticket already punched, I figured there was no point in keeping quiet while talking to the voices that only existed in my head. "Where were you? Why are you the only one that can disappear like that? That can go missing for hours at a time?"

"I don't know why I'm different than those two," he said. "Maybe I'm just a free spirit. Anyway, I was trying to get word to Sam, like I had last time."

"Ugh," I grunted, putting my head in my hands as I tried to slap him out of it. "You're just a voice in my head," I insisted. "You don't actually exist. You can't talk to other people, least of all Sam, who probably hates you as much as I do."

"You mean hate's Greg," Tom corrected, backing me up. "Look, it's not the best of situations, but it's the one we have. It's the one we've lived with for years. Greg, once you come to terms with the fact that you don't actually exist, your life will become a whole lot easier."

"But I won't," Greg insisted. "I'll never stop believing that I'm a real man. That I really exist, as something more than just a voice in a crazy girl's head."

"You do realize that you just contradicted yourself, right?" Tom said. "If you're not just a voice in her head, then neither are the two of us. Which would mean that she's no crazier than you are."

"Well, I'd say she's a great deal less crazy than Greg," Dad said. "He did kill that poor girl and tried to kill Natalie, after all."

"The point is, she can't be crazy if you're anything more than just a voice in her head."

"And, we know she's insane," Dad said. "And have the documentation to prove it. That means you're just a voice, and nothing more. Trust me. I've been here longer than the both of you combined. I've been there for your whole relationship. I know everything, even the stuff that she won't allow herself to remember about you. So, back down, back off, and learn your place."

"Or, what? You're going to beat me too?" Greg asked. "I'd like to see you try, old man."

"Old? I was as old as you were when I died."

"If you three won't shut up, I'll send myself to HTP," I said.

"Oh, honey, it's a little late for that," Dad said, though the three of them quieted down afterwards.

I could see Sam arguing animatedly with the detective. He was flinging his arms around to make himself look bigger. Though with Bently's round belly, there weren't many people bigger than him. Still, that left me there alone, sitting in one of the three chairs with my thoughts, and the voices that always kept me company. The startled face of the man in the alien costume was no longer there as no one had replaced the flier I had destroyed before. It was one less thing driving me insane. One less reminder that Angela was probably infecting her son right then. If she hadn't done so already. Maybe she had been right. Maybe they all had been right, and it really was an alien on that bridge. Maybe the second plane really had been abducted by them. Where else would that infected possum have come from? I wondered if anyone was looking for the thing. How many people it had infected before coming to our backyard? Moreover, how many would be infected before it was stopped? Before it died? And just how bad would the infection get?

The whole eye thing completely freaked me out, but maybe it would just end there. Maybe the infection would be just superficial. Maybe, once I go home, if I go home, Angela will just be worried about what happened to me, but otherwise no different from the beautiful girl that, for some reason, wanted to be with me. That would change, of course, after she found out. After she heard why I'm going back to HTP. Yet, for some messed up reason, I couldn't bring myself to blame Eric for telling on me. For telling Bently, my sworn enemy, that I threatened her life. It was probably just my messed-up mind not letting me be normal, whatever that was.

"Do you think he's avoiding you?" Tom asked.

"I don't think so," I said, pensively. "I mean, we were talking for hours, even after all of that. I'm not even sure why he said anything. Not after the night we were having. But, still, it's a bit rude that he isn't here. That he isn't trying to explain himself to me. Not that I need an explanation. It would just be nice. And it seems like the thing he'd be doing."

"Maybe he's still at the scene," Greg suggested. "He's not exactly the most senior of officers. And if they still need crowd control around wherever the body ended up, he could still be there for hours more."

"Hey," Tom said, annoyed.

"What?"

"'The body'? That's my body. Have a little more respect."

"Respect for a body that you haven't had for three years? That you're no longer physically, or should I say, spiritually, attached to? The thing is worm food, and probably looks nothing like you anymore. I'm almost surprised they were able to identify you at all."

"Do any of you look like anything anymore?" I asked. "You're insubstantial and invisible. You don't have a form. You don't exist outside of my own mind."

"Yeah, keep trying to convince yourself of that," Greg said.

I rolled my eyes at him, not wanting to take the bait. To rise to the same old argument that I had to have with each of them in turn. It was frustrating to no end to have to convince grown ass people that they weren't... well... people. There must have been some weird, twisted part of my subconscious that spawns these guys. Yet I couldn't seem to get it through my own thick skull that they're nothing but figments of my imagination with delusions of grandeur. Of sentience. Of self.

"If we don't really exist outside of you, how can it be that the four of us can have completely different opinions on the same subject?" Greg asked.

"What can I say, I'm of many minds on that subject," I joked.

With a sigh, I got up from the chair. It was only slightly awkward with my wrists cuffed. I wasn't attached to the chair. Not yet anyway. Bently glared at me from across the room. Once he saw that I wasn't going to make a run for it, he went back to his animated discussion with my lawyer. I wanted to run with every fiber of my being, but I didn't think I'd get far. Instead, I simply headed over to the main desk. The uniformed officer sitting there was doing paperwork or whatever it was that the officers did when they weren't helping anyone. Or hurting anyone. Or arresting anyone.

"What do you want?" she asked, without looking up from her desk. She was elevated above me a little, so she could probably see me even as she looked down at the desk.

"Is Eric here?" I asked, wanting to get to the crux of the matter. I just wanted to see him. Wanted to tell him that I had no hard feelings for him turning me in. After all, I understood that it was his job to look after the people of the town. And, at least as far as he was concerned, Angela still counted as people, whether or not she was an alien.

"Who?" she asked. She actually looked up from her desk to stare down at me. A look of confusion found its way to her face. I didn't remember her from before, on any of my many trips to the station. She must have been new if she didn't know who Eric was.

"Eric," I said. "Um... Officer French. Is he here?"

When her look of confusion didn't lift, as her eyes glared down at me, I was starting to worry. Had I just made Eric up? Was my condition getting worse? Had I seen him interact with other people? No, he drove me home the other day, hadn't he? And he was the one that told Bently about what I had said to him about Angela, hadn't he? Or had he? Had Bently ever said where he had gotten the information from?

"Don't be ridiculous," Tom said. "Didn't you just get through telling us off about how this whole thing really works? You imagine you're hearing voices. And we're all just... echoes, I guess, of people you knew before. You've never imagined a whole person up from nothing, have you? You're not that creative."

"How would I know," I thought at him. "How would I know what's real and what's not at this point? I can't even tell if Angela really is an alien? Besides, why would I listen to the voices in my head when they're trying to convince me that I'm sane. I'm not sane. I know I'm not. It's quite obvious to me, from the moment I wake up to the moment I go to sleep."

"Don't listen to her," someone said. My eyes darted in the direction of the voice. The blessed voice that was sure to tell me that I'm not more insane than I already knew I was. I didn't know the man's name, but I had seen him plenty of times around the station. He had never said a word to me before, but he wasn't silent when I really needed the reassurance. "She's new. But, yeah, you're right. Eric was supposed to be back from the site by now. Hey, anyone hear from Eric?" he called around the room.

"Naw, man," someone shouted from the back. "Not since we left the scene. Whose turn was it to babysit the rookie?"

"Hey, he ain't the rookie no more," someone else called out. Their voices seemed to have taken on the normal level of joking that would often be seen around an office. Among people that knew each other well. That which wasn't normally shown to the outside public. I'd almost feel blessed, grateful even, if it weren't for the cuffs around my wrists.

"Anyone been over to his place?" someone suggested. "Maybe he went home to catch some shuteye. I hear he was having a slumber party last night. Maybe he went back to finish that up, if you know what I mean."

"I somehow doubt that," I said.

"And why is that?" the last man asked. "What do you know?"

"I was the one he was having that 'slumber party' with," I admitted. A chorus of cat calls went up throughout the station.

"Wait, ain't you that crazy cat lady?" the second person asked.

"No cats that I know of," I said.

"Will you all settle down," Bently ordered. "And stop interacting with the 5150."

They all just turned to stare at me for a moment after that comment. I put my hands up in surrender, still cuffed together, and waved them around a little. "I never said anything about the crazy part. But, still, no cats. Promise."

"What are you people talking about?" Sam asked.

"Eric French," I said. "My friend, or, well, I thought he was my friend. He's the guy that tends to drive me home after this asshole pulls me in here for another one of his paranoid theories." I tried to point offensively at Bently, but it looked a lot more awkward than I intended with my hands cuffed. "Isn't he the guy that's been calling you to tell you I'm here? I never exactly get a chance to call anyone these last few times before you show up."

"What? No, I um..." Sam looked over my right shoulder, as if seeing something back there. When I looked behind me, there wasn't anything there but the same bulletin board I was sitting against before. An echo to the one that had been staring at me. The posting about the fake alien was prominent on that one, glaring at me with his hate filled eyes from his place on the bridge support. "I just get a sense that you need me here so I come. You're here often enough that it's never been a problem." He laughed a few times, but there was an odd look in his eye that I couldn't quite put my finger on.

"Okay," I said, drawing out the word in my confusion. And they call me the crazy one. "Anyway, he was the guy I was staying with last night."

"Wait, the officer that indicated you for the psych hold?" Sam asked.

"Yeah," I said.

"And he's missing?" he asked Bently.

"I wouldn't say missing," Bently said. "I just saw him a couple hours ago at the scene."

"But no one has seen him since?"

"Well, no, but--"

"Did he actually sign an affidavit?"

"Well, no, but--" Bently said again.

"But nothing. If you can't present the officer, then you have nothing to hold my client on," Sam insisted.

"No," Bently said. He stood up. His hands slammed angrily on the desk. I could see the strain on his arms when he used them as added leverage to get himself out of the seat. "We have Officer French's statement."

"But not a sworn, documented statement. That makes it hearsay and not admissible in court."

"This isn't going to a court," Bently insisted. "We have it on our authority--"

"No," Sam said, interrupting him again. "You have no authority when it comes to my client. If you hold her, I'll have an injunction shoved so far up your ass you'll be sneezing it for months. You have absolutely no standing when it comes to my client at all. Not after I filed these this morning." Sam reached into the briefcase that he always carried around with him. His shield against the injustices of the world around him. He pulled out a manila envelope and slapped it against the detective's chest with a level of authority and force that pushed his fat ass back into the overworked chair that he had only just left. The chair groaned under his weight, even starting to whine from where the metal was giving way.

"What's this?" Bently asked, at a loss for anything else to say.

"You've been served. Now will someone please get those cuffs off my client?"

I swear, Sam couldn't look any more like a knight in shining armor if he had ridden in there on a horse. He was in his element, and I was starting to wonder why he had never gone into criminal law. He seemed to have a knack for it. But, then again, I was innocent of most of the items that the detective was trying to put against me. I was, in fact, crazy, and might very well be a threat to Angela. At least, if she turned out to really be an alien. But the rest of it. The three, now four, deaths that he wanted to make into murders. That was completely ridiculous.

"Now, hold on a moment here," Bently said. He was finally regaining his composure as Sam ran out of steam. "We don't know anything about the location of Officer French. He might be caught in traffic. Or he headed home to change or shower. He had been called in unexpectedly last night and has a shift today. I'm not about to release a suspect who I think is a danger to others just because the reporting officer is late to his shift. He could be here five minutes from now. And, by the time we relocate Ms. Jennings, here," he always sounded so formal when he said my name like that, "she could have already killed someone. That would be on us, as we were well informed of it beforehand. If, as you say, you can file an injunction with the courts, on whatever grounds you find, then it would be on whichever judge signs it. But, I cannot, in good conscience, release the suspect just on your say so."

"Fine," Sam said. "But she's not to be moved from this station until I can get back here with that court order."

"Or we find Officer French and get him on the record," Bently said.

The two of them stood there, staring each other down for the longest time, as if waiting for one of them to blink. To show any sign of weakness in their stances. Neither moved, neither backed down. But, after a minute of waiting, I cleared my throat. "Maybe you could actually file that motion?" I suggested. "And call his house to see if he's there? I really am worried about him. He doesn't seem the type to just disappear like this."

"He's not," one of the officers said, nodding in agreement. "This really is not like him at all."

"Well, then, maybe there's a reason why he's missing," Bently said. His eyes bored into mine. I decided to return to the waiting room until my fate was decided before Bently could accuse me of doing something to poor Eric. My having been at the station the entire time wouldn't be enough of an alibi for Bently.

Chapter Twenty-Eight
Discovery

I sat in the police station for a few hours while Sam got the injunction. The entire time, I watched as the officers scrambled around, looking for Eric. Oddly enough, I was more worried about Eric being alright than me going back to HTP. I've spent enough time there to know how best to spend the time. On a few rare occasions, it felt like I'm more at home in those tired grey corridors than I am when I'm actually home. However, those were limited to when Greg and I were fighting.

Still, I was thrilled when Sam came back, signed documents in hand and a big smile on his face. The smile might have had more to do with the fact that Jessica was walking beside him. "Ready to go?" Sam asked, when he got to me.

"Absolutely," I said. I jumped out of my chair. My hands were still cuffed together, so Sam and I walked back over to the woman behind the desk. It was the same new recruit that didn't know who Eric was.

"Signed, sealed, and delivered," Sam said. He slid the documents across the desk to her.

The officer was on the phone at the moment. She held up her finger, asking for a moment as she finished up her phone call. I looked towards the back of the room, back over to Bently, who was looking his usual dour self. It was the way he always looked whenever he was forced to let me go. It was like he thought of me as his own little play toy and wanted to throw a tantrum whenever he had to put me away. He, too, was on the phone, calling around to all the local hospitals for the fifth time. An officer had been dispatched to Eric's house, and would be posted there to wait for his hopefully eventual return. It was starting to feel like Eric had fallen off the face of the Earth.

"You don't think..." Tom started.

"Oh, not that again," Greg said, annoyed, when he broke off in the middle of his thought.

"Use your words, Tom," I thought to him.

"I was just thinking. I mean, you don't think that this has to do with the aliens, again, do you?"

"No," I thought, quickly. "Absolutely not. Sometimes, a missing person is just a missing person." I didn't want to think of him lying in a ditch somewhere, probably dying after his car was driven off the road or something. But I had to admit, it was the more likely possibility than that he was abducted by aliens. Besides, if he was in a ditch somewhere, we'd at least be able to find him, even if it was too late to help. If he's up on the mothership, we'd never know what happened to him.

"Who said anything about a mothership?" Tom asked.

"They're aliens," I thought. "Don't all aliens have a mothership?"

"Why is it never a fathership?" Dad asked.

"Because fathers don't give birth to babies," Tom said. "Babyships come out of the mothership. Fatherships would be like big ships that the mother can't carry herself but were never designed to carry other ships, or even fighters, with it."

"So, the support ships," Dad said. "I can get behind that. There's probably plenty of fatherships up there."

"God, will you guys stop with the alien talk?" I thought at them. "If there were ships up there, we'd know about them. They'd show up on radar or satellite or telescopes somewhere."

"Space is big," Tom said, as if that answered everything. "Besides, maybe they can cloak them."

"Oh, please, that's ridiculous. You can't turn something that big invisible."

"Not invisible," Tom said. "Just hard to see. It's more a matter of projecting a visual that would make it hidden against the background. It's more like active camouflage. Like what those lizards do."

I would have tried to come up with a good way to disparage his theory, but Bently had just finished his call and was making his slow way across to us. Just as he showed up, the officer behind the desk hung up her phone as well. She picked up the papers that Sam had placed on the desk, as if she knew what she was actually looking at. Before she could read more than a few words of it, Bently snatched them out of her hands.

"That was quick," he said. The words came out thick, heavy, as if the court order was for his own execution, rather than my release.

"Like I said," Sam said. "It was quite easy. The judges were falling over each other to get the opportunity to sign it first." I very much doubted the truth of that statement, but I wasn't in a place to verbalize it.

"Uh huh," Bently said. He sounded similarly disbelieving. "Let it be on your head when she kills Angela, then." Reluctantly, he fished around in his way too tight pants until he was able to find the key to the cuffs. It only took him a few seconds to unlock them. It felt like he twisted them as they came undone. Despite the cuffs not being that tight to begin with, the blood rushed back to my hands all at once, and a throbbing started to flow through them. "If I were you, I'd still bring her back to the nuthouse, just to be on the safe side."

"Thanks for your advice," Sam said. "I will definitely not be following it."

"Suit yourself," he huffed as he headed back to his desk. As I watched him go, I wondered if they would continue pulling up all the stops to find Eric. Now that my impending commitment was no longer an issue, I just wanted to know that he was alright, even if he had turned me in.

"Now, then," Sam said, making me cringe. "Ready to go?"

"Absolutely," I said. He nodded as we started to head back down the hallway. A hallway that I didn't think I would be heading down again. At least not while free.

"Jessica will be taking over your case," Sam said, once we exited the building. I had been inside for so long that I had figured it would have been dark outside already. Instead, the sun was only just past its zenith, heading off towards the south west.

"Wait, what?" I asked. "I thought you--"

"I'll be handling the lawsuit," he said, correcting himself. "It's becoming increasingly apparent that you need a criminal lawyer as well. That's where Jessica is going to be coming in."

"Oh, okay," I said. I smiled, nodding in her direction, with a question in my eyes. She was leading the way to a lone, unfamiliar car in the guest parking lot. He just smiled and nodded back, answering my unasked question that they were back together. I liked that thought. They had seemed happy together those few times that I had seen them as a couple. It was a little sunshine in my otherwise dreary day.

"What about the actual sun over our heads?" Tom asked, being literal as always.

Jessica came up short next to the car, heading towards the driver's seat. She fumbled with the dongle on her keys until the locks clicked open. She pulled her door open before Sam could think to. Reaching inside, she pulled out a small object that fit nicely in the palm of her hand. "Here," she said, placing it in my hand before I realized she had taken it. "It's a cell phone. My number is already programmed in. The next time you're arrested, or pulled in for questioning, or even looked at in the wrong way by a cop, call me."

"God, thanks, you guys," I gushed. "I don't know how I'm ever going to repay you. Or, you know, actually pay you. I'm not exactly working right now."

"Don't worry about it," Sam said. "The firm takes care of its own. Besides, this can all be grouped in with the expenses for the lawsuit, which we're doing on speculation. So as soon as we win that--"

"Or settle," Jessica added. "With the cops, they're more likely to settle, once it's clear just how much Bently had stepped over the line."

"Right," Sam said. "Once the case is settled, we'll be paid."

"And, as for working, I've talked it over with Sarah, and, we think that, once the lawsuit is settled, you should be able to start back at the firm," Jessica said. "We'll start putting the paperwork together so that you can start up on the very next day, so we don't have to wait for processing and all that."

"Really?" I asked. "Wow, that would be amazing. Thanks. Thanks so much. You have no idea what this means to me."

"Oh, I think we have an idea," Sam said, a smile starting to spread across his face.

"Now, where are we dropping you?" Jessica asked. "Back at the cop's house? Did you leave your car over there?"

"Um, no, I think that Angela still has my car. I walked over to Eric's. You should probably just drop me off at home."

Jessica and Sam exchanged a knowing look before turning back to me, sighing deeply. "Is that really a good idea?" Jessica asked.

"What do you mean?"

"She means... well, you're not really going to kill Angela, are you?"

"What? Of course not," I insisted.

"Seriously, we wouldn't really blame you if you did," Jessica said. "She can be a bit of a bitch sometimes."

"Hey," I said, protectively. "Honestly, I think Eric was right. All I really needed was a little time and distance from her. I don't know what it was that I saw, but it couldn't have been what I was thinking it was. She's not an alien, she's my friend."

"Your friend who just happens to be an alien," Tom said.

"Alright," Sam said. "But if you go and kill her, we're going to have to drop the suit, rescind our offer of employment, and start billing you for our time." He sounded like he was trying to make it into a joke, but the look on his face made it very clear that he was being dead serious. I just hoped that it wouldn't come to that. That there really was no need to kill Angela.

"We'll see," Tom said, menacingly. "I resent the assertion that I sound menacing."

"No, you really did sound menacing," Dad said.

"Thank you," I thought to him, as I climbed into the back seat of the car.

Sam and Jessica started talking over some of the finer parts of the case as Jessica drove me back to the house. I wanted to pay attention to them, but it felt so weird, them discussing strategy about my own case. It was completely different from the cases I had worked on in the past, because I had my own personal stake in it. It was like why doctors don't treat themselves, or family members, or whatever. They just couldn't get out of their own way to get to the heart of the matter. So, instead, I watched the town fly by outside the window as we took the familiar path away from the station. Only, instead of turning down Main towards the apartment, we kept going up to the house.

In what felt like no time at all, I was staring up at the house, lost in my own sense of dread. It was quite separate from Tom's, because mine was centered around the woman. Around Angela. Around what we had been trying to build the night before. The blossoming relationship that we were trying to see if it would go somewhere. The windows were dark as they reflected the day around me. They seemed like a metaphor for whatever it was that had taken over her.

I wasn't even sure that I still wanted to see if anything was there. The relationship was somehow tainted, on both sides. Her for seeming like she was infected by an alien disease. Me for running off on her when she needed me the most. Maybe I should have stayed. Should have tried to help her overcome whatever it was.

"But, then again, maybe you running was the only thing that saved us," Tom said.

"You alright?" Sam asked, when I didn't immediately leave the car.

"I'm fine," I said, shaking myself. Before heading off into the aging afternoon, I looked around the back seat for a little bit, making sure I hadn't left anything behind. This was despite the fact that I had left the restaurant the night before with nothing but my purse. That was safely clutched in my hands, along with the new cell phone. "Call me if anything comes up in my case, will you?" I asked.

"Sure," Sam and Jessica said together. I just nodded to them before closing the back door behind me.

I took my time heading up the sidewalk, procrastinating more than I had when I had come that day that I was moving back in. Back then, all that the house held were the old memories, the ones that I had tried to run away from. Now, though, no matter how much I tried to convince myself otherwise, there was something that might be a very real threat within. Whether that threat was to my heart or my mind I wasn't sure. Both were easy targets.

The front door squeaked ominously as I opened it. My eyes darted around the front hall and over towards the playroom. Doug was sitting there, alone, in a little playpen in the corner. He looked up at me. His eyes seemed normal, the usual blue that he had inherited from both parents. As usual, they looked towards me inquisitively, showing no obvious signs of alienness. Perhaps I wasn't the best judge of those things.

My hand stayed firmly on the door handle. The door was still open, letting in the late fall air. The heat ticked on, making me jump in place in startlement. But nothing jumped out at me. A shiver ran up my spine as my eyes scanned the hallway, looking for Angela. Looking for the alien that had taken over my friend. Looking for the love that was only just blooming between us. They found nothing but the norm, the usual odds and ends that cluttered the room. Reluctantly, I turned towards the door, closing it behind me as to not let the heat out. As bad as Dad had been at controlling his temper, he had taught me not to waste the heat to the outside world.

"Well, at least I did one thing right," Dad said.

"Natalie?" came a voice from the top of the stairs. Every hair on my body seemed to stand up on end, yet my heart ached for the woman that spoke. Anxiety filled me like never before, the stark contrast between my body's desire to run and my mind's desire to stay. Or was that the other way around? "Is that you?" Angela asked.

Slowly, I turned back around. I looked towards the stairs, towards the voice that haunted my every waking thought. I was relieved to hear that it sounded normal, back to her usual soprano, rather than the guttural, demonic voice that I had heard at the restaurant. When I finally turned around to the stairs, they were still empty, though I could hear her footsteps, heavy through the carpeting that covered them.

Angela turned around at the landing, coming into view all in one go. She was stunning, ten times more beautiful than she had been the night before, for our date. Her hair flitted down, carried on the very air that flowed around her, singing her name. Though she wasn't wearing much makeup, her face seemed radiant. Far more beautiful than any supermodel that had ever lived. She was wearing a skin tight, strapless dress. Her nipples showed through the fabric as it clung to every inch of her. It only came down to just below her bum, leaving her long legs exposed to my eyes. They seemed to glow in the light coming through the windows behind her, as if she were descending from heaven itself. Although, the look in her eyes, and the body itself, seemed designed to promise nothing but lust. A hellish temptress dedicated to pulling me down to the depths of the fiery pit from which she came. Her shoes, fire red strappy sandals, were perfectly designed to show off those curves, and little else.

My eyes drank in the sight of her as my body yearned for me to move forward. To succumb to her arms, her body, her folds within. To the lust that they promised dwelled there. Yet, the fear lingered, keeping my feet securely planted where they were. The hardwood floors like tar beneath them. My hand stayed where it was on the door handle, squeezing the life out of it. As if the feel of the metal on them could release me from her spell. Neither had much resistance left in them in light of that beauty, that glory that stood before me. I was lost before I ever stood a chance against her.

"Hello, Honey," Angela said. She moved gracefully down the stairs. Not so much as a strand of her hair moved in a way that wasn't seductive, wasn't irresistibly gorgeous. She came over to me, lightly kissing me on the lips. Hers tasted like strawberries and promises that she would stay with me forever, if I would only just ask. "I was wondering when you'd be home."

"She's acting weird," Dad said. This seemed weird to me. Almost startlingly weird. He would normally be the one yelling at me to jump her bones. "Well, I still think you should, I just think she's acting weird."

"Kill her," Tom said. "Kill her now before she can infect us."

"Us?" I thought to him, trying to clear my mind enough to think.

"What makes you think she hasn't already infected us?" Greg asked. "What do you think that kiss was about?"

"She was just welcoming us--me home after being gone for so long," I thought.

"That's what she wants you to think," Tom whispered, as if Angela were capable of hearing him, now that she was... whatever it was that she had become. But, seeing her there, standing in front of me, her hands playing with my clothes, I had a hard time thinking that it was a bad thing. "Yeah, you're having a hard time thinking at all," Tom accused. He wasn't wrong.

"Is everything alright?" Angela asked. Her eyes looked into mine, searching them for an answer to her question. I looked right back into hers, looking for that circle of darkness around her iris, but finding none. If anything, they seemed to glow, to radiate light out from within, much like the light from the window behind her caressed her body.

"Fine," I said. My voice sounded two octaves higher than usual. I cleared my throat and tried again. "I'm fine."

"Good," she said, smiling at me. "We never did get to finish that date. What happened to you? I was so worried when you ran out like that."

"I'm... it... it was nothing. I just had... an episode, I guess."

"She's an alien," Tom insisted. "Just because she's looking heavenly doesn't make her an angel."

"She smells heavenly, too," I thought to him, barely getting the thought through my fogged mind. "I'm better now," I promised her.

"Good," she purred. Her lips extended towards mine, offering me a drink that I was powerless to resist.

"Oh, no you don't," Tom insisted. I could feel him resisting, pulling at me with his thoughts. But he was still insubstantial. Still powerless to affect the real world. He was still only in my mind.

My lips found hers and I lost all control. My hands pulled her into me, pressing her body against mine. She was everywhere, yet it wasn't enough. I wanted to be with her. Be in her. Be a part of her. Be one with her like never before. It was completely different from how it was with Greg. Completely different from anything I had ever experienced. I couldn't stop myself even if I wanted to.

Her dress was on the floor before I even realized I had pulled it off of her. Despite the shortness of the dress, the revealing nature of it, or perhaps because of it, she wasn't wearing anything underneath it. There was suddenly nothing to get between my roaming hands and her amazing body. There was no sign of any injury, no sign of any imperfections as my hands hungrily explored every inch of her.

I stepped out of my shoes as I pushed her backwards, against the stairs. Hungrily, she pulled at my own dress, pulling it over my head and interrupting our connection. It only took a second, but it was an eternity of agony to be apart from her. My bra broke as I tore it off of me, throwing it behind me to the door. Angela pulled my underwear off with her teeth, her tongue immediately exploring the area within.

I lost all control. All restraint. All knowledge of time and the world around us as we made love right there. On the carpeting that was only there because of our ex-husband's insistence. In front of his spawn in the other room. His voice constantly whispering in my ear, directing my hands and mouth to where she was most sensitive, most enjoyed the touch of another. It was amazing, glorious, astounding, and, yet, it ended far too soon.

It was dark outside when we finally came up for air. When my head finally cleared of the fog of her, of the lust she instilled in me. She lay there next to me, on the hardwood floors, soiled by our lovemaking. Her arm was under my head, no better pillow could I have found in all the world. The smell of sex was in the air, and it was almost as intoxicating as she was. I wanted to go in for more, wanted nothing more than to make love to her for all of eternity. But I was out of breath, my hands and arms numb from exertion. I never knew it could be like that, it could be so endless, so passionate, in the arms of another woman.

"That was amazing," I managed to get out between pants.

"Seriously," Dad agreed. "Better than porn." I ignored him, ignored his attempt to take this from me as well. He had already taken my sanity when I was sixteen. He couldn't take this from me, too. Then again, he didn't have to. Angela did it for him.

"So much better than that stupid cop, then?" she asked.

My face went cold. My lust for her immediately evaporated. My gut felt like it was kicked by a horse. "What did you say?" I asked.

"Oh, don't give me that," she said. "I saw you with him last night." She hadn't moved from her place beside me, her arm still under me, as she spoke about my missing friend so casually. My mind raced ahead, further and faster than Tom's ever had. Far past the point of no return. No amounts of denials on my part could ever erase my suspicions of her.

I sat up, sliding along the floor so that my back was up against the wall. Still, she didn't move. She almost seemed like she couldn't move, so comfortable, so blissfully complete as she was lying there. She must have felt it too. That same connection that I had only lost moments ago. Yet her smile was the same one that I had seen on the detective's face all too many times.

"What are you talking about?" I asked, trying to deny what I already knew was true.

"I'm talking about that stupid, silly man you went to last night, when you ran away from me at the restaurant." Only then did she sit up, using the railing on the stairs for support as she spun around to look at me. She leaned against the railing, her head rocking back and forth a little, almost playfully, as her smile deepened. "I know why you went to him. Why you slept with him. You couldn't handle it. How my very presence affects you. You weren't ready. But you are now. We can be together now. Forever. No one would need to know, if that's what you're afraid of, though no one would really care. This is New York, not Texas. We love each other and that's all that matters, right?"

"What did you do?" I asked. My voice barely registered in my own ears, yet she seemed to have no trouble hearing me.

"You know what I did," she said, almost teasingly. "He was an obstacle between us, so I got rid of him."

"What?" I asked. Even confronted with the evidence, with the straight admission of guilt that only confirmed my worst fears, I couldn't wrap my head around it. I couldn't believe that it was true. That she would be capable of that. Of killing my friend. Of killing a cop.

"See?" Tom said. "I told you she was an alien."

Chapter Twenty-Nine
The Failed Attack

"You did what?" I asked.

"I told you she was an alien," Tom repeated. "I did tell her she was an alien, right?"

"Oh, yes, several times," Greg said. I could practically hear his eyes rolling in the tone of his voice.

"No, not you," I said. "Her." I pointed accusatorily at Angela.

Angela looked behind herself, confused. "Who are you talking to?" she asked.

"God, I'm talking to you," I said. "Angela, what the hell did you do to Eric?"

"Eric?" she sneered. "That was his name?"

"Was?"

"Yes, was. I dumped his body where no one will ever find him. No one, that is, except for me, of course. I had to prepare the place first, though. Someone had put a dead body there already."

"What?" I asked, completely confused.

"Is she talking about me?" Tom asked.

"Well, not someone, I guess, since I know it was Greg. He even told me about it one night. He thought that secrets would keep the two of us close." She let out a deep, long, laugh at that thought. "Of course, that goes out the window when you keep secrets from that other person."

"Sorry, dude," Greg mumbled to Tom.

"What?" I asked everyone, and no one. "But, why? How? He wasn't even there that day." Had Tom really jumped or was this all some elaborate plan on Greg's side? A way to control me more than he already had? A way to take the only thing I had left that wasn't him away from me? Why am I always falling for manipulative people?

"He didn't have to trick me," Tom said. "I jumped all on my own."

"I had actually come by to surprise you," Greg said. "Then I saw what happened, and, well... I didn't want you to get in trouble for being up on that roof alone with a student. So, I moved the body. I moved it to the woods where no one would ever find it. And no one had until now. I didn't know it would drive you more nuts than you already were."

"Gah," I shouted, clenching my head in my hand. "When will you people get it through your thick skulls. You're not the people you think you are. You're not real."

"What?" Angela asked. "I assure you, I'm quite real. What we just did, that didn't seem real to you?"

"What?" I asked. She moved to stand up, to come closer to me. I flinched away, seeing her for the monster that she had become. She regained her feet. Her full, stark naked body radiant in the light of the moon that came in through the bay window behind her. Distracted as we were in our love making, neither of us thought to turn on the lights. But, unlike in the sunlight earlier, she didn't look like an angel. Instead, she looked like a vampire. A seductress that was only after one thing.

"Natalie, we love each other. I wasn't about to let some man get between us."

"Love?" I asked, astonished that she would use the word. "We barely know each other. How can we possibly be in love with each other?" It was lust, wasn't it? Plain and simple. The same thing that had gotten Greg in trouble had claimed another victim. This time, though, it took down a sweet and innocent cop in the process. "Maybe it could have become more," I allowed. "Maybe. But not after this. Not after what you've done. You're a murderer, just like Greg. I guess that's appropriate, seeing as how you married him."

"You married him, too," she accused.

"Yes," I agreed. "And I've had to suffer for that for years already. Besides, it's not like my hands are all that clean, either." I could still feel Greg's blood oozing down my hands, even weeks after I had killed him.

"No," she said, she denied. "No, you will love me. I'll make you love me."

"Oh, god, this is it," Tom said. "She's going to try to infect us. We need to kill her, now, before she can get it done. She's probably already infected the baby, already knows how to do it. Greg, got any pointers on how to kill an unarmed, naked woman?"

"Hey, leave me out of this," Greg said. "I only killed the one woman, and that was out of blind rage. Plus, she wasn't naked. And... also... I regretted it immediately. Why do you think I called Natalie, trying to pin it on her?"

"Wait, you did what?" I asked.

"Oh," Angela said, pulling my attention back to her. "You're talking to them. Those stupid voices in your head. The ones that have been driving you crazy for years. No wonder why you're so confused. Why you think that you don't love me. Maybe there's something I can do about that. Something I can do to rid you of those interlopers once and for all."

"I almost want to take you up on that offer, really," I said. "But I don't want to be an alien. Or an infected human. Or whatever it is that you are now." Slowly, I stood up, getting my feet solidly under me. Keeping my eyes locked on hers, keeping her distracted, my hand reached out behind me. It blindly searched for a weapon in the playroom around the corner. It didn't help that she had already baby-proofed the room ages ago. But I knew that there was still a lamp somewhere over there. It would have to be enough of a weapon, especially since she was still naked and alone.

"What are you even talking about?" Angela asked, oblivious to my roaming hand. "I'm not an alien." She laughed, as if that thought were completely preposterous. "Is that what this is? Why you think you don't love me? Why you're so confused by my actions? You think I'm some kind of alien? Like I've been replaced by a clone or something?"

"No," I said. "I know you were infected by that animal that attacked us. You haven't been the same since that day. It was slow at first. I almost missed it. And it helped that I didn't know you that well. Not well enough to see the subtle changes until it was already too late to stop it. That's why I ran from you in the restaurant. I saw you change. You're not human anymore, and you need to be stopped before you can infect anyone else. There's just one thing I need to know before I kill you."

"Kill me?" she asked, laughing it off. "Fine, whatever. What do you want to know?"

"Did you infect Doug?" I asked.

"What?" she asked. She was completely surprised by the accusation. "No, of course not."

"So, you admit that you could have?" I asked.

"No," she said. "Even if it were possible for me to infect someone else, I would never do that to my son."

"Good," I said, right before throwing the lamp at her.

She ducked, quicker than she should have been able to. I watched as her arm came up in front of her. At first, it was angled to block the projectile. But then she caught it, in midair, when it was still a foot away from her. She clutched it, clung to it precariously, as she stared at it. She seemed as surprised as I was. A few seconds later, barely five heartbeats, the lamp shattered in her hand. Glass shards rained down onto her bare legs and feet. Where the glass hit, instead of digging in, instead of shedding the red blood that I had been expecting, they merely bounced off, cascading down to the floor below.

"Now, why did you go and do a thing like that?" Angela asked. She didn't seem the least bit affected by my having thrown a lamp at her. "I liked that lamp." She looked behind her, to the lamp's twin in the other room, as if to assure herself that I wouldn't be able to get to that one as well.

My eyes went wide. Wider than I knew my eyes could go. Wider than my head should have been able to contain. I stared at this woman, this goddess before me, showing physical prowess far beyond what any human should have been capable of. I knew that I had to do something. But I was naked and alone, cornered by her in the home that was no longer my own. It was hers, and I had somehow trapped myself within her web. If I got too close, she was likely to bite my head off. Quite literally.

"I told you she was an alien," Tom said, again, as if that statement were any help at all. "We need to kill her."

"What do you think I was already trying to do?" I yelled at him. "I'm open to suggestions."

"I have a suggestion," Angela said. "Perhaps you should stop engaging in the conversation with them. Maybe, if you just ignore them, they'll go away."

"They're voices inside my head, not annoying little children that are teasing me," I snapped at her, forgetting for a moment that I should have been attacking her physically, rather than verbally. "You're not helping, any of you. I've had to deal with these voices for over half my life. I know what will or won't work."

"Fine," she said, raising her hands in submission. Her smile creeped back on her face as I spoke to her like I normally did. As if everything was suddenly alright between us. As if she weren't still an alien, hellbent on global domination.

"Wait, who said anything about dominating the world?" Tom asked. "This isn't about stopping them from taking over the world. This is about stopping them from taking over our bodies. Angela is gone. You're just looking at her husk. Her body with an alien poured into it."

"You have to admit it's an exceptional body," Dad said, ogling her in the moonlight. And, I did have to admit it. She looked glorious. But, the look on her face, the cunning I could see beneath her eyes, and the very real fact that she had already killed my friend kept me from her arms. I couldn't let myself get roped into her trap. Not again. Not now that I know what she did. What she would probably do to me once she was finished with me.

"That's the spirit," Tom cheered. "Kill her."

"How?" Dad asked, on my side for once. "Did you see her catch that lamp? This isn't going to be like Greg or me. She's going to be the hardest kill that Natalie has ever had to do."

"Hey, leave me out of this," Greg called out. His voice was calm, remote, and quiet, as if coming from another room. He didn't seem the least bit interested in the fact that, if I didn't handle things exactly right, I might very well die at the hands of the person whom I had just slept with. A shudder ran down my spine as I was reminded of that fact. My eyes darted to our pile of clothes, littered together at the base of the stairs. If I hadn't known that she was only wearing that one dress, the one that was still on the bottom of the pile, I would have had to wonder which was whose in the gathered assortment.

"Natalie?" Angela asked, hesitantly, drawing my attention back to her body. "Are you alright? Are you done trying to kill me now?"

I didn't know what to say to that. How to approach the whole thing. That night had not gone the way I had expected at all. If I had had my clothes on, I would have made a run for it. Fled from the house without a second look back. At most, I would have come back for my car, at some point when I knew she wouldn't be there. Maybe I'd stay at Sam's. Or even

Eric's, now that I knew he wouldn't be needing it. Heck, I'd almost settle for going back to HTP, rather than sleep in the same house as a murdering alien. But my clothes were closer to where she was standing than where I was. I wasn't about to take one step closer to her.

"You killed Eric," I said, trying to make the words sound like an accusation. They just came out hopeless, drained of all strength, as the loss hit me. It wasn't like with Greg or Dad, when their deaths had been accompanied by so much more relief that they were gone. It wasn't even like with Tom, who I barely knew at the time, other than that he was a quiet student in one of my classes. Eric was the first person that I had actually cared about that was now, suddenly, dead. Yet, for some reason, I couldn't conjure his voice like I had somehow done with the other three.

"You say that like it's a bad thing," Dad said. "Wasn't it so much better in here when it was just the two of us?"

"It was better when I was alone," I thought, miserably. I tried to remember when that was, back in my innocent youth, before the blood stains started to accumulate. I felt Eric's blood there, too, though I hadn't been the one to drive home the knife.

"You killed Eric," I repeated, as if the repetition could make it any easier to believe. Easier to bear.

"Yes," Angela said, softly, almost apologetically. "He was in my way."

"He wasn't," I said. I shook my head, denying the words much easier than I could the deed.

"He had you. I wanted you. Thus, he was in my way."

"He didn't have me, though," I said, tears finding their way down my cheek. "I... he was my friend."

"I saw you two together," she said. Anger filled her voice. Rage filled her eyes. "I watched as he put his hands all over you. His shirt was already off, as if he was expecting you. Expecting you to come over on the night of our first date. I'd say he was being a bit presumptuous but, then again, you did go to him. You ran from me. Fled straight into his waiting arms. I'll bet he had been planning this whole thing for weeks, even so far back as when he first arrested you."

I tried to think back to that first time Eric had brought me into the station. It had been weeks ago, a month maybe. Before I had been forced to kill Greg. Before I even knew what really happened to Emily. Back when the case first came across the detective's desk, finding me standing over the body. Eric had brought me into the station for questioning, at Bently's request no less. How could he have possibly been planning to seduce me back then, when he barely knew me? Was that even what he did? What exactly had happened between the two of us? Were we just friends? Had a simple flirtation turned into something more? It reminded me of how I got together with Greg, of all things. It seemed so innocent in comparison. At least I was pretty sure that Eric wasn't a psychopathic killer.

"Oh, like you knew that I would kill someone on the day we first met," Greg called out to me from the other room.

"Eric isn't like that," I protested. "He wasn't like that." My voice cracked as I forced myself to start talking about him in the past tense. He was dead. For some reason, I couldn't seem to wrap my head around that thought. Not without a body in front of me or his voice in my head. "He wasn't trying to manipulate me, like you obviously are. He was sweet and innocent and kind and he didn't deserve you killing him."

"We're all killers here, my love," she purred, as if she thought the idea sexy or something. "You have blood on your hands just the same as mine." She held her hands out to her side, as if to demonstrate. It only drew attention to the fact that her perfect, blemish free skin was exposed for all to see. "Now we have that much more in common. And he was no more innocent that I am. Or Greg. Or all the other people that you've killed over the years."

"I may have killed people, but I'm no murderer. Not like you. The thing of it is that he was on your side. He wanted me to come back to you. To apologize for running off like that. To see you how you really were, not just how I had seen you in a moment of panic. Well, I certainly see you now. How can you possibly think I could ever love anyone like you?"

That was obviously the wrong thing to say. Her eyes flared, though in the normal, human way. Anger gripped her face as it scrunched up in a mask of rage. It looked like steam was about to pour out of her ears. "You do love me," she insisted. As if anything else were too hard for her to understand, to believe. As if she were the most loveable person in the world, rather than the monster that she had become. "And you will love me, now and forever."

"I don't," I said, shaking my head as I rested it back against the wall in defeat. "I can't."

"Then I'll make you love me," she said.

She stalked forward, crossing the three steps between us faster than I could blink. Expecting her to hit me, to kill me like she had killed Eric, my hands went up reflexively, blocking her advance. She swatted my hands away as if they were paper. I thought I had heard a crack come from them. I had not time to think, to see, to even feel it, before she was on me. A stalking vulture descending on a fresh kill. Only, instead of hitting me, she leaned into me. She pressed her lips to mine.

It was weird, so much more forceful, more emphatic than I had ever been kissed before. And it wasn't just her lips on mine that was weird. Her arms, cradling me to her. Her hands playing with my hair. It all seemed so alien, as if there was nothing left of the girl that I thought I knew. That I had cared for. She may as well have grown an insectoid carapace over her skin, her flesh oozing an unknown slime like in the horror movies.

I tried to stifle the urge to scream as her tongue found its way into my mouth. An experience that I had enjoyed less than half an hour ago felt like an attack. An assault on the very heart of me. All I wanted to do was run. To get away.

But her grip on me was too strong for me to break. And not just the physical one. I could almost feel the bruises forming. All I could think of was my mother, crumpled in a ball, her hand up defensively before her. And my father stalking forward, about to kill her. Only, this time, there was no kitchen knife. I was facing my attacker, rather than standing behind him. My scream escaped before I could stop it.

Angela backed away immediately. She turned her back on me as she looked behind her. It was as if she expected some cavalry to have arrived, ready to save me from her assault. That was it, my opportunity to take her out. Perhaps the only one I was going to get. I didn't hesitate. Just as I hadn't when it was my father I needed to kill. Just like I hadn't when it was Greg I needed to kill. Now I needed to kill Angela. The third person I had loved whose love was poison. Deadly to me. My health. My sanity. But I was still stuck, huddled on the floor, pinned against the wall, naked and alone. I did the only thing I could think of.

I balled up my fist, putting all the strength I could behind it, and swung forward. While it was still flying her way, Angela turned back towards me. It was just as quickly as she had dodged and grabbed the lamp. Far too quickly for my slow fist, for my human reflexes to accommodate. She saw the fist flying her way. Helplessly slow. Hopelessly outmatched by her alienness. Instead of blocking it, though, as with the lamp, her first reflex was to dodge. The voice of my father had taught me how to throw a proper punch, after the man was no longer around to protect me from the likes of himself. I already had my full weight behind my fist, planning on following through with it. Right through her face, the target of my assault.

So, I was already completely off balance as my fist flew past her, completely wide of the target. It wouldn't have even taken the entirety of her alien strength to disrupt my flow, to push me away from her and out of reach of her. But, as my fist flew, my back coming up off the wall, she did push. Right between my shoulder blades. She pushed with her superior might. I went flying, hitting the railing where she had been standing only moments before, crumpling into a pile right on top of our clothes.

Blackness claimed me soon after.

Chapter Thirty
The Sexy Officer

Flashing red and blue lights lit up the darkness, throwing shadows all around me. The smell of blood was still fresh in my nose. The quickly drying fluids still covered my hands and arms. It mixed with the dirt and leaves that I had picked up between the scene and the road. I was naked under a blanket, sitting in the back of an ambulance. I wouldn't be its occupant as it left the area. That honor was reserved for someone else.

Yellow tape was everywhere, blocking off the area from the road to the trees and beyond, framing where it happened. Where she died. Dark forms flitted through the trees as they tried to collect all the evidence there was to find, despite the darkness of the night. They would still search after dawn, but I knew those first hours were essential. There was no telling how long the body had been there, left alone and abandoned in the woods like that.

I shook in the blanket, though it was a warm morning for October. My clothes had been taken from me, soon after the group had arrived. Before they had gotten the tape up and cordoned off the area. They were in evidence, where they would stay for the foreseeable future. I hadn't been sure what to expect in those first few hours, the first couple days, lost in thoughts as the crime scene crew did their job. Uniformed officers were already canvassing the neighborhood, though I knew that they wouldn't find anything. They wouldn't hear anything from anyone about what happened just outside their door. No one would have been awake for it. Not to hear the woman's screams, let alone see the killer fleeing the scene. They would have escaped into the town that they probably lived in. Where they could easily hide among their neighbors.

After all, Emily was killed in the middle of the night. The only reason why I had been there was that stupid phone call that woke me up, making it impossible for me to get back to sleep. There should be a law against that. But I knew the cops were hard pressed enough solving the crimes that really mattered. Like Emily's murder.

"Good morning," yawned a tall, fat, balding man in a suit that stretched across his girth. The suit was obviously purchased a long time ago, before he had gained the weight. The buttons stretched to their limit. It almost seemed like he had gained twenty pounds since putting it on. From the tired look in his eyes, Tom guessed that he had been woken up just as I had, with a phone call. Though his was from his actual work. He pulled out a small pad, barely larger than his overstuffed hand. He used it to stifle another yawn before trying to talk again. "My name is Detective Ben Lee. I'll be the lead investigator on this case. Your name is Natalie?"

"Yes," I said, my teeth chattering through the word. "Natalie Jennings."

"And you found the body?" he asked, ignoring my shivering.

"That's right," I said.

"Seems like an odd place to find a body," he said.

"Really?" I asked. "That seemed like the perfect place to dump a body. It's remote and hidden from the road. No one would be likely to stumble upon it back there."

"Yes," he said, blinking at me a few times. "That... that's what I meant. I mean, it's an odd place for you to have gone, such that there was a body back there."

"Well, I didn't know the body was there. It's not like I went looking for it. There's just a nice overlook not too far from there. It's a great place to see the sunset."

"It's the middle of the night," the detective pointed out. "The sunset is usually seen in the evening. You would have missed it by several hours."

"Yes, I know," I said. "That's not why I was going there."

"Then why were you going there?" he asked.

"Uh oh," Tom muttered.

"What?" I thought to him. "What now?" His usual silence greeted my question, though. He immediately shut up, keeping his new revelation to himself. When he was active, having him figure something out was the only way to shut Tom up. But when he was keeping something from me like that, it was often to my own detriment.

"I got a call in the middle of the night," I started to explain.

"Who was calling?" he asked. He flipped open the pad of paper. A pen hovered over the page that was already half filled with notes. When he noticed that I could see it from my higher perch, he tucked it in close to his chest. It wasn't like his handwriting was all that legible, certainly not from on top of the cot in the back of the ambulance.

"They hung up right after I picked up," I said. "Though they called again soon after. Anyway, you probably know how it is, getting calls in the middle of the night."

"What do you mean by that?" he asked, glaring up at me. I already seemed to have antagonized the man, though I wasn't sure how I managed to do that.

"I mean with your job," I said. "Aren't you, I mean, when you're on duty overnight, you usually get called in, woken up by a phone call."

"Oddly enough, we don't often get murders in this town," he said. "That's the beauty of living in a small town like this. Not like in the city."

"I don't know, I meant like, maybe burglaries or whatever."

"Were you planning on going on a crime spree?" he asked.

"A crime spree? What are you even talking about?" I asked. I was completely confused, though that might have been from the lack of sleep. His yawns had become contagious, and I was yawning myself already.

"Why else would you be up in the middle of the night, 'stumbling' upon a dead body?" he asked. He even put up the air quotes when he said the word "stumbling".

"I already told you. Someone called me in the middle of the night. When I couldn't get back to sleep, I decided to go for a walk. It seemed innocent enough at the time. I didn't know that I would find a body back there."

"But you said it was the perfect place to find a body."

"I just meant that you're likely to find a body where bodies are likely to be hidden."

"Bodies?" he asked. "Plural? Just how many bodies have you found?"

"Tonight? Just the one," I said. I didn't want to bring up those other bodies that I had seen over the course of my life. The conversation was already not going in the right direction for that.

"Uh huh," he said, obviously disbelieving me. "You do know we can check your call history."

"Go ahead," I said. "It's not like I have anything to hide. You'll see that I got two calls last night, back to back. Then I walked out of my apartment, heading down this way."

"Why this way?" he asked. "Wouldn't into town make more sense?"

"Why?" I asked. "What would possibly be open right now?"

"There might have been a coffee place open," he suggested.

"Yeah, cause drinking coffee will help me get to sleep."

"Yeah, cause a midnight walk to a crime scene is going to help you get to sleep," he threw back. "I just find it hard to believe that you had come all this way, to see a view that you can't actually see, and just happened to find a body."

"I wasn't looking for the view," I said. "It was just the place I usually went when looking for the view. I was probably half asleep already."

"Half asleep when you murdered her?" he asked, practically jumping down my throat.

"What? No. What?" I was completely thrown by that accusation. But all I could think was, "Damn you, Tom, why couldn't you warn me about that."

"Sorry," Tom mumbled.

"Look, Detective..."

"Ben Lee," he repeated, though he strung the words together in his excitement, and it came out sounding more like Bently.

"Bently," I said. He didn't so much as flinch when I said it like that. "I don't know what you're thinking here, but I assure you--"

"Oh, well, if you assure me, then it's all good. I don't think I've ever had a criminal assure me that they hadn't committed the crime before. Oh, wait, they all do. Well, in that case."

"In that case, what?" I asked. I don't know if it was brave or stupid. But in my half-asleep state, all I wanted to do was go back to bed. Heck, I wished I had stayed in bed that whole time, leaving Emily's body alone in the woods to be discovered by some other person. Or, perhaps, not at all. "What, are you going to arrest me?" I asked. "For finding a body? For actually calling the police? For not disturbing the crime scene any more than I already had after finding out it was a crime scene?"

"You mean after you made it a crime scene?" he asked. "Why else would you be covered in blood right now?"

"It was dark," I yelled at him. "I didn't see the body until I had already sat next to it. You try finding a body in the dark and not get blood all over you."

"That's it. Natalie Jennings, I'm placing you under arrest."

"Under arrest for what? Seriously, are you the dumbest detective on the force right now?"

"How about for insulting a police officer?" he asked. He pulled out his cuffs, motioning for me to extend my wrists, obviously oblivious to my naked state under the blanket.

"Last I checked that wasn't a crime," I said. I extended my wrists to him just the same. Once he slapped the cuffs on me, I grabbed hold of the edges of the blanket, trying desperately to keep it in place. I ended up settling for tucking my restrained wrists under the blanket, throwing it back over my shoulders to hide within. "Are you taking me down to the station now?" I asked, staring him down.

"I still need to look over the scene, just to make sure I didn't miss anything," he said. His eyes narrowed as he stared back.

"Yeah, didn't really think that one through, now, did you?" I asked. "Like trying to get some actual evidence rather than just arresting the first person you see? If you make it a habit of arresting anyone that reports a body, you're going to get a lot less reports of them. I mean, sure, it'll mean less work for you, but then a lot of murders will just go unreported."

"Now how would you know it was a murder if you didn't do it yourself?" he asked. I was stunned into silence by the stupidity of his logic. He seemed to think it was due to him hitting close to the mark, as he just nodded at me. Then, he headed off to make sure the evidence aligned with his ridiculous theory.

I waited there for a while, in the back of that ambulance. It wasn't like I was about to run off anyway, even without my hands cuffed together. When they had taken my clothes, it was with a promise that someone would return with something for me to wear. Everyone had been so busy securing and searching the scene that it seemed I had been forgotten. I only wish that the detective had forgotten me as well. Still, I didn't like the thought of having to walk back to my apartment in nothing but a blanket. I was quite content to stay right where I was.

The day dawned while people were still scrambling around me. Part of me was glad that I didn't have a job to go to, despite the fact that it was a Monday. Or, at least, I was pretty sure it was a Monday. Days of the week were easy to lose track of when you're not subject to them. However, being that it was Monday meant that I would need to see Dr. Mendes. Assuming that I wasn't back in HTP by that point. I wasn't too sure "arrested for stumbling over a body" would be a sufficient excuse to miss my session with him. If anything, he'd probably want to explore my feelings about the whole thing. After all, it had been after seeing my father's body that my first episode happened. He'd want to make sure that it didn't stir up any new psychoses.

"Natalie," someone called out. I looked around, trying to find the source of the call. No, I thought to myself, as I fought back the memories. No, I didn't want to see him. I didn't want his voice in my ear. Not now. Not after he was...

"Natalie," came his voice again. The voice was coming from my left. Back towards the woods. Back towards her body. It wasn't her, of course. I never heard her voice in my ear. Not after she was dead. I didn't want to hear his either. That would only mean that it was true. That he really was dead.

"Natalie?" came his voice again, as Eric peeked around the edge of the ambulance doorway. "Are you Natalie?" he had asked.

"Do you see anyone else in here, naked save a blanket, and with handcuffs on?" I had asked, trying to be funny. He was cute. I remember thinking that, even from the beginning. Even though he was wearing that uniform. Even before he had started to flirt with me.

"Well, I'm Officer French. I'm here to take you back to the precinct. I'm really sorry about all of this. Detective Lee has a habit of jumping to some pretty weird conclusions."

"Who?" I asked. I had thought his name was Bently.

"Detective Ben Lee," Office French clarified. "Personally, I don't think you could have done it. I mean, who would be stupid enough to call the police while standing over a body they had just hid from sight?"

"Why is he even a detective if that's the kind of thing that he thinks?" I asked. "It just seems so weird."

"And, yet, he had solved a big case a few years back, exactly from that logic. So, the brass give him as much rope as he asks for."

"Hoping he hangs himself on it?" I asked.

He smiled at the old, worn out joke, as if it were original. "Something like that," he said. "Come on. Let's find you something that you can wear that's more... well, more than a blanket anyway."

"Thanks," I said, smiling.

"Anytime, Natalie."

My name seemed to echo as the memory ended and darkness closed in around me.

Chapter Thirty-One
She's an Alien

"Natalie?" His voice came to me again, but it sounded different this time. It sounded like he had been saying my name so many times that he had gone hoarse from it. "Natalie." No, that wasn't it. He was sounding like a completely different person. "Natalie," he screamed. The scream was accented by a slap to my cheek.

"Ow," I yelled. I sat up quickly from the shock of it. My head hit something solid, and my hand went to it automatically. "Ow," I said again, for a different reason.

"Ow," the voice agreed. The area was light, wherever I was. I couldn't keep my eyes open for long. Between the pain in my head and cheek and the brightness of the room, it was painful to open them. The voice was familiar, but I was almost certain that it wasn't his. That it wasn't Eric's. First off, it had an echo to it, coming off the walls of the room. It actually existed and wasn't just in my head. And, since Eric was dead, since Angela killed him, he would only ever talk to me in my head. Or out of some faint memory of him. Of his smile when he saw me for the first time. Of the sound of his voice as he said my name. Oh, if only Detective Bently hadn't accused me of murder, perhaps the two of us would have gotten together long before he was killed.

"Angela," I said, using the name as a curse. I remembered what she had done. Remembered what she had said. Remembered what she was. Remembered that I needed to kill her before she did something else, something worse than killing my friend.

I forced my eyes open against the brightness, letting them adjust to the light from the overhead lamp as they searched the room for her. For the woman, turned alien, turned murderer, that needed to be killed. There she was, standing in the other room, in the playroom, right in front of me. She cradled Doug to her chest, her eyes locked on me with feint fear, as if I were the threat to her child instead of her. Angela had gotten dressed while I was passed out, wearing a subtle t-shirt and jeans. Yet, for some reason, even knowing who she was, what she had become, she still looked amazing. I had to keep myself from going to her, from kissing her like my body wanted me to.

Instead, I looked around the room more, finally seeing the man sitting in front of me. He was still rubbing his head where I had bumped it. Dr. Mendes watched me, seeming as apprehensive about me as I was about Angela. It felt weird, seeing that look on his face. Such a familiar look, one that I hadn't seen in almost a year. Not since my last stay at HTP.

"Are you alright?" he asked.

Usually, I would have just automatically said that I was, not wanting to make issues. Not wanting to be shoved back into HTP because I had a sore throat. However, with Angela looking over at me and with all the stress that had been building up over the past few days, I wasn't ready to say that just yet. Instead, I took the question as it was intended. I tried to actually examine where I was, and the damage that Angela had already done to me, both before and after I had been knocked out.

There was a bump on my forehead, though I wasn't sure if that was from the railing or from Dr. Mendes's head. When I moved my shoulders, I could feel a bruise building between my shoulder blades, from where she had pushed me. I, too, was wearing clothes again, probably dressed by Angela in an effort to detract from what we had done together. That was probably a good thing, too. If I was going to be taken seriously when I accused her of being an alien, it would help to be dressed.

"That is the dumbest thing you could possibly do right now," Tom said. For once, I was pleased to hear his voice in my head. Whatever process the conversion into an alien involved, I somehow doubted that I'd be left with my psychosis after the fact. "Oh, please, aliens can be crazy, too," he said.

"But, on the bright side, nothing happened while you were out," Greg said. "She just put you in some of your old clothes."

"Yeah, really boring," Dad said. "Not even any funny stuff."

"I'm okay, I guess," I said to Dr. Mendes. "Nothing broken at least."

"Other than your sanity," Greg said.

"No more than it was already," Tom said.

"What... what happened?" I asked. I wasn't sure what Angela had told him. I wasn't even sure how Angela had known to call him.

"You had another episode," he said.

"Pfft, episode?" I thought. "I don't have episodes. Episodes have a beginning and an end. This just ebbs and flows." I have good days and bad days. This was quite obviously a bad day, but it had nothing to do with the voices in my head.

"Angela told me that you tried to attack her."

"What?" I asked, surprised.

"Well, that is one way of looking at it," Tom said. "It's not exactly the whole story, but you did attack her."

"She attacked me first," I said, trying to dispute both of their claims.

"Really now?" he asked. He seemed more willing to believe Angela over me, despite the rapport we had had for years. "Why would she attack you?"

"Careful," Tom cautioned.

"Because she's an alien," I said, ignoring him. Tom sighed in disappointment.

"See?" Angela said, pointing at me. She held Doug closer to her chest, as if I was ready to spring at her. I would have had to get past Dr. Mendes and halfway across the room to even try. And after she took me apart last time, I wasn't exactly prepared for a second attempt.

"An alien?" Dr. Mendes asked. "She looks perfectly human to me."

"Well, she's not like an actual alien type of alien," I said. "She was infected by something that's taken her over."

"Like some kind of parasite?" he asked. "Tell me, have you been watching a lot of old horror movies lately? Invasion of the Body Snatchers perhaps?"

"No, that's... I saw it, I saw the thing take over."

"And how was that, exactly?" he asked. It was obvious he was just placating me, letting me dig my own grave. But, for some reason, I just couldn't shut up.

"Her eyes turned black and her voice went low. Like super low. Like something out of hell itself."

"Wait, is she an alien or a demon?" he asked. "Just so I can keep track."

"An alien," I said. "She was infected by that thing that attacked us the other day."

"What thing?" he asked. "You were attacked?" He looked back, over his shoulder, to Angela for confirmation.

She stood there for a moment, gaping at us, at a loss for something to say. I smiled, feeling like I finally got the better of her. Like she was going to admit that she was attacked by an alien and that I was right about the whole thing. "But... Natalie, I don't blame you for that," she said. This took me completely by surprise.

"You... Well, of course you don't blame me for it," I said. "I chased that thing off."

"Chased what thing off?" she asked. "Natalie, you threw a rock through the window because you were trying to chase Greg's ghost off."

"What?" I asked, stunned. "That's not what happened. No, some wild animal smashed its way through the kitchen window. She was bit before it got away."

"Oh, right, the 'wild animal'," Angela said. There was no confidence behind her words, as if she didn't believe what she was saying. "Wasn't that a possum, though?"

"That was no possum," I said.

"Wait, did you say it was a possum at the time?" Dr. Mendes asked. He seemed content to let the story about the rock pass, at least for now. Instead, he focused on trying to catch me in my own logic spiral, as he usually did before sending me off to HTP. I knew that he would bring up Angela's cover story later.

"Well, yes, but," I started.

"But you think it was an alien?"

"Well, yes, but," I said again.

"And you think that, when it bit Angela, it infected her with some sort of parasite?"

"Or a disease or something," I said. "Something that turned her into an alien."

"Well, I can assure you that there is no such thing known to man that can do something like that," he said.

"Well, yeah," I yelled. "Known to man. But aliens are outside of that, aren't they?"

"Natalie, please," he said, calmly. His hands were up defensively, trying to calm me. "I'm only trying to help here. I'm trying to show you that what you thought happened didn't really happen. That it couldn't have really happened. Whether it was an animal, or a rock, or a mini flying saucer. Now, did she go to the hospital?"

"Yes," I said. My eyes went wide when I realized something that could actually prove that I wasn't crazy. Or, at least, not any more crazy than I already was. "They had to operate on her arm because it was so messed up. Now, look at her," I said, pointing over to Angela. "Her shoulder is completely healed."

"It's not completely healed," Angela said. She put her hand on her shoulder, moving Doug up to block his view of it in the process. "There is still some healing needed to be done."

"What? No, I saw it earlier," I said, trying to protest. "It looked like she had never been attacked."

"When did you see this?" he asked.

"Last night," I said. "She was wearing this strappy dress when we went out to dinner. There was nothing there."

"Well, I wore cover-up on it, silly," she teased, rolling her eyes as if that should have been obvious. "You never did get that good of a look at it."

"Of course, I did," I said. "I got a good look at it earlier, when we--"

"When we, what?" she asked, daring me to say the words.

"When we... made love," I said. My words lost their power as I finished saying it.

"Seriously, girl, what kind of stupid are you?" Tom asked.

Dr. Mendes looked back over at Angela again. I followed his gaze, watched as Angela put on a sweet and innocent face and lied her ass off. "I never," she said, seeming completely shocked by what I was saying. "I would never. I mean, she's a girl."

"Gee, wasn't that what I said?" I thought.

"Yeah," Tom said. "Several times."

"And, yet, it didn't stop you," Greg said.

"So, you didn't try to kiss her last week?" Dr. Mendes asked. I smiled at that, having completely forgotten that I had told him in Monday's session.

"What? No, of course not," Angela said. She looked completely grossed out by the very thought.

"What about last night?" I asked. I was hoping that I could catch her in this huge lie she was trying to get away with. "People saw us at the restaurant."

"Yeah, people saw two girls eating together," she said. "So what? We were celebrating the end of this whole drama with Greg, our ex-husband, and you possibly getting a new job. Of course, with you going completely crazy right now, that's obviously not going to happen. I should probably call Sam and tell him the bad news before they get too far on your paperwork."

"Wow, I don't remember her being this manipulative when I married her," Greg said. "I mean, even when I was trying to frame you for Emily's murder, I wouldn't have gone so far as to make you think you were crazier than you were already."

"Oh, shut up, Greg," I snapped aloud. "That was exactly what you were trying to do."

"Greg?" Dr. Mendes asked. "Your ex-husband Greg? The one you just buried?"

And the world froze around me as I realized what I had just done. What the ramifications of it were. Greg had never been in a session with Dr. Mendes before. His sudden return to the land of the living as my new voice had never come up. Worse, I had spoken to him. Directly. In front of the doctor. In front of my shrink. That was something I tried not to do with any of them, though talking to him was so much worse. It could only mean one thing, and it was too late to take it back. Too late to stop the dominos from falling. Even if I could admit that the whole thing with Angela being an alien was just a fluke, a one-time lapse in reality, there was no getting out of it now.

"I should have known," he said, palming his forehead. "Natalie, I am so sorry. Of course. It makes perfect sense now. We never really did discuss how you were feeling, now that you've seen a third person die. How long did it take for his voice to come to you this time?"

"What's... going on?" Angela asked, hesitantly.

"Angela, could you please give us some privacy?" Dr. Mendes asked. "It'll probably be safer for you upstairs right now."

"Sure," she said. "Whatever you need. I just want to help."

"Of course," Dr. Mendes said. "I'll let you know if we need anything."

Angela nodded at the good doctor. She held Doug's head against her chest as she scurried around me and up the stairs. When she got to the landing, turning around to head up the second half of the stairs, I could see her face for the faintest of moments. I saw the smile of victory, the evil, manipulative grin that said she was overjoyed that she got her way. That she made me look crazier than I really was. And that was a feat all its own, because I was completely nuts. But, then, she was gone. My last chance of possibly proving that I was right about her leaving the room. Never to be seen by me again, if she had anything to do with it. I was certain, in that very moment, that she would be the one to sign away my rights. To commit me to HTP for the rest of my life.

"I noticed that you had been spiraling lately," Dr. Mendes said. "I just thought... but you said you were taking your meds, that you were good. Maybe I just figured that we had been making progress. That the voices were a distant memory. But they've been talking to you all this time, haven't they?"

"Yes," I admitted. My voice was barely loud enough to be heard over my own heartbeat. "They helped me figure it out. Tom helped me figure out that Greg had been the one to kill Emily. That he had been trying to frame me for the whole thing."

"Wait, you knew before coming over here that day?" he asked. "Why did you even come, then? Why didn't you just go to the police?"

"Right, why didn't the crazy person tell the police that she couldn't possibly have killed Emily because her ex-husband had? That would have made perfect sense, right? They never would have believed me. Heck, Bently still doesn't believe me, even after Angela backed up my story."

"But is that it?" he asked. "Is Greg the one trying to convince you that Angela is an alien?"

"What?" I asked, surprised that he would make that kind of leap. "No, of course not. I mean, no, it was Tom that thought of it first, even before what happened at the restaurant. Even Angela thought that thing was an alien. I mean the old Angela, the human Angela, not this... But, once I saw her eyes turn, I knew that he was right. That that... thing wasn't Angela anymore."

"And was this before or after you slept with her?" he asked. He made it sound like he actually believed me. That I was starting to bring him around to my way of thinking.

"Before," I admitted. "I only slept with her earlier tonight. Before you came over. Before she attacked me. Before... before she admitted to killing Eric."

"And who's Eric?" he asked. He pulled out a pad of paper, the same kind that Bently had used at Emily's murder scene. He started taking notes feverishly, as if he was having trouble keeping track of all the crazy that was spilling out of me just then. Heck, I had trouble with it sometimes, and I was living in it.

"We're always here to help you remember," Dad said, unhelpfully. "Hey," he snapped.

"Eric is a cop," I said. "Often he seemed like the only cop worth dealing with. The rest of them seemed to be on Bently's side of everything. He was usually the one to drive me home after another one of his interrogations. He was a friend."

"'Was'?" he asked. "Are you so sure he's dead?"

"He went missing earlier today," I told him. "He was called away on business late last night and he disappeared somewhere between the campus and the station."

"The campus? Wait, you were with him last night?"

"Not with him that way. Not the way that Angela thought we were... We're just friends, we were just friends. She said she followed me over to his house, though, and saw us together. Obviously, she got the wrong idea, because she set off to kill him. She said she moved Tom's body from wherever it was that Greg hid him to where it was found by the cops last night, opening his old grave for Eric's body."

"You do realize how crazy that all sounds, don't you?" he asked. His hand was on my shoulder, trying to lend me comfort. "I'm sure that, if we were to call over to the precinct, they would have found him by now."

"I doubt it," I said. "They spent hours today trying to get in touch with him. They..." I hesitated for a moment, not wanting to confess this next part to my shrink. But I figured he was already going to be sending me back to HTP anyway. "They had me on a 5150 under his word. But without him there, they were forced to release me. Bently wasn't happy about it."

"So, wait, they found Tom's body?" he asked, finally catching onto that part.

"Yes," I said. "I told you I saw him jump to his death. So much for your theory that I imagined that part."

"Oh, I put that theory to bed ages ago, soon after you had started hearing his voice and he had officially been reported missing. But Greg hid the body?"

"So it would seem," I said.

"Why?"

"He said it was so I wouldn't get in trouble for being on the roof with a student. Not that I would have anyway."

"He said this before or after he died?" he asked.

"After... Actually, he said it only a few hours ago, back when Angela told me she moved the body."

"And when did he tell Angela? Was that before or after he died?" he asked.

"Before," I said. "Of course, it was before. He... Okay, I see that I misspoke earlier. The voice that is in my head, and doesn't actually exist, but bears a striking resemblance to him said that that was the reason why the real Greg would have moved the body. But it is no more the truth than any other guess I can come up with."

"Natalie, I'm not trying to trick you," he said. "I'm just trying to see how much work we're going to have to do during your stay this time around."

"My stay?" I asked. My heart fell with his confirmation that he was going to be sending me back to HTP.

"Well, you are overdue for your 'annual tune-up'. Isn't that what you call it? You do seem to need to spend some time there every year, ever since that first incident. Ever since we've been working together. I was hoping that you were doing better this time around. That you wouldn't need another stay. But maybe I was wrong. Was this all just because of Greg's death? Or was there another reason, another trigger? Since you were hearing them again before confronting Greg, before killing him. There must have been some other trauma that had started up. Was it the divorce? That was almost a year ago, though, soon after your last stay, wasn't it?"

I snorted at that comment. "Greg had them serve the papers as I was leaving. Part of me wanted to just turn around and head back in."

"Sorry," Greg said.

"It's not your fault," I thought to him. "I don't blame the voices for what the people did. That would be rude, seeing as how you're not really them."

"Yet calling us nothing more than figments of your imagination isn't rude?" he asked. I didn't dignify the comment with a response.

"But, was that what triggered it? Why the voices came back?"

"No," I said, honestly. I knew exactly why the voices came back, and it had nothing to do with any new trauma. It was the fact that I was on half dosage, and nothing else. I wasn't about to tell him that.

A car horn sounded outside the house, drawing my attention to the door, as if I could see through the wood itself to the source. "Well, we'll have plenty of time to figure that out, won't we," Dr. Mendes said. He rubbed his hands together, excitedly, as if the work we were going to be doing would be actual, physical work. That we were getting ready to do it immediately. I knew that neither would be the case. He would probably drug me up to my full dosage before we even start. Perhaps even higher since he wasn't aware that I wasn't taking the full dose. "That should be the van to take us over. Angela?" he called up the stairs.

"Yes, Dr. Mendes?" she called down. Her voice came instantly from the top of the stairs, as if she had been sitting there the whole time, listening in to our impromptu session. Given what I knew about her, that wouldn't surprise me. Did aliens even have a sense of privacy?

"Did you manage to pack a bag for Natalie?"

"Yup, it's right here," she said. She came back down the stairwell. Quickly at first, but, once she came into view again, she slowed down. She came to a stop a few stairs up from where I was sitting. "You're not going to try to attack me again, are you?" she asked.

"Oh, I don't think she'll be a problem for you, dear. Will you, Natalie?"

"No, of course not," I said. I tried to keep a straight face. The fact of the matter was I would love to shove something sharp, hard, and metal through her alien heart for what she did to Eric. But it wouldn't help things. First off, I didn't exactly have a sharp, hard, metal item right then. Then there was the fact that Dr. Mendes would probably try to stop me, and get himself killed in the process. The last thing I needed was a shrink as a fourth voice in my head. He'd probably want daily sessions with me after that. Besides, I still wasn't sure just how strong and fast Angela really was, yet.

"Good," she said. A smile came easily to her lips as she practically bounced down the last few steps. She placed my suitcase on the floor next to me. It was the one that I had only just unpacked a week ago. Then she wrapped her arms around me and pulled me into a hug. "Do get better soon," she said. Then she whispered, in one of the most seductive voices I had ever heard, "I want my little sex toy back soon."

Chapter Thirty-Two
Back in HTP

The van to HTP always smelled bad, from the moment I got in it to the moment I got out. Somehow, it also left a bad taste in my mouth. The fourth time I rode in it, I tried to keep my mouth shut the entire time, even holding my breath for as long as I could. Yet I still came out with that same taste. It was weird, like a phantom flavor that just never went away. It was almost like the voices' last attempt to get me out of the van. To stop me from heading back to HTP. Back to silence them for another few weeks, months, perhaps even years if it ever actually lasted that long. Not that I wouldn't be thrilled for their complete silence. But they had to know that I dreaded that place as much as they did.

Holy Trinity Psychiatric was in upstate New York, a good two hour drive north of Tarrytown. It was closer to my hometown, to where Mom still lived, than my new home. Yet, for some reason, no matter how hard I tried, I could never completely escape it. Even if I flew halfway across the country, they would, no doubt, find some way to drag me back there. Kicking and screaming if need be.

After coming there for so long, almost twenty years, I'm what you might call a frequent flier. I knew the place inside and out. I knew where all the shrinks went to smoke, on the roof by the emergency exit that had been disabled before I even started coming there. I knew practically everything about the place, except for a way out that didn't involve the front door and proper discharge papers. No matter how sane I felt,

I wasn't going to get out until they were good and ready to let me out. And there were quite a lot of good days when I was there. When the voices were silent and the fog from the meds hadn't rolled in just yet.

Being a frequent flier, they let me pass through some of the usual checkpoints that most people had to go through when coming into the place. Don't get me wrong, I still got my stuff tossed and had to do the same strip search that everyone else had to endure. It seemed to get easier and less invasive every year. But they didn't bother doing any sort of evaluations or checking my vitals to determine which pharmaceuticals I'd react well with or anything. My treatment plan was part of my file. They would refer to that as needed. It made it a lot easier for me to come in this time around, when I was arriving so late at night, after most of the staff had already gone home. They even had my usual bed ready and waiting for me. I knew my approved belongings would be in my dresser when I woke up.

"Nat's back," someone screamed in my ear, first thing in the morning. It was so early that the sun still hadn't shone straight through the blinds and into my eyes like it usually did in the mornings. That always woke me up instantly. I searched for the source of my annoyance, though I knew who it would be before I even saw her. Veronica was my roommate my fifth year there. She spent more time inside than I did. After a brief disagreement and an incident involving a spork during my seventh visit, she had been moved down the hall from my usual room. But that didn't stop her from coming into my room to wake me up every time I visited. "Welcome back, Nat," she said, when she saw that my eyes were open, though begrudgingly so.

"Go away, Roni," I muttered. I buried my head into my pillow, trying to grab a few extra minutes of sleep before they started rousing the patients.

"I was supposed to greet you when you came in," she said. "I'm supposed to show you around the place."

"I know the place better than you do," I accused. "And I somehow doubt they meant for you to show me around when we're not even supposed to be up yet."

"They said as soon as you came in," she insisted. She didn't clarify who they were. She was schizophrenic, like me, which was why we had been paired that first year. So, the "they" she was referring to could just as easily have been one of the voices in her head as one of the orderlies that took care of the patients during the day to day.

"And how is Mark these days?" I asked, knowing she wasn't about to leave me alone anytime soon.

"He's still mad at you," she said. "He still doesn't like that he can't talk to your dad. Why won't you let him talk to your dad?"

"Because my dad is dead," I said. It was the same answer I gave her every time she asked. "I just have a voice inside my head that thinks he's my dad. He doesn't talk to other voices, because they don't actually exist and can't interact with anyone. Let alone another person that doesn't actually exist."

"Mark talks to everyone," she said. "They just don't know how to listen to him."

"Well, then tell him that he can talk to my voices all he likes. It doesn't mean that they're going to talk back to him."

"Some people can be so delusional sometimes," Dad said.

"Yeah, like imaginary people with delusions of existence," I thought to him.

"Anyway, come on," she insisted. "Up and at 'em, as they say. Breakfast is going to start in a few minutes and you're going to want to get there early today. The eggs are new since you've been here last. They have a tendency to go bad after the first half hour or so. People have been waking up earlier in order to wait in line for them."

"Wow, do you mean you waking me up at the ass crack of dawn is actually you trying to be helpful?" I asked, spitefully. I hated having a helpful nemesis. It made it that much harder to hate her. But at least I was only exposed to her when I came to HTP. When I was out in the real world, I never had to think about her. And I rarely did.

"Come on," she said again. "Get dressed and let's get going. I can't wait on you forever."

"Fine, I'm up," I said, throwing back the covers. "And I'm as dressed as I need to be for this place." I wouldn't be the only person walking around the place in the hospital issued nightgowns. At least they weren't the medical kinds with the backs open. They were just plain gray, matching the walls, and had the HTP logo over the right breast.

"So, how long do you think you'll be back for this time?" she asked. Her voice was an almost constant buzzing in my ears as we made our way down the hall towards the cafeteria. "Think you'll be back for good?"

"Oh, hell, no," I said. "I'm just here for my--"

"Annual tune-up," Roni finished for me, interrupting me saying it myself. "Just think, you'll be home for Thanksgiving. It's next week, isn't it? I have so much trouble keeping track these days."

"HTP has never been my home," I snapped at her, knowing full well what she meant. It was her home, despite the fact that it had never been mine. I wasn't sure, but I think she stayed there year-round. She was always there when I was, but I never heard her say anything about getting out. She seemed to be as permanent a part of the place as the plastic plants hanging from the ceiling in the day room. Then again, since I almost always came there for Thanksgiving, it might have just been the holidays that made her come back. Some of the people there had trouble dealing with being alone around that time of year. It never seemed to bother me much, until Greg came along.

I glared at the walls, as if they were actively trying to keep me there. Keep me contained to that place. Only shrinks would think that the dull, gray walls of the place would be soothing and beneficial to our healing. To me, they seemed like a prison. And, considering that I wasn't allowed to leave on my own volition, it might as well be.

"That's only because you actually believe them," she whispered to me, harshly.

"What?" I asked, confused.

"You believe the shrinks when they tell you that you're healthy enough to go home," she said.

"Well, yeah, that's just when I can get out of here. And the sooner the better."

"And, then, you're back here a year later," she said. "If you were really healthy enough to go home, you wouldn't be back so soon. See, I know they're lying when they say it to me. That's why I don't go. When they tell you it this time, insist on staying. That's what I do."

"But then I'd never get out of here," I said.

"Exactly. It's so much easier in here anyway." I just rolled my eyes at that thought. There was no way I was staying there a minute longer than I had to.

"Besides," Tom said. "You need to get out of here so you can kill Angela."

"And why am I doing that again?" I thought to him. I knew that I wouldn't be hearing him much longer, so I might as well humor his rising paranoia.

"Because she's an alien."

"Yes, we've covered that. But why are we killing her? We need to have her arrested for killing Eric, obviously. But why kill her?"

"Because she's going to infect everyone on the planet, if she has the chance. We have to stop the invasion in its tracks, while we still can."

It was during that lovely thought that we had gotten to the cafeteria. As Roni had said, the place was packed, though we were still not supposed to be up yet. The line ran the entire length of the room, which could easily seat a hundred patients. There was no sign of them starting to serve anything, least of all eggs. But, then again, I couldn't really see much at the other end of the room, around the mass of bodies before me.

"Dang it," Roni cursed, when she saw the long line.

"Late again," someone called from near the back of the line. "Enjoy the crappy eggs, Roni."

"Kidnap any families lately, Mary?" Roni snapped back at her. "If you had just gotten up when I told you."

I shrugged apologetically to her, before turning back to the voices inside my head. "But what about the possum?" I thought. "Isn't that still out there? Still infecting other people? There might be an army of the things when we get home."

"One problem at a time," he insisted. "We'll need to handle the one we know about before heading off to find and kill the others."

"Ah, Natalie, there you are," Dr. Mendes said, interrupting Tom. I was surprised to see him there; he usually only came in on Sundays. The trek from his other office was always so long of a drive. In my less stable days, I sometimes get a little paranoid on why he would be affiliated with a psych hospital so far from the city. He had told me once that he had done his residency there and always had a spot in his heart for the place. For me, it could burn to the ground for all I cared, as long as I never had to come back. "My schedule was empty today, so I figured we could still have that session we already had planned for today," he explained.

"Oh, right, it's Friday, isn't it," I said. The days really get away from me when I'm plotting someone's death.

"Oh, like you've been plotting anything," Tom said. "It's been me pushing for her death. You've just been having sex with her all this time."

I shrugged, smiling a little at his comment, before turning back to the good doc. "Sounds fine with me. After breakfast? I've heard the eggs are to die for." Roni snickered at my comment, trying to keep her eyes on the line.

Dr. Mendes eyed me knowingly. Now that he knew the voices were back, probably suspecting that they never truly left, he was being more observant. More cautious. And more dangerous, as he always was when he was like this. At least to me and my freedom. "Sure," he said, hesitantly. "Take all the time you need. And do yourself a favor, say goodbye to those voices of yours. I'm committed to not letting you leave here until they're completely gone, and not just medicated away."

I liked the sound of that. Liked the idea that I would be able to be myself without the voices. But I knew it wouldn't be that simple. Besides, more work inside meant I would be there longer. My freedom would be a fond memory before I got it back. I wasn't sure I could wait that long. Wasn't sure I could trust Angela to not destroy my life while I was stuck in there. She already killed my friend. What else could she do?

"What else do you have left that she could take away from you?" Tom asked. "It's not like you talk to your mother anymore. The chance of you getting your job back are pretty much history now. And any impending arrests from the detective would be tainted by your incarceration here. What is there to go back to?"

"There's her," Dad said. I could hear the smile in his voice, as if he would like nothing more than to see his daughter in the arms of another woman. He probably got a kick out of our lovemaking session from before, too. "I didn't hate it," he admitted.

"I don't think you have much to worry about on that account," Greg said. "The only reason she killed Eric was because he was in the way of her getting what she wants. And what she wants, at least for now, is... Well... You."

"And what is it that's in her way of that now?" Dad asked.

I looked over to Dr. Mendes, to the only man, the only person that was standing between Angela and what she wants. Namely me. I did not envy his position. I should probably try to get out of there as soon as possible, for his sake as much as for mine. He looked at me, eyeing me as if expecting a response. As if knowing full well that I was having a long, drawn out conversation with the three of them.

"Sure," I said, giving him a half-hearted shrug. "Sounds like we have a lot of work ahead of us."

"That we do," he agreed, before leaving me and Roni alone to wait for our breakfast. I watched him head out of the room, knowing he was a dead man walking.

Chapter Thirty-Three
The Extra Session

I didn't know what Roni was talking about. The eggs started out pretty terrible to begin with. There was no way possible for them to get any worse, no matter how much time was given to them. They were obviously from a powdered mix, those designed to be used after the end of the world. Or at least the end of other flavors in the world. They were not sitting well with me. The only good part about them was they got the bitter, lingering taste from the van out of my mouth. Although, it wasn't that much of an improvement. Still, I hadn't eaten much the day before, so I ended up getting two helpings of the crap. Then I went off through the familiar halls to Dr. Mendes's borrowed office with an overly full belly.

"Okay, I have an idea," Greg said, right before we came to the office door. "I'm going to have to go somewhere, though. I'll be back, I promise."

"Hey, don't come back on my account," I said to him. I eyed the hallway, up and down the length of it, making sure that it was as empty as I thought it was. There was no sign of anyone peeking out from the doorways. The entire hallway was dedicated to the shrinks that worked there, with offices on both sides of the hall. They were probably all in session, or waiting on the late arrivals from breakfast like myself. "If you can go away and never come back, then by all means, please do. And take these two with you, while you're at it. That would pretty much solve all my problems. I could get out of here, go home to my waiting... whatever the hell Angela is to me right now."

"Your waiting girlfriend," Dad clarified, reveling in the word.

"I'm thinking you're going to want me back here, sooner rather than later, if I'm actually successful in what I'm going to try to do," Greg said.

"And what, pray tell, is that, exactly?" I asked. I already knew that he wasn't about to tell me anything. He had taken well with Tom and had picked up some of his more annoying habits of keeping things to himself.

"Well, if you know I'm not going to tell you, why do you even bother to ask?" he asked. "I'll be back." His voice faded down the hallway. It felt a bit eerie to me that I could tell the distance from the voices so clearly, despite the fact that Greg was the only one that seemed so loosely tied to me. And, yet, I couldn't hear his footsteps as he fled from my impending session with Dr. Mendes.

"That's it, isn't it," I called after him, forgetting to keep quiet. "You're just afraid to be in the same room as the shrink."

"He didn't disappear when we were back home," Tom pointed out. "Or in the cafeteria. It's just the main, non-impromptu sessions that he's been skipping out of."

"Yeah, and being annoyingly smug about it, too," I said.

I reached over to press the button next to the door, to announce my presence to the shrink within. Before I hit it, he called out to me. "Come on in, Natalie, if you're done talking to your voices and are ready to rid yourself of them once and for all."

I smiled at that thought. The lingering hope that I feared would never be fulfilled for as long as I lived. I reached over to the knob anyway, pushing the door open. The stark contrast between that borrowed office and the one he had in Tarrytown always struck me whenever I walked in there after a long time away. It was like that feeling of coming home after a long vacation away. You get used to that other place and, when you return, with everything just the way you had left it, it feels weird that it hadn't changed while you were gone. Instead of a large sweeping office, taking up much of the space available to him, the office was small. There was only enough room for a desk, which he sat behind as usual, and a single chair in front of it. The desk took up most of the room. I often wondered how he could squeeze his heavy, wide body around it. Although sessions tended to last longer on the inside, the chair was one of the most uncomfortable ones in the world. They always reminded me about the ones at home in the dining room that Greg had proudly picked out. I would have accused him of doing it intentionally, a constant reminder of how insane I truly was. But, as he had said, he had stepped away for the moment.

As I sat down in the chair across from Dr. Mendes, I was hit with a flash of nostalgia. A reminder of all the years I had been there. All the times that I sat in that chair, across from him, promising me that he would rid me of the demons that I had been forced to carry all these years. He had never succeeded at that, not on the long term at least. But that never stopped him from making that promise, one that he would never be capable of keeping, and meaning it just as wholeheartedly as he had the year before. Anyone else would have probably given up on me by now. Locked me away in that place and thrown away the key. I had a lot of reasons to be thankful for Dr. Mendes, which made the usual time of year of my returns that much more appropriate. At least this time I wouldn't be leaving there to divorce papers and a new apartment.

"So, you think you can cure me, doc?" I asked. It was the usual thing that I said to start off my first session back at HTP, every year. He laughed as he remembered it as well.

"First off, I'd like to get some of the lies and omissions out of the way, if that would be alright," he said. This took me a bit by surprise. It was an approach that he hadn't tried before. "I see in my notes that you had responded very well to the meds last time around. The voices were gone after a few days on them. True or false?"

"True," I confirmed. He nodded, as if he could somehow tell that I was telling the truth. He had never shown the ability before.

"How soon after leaving here last year did you stop taking them?"

"I never stopped--"

"Natalie, can we please put away the bullshit?" he asked. "I'm only trying to help you."

"I never stopped taking them," I said. "I... cut my dosage in half."

"Why?" he asked.

"It always put me in a fog. It barely even registered to me that my marriage was over until like two months later. I didn't even read the papers until after I had already signed them. After I had given up so much of my stuff back at the house. If Sam hadn't helped write the papers up in the first place, I might have ended up coming out of that with nothing, rather that the alimony that I had for the past year. Although that's gone now, too."

"And you've been doing this every year?" he asked.

"Every year that I've been on this one, yeah. The last one wasn't so bad, but..."

"But that one stopped working when Tom joined in," he completed for me. "We kept trying to get the balance just right on that. But then it just stopped working all together. I'm wondering if the same would have happened this time around, even if you hadn't backed down the dosage."

"This time around?" I asked, feigning ignorance.

He just frowned at me for a moment. "How long after killing Greg did his voice come to you?" he asked.

"I don't know," I said, truthfully. "Maybe minutes, maybe a couple of hours. I don't really remember that day all that well. It's a bit of a blur."

"Perhaps Greg would be able to tell you," he suggested. "Any chance I could have a talk with him? Get to know him a little better? How his presence is going to impact you going forward?"

It was an exercise that we had tried from the very beginning, when I first met Dr. Mendes there after my first time being committed. That was back when I was only plagued with the one voice, the voice of my father. He was under the impression that Dad was there as a protector. Someone that would watch out for me. Something that my real dad had been meant to do, but hadn't, had failed to do. Tom, on the other hand, was there to help me figure out things. To help me deal with things that had started to build up against me. His clear, almost heartless logic meant that he stemmed from that part of my mind, giving voice to a part of me that I had been ignoring. I wasn't sure just what he would think of Greg, but it wasn't something I was going to figure out just yet.

"Uh, he's not in right now," I said. "Can I take a message?"

"What do you mean he's not 'in'?" he asked.

"Well, he stepped out for something. He said he had something that he needed to do. Really, I just think he doesn't want to be in this session with you." And, honestly, he wasn't the only one. "He's never been in any of the scheduled sessions with you."

"You mean he actually disappears? Or he just goes silent?"

"No, he disappears," I said. "I can't even feel his presence during those times. I mean, usually I don't notice when he's gone. It's just like it had been before he joined in. Just the two of them hanging around me, watching everything that I'm doing. I've long since got over the loss of privacy. But their constant presence is like a weight behind my eyes or something."

"And that goes away without him there?"

"Well, it doesn't exactly go away. Not completely. It's more like it lessens. But it's so little, compared to the rest of it, that I sometimes don't even notice. Honestly, I don't know how it would feel if it ever went away completely."

"That is the goal, of course," he said. "But you have to understand, that's going to take a lot of work. I had been hoping that the medication and talk therapy would be enough. But I'm wondering if we should go a different route."

"You're not talking about shock therapy, are you?" I asked. I shuddered at the thought. Even in this day and age, when the procedure was a lot less dramatic than it was in the old days, it still had its stigma, even among the crazies.

"I never liked you calling yourself crazy," Dad said. "You're my daughter. You're just... unique."

"Yes," I thought to him. "Clinically unique."

"There are other avenues that we can consider before heading that route," Dr. Mendes said. He seemed as apprehensive of shock therapy as I was. "I'm hoping that it won't have to come to that."

"Good," I said, nodding my agreement.

"However, in the meantime, we'll need to get you settled back into your normal schedule here at HTP. I'm going to try a new medication for you, something that might not put you in as much of a fog this time around. Let's see where we're at once we've stabilized you on it, alright?"

"Fine," I mumbled. I wasn't thrilled about being medicated again. But if it works without me feeling like I'm asleep all the time, then it's better than being stuck with the voices. Besides, it wasn't like he was giving me a choice in the matter.

"Well, we'd shut up if we could," Dad said, helpful as always. "Well, okay, maybe not even then."

"I've already signed you up for your usual activities while you're here," he continued, oblivious to my internal conversation as always. "But I'm afraid I'm not going to be able to approve for you to see visitors. At least not for the first few weeks."

"Weeks?" I asked. Usually it only took me a week to get back on the right balance of meds, at least how they see it, and a few more days to get approved to go home. The way he was talking, it sounded like I'd be there for months.

"Well, we're not going to be doing the same old thing this time around," he said. "It's new meds, new processes with therapy. So much more to do than normal, because the normal isn't working. You know what they say the true definition of insanity is, right?"

I glared at him, wondering if he was going to say that I was the normal definition of insanity. Like that old joke about your picture being in the dictionary next to gullible.

Dr. Mendes, seeing the glare I was giving him, put his hands up defensively. "Doing the same thing and expecting different results," he clarified.

"Oh, right, that one."

"So, yeah, it might take a while, and I'll need to see where we're at after the first couple of weeks before deciding on who can come visit you."

"Who would even want to come visit me?" I asked. "It's not like I have any friends left. None that would come all the way up here for me anyway."

"Well, there's your mother, for one," he said, knowing full well that I hadn't spoken to the woman since the third time she committed me, pulling me out of college to do it. "And I've already heard from Angela, who was halfway up here this morning before she bothered to call. I had to tell her that it wasn't the best of times, and that I'd contact her when you were ready. I'm not even sure if it would be strictly safe for you to see her anyway."

"What? You think I'm going to try to attack her again?" I asked.

"No, I mean safe for you. She seemed to have some effect on you. A trigger of something that I hadn't seen in you in all the years I've been treating you. I don't know what really happened between the two of you, and we'll need to address that at some point. But it would be best if she just stayed away for now. I'll tell you that she was not happy about that when I told her."

"Uh oh," I thought, my face going pale as my eyes went wide. The last time she thought someone had gotten between her and me had been with Eric. We all know what happened to him. Wasn't that what Tom was just saying before we came in there?

"Yup, I think it was," he gloated. "I'm so glad we're on the same page, for that one at least."

"Are-are you sure that's the best of ideas?" I asked.

"Do you think you're ready to see her?" he asked, putting it back on me.

"No, probably not. Not if what I'm thinking... Well, I'm more worried about what Angela would do--"

"I assure you, Eric is fine," Dr. Mendes said, reading my meaning easily enough.

"What?" I asked, elated. "You've heard from him? He's back?"

"Well, no," he said. "I haven't heard anything specific from the precinct. But which makes more sense? Angela is a jealous alien that saw Eric as a threat to her relationship with you and killed him, burying him in some mysterious location in the woods. Or Eric got lost coming back from the crime scene. Or, better yet, ditched out on work for being called in overnight before another shift, and is just avoiding calling in so he doesn't get in trouble."

"Well, knowing Eric, even as little as I do, I'd have to say Angela being an alien sounds much more likely than that Eric ditched work. I had never seen him shirk off before. I think the cops at the precinct would have said something if that was his habit. They were all very worried about him, and not just because it meant I was getting off of the 5150."

"I'll reach out to the precinct later today, if that will make you feel better. But I'm pretty sure that he'll be just fine. He's a fully trained officer, and quite capable of handling himself, especially against a little slip of a girl like Angela. He could probably bench press the poor woman."

"Dang right, he could," I thought, remembering the sight of his arms when he wasn't wearing a shirt. "But Angela has her own strength, alien strength. She might be able to take him, especially if he wasn't expecting it coming."

"And who would expect anything from Angela?" Dad asked. "She looks so innocent."

"When she's not all aliened out," Tom said.

I let the point slide. Dr. Mendes wasn't going to budge on it. It would take him actually seeing Angela alien out before he believed me. Before anyone believed me. I was on my own, with just my trusty voices by my side. And that was probably the scariest thought yet.

"I have to admit, I feel a little sorry for the girl," Dr. Mendes said, taking me a bit by surprise.

"Sorry for her?" I asked. "Why? Because she's an alien now?"

"Stupid," Tom said.

"No," he said. He stopped there, looking at me in a weird way, as if not sure where I was coming from or what to even say to that. I did have to admit, it was one of the craziest things I've said in all the years he had been treating me. "No, because she just lost her husband, whom, from what you had been telling me about your own dealings with him, had probably been abusing her. Honestly, I'm not even that surprised that he had been responsible for Emily's death, all things considered. And, now, after all that she's been through, she makes a new friend, who has also been abusive to her. Honestly, Natalie, I would have thought more of you."

I sat there, not sure what to say to that. Not sure where to go from there. Even setting aside the whole rock thrown through the window crap that Angela had come up with to explain away the animal attack, I had supposedly attacked her right before she called him over to take me away. That time, at least, I had actually tried to strike her. It was only her alien moves that had kept me at bay. Still, I couldn't even deny the allegations against me. Not without lying my ass off.

"Which you're terrible at, by the way," Dad said. "Always have been, always will be." I nodded at that comment, lowering my eyes to the floor in shame.

"And, now, even after everything she's been through, everything you've put her through, she still wants to see you," he said. "Pretty badly, too. You should have heard some of the things she said when I told her she couldn't see you. That girl has a mouth on her, I'll tell you. If I didn't know better, I'd almost think that she'd go after me."

My eyes darted back up to his, shocked, horrified. This was exactly what I was worried about. What I feared the most. Angela wasn't going to stop at just killing Eric. She'll go after Dr. Mendes as well, unless I could stop her. I just had no idea how.

"Kill her," Tom said, again. "It's the only way to stop aliens. You have to kill her before she kills the doc."

"But how?" I thought to him. "It's not like I didn't try before. She's too strong, too fast. Even if I could get out of here before she kills him. Even if I could get to her, get close enough to kill her. She'd still throw me away like I was a ragdoll. I wouldn't stand a chance against her."

"Maybe you don't have to kill her," Greg suggested. I smiled, actually happy that he was back from wherever it was that he had disappeared to this time. "Ah, shucks. And, well, I'm sure you'll be even more happy to hear from the person that I brought with me. 'Cause I didn't come back alone."

I rolled my eyes at that thought. As if he had actually gone anywhere. Where exactly would a voice that only existed in my head go, anyway? Other than away, which I always wished they would all do.

"I went where Angela had said she put his body, of course. He was standing right there, looking completely lost. Go on, say something. She can't see you, just hear you."

"No one can hear me," someone said. I gave out a heavy sigh, palming my forehead for a moment. But, then, I recognized the voice.

"Oh, no," I said, aloud, completely forgetting that the doctor was sitting there.

"What is it?" he asked.

"Wait, she can hear me?" Eric asked.

"No," I insisted, rejecting the thought. The truth that was staring me in the face. "No, no, no."

"But, if you can't hear me, then why did you answer me?" Eric asked. As if my denial of him, of what was happening, was an answer to his question.

"No, you can't be here," I insisted. "You shouldn't be here."

"Greg came back?" Dr. Mendes asked. "Can I talk to him?"

"Greg came back," I agreed, turning back to him. "And he wasn't alone. He brought Eric with him."

"Wow," Dr. Mendes said, taken aback. "That's a new one on me. But I guess with the recent death of Greg that you still haven't dealt with, anything is possible. I mean, it's a bit out of the norm, having two new voices so close to one another. At least it is for you. I'm not sure if this is a good thing or a bad thing. Maybe your subconscious is fighting against what we're trying to do here."

"What are you even talking about?" I asked. "Eric can't be here. I didn't see him die. Why is he here?"

"Eric isn't dead," Dr. Mendes said. "That's just part of your condition, that you think he is. That you think you hear his voice right now. This is just another part of the same breakdown you had when you were forced to kill Greg. You're feeling some added guilt over what you think is Eric's death, so you've started hearing his voice as well. That's all this is. The same guilt that you've been dealing with since killing your father. We need to get to the root of that guilt. Let you assimilate it, and the feelings that have been stirred up over it. So that we can move forward. Move towards health and fitness of the mind."

"No, no, no," I said. "I didn't see Eric die. That's always been the rule. The only rule that's been keeping me from a complete breakdown. I only hear the voices of those that died in front of me."

"No, you only hear the voices of the people that you think you're responsible for their deaths. Once Eric comes by, we can start getting to the heart of this. In fact, I think that is a great idea. I think we've finally had a huge breakthrough with this new development."

"Development?" I asked. "A breakthrough? You're calling another voice in my head a breakthrough?"

"Breakthroughs happen in the strangest ways sometimes," Dr. Mendes said. "Seeing Eric alive and well will help with your healing. With finally learning to put aside the guilt. Not just for his death, which still hasn't happened yet. But over the deaths of all of them."

"I don't feel guilty over Tom's death," I insisted. "He jumped all on his own. I was just there."

"You were there to stop him," Dr. Mendes said. "You admitted as such a while back. You failed him, and that's where the guilt over him comes from. How long ago did you first think Eric was dead?"

"That was almost a day ago, I think," I said. "I started worrying about him when he didn't show up at the precinct."

"But you didn't think he was dead then, did you? You just thought he was missing."

"Well, yeah, I guess it wasn't until..."

"Until after you slept with Angela and she said she killed him," Greg supplied.

"Wait, she slept with Angela?" Eric asked, shocked. "I didn't think... I mean, you don't look... I mean, you were totally flirting with me, earlier, right? I mean, that wasn't one sided, was it?"

"Oh, god, Eric, you're dead and you're actually jealous of the woman that killed you?" I thought to him.

"Right. Good point."

"Anyway, I think this is the perfect place to stop for today," Dr. Mendes said.

"Wait, what?" I asked. I looked over to the clock, trying to guage how long I had been in there. I didn't remember when the session started. "It couldn't have been an hour already."

"Oh, Natalie, you know sessions work a little differently in here. Besides, I need to take some time to call over to the precinct, to see if they've been able to find Eric yet. I'll see if he's available to come visit this weekend. I know I said no visitors, but I think I can make an exception for him. It'll be immensely therapeutic to see him alive and well and worried about you. Maybe it'll even help you focus away from those delusions you were having about Angela. Really, those were not healthy."

"What?" I asked.

"Wasn't he the one pushing for you to sleep with Angela?" Tom asked. "Well, him and Dad, that is."

"Don't call me Dad," Dad insisted.

"Why don't you head out and see about getting re-acclimated to the facility while I make some calls."

"Um... okay," I said. I was completely numb and at a loss for what was going on. My condition had always been a constant for me, changing only as often as I saw someone die. The constancy of it had been the only thing to help me get through it. And, now, maybe, just maybe, something was seriously wrong with it. With me.

Numbly, I got out of the chair, walked out of the office, and closed the door behind me. Once the door was closed, I ran as fast as I could back to my room.

Chapter Thirty-Four
Guilt

I was pacing the small room. More specifically the tiny portion of the floor that wasn't covered by furniture. My bed was the only one that had covers on it. The other was stripped bare. The hole in the mattress that had been there for years was sticking its tongue out to me. I was very glad that I didn't have a roommate this time around. My complete and total meltdown would be so much more awkward if I had an audience.

"How are you even here?" I asked, for the third time since getting back into the room. He had yet to give me an explanation that made any sense, given the fact that I was already crazy.

"We already went over this," Greg said. Eric hadn't said much since he showed up, leaving Greg to do most of the talking. "Angela told us where she left the body. Well, she told us that she used the same place that I had for Tom's body."

"Yeah, I'm still a bit freaked out about the fact that you hid and buried my body, dude," Tom said.

"Seriously, why didn't you know that I did that before?" Greg asked. "You were there, then, right?"

"No, actually, I was following this one around."

"Or so he always says," I said. "I didn't really start hearing him for a couple of hours afterwards. He kept complaining that my being there had 'ruined his suicide', of all things."

"Well, you did," Tom said. "The whole point of me killing myself was because I was feeling so alone that no one would notice if I was gone. You being there when I did it, and immediately reporting it to the cops, completely ruined it. But... well, I guess from one point of view, Greg did me a favor by hiding my body."

"What?" I asked, completely confused.

"Well, it sort of repaired the damage you had done. With no body, and you having a history of mental issues, that meant that no one believed that I was dead. Just missing. I mean, yes, they knew I was missing, which, still, ruined the whole point. But it came closer. It took them three years to realize I was actually dead, like you said."

"Yeah, and reporting it to the cops immediately, despite the lack of a body, obviously meant that I did it," I said. "Stupid Bently."

"Seriously, if we get out of this whole mess, we should sue his ass," Greg said.

"Greg, where the hell have you been?" I asked. "We're already suing him, or the police force or something."

"Oh, right," he said.

"Anyway," Eric said, loudly and right in my ear, as if I had been having any trouble hearing him since he arrived. "Greg found me pacing by my corpse, or where it was buried anyway, and brought me here."

"I still find it hard to believe, hard to understand, how a voice in my head could travel across the state, in a matter of minutes, find a body in the middle of the woods, that he only could have known if he was the real Greg, and return, again in a matter of minutes, with the voice of the person who had just died." I felt like I needed to be insane just to understand the sentence that I just said.

"Oh, god, she really thinks she's crazy," Eric said. "Well, I guess I didn't help much with that. Sorry about the whole 5150 thing. I guess you're in here because of me."

"Actually, no," I said. "When you didn't show up... Oh, god, why am I even explaining this to some weird voice in my head. I was there, I know what happened. You're a part of my mind, and, therefore, you should know as well."

"That logic fails," Greg said. "If that were true, the reverse would be true as well. That would mean that you'd know where Eric's body is."

"Uh, no, because you don't know where it is either," I said. "You just think you know where it is because you're fashioned after a person who does."

"But Eric is here," he said, holding him up as if his very presence disproved my explanation.

"Which you still haven't actually explained," I said. "I mean, seriously, did you use a taxi? Hail Ghost Rider? How can you possibly explain being able to get back down to Valhalla and back here before my session with Dr. Mendes was over?"

"Well, the place is called Valhalla," Greg said, as if that explained anything. "It's named after the Norse afterlife. Where else would the dead be able to travel to so quickly?"

I stared in the direction that his voice was coming from, a spot on the wall that looked like the profile of Aslan. I almost expected that it would open its mouth and speak sense when the voice itself was saying nothing but stupidity. I was just trying to find some semblance of truth in the crap that was coming to me. Coming out of the voice that couldn't possibly exist as anything but a broken off piece of my psyche. It had taken me a long time to come to terms with that explanation when it first started happening. When Dad first came to take up residence in my head. It was too slippery of a slope back down to complete insanity to consider anything else as being even likely. But there was one problem with that thought process.

"How does someone that you didn't see die suddenly show up, a day late and a dollar short, in the middle of a session with your shrink?" Tom said, supplying the question that I had been trying to get out since running from the office. "Especially given all that we already know about your condition."

"Well, if you were paying attention to Dr. Mendes back there, he had a perfectly good explanation for why it all happened," Dad said.

"I'm sorry. I was too busy freaking out about the fourth voice in my head to notice what he was saying," I said.

"You didn't see him die, but you feel responsible for his death," Dad said. "That's the real reason, the real trigger, behind the voices coming to you. It just took you longer to realize that he was dead. That you had a hand in his death and that you were feeling guilty about it. And, of course, this still applies even if he isn't really dead. Even if Angela didn't really say what you think she said. What we all heard her say. Even if Eric is still alive, you still think he's dead and feel responsible."

I felt such pride, relief, and gratefulness for Dad's explanation. It was the first real explanation that made some semblance of sense. I wanted to hug him. I didn't even remember hugging my real dad back when he was alive. But it was all I wanted to do. If only he was substantial enough to actually hug. But he wasn't, so I just hugged myself, as I sat back on my bed. Finally, I could start to calm myself down, now that there was something I could point to. Some explanation for all the crazy that suddenly crashed through my life. I was delusional, but that wasn't anything new.

"Okay," I said, nodding. "Okay, so if Eric is alive, like the doc thinks he is, like I hope he is, he'll find him and have him come by for a visit. Then I can start to get well again. To heal up. Maybe get to a place where I could leave here again. Hopefully leave here and never return."

"Why?" Greg asked. "Seriously, I never really understood that part of the whole thing. Those times that it was me signing you away in here. What's so wrong about this place? It looks pretty swanky to me."

"It's not so much the place as the not being able to leave here," I said. "Besides, the people in this place are crazy."

"But so are you," Greg said. "Doesn't that mean you should feel right at home?"

"Yeah, come back and tell us that after being stuck in here for a week or two every year for decades," Dad said, coming to my defense. "At least it's never been so bad that we've had to stay here for months. Not since that first time."

"Yeah, why do you think I call it my tune-up?" I said. "I'm just here to get my head straightened out again. Then I'm right back out of here."

"Plus, people have a tendency of shouting in the middle of the night," Tom added, in a small voice.

"But it's something that I've put up with before," I said. "It's something that I'll have to deal with every year unless I get better. So, I think the doc's right. I think I should just suck it up, for a few more weeks. One, slightly longer, but last, time here. I get well, really well. Then I can go home. Then I can figure out exactly what's happening with Angela and, if I need to, I'll put a stop to whatever it is."

"Except..." Eric said, dragging the word out for several syllables.

"Oh, not you, too," I said, exasperated.

"Yeah, that's my job," Tom said.

"Except for what?" I asked, ignoring Tom.

"Except she really did kill me," Eric said. "I was driving back from the crime scene. Or, at least, what we thought was the crime scene. Where we found the body. She was just standing there, out in the middle of the road, right where it bends that sharp left after the bridge. I had to slam on the breaks, because I hadn't seen her until I was right on top of her. The car stopped right in front of her. But, in a blink, she was suddenly next to me, pulling my door open. And I mean, she was pulling my door open. Like completely off my car. She threw it into the woods like it was a frisbee. Then, she was pulling me out of the car like I was ragdoll. Not even bothering to take the seat belt off of me. After that, well, it all went to black until she was burying my body in a hole in the middle of the woods. That girl is nuts. And I mean seriously nuts. And dangerous as hell. She has to be stopped before she hurts someone else. And, I'm sorry, but I don't think you have the time you think you do to 'get healthy'. Or whatever you want to call it. You're healthy enough already."

"But she's not going to believe you," Greg said, and he was right. "As long as we are just voices in her head to her, she's not going to put any weight behind our words. We could just be telling her what she thinks she needs to hear to keep her insane. To get her to escape here."

"Oh, please, like there's any way out of here that doesn't involve the front door," Tom said. "I've been analyzing this place for years."

"Let's not go there," I said. I didn't want to go on that very dangerous thought path.

"Except that we actually have a way to prove it now," Greg said.

"Prove what?" I asked. "That I'm crazy? We all know that."

"No," Greg said. "Exactly the opposite. I want to prove that you're not crazy. Or, at least, no more crazy than I am."

"Oh, that's a real comfort," I said, sarcastically. "You're a voice inside my head. So, by definition, I am exactly as crazy as you are."

"That's no--"

"And even if I did believe it. Even if you really were the real Greg. And Tom and Dad and Eric here are just, what? Ghosts talking to me? Even if that were true, the real Greg was not exactly the best measuring stick to use when measuring one's sanity."

"Hey," Greg said.

"I mean, seriously. You kill your girlfriend because you don't want her to tell your wife and you try to frame your ex-wife for it? What motive did I have to kill her again?"

"Jealousy," Greg, Tom, and Dad all said together.

"At least that's what Bently was saying," Tom clarified.

"Yeah, that was a bit nuts even for me," Eric said. "I never liked the guy, even before I died 'cause he called me in the middle of the night."

"My point is that I can show you exactly where Eric's body is," Greg said. "If I can do that, not only are you not crazy, not only is Angela a killer, but you'll be saving someone else's life as well."

"Wait, what?" I asked, completely at a loss for that jump in logic.

"We were thinking that earlier," Tom said, on Greg's side for once. "Who's standing between Angela and you right now?"

"Dr. Mendes," I said.

"So, really, we'd be doing him a huge favor to just get out of here while we still can," Greg said. "It's the only way to stop Angela from killing him, too."

"Except, we'd also need to make it clear to Angela that we're not here anymore," I said. "And, if we could do that, can't we do it without actually getting out of here? I mean, I really do need help, don't I?"

"No," Greg and Eric said together.

"Yes," Tom and Dad said together, at the same time.

"Well, that's three to two against escape," I said.

"No, that's three to two that you need help," Tom clarified. "I still think we need to get out of here. We need to stop Angela. Only once Dr. Mendes is safe can we get the help we need. Without him, we'd be hopeless."

"There are plenty of other shrinks out there," Dad said.

"But what's to stop Angela from picking them off one by one?" Tom asked.

"Sheer numbers?" I said. "She can't kill them all."

"No, but doesn't it take time to get a new one up to speed?" Tom asked. "As long as we're going through shrinks left and right, we're not going to make any progress."

"Let me get one thing straight with you all," I said. "It's me that needs the help. Me that keeps hearing voices that no one else is hearing, whether they're real or not. I'm the only one that needs help here."

"Except you're not," Eric said. "I mean, you're not the only one that needs help. If we're not just in your head, like Greg and I think, then we're ghosts or spirits or something. Something left over from who we used to be. We need help, too. Help to move on or... whatever it is that we do."

"And Eric needs help to get justice for his murder," Greg said. "That's something the rest of us will never get."

"Hey, don't look at me," Tom said. "I was never murdered."

"Neither were Greg and Dad," I said. "Those were self-defense."

"Exactly my point," Greg said. "Eric was murdered, and he needs to make peace with that. The best way for that to happen is for his murderer to be stopped, captured, and/or killed. And, since, currently, only the five of us even know that he's dead--"

"Six," I corrected. "Assuming this all is actually happening and I'm not completely losing my mind, then it's the five of us, plus Angela, seeing as how she's the one that killed him."

"Right, six," Greg said. "Since the six of us are the only ones that even know he's dead, and since Angela isn't likely to turn herself in and the four of us are completely hopeless in interacting with the outside world, it's up to you, Natalie. You're the only one that can do anything to stop her. And you can't do that from in here."

"So, you need to escape," Eric said. "Yes, I know, it's odd, maybe even a bit ironic, for the one cop in the bunch to be the most boisterous about escaping from a mental institute. But you don't really belong here. It's about time that you prove that to the world."

"Except this whole argument is a bit moot at this point," Tom said. "There's no way to escape this place."

"Actually, something tells me there is," Greg said. "And that Natalie knows exactly how to do it."

"No way," Tom insisted. "There's no way that she has figured something out that I haven't. Especially since I was trying to, every time we've been here. I'm the smart one in this whole relationship."

"This isn't a relationship. This is insanity. Or, if I'm not actually crazy, it's a haunting," I clarified, sensing Greg and Eric about to protest.

"Still, there's no way you're going to be able to figure a way out of here in the next few hours."

"Oh, I already know how we're getting out of here," I said. "Or, at least, I know how we're getting out of the building. The question is how are we getting back to Tarrytown and Valhalla. It's not like cabs are likely to drive by this place."

"Okay, so we need a phone," Greg said. "Any chance we can get a hold of one?"

"Not in here," I said. "Not unless..." I stopped in mid-sentence, remembering something that happened the other day. Something that might have been the solution to all my problems. I left the rest of them guessing as I started to comb through my bags. They were still packed up and just sitting around at the foot of my bed. In years past, they had actually unpacked for me. This had been the first time that I had come into the facility in the middle of the night. I was hoping that that would work in my favor, for once.

I cheered in triumph when I pulled out the small piece of folded plastic from my purse. The cell phone that Jessica had given me when we left the police station the day before.

Chapter Thirty-Five
Escape

"Hey, Natalie," Dr. Graves said. He waved to me as I came out onto the roof of the building. "I didn't know you were back."

"Well, it is that time again," I joked. My stomach was in complete turmoil. I knew that I would have to wait for someone to be up there for my plan to work. For someone to be on a smoke break. But why did it have to be Dr. Graves? Granted, he was one of the cuter smokers that came up to the rooftop multiple times during the day. But he was also the most observant and most strict when it came to the rules.

"You know you're not supposed to be up here," he said, before I took more than a couple of steps out from the stairwell. Behind me, the door slammed into the brick that was holding it open. There was no way to reopen the door from the outside, if anyone was out on the roof. But someone had smuggled in the brick ages ago. The thing had been holding the door to that rooftop open longer than I had been coming there. The problem was that you needed a badge in order to open the door to the roof. The staff always made sure the door was secure when no one was out there. That meant that the only times I could get out there was when someone was up there cultivating a very disgusting habit.

"I know," I said, waving his concern off as if it were nothing. "I just really needed to bum a smoke, and I saw that someone was up here."

"You smoke now?" he asked, surprised. And he should be. I wouldn't normally be caught dead with a cigarette in my hand. That was a phrase that had suddenly developed a whole new meaning to me considering who I've been hanging around with. Still, it was the only excuse I had for being up there. And I needed to be up there.

"I started a few weeks ago," I said. "You may have heard about my recent troubles with the law. My lawyer got me hooked."

"Oh, well, that wasn't all that nice of him," he said. "It really is a disgusting habit. You should probably fire him. After all, he didn't exactly keep you out of here, now, did he?" I snickered at that. He didn't know the half of it. "Anyway, I shouldn't be giving you one. But what the hell. I hate hanging out here alone." He waved me out onto the rooftop, pulling a fresh cigarette out of his pocket.

I smiled at him as I headed over to his side. For the first time, my continued presence here, my years of familiarizing myself with the staff, had actually worked in my favor. Instead of just being stuck there in that prison of a hospital, it was almost like a second family. The people trusted me, because they knew me too well. They knew that I was always working hard to secure my release. And that, usually, meant that I would work the therapy, take the meds required, and be as friendly as possible. For once, though, I had my sights set on a different way out. I shuddered a little at what they would think of me once I burned that trust to the ground, if I ever had to go back there.

"It really does look a lot higher than it is, doesn't it," Dr. Graves said, pointing towards the ground below.

We were five stories up, with the hard, solid, black asphalt of the parking lot below. It was specifically the visitors parking lot that we were over just then, which was much less crowded than the faculty parking lot on the other side of the building. I smiled as I wondered if he was outright making this easier for me.

I took the cigarette, sticking it between my lips, as he pulled out a lighter to light it for me. When I moved to take the lighter from him, he pulled it back, just out of my reach. "You know I'm not going to let you have my lighter," he said. "There are rules, and then there are rules. I'm breaking them enough as it is without giving you something that can be used as a weapon to hurt yourself."

"Ha," I laughed, thinking of the fact that I could be sealing my own fate already just by smoking that one cigarette. Sure, cancer tends to require continued exposure, but I had a habit of proving to be the exception to many rules.

"It may be small, but it gets the job done," he said, missing the source of my humor.

"No, I was just thinking that I could just as easily hurt myself just being up here," I said. I nodded my head towards the edge of the rooftop. "You know the second person that I saw die jumped from a rooftop not nearly as tall as this one is."

"But you're not suicidal, like I was," Tom said. "Right? You know you can't just jump off of the roof and expect to survive it."

I smiled at his words, enjoying the fact that I still hadn't told him how I was going to be escaping. It was a difficult feat, considering the fact that the voices had a tendency of reading my mind. After all, that was where they lived, wasn't it? But, still, I did all I could to think of just enough to get the job done. I wanted him to experience a taste of his own medicine.

"Yes, I guess that's true," Dr. Graves said. "But you're not going to get me in trouble by doing something stupid like that, are you?"

"Maybe," I said, smiling at him and Tom conspiratorially. "I do need to get out of here as soon as I can, though. It's just that leaving here that way won't exactly help things."

"Right," he said. He drew out the word, as if he wasn't entirely sure what I was talking about. And, of course, he didn't. "Maybe we should head back down." He made to move back towards the door, back towards the stairwell and the hospital within.

"What's the hurry?" I asked. I motioned my still unlit cigarette at him, like I still wanted to smoke it. Or ever wanted to smoke it. What I was planning on doing, my only method of escape for that hospital, required me to be on the roof alone. But I knew that Dr. Graves wasn't about to leave me up there unattended. Others might have, maybe some of the orderlies that tended to catch smoke breaks in groups near the end of their shifts. But I didn't have the time. I couldn't afford to wait for someone else to come by. It was now or never.

I looked over the edge of the roof, down to the parking lot below. There weren't many cars in the lot, just a few in the first row near the building and a single car in the last row. I squinted towards that car, the familiar looking minivan, trying to see if it was Angela's. It was too far away to make out the plates. Right before turning back towards the doctor, I thought I saw motion in the front seat. Someone shifting around inside to get a better look. To stare right back at me perhaps.

"Natalie, please come away from there, you're starting to make me nervous," Dr. Graves said. His voice claimed my attention away from the parking lot. He was already standing over near the exit, the door held open. The brick had fallen over when the weight of the door had come off of it. This was a tendency it had picked up in recent years from the wearing away of its formerly solid form, due to use and exposure to the elements.

"You're right," I said, amicably. "Sorry, doctor." I walked over to his side, picking up the brick, moving as if to place it down in its usual cubby, a hidden slot next to the door that had been worked into the stonework.

"Thank you," Dr. Graves said. He pulled the door open further to let me through first. He was obviously not going to trust me to be up there on the roof a moment longer.

"Very sorry," I said, quietly.

Putting my full weight into it, I swung the brick around at him, slamming it into the side of his head. Dr. Graves went down heavily, collapsing at my feet with an audible grunt and groan. Blood stained the already red brick in my hands and streaked against my face. I knew that I must have looked pretty gruesome, but I couldn't afford to spend the time to clean up.

"Are you crazy?" Tom yelled at me.

"Yes," I said. "Obviously. I'm talking to a voice in my head, aren't I?"

I bent over the prone body, feeling for a pulse in the man's neck. When I found the beat, slow but steady, I gave a deep sigh of relief that I hadn't killed yet another person. I had enough blood on my hands as it was. Both literally and figuratively. Quickly, I stashed the weapon back into the cubby before pulling Dr. Graves back out onto the roof by his feet.

"Quick, grab his badge," Greg said quickly.

"That's not going to do us any good," Tom said. "Even if we had a badge, they wouldn't let us out. Not in the middle of the day. All the badged doors are guarded by staff, except for this one."

"Besides," Dad said, as the door off the roof clicked shut. "We're locked out of there right now. We'd have to wait for someone else to come up here for a smoke break. They'd see the body and know what we did. You'd better have a different idea on where to go from here."

"Of course," I promised him. "I didn't want it to have to come to this, but I needed to be on the roof. This was the only way that was going to happen."

"By almost killing someone?" Tom said. "Haven't you killed enough people by now?"

"Says the guy that's insisting that I kill Angela," I said. "Trust me, I know what I'm doing."

"That makes one of us," Tom said. "Because you refuse to tell me the plan."

"Infuriating, isn't it," I said. "Now you know how it feels. So, next time you've figured something out, why not tell us instead of just gloating."

"Okay, everyone," Eric said. "Escape now, argue later. What's the plan?"

"Seriously?" I asked. "Isn't it obvious? I mean, come on, I can't be the only one here to have seen Die Hard."

"What are you..." Tom started to ask.

I looked over to the side of the doorway back into the stairwell, back into the building beneath my feet. Attached to the side was a long length of fire hose. I remembered seeing it there the first time I had snuck out onto the rooftop. At the time, one of the orderlies that worked there had a huge crush on me. He would take me out there on a regular basis. It was before Tom had shown up, before he had jumped from the building. So, he wouldn't have remembered it. Since then, it had always been there, in the background. A normal part of the landscape that was that place. But back when I had spent more time on the roof, I had always wanted to try swinging down from it, down to the parking lot below.

"No," Tom said. "No, it might not reach, you might fall. Then where would we be?"

"Well, if I fall, it'll be from further down that this," I said. "I might survive it, if I land just right. But, if it doesn't reach, well, then we'd just be stuck in the middle of the building, swinging in front of a window for all to see. We'd probably get more restrictions for almost killing Dr. Graves. But I don't think we'll have to worry about that for long. Not if you're right about Angela wanting to kill Dr. Mendes."

"Of course, I'm right," Tom insisted. "Isn't that her minivan out in the parking lot?"

"If it is, isn't this exactly what she wants?" Greg asked. "Us escaping and running right into her arms?"

"What would be so bad about that?" Dad asked. I could sense him picturing Angela and me being together again. That was something that would never happen if she really did kill Eric. "Aw," Dad said, disappointed.

"It might not be her car," I said, hoping I was right. I wanted to have a lot more in place before I confronted her again, about any of this. The last thing I wanted was the shrinks to be watching me through the windows when I was forced to kill Angela, especially if they're too far away to hear the reasons. I'd look more crazy than I actually was. They'd be likely to just lock me up for the rest of my life, especially given what I did to Dr. Graves.

"Oh, please, the asshole had it coming," Dad said. "I heard he used to take patients down to the basement and--"

"Oh, come off it, Dad," I said. "Those were never substantiated. And do you honestly think he'd still be working here if they were? That was one patient, and she had an unhealthy fixation with him. That's why they transferred her to another hospital. There haven't been any reports since."

"That doesn't mean there wasn't any truth to the first reports," Dad muttered.

I looked over my shoulder to the still prone form of the good doctor. I hoped that he would be alright, stuck up there and unconscious while I made my escape. Given the habits of the hospital staff, it was likely he'd be rescued quickly. Even if no one came to the roof before he woke up, he could just bang on the door until someone heard him. As long as he didn't die of his injuries, he'd be fine. I tried to reassure myself of that fact as I unwound the firehose.

By the time I had the hose unwound and unhooked from the wheel, Tom had started chanting. "Oh, god, oh, god, oh, god," he kept saying, over and over.

"Oh, what now?" I yelled at him. "Can't you see I'm trying to get out of here? This was your idea."

"Getting out of here, yes," Tom agreed. "But not like this. Not this way. Couldn't you have come up with some other way to get us out of here?"

"Us, sure," Greg said. "I could teach you how to decouple from this woman and we could just run off together."

"Yes, please, do," I said. The hose was heavier than I would have thought it to be. The weight was mostly on the ends, where the metal connectors were. I hoped they would be heavy enough to keep the hose in place while I descended. It wasn't exactly like I had many options for an anchor.

"Oh, god, oh, god, oh, god," Tom repeated.

"Oh, shut the hell up," I yelled at him. "What's so wrong with this option. It's not like you're afraid of heights or something."

"Um... well..." Tom said, hesitantly.

"What? Seriously?" I asked. "You threw yourself off a building. Was this sudden fear of heights something you had before or after doing that?"

"Well, jumping off a building to your death is certainly enough of a reason to be afraid of heights," Dad allowed.

"Uh, no, well, I was afraid of them before throwing myself off a building," Tom admitted. "I don't know. I just thought going out that way would be almost poetic. It would be like embracing my fear, rather than conquering it."

"Well, then, close your eyes and I'll tell you when it's over," I said. "It's too late to back out of it now."

"Especially since Margaret is about to come through that door any second, now," Dad said.

"What?" I asked. "Who's Margaret?"

"The head nurse," Dad said. "You know, the hot one."

"I... what?"

"The nurse that checked us in last time we were here. She always comes up for a smoke right before lunch. That would be about now. So, please, stop dawdling. Unless, of course, you want to sleep with her, too. I'm not sure you're her type though."

"Alright, alright," I said. I tossed one end of the hose over the side of the building, holding tight to the other side with both hands and planting my feet. Still, as the hose went taught, I was pulled forward by the momentum. I slammed into the wall that ran along the length of the roof, almost going over myself. "Ouch," I shouted.

"Oh, god, oh, god, oh, god," Tom repeated.

"Dad, can you please shut him the hell up?" I asked. I knew full well I wouldn't have any ability to. I never had. I heard what sounded like a hand slapping someone in the face and Tom's words stopped immediately. "Um... thanks?"

"No problem," Dad said. "I've been wanting to do that for years."

I slowly slackened my grip on the hose, but, as I did, it started to slip further down. Holding it steady, I peeked out over the edge of the roof. I saw the other end of it dangling, still a few feet off the ground. It was too difficult to tell just how far of a drop it would be, but the end looked like it was close enough for me to drop down safely from it. "The only problem is getting an anchor to hold it in place up here," I said, thinking out loud. After all, there wasn't anyone there that couldn't already hear my thoughts anyway.

"Yeah, you didn't really think this one through, now did you?" Greg accused.

"I'd like to see you try to make this whole thing dramatic without revealing it to someone that can read your mind and get it to work without a hitch on the first try," I said.

"Oh, yeah, blame it on Tom," he said. "After all, it was his idea to get us to break out of here, wasn't it?"

"Just wedge it in over there," Eric said.

"Over where?" I asked. I looked around, as if I could actually see his finger pointing somewhere.

"Oh, right, sorry, I forgot I was dead again," Eric said. "Over there, that vent thing poking up out of the roof."

I continued to look around us, trying to find what it was he was talking about. Off in the far corner, back closer to the staff parking, was an exhaust vent. It was probably for the air conditioning system or something. The vent pointed outward a little, giving a nice little section beneath it. Just enough room to lodge the end of the hose into.

"Well, it's better than nothing," I said. "But it's a little closer to the staff parking than I would have liked and I've already lowered the hose over here."

"You can just leave it lowered and swing it around the building," Eric suggested.

"People are going to see that, aren't they?" Greg asked.

"Oh, what are they going to think?" I asked. "The inmates are going to think they're seeing things and the doctors aren't going to know what to think. Besides, there's no time for another plan. Let's get this over with this before someone comes up here."

Without any further discussion, I ran over towards the vent. I kept along the edge of the roof so I wouldn't need to pull up the hose. I held it a few inches over the edge so it wouldn't catch on anything. By the time I was halfway there, I heard a beeping sound over by the door. It was the unmistakable sound of someone badging the door open. I didn't look around, couldn't afford the time to spare to look towards the door. I rushed as quickly as I could over the uneven ground, littered by the gravel that covered the rooftop. The door opened behind me, hitting Dr. Grave's prone form.

"What the hell?" someone yelled; a woman's voice.

"Yup, that's Margaret," Dad said.

"Oh, shut up," I said, as I lodged the hose in place. I looked over the edge of the roof, making sure that the hose still hung down freely. On this side of the building, the black asphalt was just a narrow strip, where they stuck the dumpsters when they weren't being unloaded. Beyond that was a wooded area that extended into the distance, reminding me a lot of a very different rooftop.

"Oh, god," Tom said, one final time.

I gave the hose two experimental tugs, though I couldn't spare any more time for caution. I climbed up onto the ledge, with just a single glance towards the door, where a disembodied arm was reaching through the crack to feel around Dr. Graves's leg. "I've always wanted to do this," I said, as I grabbed hold of the hose with all my might. "I just wish I had more time to enjoy it."

The door slammed open and I jumped off the edge, sliding down the hose like it was a pole. Hand over hand, I descended, heading quickly for the ground below, until the anchor finally gave way.

And I was falling.

Chapter Thirty-Six
Graverobbing

My limp grew more pronounced as the day grew darker. The bus faded into the distance behind me. The two buses and two trains that it took to get there faded from my memory. My focus was set on the road forward, my destination. The last place I wanted to be just then was the only thing I focused on. It was the only thing keeping me moving forward when all I wanted to do was go home and crawl into bed. I wouldn't even allow myself to wonder if I would be doing that alone.

"Are you trying to make me jealous?" Eric asked.

"Jealous of the woman that killed you?" Greg asked.

"Well, who else was going to be crawling in bed with her?" Dad asked.

"Will you four shut it," I said. I huffed with the effort of walking.

"Hey, I didn't say anything," Tom said, defensively.

Greg insisted that Eric's grave was close when he told me to get off the bus in the middle of the otherwise deserted street. We were in the no man's land between Tarrytown and Valhalla, a section littered with woods where no one would want to be in the middle of the night. It was just the kind of road that a certain someone attributed to our neighbor to the north had stalked his victims, looking for his missing head. The bus driver had barely sent me a curious glance over his shoulder as I descended the back stairs. That suited me just fine. I didn't want him to ask questions that I wasn't able to answer.

I tried not to think of the fact that I had broken out of HTP and came halfway across the state on the word of the voices inside my head. I was well off the reservation, with no way back. Only the road ahead to keep me going. If I was found, if I was stopped, I'd be going straight back there, with no hope of escape. No hope of ever leaving there. But luck seemed to be on my side for once. I had stayed ahead of the news of my escape. No one knew where I was heading, or why. Otherwise, I would have already been surrounded by the boys in blue, ready to send me back to the men and women in white.

"So dramatic," Greg said. "Just relax. This is almost over. Once we find Eric's body, we can call in the cops and have them arrest Angela. Then we can go home, alone, and crawl into our own bed, alone." He overly stressed the word "alone", making it clear that he didn't want me with Angela any more than Eric did.

"That's assuming we ever find the place," I said. "I can't see a thing past that first row of trees."

"Your eyes will adjust," Greg said. "Just like they did the night you found Emily's body."

I laughed a little at the similarities between the two nights. At the time, I hadn't known Emily was dead, or that Greg had killed her. Yet, now, I was almost positive that Eric was dead, that his body was somewhere in the woods around me. I also knew that, if I did find him, I was most likely going to be blamed for his death, one way or another.

"Not this time," Eric promised. "We'll make sure that Angela doesn't get away with it."

"Like you had kept Greg from getting away with it before?" I asked. "How did that end again?" The reminder brought the eternal feeling of blood covering my hands to the forefront of my mind. It became a new obsession to fill in the gaps of my focus. Unconsciously, I rubbed my hands down my tattered shirt. It was the remnants of the outfit that I had put on earlier that day, after breakfast.

"Turn here," Greg said. He didn't sound as sure as I would have liked, given the area we were in. Reluctantly, I followed his instructions, turning off the solid ground of the road and into the murky muck of the woods. The road seemed to instantly disappear, though I could still make it out through the trees. It was just hard to see without any street lights to guide me and the moon still asleep. Getting lost there would certainly solve some of my problems, but cause a lot more of them. I wouldn't be surprised if I woke up dead the next morning. "Oh, you're not going to get lost," Greg said. "We're not even going to lose sight of the road. Besides, the four of us can fan out and look for it if we do."

"Said the voice inside my head. My own personal siren baiting me into the dark and scary woods to be eaten alive by wolves and worse."

"This is nothing," Greg insisted. "Just wait until you have to go home and handle the wife."

"We're not going to be doing that, right?" Eric asked. "We're calling in the cops. I would have liked it if we had called them before leaving HTP, rather than breaking out on our own. But I knew they wouldn't believe you. Not on the word of a voice in your head."

"Bently will never believe me," I reminded him.

"Well, it's a good thing that we don't have to call him, then," Eric said. "We're calling the Valhalla PD, aren't we?"

"If we actually find your body, I'm only going to be making one phone call. And that's not to either town's police department. It's to Jessica." I pulled the small cell phone out of my pocket, holding it in my hands as a safety blanket. A friendly reminder that I wasn't completely alone in the world. It was my one tether to sanity. My last bastion of safety as I descended into the dark abyss surrounding me.

"It's just the woods," Greg insisted. "Besides, we're here."

"We're where?" I asked, looking around me. I could still just make out the clearing that signified the road in the distance behind me, but I could no longer make out the black asphalt apart from the black night. It was too late to go back, to wait for the bright of day before handling things. My imagination was running ahead of me, conjuring images of Eric's dead body, rising from the grave to drag me back down with it.

"I wouldn't go and do a thing like that, now would I?" Eric insisted.

"That would suggest that you're real," I said. "And in control of your body. I somehow doubt both of them could be true at the same time."

"Hey, anything is possible," Eric said. "A petite blond killed me without breaking a sweat. I wouldn't put it past my ghost to be able to possess my own dead body."

"A petite blond alien," Tom amended. "I don't think she would have stood a chance against you before this whole thing started."

"Too right," Greg agreed. "I remember when she overloaded her suitcase for our honeymoon. She couldn't even lift the thing into the trunk. But it was easy enough for me to get it in. I could do it one handed."

"Honeymoon?" I asked him. "Was this before or after you divorced me?"

"Man, you're touchy tonight," Greg accused.

"She has a right to be," Dad said. "We broke out of a psych hospital to go traipsing, near a dead body, in the middle of the night, while on the run from men in white uniforms. And her ex-girlfriend, who just happens to be a homicidal maniac alien. I think we all have a right to be a little afraid, and the four of us are already dead."

"Not so much near as... well... on," Greg said.

"What?" I shouted. My shriek echoed off the trees around me, as I jumped up and away from where I was standing. "Ew, ew, ew," I chanted.

"Hey," Eric said, offended.

"Oh, shut up," I said. "I'd like to see you not be grossed out by your own dead body. It's been over a day since you died. You're probably all bloated right now."

"Yeah, but where are you?" Tom asked. "Where was I? All I see is the leaf cluttered ground."

"Should we have brought shovels?" I asked. "Or, well, I guess one shovel. It's not like the rest of you can exactly help me dig him up."

"Will you just relax?" Greg said. "Turn around." I turned around in a circle, quickly, trying to see what it was he was talking about. Angela couldn't have just left the body out for everyone to see or wild animals to attack. Tom's body would have been found years ago if Greg had done the same. Still, it all looked like a normal forest floor. "No, slower," Greg ordered. I slowed my spin. "There."

I could feel his disembodied arm pointing towards the base of the tree in front of me. It was the one I had been standing next to, about to lean into, just moments before. It looked like any old tree, though it was tall and thick, twice as wide as I was. The rest of the forest had grown up around it, interlocking into its branches above and playing footsie with its roots below. It was easily the biggest tree around. But, other than that, there wasn't anything remarkable about it. No clear cavity or section that could hide something as large as Eric's body.

"Are you saying I'm fat?" Eric asked. "Or was, anyway?"

"What? No," I said. I was surprised that someone that had looked that amazing could possibly have body issues. I remembered the sight of him, without his shirt on. Remembered lusting after the glimmering pecks, the strong muscles. Remembered that I had wanted to pull me close to his chest and never let go. "You were perfect, and hopefully still are, if you're not really dead."

"So, you're saying you want to be completely crazy?" Tom asked.

"Well, it beats having someone be killed because they were your friend," I said.

"Not by much," Dad said.

"Can we focus?" Greg asked. "I really don't want to be out here all night."

"Well, whose idea was it to come out right now anyway?" I asked.

"There, at the base of the tree, is a shovel," Greg said. Again, I could feel his arm, reaching out towards the tree, as if he could pick up the shovel himself and present it to me.

With a huff of exasperation, I went back over to the tree. I looked around for a shovel that I was sure couldn't possibly exist. At least it would stop me there, settling everything once and for all. If Greg said there was a shovel here and there was no shovel, then, obviously, I was completely delusional, and should turn right back around and head back to HTP.

"Unless Angela took it with her when she buried Eric here," Greg suggested.

"No," I said. "If I can't find a shovel, I'm going back. What exactly do you expect me to do? Dig him up with my bare hands?"

"You won't have to," Dad said. "Look. Over on your left."

"What?" I asked.

My hands automatically went that way, grazing across a hard, cold piece of metal that I couldn't see in the darkness of the night. Even with hitting it there, it took me another minute or so to actually find it, and another to pull it free from the foliage around it. "What the hell?" I asked. I was completely stunned when I looked at a very old, very rusty, but very real shovel in my hands. The handle was warped by being outside for so long. The blade was rusted. But there were no signs of holes. No signs that the thing would fall apart at a moment's notice. And, assuming Angela had used it just a couple of days earlier, it was probably still good enough to dig up a dead body.

"What the hell?" I asked, staring dumbfounded at the shovel in my hands. Why would there be a shovel out in the middle of nowhere? How would I have even found such a thing, in the dark, in a place that I was told it should be by the imaginary voices inside my head. "I know this. How could I know this, Greg? Did you tell me? When you were alive, did you tell me? Like you told Angela? Do I just not remember?"

"No," he insisted. "I never told you. You don't know this. You never knew this. You only know now because I told you now. I'm real."

"No," I shouted. My voice echoed through the woods around me, around us. "No, you can't be real. It's not possible. And if I believe that, if I let myself believe that you're real, then I truly am lost. That's when I'm too crazy to know the difference between what's real and what's not. Then I might as well check myself back into HTP right now."

When a professional tells you that you're crazy, you kind of have to believe them. When the voices inside your head tell you their real, you ignore them as long as no one else can hear them. But, when the voices inside your head tell you something that no one else should be able to know, when it turns out that what they're saying is true, how do you handle that? How do you even begin to explain away something that couldn't possibly be real?

"I'm as real as you are, babe," Greg said. His voice sounded overjoyed, as if he were smiling broader than his mouth should have allowed. But he didn't have a mouth. Not anymore. At least not one attached to the source of his voice. But what was the source of his voice? Where was it coming from if not from inside my head? And why was it that I was the only one to hear it? To hear him? To hear them?

"You're special," Dad said. "I've always known that. I just wish that I had appreciated it more back when I was still alive. Back when I was still your father."

"No," I said, shaking my head in denial. Not after all this time, after all these years hearing my father's voice in my head, thinking that I had just gone crazy, not that I was... "I'm haunted," I said. "That's what it is. I'm haunted by the men that affected my life the most. They're all dead, but none of them should have been."

"Can we get to digging up my body now?" Eric asked. "I'd like to get justice for my death sometime soon."

"No," I said again. "No, I shouldn't dig you up."

"What? Why not?" Eric asked.

"Because this is a crime scene," I said. "I already stumbled upon one crime scene and almost got arrested for the crime. I'm not about to contaminate another one." Carefully, I placed the shovel back against the tree. Not where I had found it in the growth that had been built up around it, but against the main trunk. "Besides, I don't want to see you like that."

"Then what's the plan?" Tom asked. "Are you satisfied we're more than just voices in your head now?"

"Yes," I said. "And no. But, I'm ready to proceed under that assumption. I'll be completely damned if I'm wrong. Condemned to live the rest of my life as a crazy loon. But I can't overlook this evidence that this was all real."

"Gee, if I knew that some random shovel in the middle of the forest was enough to convince you I'm real, I would have shown you here a long time ago," Greg said.

"Greg, you should have shown me to Tom's grave a long time ago anyway, even before I killed you," I said. "That was just mean to keep that to yourself all this time."

"Yeah, man," Tom said. "I have parents too, you know. Maybe they would have liked to have grieved for me properly."

"Maybe they would have wanted their son to be alive," Dad said. "Did you ever think of that?"

"Pfft, like they even noticed I was alive when I was...
well, you know, alive. They probably noticed my absence
more than they ever noticed my presence."

"Yeah, if only I could have ignored your presence," I
said. "Alright, where the hell is the stupid road now?"

"It's on the other side of the tree from where you're
standing now," Greg said. "See? We didn't get you lost at all."

"On the other side and how far off?" I asked. As I made
my way around the tree, still too far away from the road to see
much of anything, I pulled out the cell phone that Jessica had
given me, flipping it open to see the screen. "Great, I have no
signal. How the hell am I going to be able to direct the cops
here without actually being here to direct them?"

"That's what the mile markers on the road are for," Eric
said. "But why aren't you going to be here to direct them?"

"Because I have an alien to slay," I said. It came out a lot
more ominous than I had intended.

Chapter Thirty-Seven
Stalking

I was halfway back into Tarrytown, walking the entire way, before I got a signal on the cell phone. Immediately, I called Jessica, giving her as much information about the whereabouts of Eric's body as I could. This included telling her about a dozen times that I had nothing to do with his death, but that I was going to confront the person that did. She didn't like the sound of that. To be honest, neither did I. But it had to be done. Angela had already killed Eric. There was no telling what else she did while I was stuck at HTP. I wasn't about to let her do anything else. Not without at least trying to stop her.

"And the only way to stop her is to kill her," Tom said.

I was just turning down my street. The house was visible in the distance. What little money I had brought with me during my escape had been spent just getting me back into the area. The two bus tickets and two train tickets drained almost all of it, with a small meal here and there to tide me over. I had left most of my stuff, including my purse, back in my room, not wanting to tip anyone off to my escape attempt. Either way, I would be returning to HTP when this was all over.

"Assuming you're still alive when this is all over," Eric said. "It's not too late to just call the cops on her."

"Yes, it is," Tom said. "She's long past their authority. Technically not even in their jurisdiction."

"She still lives in Tarrytown," Eric said. "That is their jurisdiction."

"No, she's an alien," Tom said. "Only the MIB can handle her now."

"What does the Medical Information Bureau have to do with this?" I asked.

"Wait, what?" Tom asked. "No, the Men in Black."

"Oh, so you want to turn to a non-existent organization rather than the very real men with very real guns?" Eric asked.

"You're non-existent," Tom said. I laughed at that, wishing I could still agree with the sentiment. But I had seen too much to still believe that the voices inside my head were only that. I yearned for the more innocent times when I still thought I was only crazy.

"Why do you think that is?" Dad asked. He seemed to be referring to a conversation that we weren't having. "Why do you think that you can hear us but others can't?"

"I'm psychic?" I asked, more than said. "I don't know. Why do some people see or hear ghosts when others don't? If they're not crazy, that is."

"Maybe it just means you're special," Greg suggested. "Of course, I've always known that you were special. Why else would I have married you?"

"Because you're a homicidal, anti-social, sociopath," I accused. "Just like all lawyers."

"Said the paralegal," he said.

"Paralegals aren't lawyers," I said. "We do the grunt work of lawyers for a fraction of the pay. You're the ones with the egos the size of Texas."

"Can we focus?" Eric said. "We're here. What's the plan?"

"Honestly, I was hoping that a plan would come to me on the walk over," I said. "Angela scares the hell out of me right now and I want to be anywhere other than in there." I looked up at the big, dark house, wondering just where she was inside. The display on the cell phone showed that it was past midnight. The walk from the middle of nowhere had taken hours. Usually, that would mean she was in bed, on the far side of the house. However, as the curtains on the window to the baby's room seemed to flutter back into place, I somehow doubted that she would be sleeping. Perhaps more accurately, I doubted that it would be that easy to take her unguarded.

"Well, it's not just up to you to come up with a plan this time," Tom said. "We're here. And we're all really here. How do we want to handle this?"

"Call the cops," Eric said, again.

"I think that I would have heard from Jessica by now, if she had actually got a valid response from them about what was happening. If she had gotten some kind of indication that they believed me. That they didn't think I was responsible for Eric's death," I said.

"How exactly would you have been responsible for my death?" Eric asked. "You would have needed to kill me, get rid of my body, and get back to my house in the span of less than an hour. The cops deserve more credit than that."

"Even Bently?" I asked.

"Well... maybe not him. Sure, he'd probably suspect you of being able to teleport around like a witch."

"Besides, does anyone know the exact time you disappeared?" Greg asked. "They'd need to build out a timeline for that, won't they?"

"Actually, no," I said, remembering something. "Bently's last theory had me working with Angela to kill you. He'll just think we did it again, keeping me alone at Eric's place as an alibi while she did the deed. I'd put my money on that being exactly what he's thinking right now."

"Yeah, you're right," Eric agreed. "Alright, the cops are out, then, unfortunately."

"We could just go," Dad suggested. "Disappear, tonight. Head off into the world, never to be seen again. By the cops or by Angela. The cops are bound to arrest her eventually, for

Eric's death or for Greg's. Either way, she'd be stopped, and you'd be safe."

"Except I'd be on the run the rest of my life," I said. "And, plus, what chance do the cops have against her with that weird super strength of hers?"

"What chance do we have against it?" Eric asked.

"Ooh, I know that one," Tom said, celebrating the fact. "She loves her. Did you guys see how she looked when she pushed Natalie into that railing the first time? She was horrified. Scared she accidentally killed her. She'll be careful this time around, trying not to hurt her."

"So, let me get this straight," I said. "Angela is an alien and, therefore, a monster. But she still cares about me, perhaps even loves me, and we need to kill her?"

"Well, yeah," Tom said.

"Maybe, and I know this is perhaps a rather wild idea, but, maybe we just try to convince her to turn herself in," I suggested.

"Nope," Eric said.

"No," Greg said.

"Not going to happen," Tom said.

"Well... yeah, no," Dad said.

"The whole reason she killed me was because she thought I was in her way," Eric said.

"The whole reason why Dr. Mendes is probably dead right now is because he was in her way," Tom said.

"Wait, what?" I asked.

"I mean, unless he was able to convince her that you really weren't there," he said.

"Wasn't that her van at HTP?" Dad asked. "She would have seen us escape, right?"

"Then why didn't she chase after me?" I asked.

"If that was her, are we sure she's not still there?" Greg asked.

"The van's here," I said. I pointed towards it in its usual spot in the driveway. My own car was parked right behind it, lending to the theory that it wasn't her van there at all.

"We're just talking in circles, here," Dad said. "Do we have a plan or not?"

"Not," I said. "Obviously."

"We need a plan, right?" Tom asked. "I've never done something like this before."

"Tom, none of us have come home to kill an alien who is alone, asleep, in bed," I said. "No one has. It's just so out of the norm, I... I don't think any real plan would work."

"What are you talking about?" Tom asked. "We have to have a plan. We didn't have a plan last time and look what happened."

"Last time, we weren't sure she was really an alien," I said.

"I was sure," Tom said.

"We had no idea that she was so strong, or fast," I said. "In fact, we have no idea what other powers she actually has, if any. Maybe we try to sneak up on her while she's sleeping, only to find out that she doesn't sleep. Maybe we try to blow up the house only to find out she's impervious to fire."

"Well, I like that idea," Dad said. "Can we revisit the blowing up the house idea?"

"What about Doug?" Greg asked.

"Yeah, we don't know that she infected him," I said. "We can't risk him dying unnecessarily."

"I'm not sure I want him dying even if he is an alien," Greg said. "Something about paternal instinct and all that."

"Do you even have paternal instinct?" Dad asked.

"Do you?" I countered.

"Can we stop arguing with each other?" Eric asked. "Natalie's right. We don't know anything about Angela right now. Just that she's strong, she's fast, and she needs to be stopped."

"And she's infected by something alien," Tom added.

"Or was replaced by something alien," Greg suggested. "No one's ever suggested that. It's possible that Angela is still alive out there, still human, and this alien is the only way we find her."

"Greg, get over it," I said. "We all saw her go over to the... well, the alien side of the force."

"So, what? The plan is like the spoon?" Tom asked.

"Yeah, I think it's time for plan spoon," I said. "I don't want to go in there, but I know I have to. Perhaps the best way to stop Angela is with her help. Maybe there's still some of the old Angela in there that can help us stop her. If not, we'll have to kill her, or die trying."

"Well, you'll have to die trying," Greg said. "The rest of us are already dead."

I gave that comment just a cursory smile. I wasn't even sure if it constituted an actual joke, or if it was just gallows humor. The last quip of a group of people heading for their doom. Even if the rest of them were already dead, I was their only connection with the land of the living. The only person that even knew they were there, let alone could hear them. Without me, they were as good as dead. Still, none of them let on that they had anything to lose. That they were afraid at all about what was inside that house.

And, truth be told, we had no way of knowing that Angela didn't have some capability to not only see and hear them, but end them for good. Taking them out of this world more permanently than they already had been. No one wanted to mention that. That uncertainty. The unknown that plagued our every step towards the dark house in front of us.

I took my keys out of my pocket before I even made it to the sidewalk, heading for the door. Their cold, hard metal felt good in my hands, as if their very presence was enough to combat the uncertainty I was feeling. Their twins were still locked away in evidence at the station. The ones that I had used barely two weeks earlier to end the first threat. I wondered if I would ever get those back, or if I'd ever be able to use either set again. Whatever happened inside would decide my fate for the foreseeable future. Or if I had a future at all.

My shoes hitting the cement for the first time made me jump. The change in the sounds of my footsteps made me think that something was wrong. It was like maybe I was stepping into a territory that I shouldn't be in. Like Angela's very alienness had been enough to corrupt the property that I had bought, the home that I had lived in for years before she was even a blip on Greg's radar. It felt wrong, somehow. Like the aliens had already won. Had already taken over the entire world, rather than just my corner of it.

I looked around at the other houses in the neighborhood, wondering just how many of them were similarly tainted. Had Angela already started spreading the contagion? Would killing her do nothing to stop the alien invasion in its tracks? Perhaps it was already too late. Perhaps the aliens had already taken over the entire world, missed by me during the walk from Eric's shallow grave. That would certainly explain the lack of calls from Jessica.

The cell phone felt cold and dead in my pocket, beating against my leg with each step. It was a constant reminder that, despite ties to the outside world close at hand, I was still alone. Still vulnerable and unprotected as I walked straight into the alien's den. I wanted nothing more than to be wrong about everything. To really be as insane as everyone thought I was. To know, or even consider it a possibility, that Angela was as human as I was. But that wasn't to be. There was no magic wand to make that true. No rewind button to take me back to before she was corrupted by the beast that attacked us.

I missed the girl that she used to be. Missed the love that we could have had. I had wasted so much time fighting the feelings that were developing between us that I missed out on everything. I had missed out on what could have been an epic love story. One they sang songs about. One that shadowed what I had, what either of us had, with Greg. By the time I got to the door, touched the cold metal of the door knob, a perfect mate to the keys in my other hand, I had almost convinced myself that it could still work. That I could overlook her being an alien. Her having killed Eric to get to me. Her obvious plan to take over the world.

Almost.

The lock gave a satisfying click as I turned the key in it. The door whined in protest as I opened it, as if complaining about my intent. Or, better yet, in a futile attempt to warn Angela about that intent. Not wanting its continued sounds to warn her any more than it already had, I left the door open. I took three long strides across the hardwood floors of the entry hall, setting my feet down as lightly as I could. Once I made the stairs, and the carpeting that coated them, I was home free. My feet were properly muffled as I ascended toward my target. Towards the woman, the alien, that I needed to kill.

Knowing the house, my house, as well as I did, I easily stepped over the loudest of the stairs. No squeaks or groans of the underlying wood would sound an alarm like the traitorous door. I paused briefly at the top of the stairs, sending one, short, fleeting look towards my right. Down towards my room. Or, at least, the room that I had taken residence in during those nights that I hadn't been sleeping next to Angela. For an instant, I wanted to just go to my own bed. To spend one last night of freedom before I condemned myself to whatever fate would befall me after I did my duty. I knew full well that no one would ever congratulate me. Never thank me for what I was about to do, despite the fact that it would save the world from aliens. More than that, it would save its people from a fate far worse than death, the stealing of our bodies by those aliens.

With a subtle shake of my head that only the voices, the ghosts, could see, I turned towards my intended target. Towards my left. Towards her room. As I took those last few fateful steps, I was thankful to the four of them for remaining quiet as I ascended into the house. I didn't know if I trusted my nerves to take their constant voices in my ear as I tried to be as quiet, as stealthy, as I could. Walking through my house as if it were still mine.

"The other two stayed outside," Tom whispered. "I don't think they liked the idea of killing her. But we know it's necessary."

"We're with you, my daughter," Dad whispered. His words left me with a reminder that he really was my father. That all this time spent with him was more quality time with him than all the years he had been alive. It also put a lot of things he had said over the years in a much more perverted light. But I tried not to dwell on that. I tried to focus on the task at hand.

The door to Doug's room was wide open. The moon, finally rising, shined through the windows and bathed the room in an almost ethereal light. Doug's sleeping form could be seen in the crib in the corner. His face was turned towards me, showing a serenity only known by babies. I wondered if he really was still a baby. Still human behind that guise of innocence. Or if the same perversion that led Angela to kill Eric ran through his blood. Controlled him as surely as it controlled her. I couldn't risk waking him, though. I didn't dare check on his humanity, for fear that his cries would wake Angela.

Thoughts of Doug's cries reminded me of Angela's first attempt to get me to move in with her. I remembered her thinking that Doug was having trouble sleeping through the night. That her nightmares of Greg weren't the problem keeping her up at night. That the child was having more trouble adjusting to his death than she was. A lot had changed in so little time. I doubted that she would ever be that innocent again. That troubled.

Angela's door, too, was wide open, leaving the path between her and her child free of barriers. She would hear him if he stirred. Hear him if he needed her. He would hear her, too. But would he have the capacity to know it? To know that his mother needed help? Know that he was incapable of helping her at all? It wasn't like he could get out of the crib. He couldn't call the cops or even do much more than cry. His piercing screams would rend the night. But it would go unanswered. Unnoticed by the world around him. For the only one left standing to tend to his cries would be the very woman that needed the help.

Two steps into the room took me to Angela's side. My side of the bed was vacant, as it always was since that first kiss. She had pulled back the sheets, leaving the bed open on that side, as if inviting me to join her. As if she knew to expect me to return to her. As if her spell over me was still in place, the one broken only by her alienness. Yet, even knowing what she was, I still felt that draw. I still felt the desire to crawl in bed next to her. To snuggle up to her. To hug her close and never let go.

My eyes focused on her sleeping form next to me. They focused on her face, serene in sleep.

So, I saw it when her eyes flicked open. The darkness that I had seen at the restaurant was back again for a split second before her familiar blue eyes returned.

I wanted to scream, to run. But I was completely frozen in place by her eyes.

Chapter Thirty-Eight
Going in for the Kill

The keys were still in my hand. An echo of the previous death, the previous day. A very different day. One where I didn't know I was going to kill. When I came for Greg, I wanted him to deny it. I wanted him to refute my suspicions of his involvement in Emily's death. That night, I came for a very different reason. I came to kill. It looked so different from the other end of the spectrum. I wanted to ask Greg how it felt to kill Emily when intending to do her harm. But his voice was absent from my mind. I could feel Tom and Dad trying to pull away from me. Trying to escape that cold, hard gaze that entrapped me. If they could abandon me like Greg and Eric had, they would have. But, for some reason, perhaps our many years together, they were tied to me so solidly that I could feel them pulling at that very real, very tangible tether that joined us.

If I was able to, I would have run too.

"Natalie," she said.

My name. So simple. So subtle. But everything coming from her lips. It was intoxicating, being that near to her again. Letting her be so close to me. I wanted to join her in bed as much as I wanted to flee. But I knew I could do neither.

She sat up in bed. The covers fell away from her naked form. Her eyes, locked onto mine, promised pleasure and lust beyond anything that I had known before. In anyone else's arms, man or woman.

"Hi," I said, moronically. Even in such a small syllable, my voice quivered with fear. She smiled at me, perhaps thinking there was a very different source of the quiver.

"You came back," she said, she cooed, as her arms reached out for me. Reflexively, I took a step back. Her eyes missed nothing, but her smile didn't slacken in the least. "I was worried that I'd never get to see you again. Were you released already? I kept trying to get in touch with that doctor of yours, but he wasn't taking my calls."

A sigh of relief escaped my lips against my better judgement. If she was still trying to reach him, perhaps it wasn't too late to save him from her. Then again, perhaps she was just saying that. Trying to throw me off her game. Trying to stop me from thinking the worst of her. She needn't have bothered, if that were the case. I already thought she was a horrible monster that couldn't be allowed to live.

"The cops will be looking for me," I said. I don't know why I said it. Her eyes bore into mine, as if searching them for something. For information. For why I was there. For how I was there. Yet, I would have told her anything, if only she would ask.

"Why?" she asked. "What's going on?"

"I found Eric's body," I said. "I told them where to find it."

"You found... How? That's impossible. No one knows where that place is. It's in the middle of nowhere. That was the whole point. The whole reason why Tom was never found."

"It doesn't matter how I found it," I said. "The point is that I did."

"But I don't understand," she said. "He was trying to get between us. To steal you away from me."

"He was my friend," I yelled at her. She didn't so much as flinch. "He was my friend and you killed him. Why? Because you were jealous of him?"

"Yes," she admitted. "I was jealous of him. Of the things he could do to you that I can't. To fill you in ways that I can't. I saw him, standing there with his shirt off. Offering you the world. And I just saw red. I had never experienced that kind of rage before. To know that you had run from me at that restaurant to go to him. Why? Why did you run from me? Did you just want him more?"

"What?" I asked. "No." My hands moved towards her, unbidden, under some control that was not my own. They didn't move to kill, but to comfort. I had to stop them before they went too close to the killer before me. "I didn't know I was... I didn't plan on going to him that day. I was... I was scared. You scared me."

"Me?" she asked. "I scared you? How? Is my love for you that scary?"

"Not your love," I said. "It's the fact that you're an alien."

"An... what?" she asked. She fell backwards, sitting back on the bed as she stared at me in utter confusion. "What on earth are you talking about?"

"Oh, don't give me that," I yelled at her. "Don't try to pretend that something is happening here that isn't. It's just the two of us. You can drop the whole act."

"Wait, you mean that whole thing that you were talking about yesterday?" she asked. "About that creature that attacked us? I thought you were having some kind of episode. About the whole thinking it infected me with something. That was why I called Dr. Mendes."

"Oh, yeah? Then what about that whole thing about me attacking you? Huh? Where did that come from?"

"Natalie, you need help," she said. "You... You weren't released, were you. You escaped? Is that why the police are after you?"

"Don't... Don't start that whole innocent act again," I said. "I know what I saw at that restaurant. You know what I saw there. You're not Angela anymore. You're that thing that took her over."

"Natalie, I assure you, it's still me," she said. She reached out, taking my hand before I noticed. Faster than she should have been able to. Her speed belied her denial. "I'm still the girl that you were starting to fall for, before he turned you from me." Her voice got dark when she brought up Eric. A flash of the same darkness crossing her eyes, momentarily, before she came back to me.

I wanted to believe her. I wanted to believe that the girl I had been falling for was still in there. Not only still in there, but was dominant. Was forefront in that complicated mind of hers. Perhaps the alien was only coming out in the anger, making it harder, sharper. Like a knife, to stab out at the people around her. Perhaps it wasn't too late to save her. To free her from the enslavement that was to come.

But the world didn't revolve on perhaps, certainly not my world. In my world, perhaps was as dangerous as a gun, something that I wished fiercely that I had brought.

"That girl I was falling for wouldn't have killed someone," I said. "Not for any reason. Certainly not out of jealousy." Despite my words, my denial of her, she pulled me towards her. And I came willingly. My arms wanted to wrap themselves around her, to pull her towards me, into me. But she held them, preventing my escape as much as my embrace. "I want to believe that you're still in there. That you're still you, but--"

"But I am still me," she said. "See? This is me."

"But your eyes," I said. "Your strength, your speed."

"Yeah, that was why I didn't want you to tell Dr. Mendes about that creature," she said. "It's a bit scary, I know. But that doesn't mean I'm an alien. The thing just... well, it gave me superpowers. That's all. Instead of a radioactive spider, I had a weird... possum... thing. We need to be careful about who knows. Then you go and attack me, accusing me of being an alien. Natalie, you were talking crazy.

I just thought you needed a night to think things through. I remembered Greg telling me about having to have you committed when you started saying crazy things like that before. I just figured..."

"You, what? You figured you'd have me committed for a night? They'd see nothing was wrong with me? Then I'd come crawling back to you? To your bed?"

"Well, yeah," she admitted. "And now you have. You're here."

"No," I said. I stood up, pulling from her grasp. Pulling out of her arms. And she actually let me go. I could see the surprise, the shock in her eyes when I did that. I could see her, the real her. Angela, my Angela, coming to the surface finally. Pain flitted across those eyes. Pain and loss and a little of something else. Perhaps even guilt. "No," I said, again, this time quieter. "You don't get to do that. You don't get to kill someone and just think everything is going to be okay."

"But... But you killed Greg," she accused.

"And Greg killed Emily, and was about to kill me. That doesn't make it right. I still feel his blood on my hands. I still remember the look in his eyes as the keys went into his neck. Watching as the life slowly drained from him. How could you have done that, willingly? How could you take the life of another person when you didn't have to?"

"But I did have to," she insisted. The alien rose back up. "He was taking you from me."

"So?" I asked, not allowing the point but going past it. "So what if he was? That doesn't mean you get to kill him. You stole Greg from me; does that mean I should be allowed to kill you?"

"What?" she asked, stunned by that thought. And she was back again. My Angela. Sitting there looking amazing as the horror and regret played across her face. If I could just figure out a way to keep her there, to keep her with me, maybe I could free her from the embrace of the alien. Still working its way through her. Still trying to conquer her. The fact that she was still struggling with it gave me hope. Hope that I would save her. Hope that it wasn't too late. That she hadn't started infecting the world with whatever it was that took her over. "But... But you already lost him."

"And you had already lost me," I said. "Not by anything you did or said, but by what happened to you. It scared me. Scared me more than I would have liked to admit. I cared about you. I still care about you. I still want you. But I can't see past what you did."

"Never?" she asked. That one word caught me off guard. It broke my heart into a million pieces. It was full of all the despair that had kept her with me. That had chased off her inner demon. The one that had caused all these problems.

"Maybe," I admitted. "But maybe not." She looked up at me, through her eyelashes, as tears started to spill down her cheek. She looked so beautiful, so enticing. I wanted to go to her. To hold her close and tell her that everything was going to be alright. But I couldn't, because it wouldn't. Not as long as whatever it was had its hold on her. "It wasn't really you," I said. "Not the real you, anyway. It was that thing that's in you. That thing that has possessed you. It made you do it, made you kill my friend. And that was all he really was, my friend. Maybe we could have been something more. But so could the two of us. You and me, Angela. I still want to be with you. Just not... not like this. We need to get you better. Then we'll see. Alright?"

"I can't believe this is actually working," Tom said. "Can we really save her?"

"Not if she doesn't want to be saved," I thought back to him. But I reached out my arm, reached out towards Angela, inviting her to me. Inviting her to get the help she needed. She smiled up at me, reaching her hand out, taking mine. I pulled her towards me, wrapping my arms around her. With her so close, kneeling on the bed, she was a good three inches taller than me, reversing our usual height difference. For once,

I wished I was wearing heels, so we would be on the same level.

Tentatively, tenderly, she leaned down, letting her lips lightly touch mine, teasingly, before pulling away. She was smiling, a tender, loving smile. My smile. The one she always had for me. I thought, for that one, happy, beautiful moment that I had done it. That I had saved her from that demon that had possessed her. The moonlight struck her just right, making her skin radiant, glorious in my arms.

But, then, her smile turned. It became the same one that I always saw on Bently. Suddenly, it was like I was holding him, embracing him. And it was all I could to not throw up. "Aw, that's so sweet," came the voice that I had heard at the restaurant. The deep, guttural, demonic voice that told me the alien had full control again. "There's just one problem."

I stepped back from her again. In disgust. In despair. In loss. Unsure what to do. Where to go from there. If I couldn't bring my Angela back, what was there left to do? "What's that?" I asked.

"I'm not going anywhere," it said. The alien said. "I can't. Not anymore. Maybe at first, back when I was only just ingratiating myself in here. But not anymore. See, I'm not just some alien to be eradicated. Some plague that is going to take over the world." It laughed, an almost maniacal laugh, as she stood up in front of me. I gave ground, backing away from her naked form, as she approached me. "I am Angela. I am what she's always wanted to be but was too afraid to be. I am everything that she was ever capable of becoming. And, more importantly than anything else, I like being who I am. Me, Angela, the one you're so hellbent on saving. There's no one to save. No one that needs saving. I am me. Just a better, stronger, smarter, faster me than I was before. Those nightmares, the ones that woke me in the middle of the night. You remember those? They're gone now. I used to blame my little one, my beautiful Doug, for waking me. I've never slept better."

Her voice gradually became her usual voice, somehow taking on a more nefarious tone as it did so. Once it was completely back to her normal voice, her eyes flashed once more, turning completely dark before returning back to normal. Although, it could have just as easily been a trick of the light. And something deep within me told me that whatever had started the other day, back when it first started taking over at the restaurant, had finally run its course. Whatever it was that had taken over Angela, it had finally won. And there was no one left to save.

"I told you," Tom said.

"Run," Dad ordered.

I wasn't exactly in a place to argue with him, standing there, alone, in that room with the beautiful, naked alien that either wanted to kill me or keep me as a pet. It was too close to tell. As vulnerable as she may seem, I knew that looks could be deceiving. Especially when it came to this alien.

So, I did the only thing that came to mind at the moment. I turned around and ran straight out the bedroom door. It was already close at hand, just two steps before I was in the hall. Four more strides and I was turning down the stairs. The carpeting, perfect for muffling my steps earlier, did nothing to muffle my stomping feet as I ran for my life. Yet, for some reason, there were no sounds of pursuit behind me. I didn't try to look back. I wasn't brave enough to see the rage in her eyes. Or maybe to see the alien in her causing her beautiful, lustful body to transform into something else. Something perverted. Something monstrous. When I reached the landing at the middle of the stairs, half of me wanted to just run backwards down the last few. Keeping my eyes away from her. Away from the pursuit that I knew was coming. It was a good thing that I hadn't.

My planted foot slid, digging into the carpet, as I pivoted in place. I used my momentum to propel me further down the stairs. Before I took another step, however, something dropped down from above in front of me.

Something that I couldn't make out at first in the darkness of the stairwell. Then she stood up, coming to her full, yet petite, height in front of me. Still naked. Still looking very much like Angela. She glared at me menacingly, as if asking how I dare reject her. How I dare run from her side. I made to run back upstairs, back the way I had come. But, when she saw my movement, she crouched down, as if she were quite capable of making the jump in reverse. From what I had seen of her prowess so far, I wouldn't have put it past her.

"There's no getting away from me, Natalie," she said. She said it in her normal voice, which made it sound almost cute. Except for the look in her eyes as she stared up at me. "You're mine. No one will ever love you the way I love you."

"Do you mean possessively?" Tom asked. "Seriously, why do people always say that?"

"Let me go, Angela," I said. I tried to make it sound strong, barking it like an order. But it came out sounding more like the cornered animal that I had become, thanks to my psycho ex-girlfriend.

"She's more like your psycho ex-lover," Dad countered.

"Not now," I whispered to him, not trusting my thoughts to get past the internal screaming that had started up the moment I started running from her.

"But this is your home," she said. "Where would you go?"

"That's a good question," Tom said. "HTP?"

"The police?" Dad suggested.

"Eric's place?" Tom countered.

"What?" Eric asked, calling from the door. "Oh, never mind," he said, perhaps the moment he saw my predicament.

"Coward," I called out to him.

"What?" Angela asked, shocked that I would say such a thing to her, considering the state we were in. "How am I a coward? Because I don't want to share you? Because I don't want to let you go? I can't lose you. Not like I lost Greg, long before you ever killed him. I love you too much to let you go."

"Haven't you ever heard that old saying? If you love someone, set them free."

"Except I know you'll never come back to me. Not until I make you understand. Not until you're no longer afraid of me."

"Well, you're off to a great start," I said. "Cornering me on the stairs like this."

"Isn't there a window behind us?" Tom asked.

"Yeah, but I don't think I'd be able to get it open," I whispered to him. "Not before she's on me."

"Bow, chica--" Dad started to say.

"Not now," I barked at him.

"Those voices are still talking to you, aren't they," Angela accused. She looked over my shoulders, one after another, as if trying to see the sources of those voices. Given the fact that I now knew that they were real, that they really existed, more than just in my mind, I got this gut-wrenching fear that she really could see them. That she could tear them out of my mind. Rend them from the world itself. "I guess I'll have to share you with them. But only until we can get you the right kind of help. Or... maybe I already have the right kind of help for you." She trailed off as she thought over whatever idea had just popped into her head. I had to admit, whatever it was scared the crap out of me, even without knowing what it was.

"You're right," I said. I was trying to distract her from whatever twisted line of thought her mind had wandered down. "Perhaps I should head back to HTP. Get my mind in order before coming back here. Maybe then we can, I don't know, start over. Perhaps we'll find our way back to each other. Maybe it'll even help me get over this whole you being an alien... thing. Just, please, don't kill Dr. Mendes when he doesn't let you come see me."

"Kill Dr. Mendes?" she asked. She was completely shocked that I would even suggest such a thing. "Why on earth would I ever have killed Dr. Mendes?"

"Be... 'cause he was keeping me from you?" I asked more than said.

"He was making you better, or at least trying to. I love you, Natalie. I want what's best for you."

"Even if what's best for me isn't... well... you?" I asked.

"Wow, that was stupid," Tom said.

"Of course," Angela said.

"Wait, what?" Tom asked.

"But we both know that's not the case," she continued, uninterrupted by Tom's amazement. "We belong together. Neither of us will ever truly be happy without the other."

"Then let me go," I said. I begged. "If that's really true, then I'll come back to you, obviously."

"You're right," she said. "You do need help. Help to see that we're perfect together. Help to get rid of those voices, once and for all. Of course. Why don't I drive you back to HTP myself? We can talk on the drive."

"Yeah," I said, reluctantly. "Sure. That sounds... nice."

"Nice?" Tom asked.

"Shh," I hissed at him.

"Great," Angela said. "Let me just get my keys."

"And maybe some clothes," I suggested.

"Aw," Dad whined.

"Clothes?" Angela asked, looking down at her naked body. "Oh, god, right. Sorry. I must look insane, standing here, naked, threatening your life if you leave me."

"Just a little," I said, pinching the air.

"Alright. I'll be right back. Don't go anywhere. You know I can run after you fast enough to catch you wherever you go."

"Right," I said, nodding.

I half expected her to jump back up to the hallway above. But she actually took her time, walking up the stairs like a normal human. She even gave me a wide berth, giving me the space that I needed to not jump out of my skin. As she passed, I couldn't help but notice that she smelled amazing. Like something I couldn't even describe. Once she was out of sight, I slowly made my way towards the open door, once again doing my best not to make a sound.

However, the hardwood floors conspired against me. Halfway between the bottom step and the door, the floor gave out a loud, almost ominous creaking as it bore my weight. I froze, my foot only halfway down, holding my breath, as I tried to ease it off again. Tried to undo the damage that had already been done. But it was obviously too late. Alien strength, alien speed, and, obviously, alien hearing.

It felt like a breeze. Like the wind from outside was simply pulling at the air inside, bringing it through the door. My mind took a few moments to register what I was seeing. Suddenly, directly in front of me, was Angela. Now fully clothed. Standing before the now closed door. Part of me was more disappointed that she had gotten dressed so quickly than that she was barring my passage.

"Now where exactly were you planning on going?" she asked. There was fire in her eyes. Not literal fire, but I wouldn't put it past her, given all the powers she's been showing me. She glared me down, daring for me to lie to her. I didn't disappoint.

"I was heading out to the car," I said. "I didn't think you would be gone long. I'm glad you didn't disappoint on that front."

"Did you forget about Doug?" she asked. She seemed to play along, though her ire never faded. "Did you think I'd bring him along in the middle of the night? I was about to call for a sitter."

"A sitter?" I asked, trying to play dumb. "In the middle of the night? Isn't that expensive? We are still on a budget, aren't we? Why can't we just bring him along? Won't he just sleep the whole way anyway?"

"How dumb do you think I am?" she asked. She stalked forward, slowly taking those two steps that separated us. "Remember, I have enhanced intelligence now, thanks to my new powers. I knew you were just playing along. I just wanted to see how far you would take it. How long until you showed your true colors." Lightly, she touched my face, tracing her finger down the edge, before grabbing forcefully at my hair. She pulled me towards her, forcing her mouth on mine in an aggressive kiss. Fortunately, it didn't last long before she pushed me back. I hit the railing again, though this time in my back rather than my head. Still, the railing groaned with the impact, echoing my own sounds of pain. "When are you going to realize that you're mine, Natalie? There is no escape. Not for you. Not from me."

Her Cheshire cat smile was back, reminding me again of Bently. It almost made me wonder if Bently was infected too. If he was an alien as well. Although, I had no idea how he would have been infected. If he had, it must have been before I met him. But, given the fact that the creature that attacked Angela was out there for who knows how long, anything was possible.

I ran from her, heading towards the kitchen and the backyard beyond. It was the same path I took to flee from Greg. Only, this time, I didn't get that far. She pounced, knocking me to the floor in the living room. My momentum had me sliding across the floor, hitting the end table next to the couch. Stunned, I lay there for a moment, listening to something above me, something on the table that I had hit, rocking back and forth before settling back into place. I wanted to roll over. I wanted to jump to my feet and keep running. Wanted to give up. To give in and let death, or whatever Angela had planned for me, come. Instead, I just rolled over, seeing Angela standing over me with that grin.

"Are you done?" she asked. "Are we done playing? Are you ready to surrender to me?"

"Is that what love is to you now?" I asked. "One person surrendering to another's will?"

"Hasn't it always been like that?" she asked. "I surrendered to Greg, as did you. Now it's your turn to surrender to me."

"What if I don't want to?" I asked. "What if it's you that should surrender?"

"That's not going to happen," she said. "Not now. Not when I'm like this." As if to demonstrate, she reached down, grabbing me by the front of my shirt and pulling me to my feet in front of her. The smile didn't look any more attractive from up close. "I could break you in half if I chose to, just like I had done with Eric. You never did see his body, did you? Before you called the cops on me?"

"No," I admitted. "But I knew he was down there."

"It's no matter. That stupid Bently guy will just blame his death on you. But you were insane. Lost to the voices inside your pretty little head. We'll get you sane again. Really sane. Then we can be together, forever. We'll just have to make you a little less breakable, first. I wouldn't want to have to hold back when we make love. Ah, if only you hadn't chased off that weird possum. We could have just had it bite you, too. But we'll figure something out. There's gotta be a way to transfer at least some of my abilities to you. You'd like that, wouldn't you? To be a superhero like me?"

"You're no superhero," I said. Hanging there by her hand, I had no real leverage to fight her with. Instead, I reached back, my hands grasping whatever it was that had been rocking back and forth on the table. I threw it down with all my strength. The lamp, the twin to the one that had been destroyed in our previous fight, smashed over her head. The glass streamed down to the floor. The shards cut deep gashes in her face. But even as I watched, they started to heal up. "Superheroes save people. They don't kill people. They don't enslave people. You're more of a--"

"Don't say it," she shouted in my face, before pushing me away from her. I hit the sofa before tumbling down on the coffee table in front of it. Fortunately, the wooden coffee table held my weight, keeping me from falling further and not impaling me on anything. "I'm not a supervillain," she snapped. As if in defiance to her own words, she jumped forward, jumping on top of me. The added weight of her on top of me smashed the coffee table to splinters. I felt it as the spike of wood, broken off from one of the legs, lanced me through my back. It sliced through my body as if it were butter.

I lay there for a short eternity, or a long instant, thinking that she had actually done it. Angela had killed me. Obviously, she hadn't meant to. The alien fed rage had full control over the creature that she had become. Still, I knew, without needing to look, without needing to hear from a doctor, that I was dying. That my life's blood was pouring down onto the pile of wood that had once been the perfect coffee table for the room it was in. Part of me wished I had brought it with me to my apartment, forcing them to replace it like they had the couch. It matched the couch, the one that was now in storage. Much better than the one that Angela and Greg had chosen. Yet, it didn't matter. It mattered little if it was the coffee table that I had painstakingly chosen or the one they had bought on a whim that had done me in.

Angela's eyes were right above mine, staring down at me. They echoed the disbelief that must have been in my own. Except she wasn't looking at me. She wasn't looking in my eyes. Instead, she was looking at my left hand and, more importantly, to what was in them. Her hand clung to mine, holding it at bay. Holding the keys that were gripped between the fingers, pointed towards her. The longest of the lot, the car key, was stuck up between my middle finger and my ring finger, seemingly almost metaphoric as it reached up into the air. Reaching, almost on its own will, towards Angela's neck. I pushed against her hand. Pushed with all the strength in me.

Pushed with all the power my dying body had in it. And, when her grip held, I pushed more. I pushed harder than I ever thought possible. I could feel the adrenaline coursing through my body, its last-ditch effort to save me. Although, I already knew that I was beyond saving. I'd be damned if I didn't bring her with me, though.

"But I love you," Angela said. It was one last attempt to beg for her life. To stave off the blow that I already didn't want to land.

"I know," I said, as my strength finally got the better of hers. My hand, and the keys with it, slid free of her grip, cutting through the flesh under her neck. Blood spurted in my eyes, but I refused to close them. To look away from hers for a second. My eyes locked on hers. I saw as they flashed, not with life or with a sudden burst of knowledge, of understanding. But with the darkness that had consumed the woman that I loved. With one last cough, one last gasp for air, her dying breath, a blast of orange mist flew through the air.

I breathed in, reflexively.

Epilogue
The Awakening

The flashing red and blue lights gradually brought me back to consciousness. When I had left it, I never thought a return trip was in the cards. The pain in my back had lessened greatly. It had become more of an uncomfortable soreness like when I overdid it at the gym or if I'm lying on my back for too long. I opened my eyes slowly, expecting them to resist. Expect an impending death to still hold them secure.

Angela's dead eyes still stared into mine. The orange mist that had clung to her mouth was gone, having evaporated or simply poured down on me completely. I wasn't sure. There was nothing left of her but a husk. The gaping wound in her neck was an echo to the one that had ended Greg. She was no longer bleeding, but the very real blood, still the dark red of human's blood, stained my hand as it had done before. As it had never really left it.

A key in the lock brought my attention towards the front door and away from the corpse that was my blanket. The girl that should have been my girlfriend. That had been my lover. I racked my brain, trying to come up with an explanation. Something to say besides the overused "this isn't what it looks like". Admittedly, it was exactly what it looked like.

I had killed, for the third time. And this time I had gone there with that intent. There was no getting out of it this time. No alibi. No being too young or having defense as an excuse. I may have been defending the human race from an alien incursion, but no one was going to believe that. Besides, there wasn't exactly an imminent threat. Angela still hadn't figured out how to contaminate someone with the alien contagion.

"Yeah, if you believe that crap," Tom said. I looked in the direction of his voice, no longer sounding like it was coming from inside my head, only to see someone standing off to the side. He was young, perhaps just out of his teens, and leaning against the railing like he lived here. His ratty t-shirt looked familiar, advertising a concert that took place over a decade ago. I wanted to yell at him to get out of my house. To get this woman off me. But something about his look, the sheer hopelessness on his face, told me he wouldn't be much help with either of those. "I still say she infected her baby at the very least. Maybe not intentionally. But perhaps with breastfeeding him or something," the boy said, with Tom's voice.

"Oh, nonsense," Dad said. I recognized him immediately, where he was standing by the door to the kitchen. What surprised me more than actually seeing him, seeing the man that had been haunting me for decades, ever since I killed him almost twenty years ago, was the fact that I could see everything in the room. I wasn't sure how long I had been lying there, but it had to have been hours. The moonlight was no longer coming in through the bay windows behind me. But I could see the room as if it were the middle of the day, with sunlight pouring in everywhere. Knowing the events that led up to that moment, I knew that it wasn't a good thing. "Yeah, no kidding, kid," Dad said.

"Do you think the tether will break soon?" Tom asked. "I'd really like to run from her, like Greg and Eric have, before she goes full alien on us."

"Angela couldn't see us," Dad said. "I don't think we have much to worry from her. We'll probably just go right on haunting her for the next few years until someone kills her."

"What are you talking about?" I rasped. My throat was drier than it had ever been, like I hadn't drunk anything for weeks. "I'm not an alien."

"Not yet," Tom said. "It's only a matter of time, I'm afraid."

"Never going to happen," I said.

"Then how can you see us right now?" he asked.

"What?" Dad asked, surprised. "What are you talking about?"

"She's looking straight at us when we're talking about her," Tom said.

"Well, you are talking about me like I'm not in the room with you."

"Go," someone shouted, right before something solid bashed open the front door. It swung open, unhindered by the lock or latch that had held it in place only moments before. The knob knocked into the rubber nub that I had insisted on Greg installing after the third time he had almost bashed a hole in the wall. Guns led the way as three men in uniforms stormed in, pointing the weapons in every direction as they searched for their target.

"In here, you guys," I said, waving my hands from where I was pinned beneath Angela.

"Natalie Jennings?" one of the men asked.

"That's me," I admitted.

"You're under arrest for the murder of Officer Eric French and... and this woman as well. You have the right to remain silent." He listed off my rights in a flurry of words as the three of them closed in around me. Their guns were trained on me the entire time. I tried to ignore them. Tried to focus on the familiar faces near the door. Sam was in the middle, gawking at me openly. Detective Bently was on his right, his Cheshire cat smile firmly in place. His hands were rubbing together, as if him finally getting to arrest me was a feast he had been starving for for years. Jessica was standing on Sam's left, looking afraid. Although, I hoped she was level-headed enough to remember that my insanity plea practically wrote itself.

I'd be heading back to HTP, of course, to take up one of the residential spots. I really would be home for Thanksgiving, and I couldn't even deny that it would be my home from then on. After all, it wasn't like I didn't really hear voices. No one was going to believe me that their sources, the ghosts of the people I've seen die, were as real as I was. Not to mention the fact that a fifth one, that of Angela, was scheduled to make an appearance at some point. I wondered if it would be her real self or the alien version of her that would be with me for the rest of my life.

"Oh, I don't think you're going to have to worry about that," Tom said, pulling my attention back to him. His voice had become quiet, almost hard to hear over the incessant droning of the officers as they told me my rights. When I looked over at him, his form, the body that I shouldn't have been able to see, was fading as well. "I already feel the tether fading," he said. "We'll be free of you soon enough. I'm sorry about how things turned out. I'm sorry for having haunted you for all these years. I'm.... I'm just sorry for a lot of things."

"Take care of yourself, kid," Dad said. His form was already gone, his voice nothing more than an echo. "I'll look over you from wherever it is that I'm going."

"Dad?" I asked. The cop stopped telling me my rights as the three of them stared at me in confusion. I wasn't even sure if they had finished or if they were reacting to me calling out for my dead father. "Tom?" I called, looking over at the empty stairs. "Don't go."

After all this time, after the years that I had wanted them to just leave me alone, the voices that had made my adult life a living hell, all I wanted was for them to stay. I could no longer feel them there. The presence that had always been just behind his eyes. Right where they should have been if they really were just voices in my head. Instead, it was just gone.

And I was finally alone with my thoughts. Something that hadn't happened in almost twenty years.

I didn't know what to do with myself.

Finally, the three cops pulled Angela's dead body off of me. I expected to see the shaft of wood that I had been impaled on protruding from my stomach. Instead, as the literal dead weight was lifted off of me, the piece of wood simply fell off to the side. There was a bloody hole in my shirt, right where the pain had been. But the flesh beneath it was whole. There wasn't even a sign of a scar. The familiar flesh was unmarred as it always had been. As smooth as a baby's.

"What about Doug?" I asked, remembering the child still asleep upstairs.

"Don't worry," Sam said. "I have Doug. You just worry about yourself. Get yourself healthy again."

I looked towards him, and he stared at me, at a loss for anything else to say.

It made me wonder if my eyes had suddenly gone dark, or if my voice had gone deep without my even noticing.

I just hoped I wouldn't grow antennas.

###

About the Author

Cassandra Morphy is a Business Data Analyst, working with numbers by day, but words by night. She grew up escaping the world, into the other realities of books, TV shows, and movies, and now she writes about those same worlds. Her only hope in life is to reach one person with her work, the way so many others had reached her. As a TV addict and avid movie goer, her entire life is just one big research project, focused on generating innovative ideas for worlds that don't exist anywhere other than in her sick, twisted mind.

Other books by this author

Please visit your favorite ebook retailer to discover other books by Cassandra Morphy:

Crowbarland Chronicles
In Time for Prom
The Awakening
Demons Force
Angels Innocence
Crowbarland Prep
Light Through the Windows
Last Scientist
Missing Mars

The Delnadian Invasion
Alien Fireworks
Alien Life
Alien Death
Alien War

Desparian Legacies
The Prophecy
Mountain Princess

Doors of Despair
The Mind's Door
The Door in the Sky
Gates of the Inferno
Heaven's Door
Door to Victory

No One Can Hear You
Travel
Train
Thrive
Fly
Spy

www.ingramcontent.com/pod-product-compliance
Lightning Source LLC
Chambersburg PA
CBHW071552150726
48000CB00004B/1436